JELLY

THE MAN IN THE MIRROR

A Novel

by Mike Conti

SABER PRESS
North Reading, MA

JELLY BRYCE

THE MAN IN THE MIRROR

A Novel

by Mike Conti

Jelly Bryce: The Man in the Mirror
A Novel
by Mike Conti

Copyright © 2016 by Mike Conti

ISBN13: 978-0-9965302-9-3
ISBN10: 0-9965302-9-0

First Edition

Printed in the United States of America on recycled paper.

Published by Saber Press®
153 Main Street, PMB 138
North Reading, Massachusetts 01864, USA
Tel./Fax. (978) 749-3731
Email: admin@sabergroup.com
Website: www.sabergroup.com

SABER PRESS, SABER GROUP, INC., and the
"sword and shield" design are trademarks belonging
to Saber Group, Inc.® and registered in the United States
Patent and Trademark Office.

Description of Tequila and the relationship between a man and
his little dog courtesy of Pat and Mugzee.

The Guy in the Glass, by Dale Wimbrow was first published in
The American Magazine, 1934. Used with permission.

Cover image of Jelly Bryce provided by *The Oklahoman* from
their archives. Used with permission.

Images of Jelly Bryce at end of book courtesy of the Bryce family.

Please note that this is a novel. While inspired by actual persons
and historical events, the characters and all other persons, businesses,
places and events depicted in this novel are fictionalized. Certain
characters' names have been changed, some main characters
composited or invented, and a number of incidents fictionalized.
All rights reserved. Except for use in a review, no portion
of this work may be reproduced in any form or by any means,
electronic or mechanical, including photographing, photocopying,
recording or videotaping, or by any information storage and retrieval
system without the written permission of the publisher.

To Delf and His Family

*And a special dedication to the memory of
Patrick "Duke" McAdam
who crossed the river much too soon.
We'll see you on the other side, my Brother.*

The Guy in the Glass
by Dale Wimbrow (© 1934)

When you get what you want in your struggle for pelf,
And the world makes you King for a day,
Then go to the mirror and look at yourself,
And see what that guy has to say.

For it isn't your Father, or Mother, or Wife,
Who judgement upon you must pass.
The feller whose verdict counts most in your life
Is the guy staring back from the glass.

He's the feller to please, never mind all the rest,
For he's with you clear up to the end,
And you've passed your most dangerous, difficult test
If the guy in the glass is your friend.

You may be like Jack Horner and "chisel" a plum,
And think you're a wonderful guy,
But the man in the glass says you're only a bum
If you can't look him straight in the eye.

You can fool the whole world down the pathway of years,
And get pats on the back as you pass,
But your final reward will be heartaches and tears
If you've cheated the guy in the glass.

PROLOGUE

Shangri-La Resort
Grand Lake O' the Cherokees, Oklahoma
12 May 1974

FRANK BRANDT SLID ONE of the tall glasses of ice cold beer toward the younger man seated beside him at the bar. With his other hand he slid a dollar bill toward the bartender and said, "Keep it."

The bartender nodded his thanks and moved on down the line to the next customer. The bar was hopping busy, every stool filled, lines of people trying to get barside so they could put in an order.

"Thanks, Frank," Jerry Hennigan said as he wrapped his hand around the glass of cold Schlitz and raised it up. "To your health." Little rivulets of condensation ran down the glass. The cool drops felt good under his fingers.

Brandt picked up his own glass, nodded, and took a long drink. Turning around on the bar stool so he faced the banquet room he scanned the crowd. "Good turnout."

Hennigan rotated the seat of his own stool so he could take in the view. "Are they always this well attended?"

Brandt took another drink before replying. "I don't really know. This is only the second one I've been to."

The banquet room was one of several in use that Sunday evening at the Shangri-La Resort. Standing on the shore of a 60,000-acre man-made lake, the resort had recently been completely renovated. It was decidedly upscale. In addition to the lake and marina there were two golf courses, indoor and outdoor tennis and racquetball courts, conference rooms, restaurants and tastefully-decorated lounges. The room they were in had been rented by the Society of Former Special Agents of the FBI for their annual two-day reunion. Both Brandt and Hennigan were current active duty members, there to assist with the event. While Brandt was a veteran agent with nearly twenty years on the books, the twenty-six-year-old Hennigan was a relative new guy having just completed his second year with the Bureau. He'd tagged along with Brandt since they both worked out of the Oklahoma City Field Office and were the only two agents not on call that weekend.

"Kind of like getting a glimpse of the future," said Hennigan, a gregarious second-generation Irishman with an easy laugh, head full of thick, black hair and a horseshoe moustache close to the edge of violating the Bureau's 'professional appearance' grooming standards. "How many more years 'til you qualify to join?"

Brandt smiled at the comment. He remembered needling older agents the same way. Fifty-seven had long been the mandatory retirement age, making a career in the FBI a relatively young man's game. *'Or young woman's game,'* he mentally corrected himself. The first female agents had graduated from the academy a mere two years before.

"Still got a ways to go," replied Brandt as his eyes moved over the people in a grid search pattern. His own black hair hadn't started thinning yet, but there was a little gray showing at the temples. "Tell you what, though, Jerry–lot of experience in this room, my young friend. Lot of talent."

Hennigan took in the scene: a mix of mostly older white men and women. Many were seated at large, round, table-cloth-covered tables waiting for dinner to be served. Others stood in little groups, drinks in hand. All were talking animatedly; many smiles and much laughter. To Hennigan, they all appeared to be well dressed senior citizens. *'Room looks like a box full of Q-tips with ties,'* he mused silently to himself. "Talent. I bet," he replied, but in his mind he only half-believed it. Things had changed completely since the days most of these old timers were on the job. He smiled as he imagined them trying to deal with the modern realities of organized crime and intricacies of white collar criminal investigations.

After a few minutes of sitting, watching and drinking, Hennigan noticed a subtle change in the senior agent next to him. Brandt had spotted someone of interest. Hennigan could tell by the way Brandt moved. They'd worked together on more than a few investigations, and Brandt had a few "tells" Hennigan had come to recognize. "What is it?" he asked.

"I'll be damned."

Curious, Hennigan zeroed in on the subject of Brandt's gaze. All he could see were more old people. "What?"

"I thought he was dead," Brandt said quietly. Then he used his glass to indicate the table he was looking at, off to the side near the wall.

Three conservatively-dressed men sat at the table, talking quietly. All were small statured, each well under six feet, Hennigan estimated. One of them, a lean and rather frail looking man with thinning hair, held a small gray poodle in his lap, rubbing its ears as he spoke. The second man at the table was nearly bald and about forty pounds overweight; his face looked bloated and rather washed out. The third man, while appearing the same age as the other two, had a markedly different look about him: he sat ramrod straight in his chair and appeared capable of springing to his feet and into action if necessary. He was also scanning the room at regular intervals. As his gaze passed over the bar, Hennigan got a good look at his face. Even from across the room the man's eyes had a steady, penetrating quality. *'Apex predator,'* Hennigan thought, remembering the term from one of his classes at the academy. Assuming the intense looking man was the subject of interest, Hennigan leaned toward Brandt and asked, "So, what's that guy's story?"

Brandt smiled before taking another drink. Then he sat back on his stool and began talking. "That man, my young friend, is a living legend of the FBI. D.A. Bryce. The D.A. stands for Delf Albert, but most people knew him as Jelly."

"*Jelly?*" Hennigan repeated, amused. "How the fuck do you get a nickname like Jelly?"

Brandt glanced at Hennigan and smiled. "Jellybean was something people called a fancy dresser way back when–nineteen-twenties and such. The story I heard was that a dying bank robber called him that right after Jelly shot him to pieces in a gunfight. Supposedly the guy looked up and saw Jelly all decked out in a fancy suit, and said, 'I can't believe I was killed by a jellybean.' Or something like that. The crook died at the scene. But the Jelly stuck."

Hennigan smiled. "Good one, the jelly *stuck*."

"That man right there, kid, you have no idea," Brandt continued, ignoring the comment. "That one little old man has put more criminals in their graves than probably all the other agents in this room combined. I've heard numbers as high as twenty that are known about."

"No shit?"

"No shit. And the word too, things I've heard from some of the older guys, is that he was also involved in a lot of off-the-books operations, you know, during World War Two and after. God only knows what he's seen and done. But I will tell you this–" Brandt looked at Hennigan and held his gaze– "I've been told by more than a few serious men that Jelly Bryce was no one to fuck with if you valued your life. Not only was he dangerous, but he was so freakishly fast with a pistol, they used to say if you blinked when you went up against him with a gun, you'd die in the dark."

Hennigan's eyes narrowed. Then he smiled. "C'mon," he said dismissively.

"I'm telling you. No bullshit. You hear something now and then, you take it with a grain of salt. But this guy," again motioning with his glass toward the table, "this guy is a for real, old school gunfighter. Recruited personally by Hoover himself during the gangster wars of the thirties. Living fucking legend, my friend. I heard him give a speech years ago, and you could have heard a pin drop in the room. A room full of crusty old hard-boiled agents I might add. They hung on his every word. I had a chance to meet him briefly afterwards, and I gotta tell you, he was one of the nicest guys I've ever met. Really interesting man."

Hennigan stood up and drained his glass. "Okay."

"Okay what?"

"Finish your beer and let's go say hello." Hennigan placed his empty glass on the bar and looked at Brandt. It was a challenge.

Brandt didn't respond the way Hennigan had anticipated. He actually looked a bit apprehensive. "I don't know, Jerry. I don't want to bother him."

"Oh, come on," Hennigan chided, "You're gonna drop all that living legend stuff on me and then not introduce me? Why else is he here? He wants to meet people, obviously, right?"

"I don't know..."

Hennigan looked squarely at his friend. "C'mon, Frank, I'm a people. I qualify." He smiled.

"Barely," replied Brandt, smiling back. "All right–but don't embarrass me." He stood up, finished his beer and put the glass on the bar. Then he waved the bartender over and pointed to the table. "I'd like to buy that table a round of whatever they're having," he said, and slipped the bartender three dollars.

"No problem, sir," replied the bartender. He caught the attention of a waitress and pointed at the table, then pointed his index finger straight down and made a circling motion.

"All right, junior," Brandt said to Hennigan, "Come on–but I'm serious, do not embarrass me here. Watch your language. And none of your wise guy, hippie shit comments. These guys probably won't get your humor."

Hennigan grinned at his clean cut partner. "Hippie? Really?"

Brandt's eyebrows lifted in question as he pointed at his own upper lip and waved his index finger back and forth.

"No problem, Boss," said Hennigan, making a show of stroking his own index finger and thumb down the sides of his long moustache. "I promise, I'll be as humorless and square as you." He grinned.

Brandt rolled his eyes and turned toward the table. "Come on."

The two agents walked across the room toward the small group of retirees. Brandt could tell they were noticed making their approach right away. The three men shifted subtly in their chairs, even while pretending they were unaware of the impending intrusion.

"Excuse me, gentlemen. I'm so terribly sorry to interrupt..." Brandt began.

The three older men looked up kindly at Brandt, though their eyes expertly scanned both him and Hennigan. None of them spoke.

"My name is Frank Brandt, special agent out of the Oklahoma Office. This is Agent Jerry Hennigan. We're here helping out with the reunion this year, and I–*we* just wanted to pay our respects, gentlemen."

"Very kind of you," the man with the penetrating stare

said as he stood up and extended his hand. "I'm Walter Walsh, retired."

Hennigan shook the man's hand after Brandt, surprised both at the strength of the old agent's grip and that he wasn't Jelly Bryce. Then the heavyset man stood and extended his hand first to Brandt, introducing himself as "Jim Rutherford, Special Agent, retired."

"A pleasure, sir," Brandt said while shaking Rutherford's hand; then he walked around the table to the frail man with the poodle in his lap. Brandt held out his hand again. "Mister Bryce."

Jelly remained seated and extended his own hand, saying, "Pleasure to meet you, Brandt. Please forgive me for not standing; my guard dog gets a little nasty if I make him get down."

Brandt briefly glanced at the little puff of gray fur and smiled. "Please, sir, don't get up, and again, excuse us for interrupting you–"

Just as his hand grasped Bryce's, the little poodle erupted in a snarling burst of teeth and guttural growling.

Brandt reflexively pulled his hand away. "Jesus!" he said, then smiled sheepishly as all the men laughed.

"Tequila!" Jelly snapped, pulling the dog back by its thin red leather collar.

The waitress carrying the tray of drinks Brandt had ordered arrived at the table that moment. She stopped short and said, "Oh, I'm sorry, I brought what you were drinking. Do you want tequila instead?"

Jelly shook his head and smiled. "No dear, what you have there is fine. My dog's name is Tequila."

The middle-aged waitress glanced at the dog, smiled back at Jelly and said, "Well, okay then," and set the drinks on the table. Walsh and Rutherford were drinking beer. Jelly had a Scotch on the rocks. The waitress picked the change off the tray and offered it to Brandt. He shook his head. "Keep it." She smiled sweetly at him, looked at the seated men and said, "This gentleman bought the round."

The three retired agents smiled and nodded at Brandt. Rutherford said, "Thanks, Brandt. Mighty white of ya."

"Maybe we should get the dog a drink, too," joked Hennigan as the waitress headed back to the bar to reload.

Jelly smiled. "I think he's had enough. As you can see, he's a bit of an ugly drunk."

The men laughed again.

"I hope he didn't get a piece of you, Brandt, did he?" asked Jelly, concern in his voice.

"No sir, not a problem at all. Seems like he's very protective of you. That's good."

"My wife's dog actually," Jelly replied, rubbing the dog behind the ears again.

"Oh," Hennigan said, "is she here? We'd love to buy her a drink too, sir."

Jelly's eyes went a little vacant. The other retired agents shifted uncomfortably.

Sensing he'd stepped out of line, Hennigan added, "I mean, if that would be all right with you, Mister Bryce."

Jelly shook his head again, then sadly said, "No, I'm afraid my wife passed away last year, Agent Hennigan. But thank you for the thought."

Hennigan felt like an idiot. Brandt quickly spoke up, "We're so sorry to hear that, Mister Bryce."

"Yes," Hennigan added, "We're very sorry for your loss."

Jelly nodded.

Sensing the discomfort descending on the table, Walter Walsh rerouted the conversation. "Are you gentlemen involved with the interviews?"

"Interviews?" Hennigan asked, thankful for the

reprieve.

"Yes," Walsh replied, "we're supposed to be interviewed this evening, some kind of project the Bureau's doing. Trying to preserve the history, I guess."

"I hadn't heard about that," Brandt said. "But I'll look into it right away and find out."

The retired agents nodded.

Hennigan smiled. "I bet you gentlemen have a lot of stories. I mean, I can't imagine what it was like on the job back then." He looked at them expectantly.

Brandt walked back around the table and stood next to Hennigan. "We'll be sure to check out the histories you gentlemen provide; I'm sure it will be fascinating. But for now, we'll leave you be, let you get back to your conversation." Then he nudged Hennigan with his shoulder back toward the bar.

Hennigan took the overt hint and reluctantly started to back away from the table, saying, "A pleasure to meet you gentlemen..."

Walter Walsh looked at Jelly, then Rutherford. Both men nodded. Walsh's eyes narrowed as he looked at the two younger agents and said, "What's the rush?"

Hennigan stopped and smiled. Brandt raised his eyebrows and said, "Rush?"

"Yeah, what's the rush?" asked Rutherford sternly. "Don't like our company or somethin'?"

Brandt blanched. "Of course not! I mean, no sir..."

Jelly smiled. "Grab a couple drinks and sit the fuck down, gentlemen. You're making my bloodhound nervous."

* * *

For the next hour Brandt and Hennigan were treated to a fascinating glimpse of the Bureau's history as the old timers regaled them with stories.

While Brandt was totally absorbed in the tales, Hennigan found himself morphing from jaded observer to an almost childlike state as he listened to the veterans talk. He'd had no idea what these men had gone through; nor had he ever known just how smart, funny, sophisticated and intelligent the older generation was. He felt completely outclassed and more than a little intimidated as the conversation flowed, long ago events and conversations channeled through the three men seated before him. *'Holy shit,'* Hennigan thought as the first story was told, for in the telling not only was he transported back some forty odd years, but the old men seemed to grow younger before his very eyes. *'Younger and much more dangerous.'* As that realization sank in, he stole a quick glance around the room at the other white-haired veterans, seeing them all in a very different light.

"...so as I'm putting the cuffs on the skell," Rutherford said animatedly, "he looks at me all horrified and says, 'What the fuck was that?!' And I says, 'What?' Then he says, 'That fuckin' wild Indian tried to kill me!' and I just laughed and said, 'Son, if that man had wanted you dead, you wouldn't be vertical right now.' "

The men all laughed. Rutherford looked at Jelly and said, "Remember that, Jelly? You emptied that Thompson's fifty-round drum into that car as that idiot tried to drive through the roadblock. That was a beautiful thing."

Jelly just smiled and looked down at the table.

"Although," continued Rutherford, glancing at the other men at the table and winking, "when we counted the holes in the car, there were only forty-nine. Apparently 'Mister Perfect Shot' here missed one!"

Jelly, still smiling, looked up and shook his head. "Obviously, I'd been shorted a round in that magazine."

More laughter.

Hennigan, smiling, asked, "Are you really an Indian, Mister Bryce?"

"Part Indian," Jelly replied. "Mostly Scot."

"Scot indeed!" said Rutherford enthusiastically, holding up his empty bottle and getting the waitress's attention. She approached the table and stood next to Hennigan. "Another round, gentlemen?"

"Yes," said Rutherford, "and this time, please bring us a round of Johnnie Walker Black as well, please, miss."

"Anything in it? Rocks, water...?"

Rutherford's eyes narrowed. "Shame on you, darlin', for suggesting such a blasphemy. Shot glasses will do nicely."

The waitress smiled. "My apologies," she said, adding, "Be right back," as she left.

For just a moment Brandt had thought to decline the shot as he and Hennigan were sort of officially working. Then he thought better of it. Refusing a drink with this crew would be blasphemy in itself. "Were any of you gentlemen involved in the Dillinger case?" he asked instead.

Rutherford looked at Jelly. "Were you on the Flying Squad then, Jelly?"

Jelly shook his head. "Nope, still with Oklahoma City then. But Clarence Hurt was there that night. Him and Charlie Winstead took Dillinger down."

Hennigan perked up. "I've heard of Winstead. They talked about him at the Academy. Is he here tonight?"

The retired agents got quiet.

Jelly slowly shook his head. "No. We lost Charlie about a year ago. Pneumonia."

"Oh, I'm sorry to hear that," offered Brandt.

"Good man," said Rutherford as Walter Walsh nodded.

"Great guy," agreed Jelly, "and a good friend."

"Well, at least he outlived J. Edgar," Rutherford said.

"That must've made him happy."

Jelly and Walsh grinned.

"No doubt," said Jelly softly. Hoover had died in May of 1972. Heart attack. He was 77 years old and still serving as Director of his Bureau. He'd died alone, inside his locked bedroom.

After a few moments of silence from the older men, Hennigan spoke up. "What about Bonnie and Clyde?" he asked. "Were they anything like in the movie?"

The three old timers looked at Hennigan. Then Walsh laughed. "Son," he said, "if you're looking for accuracy, the last place you'll find it is coming out of that Hollywood cesspool."

Jelly nodded. "Bonnie and Clyde were a couple of dirt bag thieves and murderers," he said with conviction. "They killed a lot of good lawmen and innocent civilians. True, they hit some banks, but Barrow mostly preyed on small country stores and gas stations, something I bet they didn't show in that movie." Nodding again, he continued, "The girl went along for the ride mostly, but she was as guilty as the rest. Thing that made those screwballs famous–before that rotten movie–were some photographs they left when they bugged out of a hideout in Joplin."

"Oh, yeah, the press loved those pictures," chimed in Walsh. "Plastered them on newspapers around the country. The girl holding the guns and smoking a cigar. People loved that shit." He smiled and shook his head.

"Same thing today," said Rutherford. "The press and Hollywood makes heroes of the gangsters, and inspire more people to be like 'em. Fuckin' ridiculous."

"I actually have Parker's glasses from the death car," Jelly said quietly.

All the men looked at him.

"How'd you end up with those?" asked Walter Walsh.

"Someone gave them to me. I took them to be polite. One of these days I'm gonna have to figure out what to do with them."

Hennigan looked at Brandt and raised his eyebrows.

"What about giving them to the FBI for the museum?" Brandt asked.

Jelly looked at him and shook his head slightly side to side. "Naw. Hoover collected enough of that stuff. Besides, weren't us that got them. Hamer and his crew took those two down. Wiped them out in Louisiana back in '34. Put a definite end to their killing ways in a Texas efficient manner."

"Texas Ranger, Hamer was," said Rutherford.

Jelly nodded. "Another good man. He passed back in '55, I think."

"I remember him from the movie," Hennigan said cheerily. "Bonnie and Clyde captured him, right? Humiliated him, if I remember right. That's why he cut them down at the end of the movie while they were just sitting in the car. Guess they pissed off the wrong guy." He smiled.

Jelly's eyes focused on Hennigan's. As Hennigan looked at them, his breath caught in his throat. He'd never seen a look like that in his life. For one fleeting moment he felt he was in danger, though part of his mind tried to reject that feeling. *'He's an old guy, for Christ's sake...'*

"Son," Jelly said steadily, "I knew Frank Hamer. Two mutts like Barrow and Parker, and all the rest of them for that matter, weren't worth a bucket of warm spit compared to that man. They never had Hamer. That's a bullshit story."

"I'm sorry," said Hennigan, surprised at his own words. "I meant no disrespect."

Jelly's gaze softened. "I know it," he said. "All you young guys know is what you see and read. But Hamer–he was somethin'. This is a guy who carried the badge all his life, whether he was on the job or not. Wounded more than seventeen times, left for dead more than once, and in his lifetime he killed nearly seventy badmen. Seventy! That's seven zero."

"Excuse me, gentlemen," the waitress said as she whirled up to the table delivering drinks. After placing the full glasses down and empties on her tray she glanced at Brandt who indicated he'd cover the tab. Then she was gone.

Walter Walsh picked up his glass of Scotch and raised it up in a toast, eyes on Hennigan. All the men picked theirs up as well. "Mister Hennigan," he began, then glanced at Jelly, "a wise man told me long ago, only believe half of what you see, and none of what you hear!"

"Lang may yer lum reek!" added Rutherford.

"May you live long and stay well," translated Jelly.

The men downed the shots of the smooth whiskey then forcefully seated the small stout glasses on the table.

"Now I've got a story for you," Jelly began, smiling at Walter Walsh. "Back in, what was it Walter, thirty-seven?"

"What's that, Delf?" Walsh asked, turning his good ear toward Jelly.

"Maine; Al Brady? Nineteen thirty-seven, right?"

"Oh, yeah," Walsh replied, "but don't tell that one. Tell about the embassy, when Hoover suspended me."

Jelly smiled wider. "You know, I almost forgot about that!"

Just as Jelly began to tell the story about Walter Walsh's unauthorized pursuit of a man into the Colombian embassy, a woman stepped up to the table. Appearing to be about forty-years old, she was accompanied by two younger men carrying audio recording equipment in boxes.

"Excuse me," she said in a charming southern accent, "I'm looking for some retired agents–" she glanced at a small notepad in her hand. "Walsh, Rutherford and Bryce? I'm Maryanne Singleton, from the history project?"

The three older men looked up at her and smiled. She was smiling back sweetly and very easy to look at. Her conservative dress and suede Pappagallo flat shoes couldn't disguise an athletic figure, and the lack of a wedding ring was immediately noted by the veteran trained observers.

"Yes, ma'am," said Rutherford. "We're your men."

"Great!" she said, smile expanding, revealing a mouthful of even, shining teeth. "I have a room set up for the interviews, just down the hallway. Who'd like to go first?"

Jelly looked at the woman's face. She was brunette. Big expressive green eyes and wide full lips. "You go first, Walter," Jelly said. "I need some time to collect my thoughts."

Walter Walsh nodded and stood up, formally introducing himself to the woman and her assistants as they all walked toward the doorway leading out to the hall. The woman paused for a moment, just long enough to look back at Jelly and Rutherford and say, "This shouldn't take too long. You two gentlemen think about what you'd like to tell us about your lives, okay now?" Then she slipped her hand into the crook of Walsh's bent elbow and let him escort her across the room. Even from the back the men at the table could tell Walsh was grinning.

Jelly watched them for a long moment then turned to Rutherford. "Jim, would you mind telling the story about Walter and the embassy? I'm suddenly a little tired."

"My pleasure," Rutherford said, turning to Brandt and Hennigan. "This is a good one..."

As Rutherford spoke, Jelly wrapped his hands around his glass of Scotch and slid it closer to him. After hearing just a few words of the tale Rutherford had begun, he retreated into his mind and memories. He'd heard and told these same stories for years. Stories that became legend and spawned other stories, many based in truth, a few pure fabrications; most a mixture of both.

But some stories Jelly had never told. Would never tell. Even though most of the people involved were now dead and gone.

Men like Edgar Hoover, Walter Walsh, Clarence Hurt, Charlie Winstead and Jelly Bryce knew something many people wouldn't understand. They knew that some stories were best left with the dead.

CHAPTER ONE

Lima, Peru
May 1941

TOM WILSON WOKE UP, his eyes wide and bulging. He wasn't breathing. Someone was on top of him, their hands wrapped around his throat, thumbs pressing on his windpipe.

If the assassin had been properly trained he could have carried out his mission in a much more efficient manner. Luckily for the veteran FBI agent, the men who'd dispatched the killer didn't regard Wilson as either a high level target or much of a threat. They'd been watching him since he'd first arrived a few weeks before and had been amused by his amateur, bungling spycraft. Not only was he ignorant of their language and culture, he was also apparently soft and weak. They'd tested him a few times, had one of their men intentionally bump into him in the bar of a restaurant one evening and try to provoke him into a fight. To the disgust of the undercover provocateur and several silent observers, Wilson cowed at the challenge, his unmanly fear evident by his frightened expression and submissive body language.

They'd actually considered just leaving him be until he was recalled by his own government–or simply broke and ran as it appeared he soon would–but then things started heating up on the border with Ecuador again. That's when the decision was made to swat the American intelligence fly, ostensibly so there would be one less potential complication in the mix. That's what the boss told his men, anyway. The man who'd ordered the hit, Capitán Alvaro

Amaru, commander of the 3rd Infantry Regiment of Security, kept the real reasons to himself.

As commander of the 3rd IRS, Amaru was responsible for security in his area. Until recently, his unit had been part of the Peruvian Republican Guard Regiment, but now with war breaking out on the border again it operated primarily as an independent military strike force under his complete control. Amaru had come to fancy himself the local governor. And everyone knew there were certain protocols that must be adhered to and enforced when operating in his territory. That's why he took such offense to Wilson's presence.

Not only had the Americans not asked for permission before sending this man to their country on whatever mission he'd been given, they'd also failed to offer any type of "tribute" in the form of cash or goods to Amaru.

"Wañuchiy chay Yankee," Amaru had muttered to his executive officer between sips of coffee. He hadn't asked for authorization nor wasted a lot of time considering things before issuing the kill order. This was "Lima the ugly" after all, and with the exception of a small contingent of US naval aviation advisors, the Americans had no great influence here. Had the intelligence agent been French, that would have been different. The French military had long been present in Peru and had established many personal, mutually-beneficial relationships with high ranking members of the Peruvian government. But now Peru's old ally France had fallen to the Germans and the world itself was poised to fall into yet another great war, a war the Americans were sure to get involved in. While the Peruvian government was well aware of the international situation, they had problems of their own. They'd actually always had problems of their own, seeing as how their beautiful South American country was bordered on the north by Ecuador and Colombia, the east by Brazil, the south by Bolivia and

Chile, and the west by the Pacific Ocean. With the exception of the ocean, Peru had been at war with one or another of its bordering neighbors as long as anyone could remember.

  Most of this information was unknown to Tom Wilson as he lay in his cheap hotel's too soft bed having the life strangled out of him. All he was truly certain of was that he was experiencing more pain than he'd ever known was possible. As the assassin's grip shifted, crossed thumbs now correctly pressing down on the sides of his throat cutting off the blood supply to his brain, Wilson's head started to feel like it was going to explode. In addition to increasing the pressure on the carotid vein and artery, the man on top of him grunted each time he pulled up and then rocked his weight back down. He did this again and again. The grunting sound was the thing that finally tipped Wilson over the edge. It activated part of his brain he hadn't been aware of before. Suddenly, Tom Wilson–seven-year veteran of the FBI, graduate of Boston College Law School, and all around caring and compassionate human being–was transformed into a feral, primal creature that very well could have been covered in scales and fur. The young and inexperienced soldier on top of him was more surprised by the transformation than Wilson. The soft, compliant Yankee beneath him started to buck and froth, now all teeth and claws and bloodlust, adrenalin pumping through his system.

  The tip of Wilson's left thumb found the inside corner of the soldier's right eye socket. While the thought of intentionally injuring anyone normally repulsed him, Wilson's lizard brain, perched on top of his spinal cord, instinctively knew the path to survival was through that eye socket. The FBI agent's thumb plunged deeply, the lizard's desperate goal being to touch the brain behind it.

  Now it was the young soldier's turn to feel pain beyond comprehension. As his own lizard brain took control, the impulse to flee was overwhelming; he ripped his head violently backwards. When he did Wilson's hooked thumb plucked the eye out. The pain was so complete it sucked the air out of the soldier's lungs. No more grunts; no scream. His mouth opened wide as he tried to take a breath, hands instantly releasing from around Wilson's throat as he flailed blindly about, falling from the bed to the floor.

Wilson rolled to the side, his own hands now clutching his throat, the arteries in his head and face pounding. He coughed repeatedly as his airway tried to re-open, gulping air. He could hear someone else gasping, groaning, and for a moment had no idea where he was or what was happening. None of this made sense. He sucked in breath after breath, certain now only that he had to escape. Stumbling toward the door in the dark room he fell over the legs of the soldier curled up in a fetal position on the floor. The weight of his body crashing down on the soldier freed the wounded man's voice and he began to cry out. In Tom's head the animal brain now took control, focusing on this new threat. Unlike the lizard brain the animal brain didn't simply react; it could process information, recognize threats, evaluate them and make instantaneous decisions. The assassin's screams would surely bring more men. The screams had to cease.

Unencumbered by conscience or philosophy like the human brain, the animal brain was laser focused on survival. It was like a wolf's brain. No concept of mercy or God or Heaven or Hell. In situations like this, its sole focus was on kill and live.

Tom grabbed for the large, triangular-shaped quartz ashtray on the table. Big and heavy, smooth, cool and solid it filled his hand like it belonged there. He raised it high then drove it straight down into the head of the man on the floor. *'Faster, harder,'* demanded the wolf's voice in his head, *'We're running out of time! Faster, harder!'* Again and again. Odd sounds were produced with each impact, sounds that would have sickened his human brain, but satisfied the animal in control. Now Tom's hand was slick with blood. He became aware that there were no more screams, no movement from the man on the floor. Tom fell back against the wall, slid down into a seated position on the floor and felt only his heart pounding in his chest.

He didn't know how long he'd sat like that when a quiet knock on the door startled him back to the completely insane, unexpected reality his world had become.

"Marcos, Haku! Hakuchi!" The urgent words were whispered close to the outside of the door.

Marcos, the dead soldier on the floor, had insisted on carrying out his first killing by himself. It was a tradition in the 3rd IRS. It was the way new members "made their bones," proved themselves worthy. The more personal and brutal the kill, the more admiration one received from his peers. Marcos had gone for the gold. He'd wanted to be able to brag about strangling the life out of the soft, weak Yankee, mano a mano. It would have been a humiliating death for the American, something Marcos and his friends could have gotten a good laugh out of while at the same time, the nature of the kill would have reflected well on the young soldier. It took big balls to kill like that. "Even more than using a blade," his friend Alejandro had assured him earlier that day.

It was Alejandro outside the door. He'd waited patiently downstairs, but now it was taking too long. They needed to go. There were other foreigners staying in the hotel and the soldiers were supposed to get in and out without being seen or identified. That's why they were wearing civilian clothing and carried only concealed pistols and knives.

In response to the knocking, Tom stood up slowly,

facing the door, eyes wide and waiting. *'More coming,'* the wolf's voice in his head said. The thoughts, *'Who are these men and why is this happening?'* never entered his mind. That would come later, when the human brain was back in control.

Tom realized the ashtray was still in his blood covered hand. He readjusted his grip on the glass-smooth quartz but when he did, blood found its way beneath his fingers and the ashtray slipped from his grasp to the carpeted floor. The words and phrases he'd taught himself in Spanish and Quechua also slipped from his grasp as his shocked, exhausted mind tried to form a plan of action. "Shhhhh, shhhh, shhhh," was the best his human mind could come up with, making the universal silencing sound loud enough to be heard outside the door. It was a desperate attempt to delay the man or men on the other side long enough so he could escape.

He was on the third floor. There was only one door. The thought of climbing out the window never occurred to him.

Tom desperately wished he had a gun. He'd naively believed he wouldn't need one on this assignment and his supervisor had actually discouraged the idea. "Not that kind of mission," he remembered Bob Waterman telling him with a smile. "A gun in a foreign country will get you into more trouble than you'll need."

'And like a fool I believed you,' Tom thought, seeing Waterman's smirking face in the dark before him. Then another face appeared before him. One of his instructors at the FBI School. The Texan. Winstead. The man who'd simultaneously amused and terrified the young recruits going through the training.

"If you ever find yourself facing a better armed man," Winstead had forcefully stated one afternoon during combatives training, "you damned sure better figure out a way to kill that man and then equip yourself with his superior weaponry."

These thoughts galloped through Tom's mind in milliseconds. He crouched down and ran his hands over the dead man's body, searching for something, anything. His thumb caught on a thin chain hung around the man's neck. He felt a small, round metal disk attached to it. He froze. It was a soldier's pin. A random bit of information from his pre-mission briefing sparked through his brain. Peruvian military personnel wore these small disks inscribed with their name and unit designation. This wasn't some local bandit. This was a soldier. He released the disk and continued his search.

In the pants pocket he found a knife. He hastily wiped the blood from his hands on the man's clothes then slid the knife from the pocket. Some type of folding knife. He pulled the blade open and held it in his right hand, then continued frisking the body with his left. A holster on the right side under the loose shirt. The handle of a pistol. He pulled the pistol out and up and tried to see what kind it was in the dim light. Some type of revolver.

At that moment Alejandro quietly opened the door and stuck his head inside. *"Marcos!"* he whispered into the darkness.

From his position close to the floor Tom could see only the silhouette of Alejandro's head and upper torso against the light from the hallway. It looked just like the black silhouette targets they practiced on at the range. He extended his left arm at the shape and convulsed his hand three times. The muzzle blasts produced a strobe light effect. Tom saw the surprised look on the young face of the shape as it fell in slow motion into the room. For a moment it didn't seem at all real–Tom was sure the gun hadn't worked as he hadn't heard it fire.

'*Am I deaf?*' he suddenly thought. '*Did the gunshots make me deaf?*' He could hear nothing. There wasn't even the high-pitched ringing tone he usually heard after shooting at the range.

Then he clearly heard a man's voice say, *"Que demonios!"* from the next room. He waited, gun pointed at the doorway. Other doors started opening in the hallway. People were talking, calling out. The complete fear he'd been gripped by earlier now turned into something else. He felt a rage boiling up inside him. He wanted this to be over. At the same time part of his mind was shocked that killing felt so surprisingly natural. It was even easy, so much easier than he'd ever imagined. It was also extremely satisfying in some deep, base way. '*This is just a dream,*' he thought. "Of course," he said aloud. Then Tom watched himself from a distance as he stood and walked boldly into the hallway, knife in one hand, revolver in the other, wolf brain in full control.

"Ay dios mio!" a woman screamed at his appearance. The few people in the hallway disappeared back into their rooms, doors quickly closing, latches snapped into place.

No one else was out there. No other killers. '*But they're coming,*' said the unfamiliar wolf's voice in his head. Then the lizard's flat, unemotional voice ordered, '*RUN.*'

Tom looked down at himself, saw he was covered with blood and dressed only in his skivvies. He took a step down the hallway, stopped and whirled back into his room, clumsily stepping over both bodies as he made his way to the bureau. Setting the gun and knife on the bureau, he ripped a pale yellow, cotton shirt from the drawer and paused before pulling it on. Instead he reached for the bed and pulled the sheet from it, using it to wipe the blood from his hands, arms, chest and legs.

"Jesus, Jesus, help me, Jesus."

His hands shook. He rolled the sheet up, used a clean spot to wipe his face, threw the sheet across the bed. "Hail Mary, full of grace. Hail Mary full of grace."

Tom grabbed the shirt again, pulled it on; then grabbed the pants he'd laid across a chair and pulled them on, stuffing the shirt inside the pants. Buckled his belt. Stuck the gun behind the belt in front like he'd seen his friend Jelly Bryce do at the range.

"Help me, Jesus, Lord help me, Jesus."

He closed the knife and slid it into his pocket. Slipped his bare feet into his shoes. Pulled on his suit coat and scanned the room, the interior visible now from the light spilling in from the hallway.

'Enough time to pack my bag?' the human voice weakly asked in his head.

'Time to go, you ridiculous creature,' commanded the wolf's voice as the lizard brain dumped more adrenalin into his bloodstream.

"Jesus, gotta gogogo. Gotta gogogo."

Maniacally energized again, Tom pulled the pistol from his waistband with his trembling left hand, stepped over Marcos' body and stopped at the doorway just long enough to look down both ends of the hallway. Seeing it was still clear, he fled, inadvertently stepping on Alejandro's hand on his way out the door toward the staircase.

* * *

By the time one of the guests on the third floor of La Casa de La Rosa had worked up the courage to get involved and telephoned the desk clerk to report the shooting, Tom Wilson was fast walking his way through the darkness down Avenida Primavera toward the US Embassy. His heart was still racing, and he'd already sweat through the clean shirt he'd put on just minutes before–but he was alive and felt like he was flying. He'd never been so scared or felt so alive in all his life. Over and over in his mind the horrible events in the hotel room replayed. So much of it was missing, though, big gaps in time between moments of shocking clarity. The terror and fear of waking up realizing someone was on top of him, feeling those big powerful hands wrapped around his throat; then suddenly he was hitting that man with something–yes, the ashtray–until the man stopped struggling. How they'd gotten from the bed to the floor Tom had no clue. Then the knock on the door, seeing the silhouette in the doorway, and firing the gun.

"It was just like they taught us at the range," Tom said to himself, marveling at what he'd done and so grateful for the training he'd been given. *'The gun,'* he thought, *'How many bullets did I fire?'* He couldn't remember. He pressed his left hand against his jacket, feeling the revolver tucked behind his belt. He'd have to check the cylinder, see what he had left for ammunition.

Smiling like a madman he kept moving, passing a giant statue of Pizarro on horseback as he scanned around and behind him every few steps. *'Too much,'* he thought, *'Gotta slow down.'* A military vehicle drove past him heading the opposite way. The driver glanced at Tom, then looked away. Tom felt vulnerable, exposed. His tan suit and open-collared shirt didn't look out of place in the city. He probably looked like any other tourist or businessman heading home after a late night at one of the many bars or clubs that catered to gentlemen of means.

"Take it easy take it easy take it easy," he repeated aloud to himself.

He tried to make himself slow down, but broke into a trot instead. It was like the time he'd taken too much Benzedrine, except this was much more powerful. He felt he was on the edge of crazy, about to lose control any moment.

He smoothed his hair; made himself breathe slower, told himself to get hold, calm the hell down, think. That's when the question surfaced, popping up in the middle of his racing thoughts like a swimmer who'd been submerged too long, suddenly gasping for air and demanding his attention. *'Why the hell would anyone want to kill me?!'* the human voice asked.

"What for?" Tom said aloud. "Why me, why now? What the hell did I do?" Then the big question dropped on him like a safe in a Laurel and Hardy short. *'Who?'* The last thought stopped him in his tracks. Not many people knew he was there, even fewer knew why. He went down the list: the American ambassador, maybe one of his assistants at the embassy; his contact here in Lima; Waterman, his supervisor back in El Paso; and the boss, Mister Hoover. Tom's eyes narrowed at the thought of Waterman, then the anger welled up again. This time it was directed at the whole fucked up assignment he'd been sent on.

Walking normally now, he took a left onto Avenida Panamericana. He could see the well-lighted front of the US Embassy building a half mile away, American flag cascading gently in the warm breeze. But something was wrong there too. There was a lot of activity in the area. Way too much for this time of night. Republican Guard vehicles were cruising slowly up and down the Avenue. Several men were gathered on corners, dressed in civilian clothing but clearly military by their posture and demeanor. Tom glanced at his right wrist to check the time. His watch was missing, replaced by a deep, bleeding scratch. His eyes returned to the embassy. He'd headed there immediately, seeing it as his only safe haven in this dangerous, hostile country, a country he'd come to despise even before it tried to murder him. One of the vehicles took a turn, heading his way.

The wolf brain which had been quiet for a bit just below the surface growled, *'Embassy's not safe. Lima's not safe. Not safe here at all.'* The lizard brain again made its desire known, kicking in another shot of adrenalin for good measure. *'Runrunrun!'*

Tom took one last look at the embassy, turned on his heel and stepped off the roadway between some long, low buildings. He'd been in this area before. He knew the railway was ahead.

"Screw this place," the wolf's voice raged, talking out loud now. "Screw this God forsaken shithole, screw that prick Waterman, screw J. Edgar Hoover in the ass and screw the FBI."

* * *

Tom Wilson woke up, his eyes wide and bulging. He wasn't breathing. Someone was on top of him, their hands wrapped around his throat, thumbs pressing on his windpipe.

"Jesus!" he screamed as he sat up on the floor of the rail car, kicking his legs and striking out with his hands at the empty air around him. He was sweating profusely, covered with dust and grime and three days' worth of stubble. He was also starving and getting desperate again for water. The last food he'd eaten had been at the hotel restaurant the evening before the attack in his room; the last water from a stream beside the tracks when the train had stopped to take on water the afternoon before. Tom had been careful as he drank so he wasn't seen by the members of the crew as they filled their leather buckets with water before passing them up to be poured into the train's tender. He'd wished he had one of the buckets, but couldn't even find an old can to save some water in.

    The train he was on belonged to Peru's Central Railway. He'd managed to jump aboard one of the open, empty cars as it trundled slowly past, a few miles beyond the Desamparados Station in Lima. How he'd avoided the patrols that were apparently searching for him he had no idea. He also wasn't sure of where this train was heading, except he believed they were travelling in a general northerly direction. It was hard to tell as there were so many tunnels, turns, and zigzags through canyons and barren, mountainous terrain. They also seemed to be climbing in altitude, as his ears kept popping every few miles and it was getting cooler. A few times he'd risked peeking out the open doorway as the train negotiated a long winding turn. It was only then he could see the locomotive pulling the train. A large, steam operated engine, it was pulling about eighteen or so cars. Most were empty, doors opened, like the one he'd stowed away on. He knew from one of the basic briefings he'd been given back in El Paso that many of the trains were used to haul mining supplies; he'd figured they were heading to the Sierras to load up on copper or something similar.

    Despite being hungry and thirsty, Tom had unexpectedly found his time on the train somewhat pleasant. Though he'd never really liked being alone, the constant movement of the car and sound of the wheels clacking along the tracks had been very calming for him, especially since each moment took him further from the nightmare Lima had become.

    Boom, boom, chick, chick, clack, clack, boom, boom, chicka, chicka, clack, clack. The rhythmic pulse was soothing, almost hypnotic.

    Climbing higher through the Andes, the train passed the ruins of immense Incan fortresses and temples. The many bridges they'd crossed also evoked images from one of his favorite books, *The Bridge of San Luis Rey* by Thornton Wilder. Thinking about the theme of the book, the search for some type of meaning in the death of people who'd perished in a train wreck in Peru, Tom had reflected on the meaning of his own life and the events that had catapulted him from steady FBI man on an interesting assignment in an exotic foreign land to hunted deserter on the run to God only knows where.

All he had with him was the pistol and knife he'd taken from the dead soldier, his wallet with his Bureau-produced, fake Massachusetts identification, and several hundred dollars in bills and change in local currency. In his haste to escape he'd left behind his sterilized passport and a money belt that held several thousand dollars in various currencies and gold coins. His watch was also missing, apparently torn from his wrist during the struggle in the room. His father had given him that watch just before Tom had left on this assignment. Tom rubbed the now scabbed over cut on his wrist where the watch had been and thought about his dad. He hadn't told his father much about the job he was being sent on, only that he'd be out of the country for a bit and that his parents shouldn't expect to hear from him for a while. His father, a successful patent attorney who'd never been enthralled with the idea of the FBI or his son working for it, had tried once more to persuade Tom to leave the Bureau and come work with him.

"You've done your part, son," he'd said earnestly. "It's time to come home. I'm not getting any younger, and your mom and I both miss you and worry about you. The business is yours to take over, you know that. You can start a family and settle down."

The words had fallen on deaf ears. Tom still loved the Bureau and felt his work was more important now than ever, considering the world was being consumed by war.

The secret mission he'd been sent on was to set up a radio station in a safe house in Lima. Once the base was established, Tom would report on any movements of Axis troops or related activities to his handler, Waterman.

It was Waterman who'd hooked Tom up with Manuel, a local man paid by the FBI to help him during his time in Lima. Though Waterman had earnestly and repeatedly described Manuel as an "asset," Tom had been less than impressed. The thirty-year-old auto mechanic came across as not very bright and primarily interested in seeing how much extra cash he could coax out of Tom. Not knowing the local languages also put Tom at a severe disadvantage, making him almost totally dependent upon Manuel.

"Don't worry about it," Waterman had said when Tom expressed concern about the lack of preparation he'd been provided. "Our asset is a solid guy; I've worked with him before. He knows what to do. You just get your shop set up and then make your daily transmissions. The rest of the time is yours to enjoy."

"Enjoy?" Tom had asked, looking for something a little more specific.

"Enjoy," Waterman had said with a salacious grin. "For Christ's sake, kid, you're what, twenty-nine, thirty?"

"Thirty."

"Not married, no kids. Jeez, I'm jealous!" Waterman said shaking his head. "You're gonna be in the land of little brown people with a bucket of cash. Everyone will believe you're a well-off businessman from a rich American export company. The broads are unbelievable there. Lima's no small, jerkwater town, you know. It's huge. Beautiful buildings, beaches, a race track. It's better than Miami, kid. Just keep your eyes and ears open, get your reports in, and spend the rest of your time getting screwed, blewed and tattooed!"

Tom remembered smiling at the advice, thinking if this is what his supervisor was telling him to do, then obviously there was very little danger in the assignment. That impression was driven all the way home for him when he'd asked about bringing a firearm and Waterman had rolled his eyes and fed him the line about a "gun getting him into more trouble than he'd need."

"Asshole." Tom said the word to the image of Waterman's grinning face behind his closed eyes. Then the thought, *'I'm the asshole,'* punched him in the face and he opened his eyes and slowly shook his head. "Never again."

His back against the wall of the car, legs stretched out on the floor, Tom felt his body gently rock as the train trundled along. *Boom, boom, chick, chick, clack, clack.* Through the open door he watched the countryside pass by. The occasional people he'd seen were dressed in traditional garb. The suits and ties worn in the cities were absent out here. The people wore strong, warm, homespun clothing and sandals. They chewed coca leaves and lived in buildings made of adobe, thatched with patches of tile. They planted and lived on a diet heavy with corn and potatoes.

He'd seen more of the "real" Peru the past few days than he had the entire time while living in Lima. It was different out here. The veneer was stripped away. The people worked in colonial mines and on plantations. They lived in villages where the local church was the center of it all, surrounded by a marketplace where they would buy, sell, trade and barter. *'Good, honest Christians,'* Tom had thought time and again.

That thought alone helped Tom feel safe out here, in the countryside. It was ridiculous, he knew, because he didn't speak the language and was probably being hunted by government agents. But he'd been overtaken by a feeling of calm since waking up from the most recent nightmare a short time before.

'Two soldiers,' Tom thought, nodding his head. "Two trained assassins–and I killed them both," he said aloud. For the first time, the thought of killing the men hadn't nauseated him, even though he still believed in his heart killing was a sin. "They came at *me*. They tried to murder me first. I never did anything to them. Screw them," he said getting angry again. "And screw this country. I'm going home."

Immediately after the words left his lips the train shuddered for a moment as it entered a tight curve. The wheels squealed as it began to slow. The engineer sounded the steam whistle a few times, short staccato pulses that served as greeting and warning to those near the tracks.

A boy leading a white llama with packs on its back momentarily appeared in the opened doorway, no more than twenty feet away. The boy glanced inside the car, saw Tom and smiled. Tom waved in response but it was too late, the car had carried him past the boy. Then Tom heard someone shout. He jumped to his feet in a crouch and moved toward the corner of the car, steadying himself with a hand against the wall. More people were visible through the doorway. He realized they were moving through a village. He wondered if the train would stop. Tom crept to the side of the doorway and looked out, expecting to see armed guards by the tracks. All he saw instead were a few Indians sitting on the ground eating vegetable stew from an earthenware pot. His stomach growled loudly.

Tom scanned the interior of the train car to make sure he was leaving nothing behind. He felt the wallet in his back pants pocket, closed knife in his jacket pocket. He shifted the revolver in his beltline, making sure it was covered by his suitcoat. Reaching through the doorway, he grabbed the thin iron rail fixed to the outside of the train car next to the door, glanced up and down the tracks and swung himself out and to the ground as casually as he could. As soon as his feet hit the ground he took a few steps to get his balance and then walked directly away from the train tracks toward the village. The train kept moving. It wasn't going to stop. Just for a moment Tom considered climbing back on board. He looked over his shoulder at the open car door. He could make it if he ran. His stomach growled again.

* * *

The next few days passed without event. Tom found the villagers to be calm, welcoming and generous people. Even with the language barrier, his needs were understood. He was hungry and thirsty. "Of course you are," the middle-aged, bronze-skinned man wearing a large, colorful flat hat seemed to say, smiling and nodding as he passed a wooden bowl of stew to Tom. "You are a human being. Eat. Drink."

The man had been sitting on the ground with three other villagers when Tom approached and tried to ask the name of the village and buy some food. The men seemed curious about him, but they weren't afraid, even when Tom couldn't respond when the middle-aged man asked where he came from– *"Maymanta kanki?"*

It was obvious the Yankee didn't understand. Instead, Tom had made an eating motion with his hand and pointed at the stew, holding a few coins out. The man with the flat hat neither rejected him nor took the coins. He'd simply pointed to the ground next to him.

Tom had smiled and said thank you in Quechua as best he could. *"Solpayki!"*

They'd smiled at his attempt to speak their language, replied, *"Imamanta!"* and then exchanged words between themselves as he watched them closely for signs of deception. Their eyes were clear, smiles genuine, Tom thought.

He sat on the ground with them and ate from a wooden bowl as they did, using his hands and drinking the broth from the bowl. They gave him cool water poured from a large jug. They constantly smiled at him and gently touched the side of his arm as they spoke in a singsong cadence. When they'd finished eating Tom smiled back and again offered them some coins. This time they accepted with the same joy and naturalness as they'd given him food and water.

Later, the man with the hat had taken him to the church. The priest spoke some English. Tom explained he was a traveler who'd gotten separated from his associates and needed to get to Mexico. The priest looked at him directly: Tom was sure the lie was obvious. But then the priest went to the door of the church and called a young man over. Speaking the local dialect, the priest gave instructions to the man, then looked at Tom and said, "This is Havier. He will guide you to Mexico. His family is very poor. Wife very ill. You can pay him, yes?"

"Yes, of course, of course, thank you, Padre, thank you," replied Tom as he extended his hand. The priest shook his hand, then looked over at a metal offering box surrounded by a half dozen votive candles and raised his eyebrows.

Tom smiled and nodded. Taking several bills from his pocket, he showed them to the priest then slipped them through the slot in the box. The priest relaxed a bit and smiled back, said a few words to Havier and the young man left.

"He will come by for you tomorrow morning," the priest said. "Tonight, you stay here, eat, sleep. I will have the woman wash and pack your clothes and bring you some better clothes to travel in. Clothes like the people wear."

Again the priest looked knowingly at Tom.

Tom nodded and thanked him again. He took a few more bills from his pocket and offered them to the priest. The priest smiled and glanced at the offering box again. Tom walked back to the box and slid the money through the slot. Then he kneeled on the wooden slat before the box, picked up a long, thin stick from a can and held the end in the flame of one of the candles. Once the stick lit, he carefully transferred the shared flame to one of the unlit candles. Tom did this slowly, taking his time to make sure the wick was burning before sliding the lit end of the stick back into the small sand-filled can. As the priest watched, Tom blessed himself, making the sign of the cross, then clasped his hands before him and bowed his head in prayer.

* * *

During the course of a week, Havier guided Tom through Peru's backcountry. They started off in the bed of a truck, then walked for two days before getting another ride, this time in a bus. They passed flocks of llamas grazing in centuries-old pastures and men planting fields using twin oxen to draw wooden plows through the rich red earth. Tom marveled at scenery so beautiful it took his breath. A winding river flowed through a lush green valley; a desert rolled out before them; mountain vistas rose off in the distance. Thoughts of the Bureau, Lima, and what faced him back in the United States faded from his mind sometimes for hours at a stretch.

They stopped several times at small villages and hamlets during their journey to spend time with people Havier knew. Tom was amazed at the way the people lived. They ate while sitting on the ground; the women wove strong, warm clothing on small hand looms; they spent a great deal of time and effort creating colorful shawls and ponchos with intricate designs they wore with pride. The clothes seemed to project the core essence of the people. While they had very little material goods in comparison to what Tom was used to, they seemed to be unfailingly happy with their lives and each other here in the high Andes. Everyone they met welcomed them with a genuine smile and a friendly sing-song greeting. As they left one small village, Havier looked knowingly at Tom, almost as if reading his thoughts and said, "Here, the people… lot work, not much eat. Good people."

Eventually they made their way down from the high country and travelled long, winding dirt roads through jungle-like terrain. The strange ache he'd been feeling in his muscles stopped as they'd descended. Though Tom wasn't aware of it, Havier had guided them from Peru into Columbia. In a village just over the border, Havier arranged a ride for them in the bed of another truck. As they lay back against their small travel packs in the truck, eating some food bought in a hamlet, bouncing along the unpaved roads, Columbia turned into Panama, then Costa Rica.

Off the truck, the next days blurred one into another first on a decrepit old bus then another flatbed truck through Nicaragua, Honduras and Guatemala. Though they passed through several border checkpoints along the way, the money Tom had provided the drivers was enough to pay off the guards so they didn't ask any questions about the two odd passengers. Throughout their trip of almost two weeks, Havier remained quiet and pensive, but never gave Tom reason to suspect he was doing anything other than had been agreed upon. The journey had become job-like, grueling. Both men had lost a lot of weight and were in desperate need of a bath and shave.

In Guatemala City, a change came over Havier. He

smiled at Tom, looked relieved.

"Here," he said in faltering English. "We here now. Guatemala. You," he said, placing his hand for the first time on Tom's shoulder in the way Tom had seen Peruvians talk to one another, "you go now by alone. Mehico." Havier pointed at an old run down bus idling by the curb across from where they stood. "Mehico," he repeated, nodding and smiling, pointing again at the bus. *"¿Intindinkichu?* Yes? Unnerstan?"

Tom nodded and smiled back, his dried, sunburned lips feeling they were going to split from being stretched. He extended his hand and the men shook hands warmly.

"Solpayki–thank you, Havier, thank you, amigo," said Tom. "I will never forget your kindness. God bless you, my friend."

Havier smiled back, clearly understanding the 'thank you' and 'amigo' but not much else. But he got it.

Tom reached into his pocket and slipped the folded bills he'd prepared into his hand. Then he reached out and shook Havier's hand again, surreptitiously passing the bills to him. Havier smiled again and nodded.

"Huq p'unchaykama," the young man said sincerely, then nodded and said, *"Yara*–care full, yes? Care full." Then Havier turned and walked away, leaving Tom alone again in yet another foreign country where he neither spoke the language nor knew the customs. His heart started to beat faster when he thought about the revolver in his pack. There were three rounds left. He'd kept the gun and knife, even though he realized their possession could have created much trouble for them had they been searched along the way. The feeling of complete vulnerability he'd experienced in the hotel room would not leave him for the rest of his life. He knew he would never be caught without a gun again. *Ever.*

He walked toward the bus and saw his reflection in a glass window of a shop; the image stopped him. He didn't recognize himself. He hadn't shaved in two weeks. His dark beard and uncombed hair framed his face. The skin on his face that was visible was deeply tanned. He was dressed as a native and pretty much blended in with the people on the street. His heart slowed down and his confidence returned. A Peruvian saying he'd read during his truncated training had stayed with him and he repeated it aloud. *"No ladrón, no mentiroso, no ocioso."* It translated as, "Do not steal, do not lie, do not be lazy." Tom repeated it quietly to himself as he approached the open door of the bus. The driver, seated behind the steering wheel, looked up from a newspaper he was reading as Tom stood in the doorway. Tom asked, *"Mehico?"* doing his best to sound like a native.

The driver grimaced at him. Tom thought of his appearance. He knew he smelled as ripe as he looked. He took out the remaining coins he had left and held them out. The driver glanced at them, shook his head.

"Quetzal," he said.

Tom produced a Peruvian bill. Again the driver shook his head. *"Quetzal. La plata."*

Tom looked into the bus. There were only a few people. A woman with two small children. An older couple holding paper bags on their laps. Tom thought for a moment then reached into the pocket of his poncho and produced the knife he'd taken from the assassin. The driver's eyebrows raised a bit. Tom smiled and extended the closed knife to the driver for inspection. The driver took the knife, turned it over in his hand, then opened it and examined the blade. He dragged him thumb sideways across the edge. It was well made and very sharp. He looked at Tom again, held out his other hand, pointing at the coins Tom still had in his palm. Tom gave the man the coins. The driver slipped the knife in his pocket and tossed his head toward the back of the bus. Tom climbed aboard.

*   *   *

Eighteen bumpy, dusty hours later Tom was in Mexico City. Though starving and desperate for rest despite having slept sporadically during the journey, he used a telephone and called his father collect. Keeping his voice steady as he could, Tom told his dad he was coming home, told him it was "time to start my real life." Then, without going into detail, he told his father he was in Mexico City and needed some money to get home. "Can you wire me some money, Dad?" he asked. His father, sounding simultaneously concerned, relieved and happy didn't hesitate. "Of course, son. I'll send it immediately."

Two hours later Tom had collected the money from the wire transfer. He bought some tacos from a vendor on the street and ate the food as he stood there, washing them down with a cold bottle of Coca Cola. Then he walked to a seedy hotel and rented a room, greeting the proprietor's skeptical expression with a handful of pesos. In the room he unrolled the brown paper package containing his suitcoat, shirt, pants and shoes and laid them out on the bed. Locking the door behind him, he left the room and went to the communal bathroom at the end of the hall and took his first bath in weeks. The warm water and soap felt like something foreign and deliciously familiar at the same time. Leaving his native garb folded neatly on a table in the bathroom, Tom went back to his room wrapped in one of the hotel's thin white towels. He ran his hands through his hair, straightening it as much as possible, then pulled on his clothes and went outside to find a barber shop.

Half an hour later he emerged from the barbershop looking like an American ex-pat but still smelling like the countryside. It was his clothing, he realized, as he held a sleeve up to his nose and breathed in. Tom walked for a bit until he found a decent clothing store. A new suit, underwear, socks and shoes completed the transformation, leaving more than enough cash in his pocket to get him comfortably back across the border.

"Across the border," Tom said quietly as he tied his shoes. "With no passport. Great." As he said this he stood up and looked at his reflection in the full length mirror. He recognized the man he saw, even though he was thinner and seemed older than he remembered. The sunburnt skin above the beard line added a strange effect to his appearance as well. Then Tom realized he was different in more than appearance. Just a few weeks ago, the thought of being completely isolated in a foreign country with no passport would have terrified him. Now here he stood not only in that situation, but with a stolen pistol tucked in his belt, on the run from foreign assassins, after having deserted his mission and gone AWOL on the FBI. An image of the dead bodies in the hotel room back in Lima flashed in his mind. Tom scratched his eyebrow. Then he began to laugh.

"Señor?" asked the shopkeeper with a smile of his own, "You like the suit, yes?"

Tom looked at the well-dressed Mexican and laughed harder. "Yes," he said, nodding. "Yes, I do."

The shopkeeper began laughing as well and then held up a paper bag for Tom. Tom raised his eyebrows and looked inside the bag. The shopkeeper had folded his old clothes and packed them up for him.

Tom shook his head. "Burn 'em," he said as he reached into his new pants pocket and pulled out money to pay the bill.

*   *   *

By late afternoon Tom was on a bus heading north toward Juarez. The money his father had wired him bought a ticket on a nice bus. A nice bus that travelled on a good road and would move all night and well into the following day. This was possible because the bus's scheduled stops included changing drivers along the route.

By early evening of the second day he stood in Juarez looking at the US border.

Tom had thought out his strategy on the ride. Though he knew SIS had people in Mexico City, he'd had no way to contact any of them. None of the agents assigned to SIS were given the identities of any of the others. "Safer for everyone this way," Waterman had told him. Tom's eyes narrowed at the mental image of his supervisor.

"Safer for me to get back alone," Tom said to himself as he approached the young American border guard in the booth facing the walking lane. Luckily for him, the young man accepted his story of having lost his passport after a night of drunken partying in Juarez. It obviously wasn't the first time he'd heard this type of tale. The fact that Tom was both polite and contrite, talked American and still had his wallet with his Massachusetts driver's license sealed the deal. Tom never mentioned anything about the FBI. The border agent never wrote down his fake information. There would be no record of his returning to the States.

As Tom walked across the border in his new suit with his stolen revolver in his belt the thought occurred to him it was actually kind of a shame he was done with the SIS and FBI–he might actually not be all that bad at this spy business.

Spotting a telephone booth at the back of the Quality Coin and Loan where he'd gone to exchange his pesos for dollars, Tom asked the clerk for the time. Nearly 5 p.m. He nodded to the clerk as he took his fresh, green American currency, then walked to the booth and stepped inside.

Picking up the receiver, he dropped some coins into the slot and dialed a number.

"FBI, El Paso office. How may I direct your call?"

The woman's voice was unfamiliar.

"Agent Waterman, please."

"I'm sorry, Agent Waterman is no longer assigned here. Is there someone else you'd like to speak to?"

Tom hesitated. "Could you please tell me who's in charge there?"

"Yes, sir," the woman answered, "That would be Special Agent Bryce."

Tom's grip on the phone tightened as he pressed the receiver to his ear. "Delf Bryce?"

Now the woman hesitated. "Um, yes, sir. Could I ask who is calling please?"

"Is he there? Can I speak to him please?"

"I'm afraid he's gone for the day," she replied, growing more cautious. Then she asked again, "Who is this calling, please?"

"That's okay," Tom replied. "I'll try again tomorrow." As he placed the receiver back on its hanger he could hear her voice asking for his name again.

"Son of a gun," Tom said brightly with a smile. Jelly was the new SAC at El Paso. He trusted Jelly, practically more than anyone he'd ever known. He could go to Jelly. Tell him what happened. Jelly would know what to do. Jelly would help him with this mess.

Tom exited the telephone booth feeling like he'd just been reborn, the awful events of Lima and the grueling trek north quickly fading into unreal memory–almost as if it had all happened to someone else. "Son of a gun!" he said again happily as he walked out of the small store and onto the sidewalk. He looked around the deserted industrial area. Many of the stores and businesses appeared to be shut down. Times were tough all over and El Paso hadn't been spared.

'Hotels are that a' way,' Tom thought, remembering the direction toward the heart of town. Then another thought elbowed the hotel aside. *'I need a drink.'* An image of his mother's disapproving face flashed in his mind. "Sorry Mother," he said aloud, "but actually, I want a drink." He smiled again and said, "Hell, I deserve a stinkin' drink!"

His eyes spotted the red glow of a fluorescent light fixture in a window a block away. *'If that's not a bar, I'm a monkey's uncle,'* he thought. *'First a drink–or two. Then a hotel, food, sleep, and I'll call Jelly at the office first thing in the morning.'* Tom stuck his hand in his back pocket for his wallet. Better to have a few dollars ready to pay in the bar. He didn't frequent these places, but even he knew it was never a good idea to pull out your wallet in a gin mill.

"Special Agent in Charge D.A. Bryce," Tom said happily, shaking his head slowly side to side. He could hardly believe it. He was sliding his wallet back in his pocket when he felt the small hard round metal rod pressed against his back.

"Move you die," the disembodied voice warned in a quiet growl.

"Wait–" Tom started to say. Then a flash of white light and the street vanished into darkness.

*   *   *

Tom Wilson woke up, his eyes wide and bulging. He wasn't breathing. Someone was on top of him, their hands wrapped around his throat, thumbs pressing on his windpipe.

"Jesus, no!" he screamed as he sat up, striking out with his hands and feet. His fists pounded into the side of a brick wall, tearing the skin from his knuckles. He was completely disoriented. Had no idea where he was, what he was doing, what was happening–or had happened to him. "Get away from me!" he yelled out, pushing now against the wall. It was dark where he was; there was dirt beneath him, vegetation, broken glass and dog feces. He recoiled from the darkness, pressing his back against the wall. He couldn't see. There was something in his eyes. His lips felt odd, his face burned in the darkness. Lima. He was in Lima. No, not Lima. Mexico. *'What the fuck is happening to me?'* His mind turned on itself. The lizard part of his brain was demanding escape and dumping adrenalin into his system; the animal brain was raging then withdrawing, unsure which way to move, what to do.

Then he froze. Everything just stopped, including his breathing. He froze in place, waiting for the pain, listening with every fiber of his being, trying to hear what was going on around him. A car horn sounded nearby. Then he heard voices. A woman and a man, talking quietly. Moving closer. As Tom's heart pounded in his chest, he felt tears gathering in his eyes. The voices grew louder, closer, then they passed. Tom felt a warm breeze flow over him. His head started to pound, blood pressure forcing his eyes to bulge. He exhaled loudly, then started sucking in air in big gasping gulps. No one hit him. No one was there with him.

He was outside. It was night. He slowly stood up to a low crouch, hand braced against the wall; a sharp pain from his ribs made his head spin. He felt blood in his mouth, swallowed some before he realized what it was, then spit the rest out onto the ground. He looked around. He was still on the street near the bar. His head throbbed. He felt a tender spot on the back of his skull behind his right ear.

"What the hell…" he said, then spun around, looking for whoever had done this. *'Done what?'* His last thoughts had been that the assassins from Lima had caught up to him.

That he was a dead man right there, right then.

Lima. He'd killed two men. Broken the sixth commandment–*twice*. His hands started shaking, then it spread to his whole body. He had trouble catching his breath. "I'm in El Paso," he heard his voice say as the words spilled from his bloody mouth. He felt for the pistol in his belt. It was gone. So was his wallet. He groaned.

Tom Wilson–veteran FBI agent, international spy, killer of trained foreign assassins–had apparently been mugged on the street in El Paso, Texas.

"Sweet Jesus," Tom sobbed. "I'm a joke. I'm a ridiculous joke. I don't belong here. I have to go home." Then he remembered his friend. His friend–Jelly Bryce.

"Jelly will know what to do. Jelly will know what to do."

Tom knew where the El Paso SAC was billeted. He'd been to the small house just on the outskirts of town before. Waterman had met him there once, just before Tom had left for Peru. Jelly would be there. Jelly would be at the house. Jelly *had* to be at the house. Tom was dying. He knew it. He knew he was dying. His mind was teetering on the edge of an abyss. He was going over in pieces. He could feel it. Only Jelly could help him. He stumbled onto the street and started walking, staggering like a rum-soaked drunk.

* * *

Tom wasn't sure exactly how he got there. He remembered walking by the road, sticking his thumb out to the few vehicles that passed him. A truck stopped. An old man driving had asked him what happened to him. Tom thought he'd said he'd fallen or something like that. Whatever he'd said, the old man had taken pity on him and driven him the few miles to the address Tom had described. Looking out the window as they neared the location, Tom said, "Here's good, please, sir."

Tom climbed from the truck up near the top of the long sand and gravel driveway, thanked the old man and stumbled down toward the house. It was moonless dark and Tom felt he was walking for too long a time when he practically fell into a black Bureau sedan. The small house seemed to materialize behind the car as he stared, then it disappeared into the darkness again. *'What if Jelly isn't there?'* the voice in his head asked. *'What if it's Waterman?'*

Tom shook his head side to side. "No, no, no," he repeated, "Jelly's there. Jelly's the SAC. Waterman was the SAC and SIS chief, so now Jelly's the chief."

Yet still…

Tom quietly walked up the steps to the porch. The small house was silent and completely dark. Not a light on anywhere. He wanted to knock on the door but hesitated.

'What if Jelly isn't here? What if it's someone else? What if Jelly is sleeping? What if this is the wrong house…?' The thoughts came one after another, holding his knuckles back inches from the wooden frame of the door.

'I can't even do this right,' said the voice in his head, *'I'm useless, useless. A failure. Dad was right. This was such a mistake.'* Tom turned his back to the door, moved a few steps to the side, and sank into a crouch. Next thing he knew his back was against the wall of the house, then he was seated on the porch, and a strong memory of the train flooded over him and he was back in the Andes, alone in the train car, listening to the distinctive sound of the steel wheels on the rails: *boom, boom, chick, chick, clack, clack…*

"Who is it?" a voice demanded from his right.

Tom froze, his voice catching in his throat. Then one word escaped: "Jelly?" he asked weakly. His voice didn't sound right to his ears.

"Who are you?"

Tom thought it sounded like his friend, though they hadn't talked in a few years.

"Jelly," Tom repeated, "Jelly, it's me, Tom."

"Tom who?" demanded the voice in the darkness.

"Wilson," Tom's voice croaked. "Tom Wilson." Tom felt relieved he'd gotten his name out. Now Jelly would help him.

Instead the voice ordered, "Stand up and walk down the steps, nice and slow. Keep your hands where I can see them."

Tom wanted to object, to reassure Jelly it was him, his friend, Tom. But the voice didn't come. All he could do was struggle to his feet and move further out onto the porch, toward the nearly invisible steps.

"Down the steps, face away from my voice. Put your hands on top of your head like in the war movies."

Again, Tom did as instructed. His heart began dancing in his chest. He felt lightheaded. The ground beneath his feet felt soft. A light came on behind him. Tom could see his own shadow on the ground. It looked as though it were stretching beneath the wheels of the sedan in the driveway. Tom's eyes locked on a glint of light reflecting off the chrome molding on the side of the car's big front fender.

"Keep your hands on your head and turn around," said the voice. If it was Jelly, Tom had never heard this tone from him before. It was pure, true menace. There was no room for discussion. Tom tore his eyes from the glinting chrome and slowly turned around, facing the light on the porch. He squinted into the glare of the yellow light, tried to make out the face of the man before him, but the light obscured the details. Though the man was naked except for his boxer shorts, Tom didn't realize it as his eyes were drawn to an object the man held at waist level. It looked like a flag. A white flag tied to the end of a stick. The absurd thought the man was surrendering flashed through his mind a split-second before he recognized the stick was a shotgun barrel. And the barrel–complete with white cloth tied to its end–was pointed right at Tom's chest.

"Tom," the voice said, the tone instantly changed and now completely recognizable as the voice of his friend. "What are you doing here?"

Tom watched the big black 12-gauge hole disappear as Jelly lowered the barrel, pointing it at the ground. "I'm one of your men, Jelly," he answered, the ground starting to pitch and swell beneath his feet as he stared at the white flag.

"What do you mean, my men?" Jelly asked, apparently so stunned by Tom's appearance he didn't even think to tell him to put his hands down.

"I'm S.I.S." A vibrating noise spun inside Tom's head like a top wavering on its point. A strange white light began flashing in his peripheral vision. *'This is it; we're losing it,'* Tom's inner voice warned over the vibrating sound.

"I need your help, Jelly," were the last words Tom got out before the vibrating sound completely filled his head, the top spinning off its point, crashing wildly and dragging him back into the engulfing darkness.

CHAPTER TWO

El Paso, Texas
17 June 1941

JELLY WALKED SOFTLY BY the spare bedroom doorway and looked in on Tom. He'd practically had to carry the semi-conscious agent into the house and onto the bed the night before. He'd wanted to get Tom a doctor but at the mention of the word, Tom had become extremely upset, insisting he was all right, repeating over and again he just needed some water and sleep. Jelly glanced at his wristwatch: 9:30 in the morning. Tom had been asleep for eleven hours.

Though he'd been restless throughout the night, at one point yelling out incomprehensibly, the injured man now lay motionless, face up on top of the blanket, breathing deeply and rhythmically. His bruised face was several shades of purple and scarlet around the eyes, cheeks and lips. Tom's top lip had been split, though fortunately, not enough to require stitches. There was a decent-sized goose egg behind his right ear that Jelly figured to be the knockout blow, most likely inflicted with a leather sap. If you knew how to wield one you could knock a man out instantly without splitting the skin. Jelly knew this because he'd seen the effects before. He carried one.

Jelly had washed the blood from Tom's face, neck and hands at the same time he'd looked the unconscious man over thoroughly to make sure there were no bullet or knife wounds that needed attending; as best he could tell, Tom had been worked over pretty good but there didn't seem to be any life-threatening injuries. None he could see, anyway.

Jelly had examined a lot of dead bodies over the years, and sometimes the cause of death wasn't visibly apparent. Something as simple as the blunt trauma caused by a single wooden garage door accidentally coming down and striking a man on top of the head could result in death without leaving a mark or a clue–and an investigation taking three days to rule out foul play because of the circumstances.

You just never knew. Because he knew *that*, Jelly was worried about his friend.

But the totality of the situation from the first moment Tom had unexpectedly arrived convinced Jelly it was best to keep this contained–at least for the time being. He'd learned that sometimes, when in doubt, it was best to follow the unofficial motto of the United States Army as Charlie Winstead had cynically related it to him: "When in doubt, *do nothing*."

Closing the door to the bedroom, Jelly walked back into the small kitchen and picked up the telephone receiver from its hook on the wall. He dialed up the office, spoke to his secretary and told her he wouldn't be in the office today but could be reached at the house. She didn't question the boss, just said, "Very good, Mister Bryce," and waited for him to hang up. He stayed on the line just for a moment, deciding whether to add anything by way of explanation, then remembered Hoover's words: "You're the boss now; you don't have to explain anything to anyone except me." Jelly placed the receiver back on the hook, picked his coffee cup up off the table and walked outside onto the front porch to drink it. Standing at the top of the steps, he scanned the area for the seventh time that morning.

He'd already walked the perimeter of the property, looking for anything that might provide a clue as to where Tom had come from or how he'd gotten there. There was nothing but some tire tracks at the top of the driveway. Jelly knew they were fresh because his car would have left tracks over them had they been there longer than the past night. He'd gotten to the house after seven. Tom had appeared around ten-thirty.

He'd also only been able to detect one set of foot prints near the fresh tire tracks. They matched the shoes Tom was wearing.

"So," Jelly ruminated aloud, "Someone dumped you off after working you over to make a point, or you got a ride from someone you knew, or you got a ride from someone you didn't know."

The first and second possibilities were highly unlikely. Anyone who knew Tom and or Jelly wouldn't have left him at the end of the road in the dark in that condition.

"A," Jelly continued, as if explaining it to a class, "because if it *was* a friend they would've helped you, and B, if it was an enemy, they would have known the consequences of leaving you alive after doing that to you."

That left a ride from someone who didn't know Tom or Jelly. That meant a taxi, or someone else Tom paid for a ride, or a good Samaritan.

Since Tom's pockets were not only empty but had been pulled inside out, and he wore no watch or had anything else on his person, Jelly doubted he'd paid anyone for a ride. Even the thought of having traded a watch–if he'd even had one–for a ride was highly unlikely. So that left a Samaritan. Most likely a neighbor on his or her way home.

If he couldn't get the story from Tom, Jelly would make some inquiries with the locals to find out if anyone had seen Tom or given him a lift. One of the best things about this part of the country was that people tended to mind their own business and keep things to themselves. You usually never even saw your neighbors unless you needed them or vice-versa; and, when that was the case, everyone willingly helped out everyone else. It was the old code of the West.

    Jelly, dressed in blue jeans, boots, and a white collared shirt, sat down on the top step and sipped his coffee. It had gone cold. He took a pack of cigarettes from his shirt pocket, shook one out far enough so his lips could snag it and pulled it from the pack like that, ready for lighting. Placing the pack back in the pocket, he fished out his new stainless Zippo lighter, snapped the cover back and spun the little wheel. The sparks hit the fluid-soaked wick, the burning alcohol-petroleum and tobacco smells blending as he took a deep drag off the smoke.

    "So if it was a local good Samaritan that gave you the ride, then the fuckstick that tuned you up and left you alive has got to be fairly close by."

    Jelly snapped the lighter's cover closed and dropped it in his shirt pocket with the smokes. Then he slowly removed the Registered Magnum from the holster on his hip, opened the cylinder and looked at the six live rounds seated in the chambers. Satisfied, he closed the cylinder carefully and deliberately and gazed up the driveway.

    It was going to be an interesting week in El Paso.

*   *   *

    Fifteen hours after showing up at Jelly's front door, Tom Wilson opened his eyes. At first he wasn't sure where he was, but as he lay there quietly, motionless, the pieces fell into place for him. He'd made it to El Paso. He was at the El Paso SAC's living quarters. He'd found Jelly. But what had he told him? Tom had very little recollection of recent events. He'd arrived in El Paso. Exchanged his pesos for dollars. Gone outside. He was looking to get a drink. Saw a bar. Then…nothing.

    No, not nothing. A gun barrel stuck in his back.

Someone–a man's voice–from behind, telling him he was going to kill him? Then nothing until he woke up on the street behind a building. Was it hours or days later? He couldn't say. He started to move but the pain hit his head like twin hammers on his temples. In response he sucked in a lungful of air expanding his ribcage and another bolt of pain shocked him, this one feeling like a dull knife plunging into the right side of his chest. He lay his head back against the pillow, feeling he was going to be sick.

"Take this."

Tom looked up to see Jelly coming through the doorway holding a glass of water and some aspirin. He struggled to sit up through the agony, doing his best to put on a brave face for his friend. The ribs felt broken. "Thanks," Tom said as he reached out for the white pills. He placed them on his tongue, avoiding making contact with his split lip. Then he took the glass and washed the aspirin down. The water tasted sweet and cold. He drained the glass.

"More?" Jelly asked.

"Please."

Jelly walked back to the kitchen. Tom could hear the water running at the tap as Jelly filled the glass. When Jelly came back to the room he handed the glass to Tom, then sat in the chair next to the bed.

"How are you feeling?"

Tom thought about it. "I feel like I've been run over by a truck." Then he shook his head and said, "I'm not…I don't know. Honestly. I think I feel more stupid than anything else."

Jelly nodded. "We've all been there." He smiled.

Tom looked at Jelly's face. He looked the same as Tom remembered. Calm, clear-eyed, confident. Tom couldn't think of anything to say. It was like he just couldn't think. He started to talk, then lost the words. Glancing at Jelly, he could see the look of concern on his friend's face. But Jelly didn't push him to talk, didn't ask any more questions except, "Can you eat?"

Tom nodded and Jelly disappeared back into the kitchen. Tom closed his eyes and faded out apparently, because it seemed like only a moment or two had passed when Jelly reappeared holding a tray with a plate full of scrambled eggs, some toast and a cup of coffee. Jelly placed the tray on the bed next to Tom who was still in a seated position against the pillows.

As Tom ate, Jelly sat in the chair and read the newspaper. Still no questions. When Tom had finished, Jelly picked up the tray with the now empty plate and cup and started to walk out. Stopping at the door, he looked at Tom and said, "Anything I need to know right this minute?" Tom paused, then shook his head. "Okay then," Jelly said in response, then added, "Ready, sleep" like the instructors used to say in the FBI School. With that Jelly closed the door behind him. Tom was asleep within a few minutes.

* * *

Jelly waited until he heard Tom's rhythmic breathing through the door before leaving the house. He walked the perimeter again, smoking and thinking as he did so. He needed to get a handle on this situation pretty damned quickly. He had an FBI office to run as well as the covert espionage wing of the Bureau that until just recently he'd known nothing about.

"What the hell, Hoover?" Jelly asked for the twentieth time since finding Tom Wilson at his front door. "What the hell have you gotten me into?"

Coming around the property to the back door, Jelly walked into the kitchen and listened. He could hear Tom snoring. He picked up the telephone and called the office. When his secretary answered, he asked for an update. The secretary, a competent woman with no obvious sense of humor, responded with a quick rundown of the status of several cases being handled, then just stopped talking. Jelly smiled and waited. Nothing. "Is that everything, Mrs. Stimson?"

"Yes, Mister Bryce. Though…" She hesitated. Mrs. Stimson never hesitated.

"Though what?"

"Well, sir, there was a telephone call yesterday. Around five o'clock. A gentlemen asked first for Mister Waterman. Then when I told him he was no longer assigned here, he asked for the name of the current SAC. I gave him your name and it seemed as though he knew you."

"But you didn't get his name."

"How do you know that?"

"Because of your efficiency Mrs. Stimson. If you'd gotten his name you would have already told me."

Jelly could feel a slight smile through the telephone.

"No, sir, you're correct. I asked several times for it, but he wouldn't give me his name."

"Made you suspicious, yes?"

"Yes."

"Good," Jelly said. "I like that very much, Mrs. Stimson. It's just too bad you didn't have the operator check to see what number the call came in from right after it happened."

"But I did, Mister Bryce," the young woman said brightly.

"Of course you did." Now they both smiled through the phone.

* * *

At six p.m. Jelly stood by the stove frying up a couple of venison steaks in a big flat iron pan. On the kitchen table stood a large round bowl filled with salad, flanked by two small decanters. One held oil, the other vinegar. Jelly had developed a taste for the dressing while living in Oklahoma City. His landlord at the time, an old Italian gentleman who'd kind of adopted Jelly, used to feed him steak and salad at least once a week. A loaf of fresh bread and bottle of red wine complemented the meal. "All a man needsa ta eat," Profetta used to say.

Over the sizzle of the meat in butter and garlic he could hear Tom walking out of the bathroom off the hallway. Jelly had left him a spare toothbrush and told him to use his shaving gear. He'd also pulled out a rolled bandage from the first aid kit and left that by the sink, telling Tom to wrap it around his chest over the bruised area to alleviate some of the pain.

"Somethin' smells good," Tom said as he walked into the kitchen. He'd shaved and showered but was still wearing the pants and shirt he'd arrived in. There was dried blood on both.

"Those clothes didn't fit you." Jelly wasn't asking. He figured his stuff would be too small for his tall friend.

Tom shook his head. "I tried washing the blood out. Didn't work as you can see."

"We'll get you some new duds tomorrow. Sit down and eat." As Jelly said the words he stuck a fork into the bigger of the two steaks and plopped it on a plate. "You sit there."

Tom sat and the two men had dinner. Tom drank three glasses of water, sipping at his wine in between. His appetite was good. Jelly started to relax a bit. *'Dying men don't eat like that,'* he thought.

When they'd finished, Jelly poured coffee for them and cleared the table. They sat and looked at each other.

"Smoke?" Jelly asked, taking out his pack and offering it to Tom.

Tom shook his head. "Never acquired the habit."

Jelly lit a cigarette and sat back in his chair. He took a long drag off the butt, blew the smoke out through his nostrils and said, "So how can I help you?"

Tom looked at him, slightly confused. "You *have* helped me. I mean you *are* helping me. What do you mean?"

"Last night when you showed up here, you said you needed my help. You said you were one of my men. Do you remember that?"

Tom placed his hand around his coffee cup and stared at the black liquid within. "Vaguely. I'm sorry to bring this trouble to you, Jelly."

Jelly smiled. "No trouble we can't handle together, Tom. Now, are you ready to fill me in?"

Tom nodded. For the next forty-five minutes he talked non-stop, starting at his being picked for SIS and including every detail of everything that had occurred since. When he got to the part at the hotel in Lima, his eyes went a little vacant and his hands started shaking. Jelly could see Tom's chest was tightening. Tom looked like a little kid as he asked for more water. Jelly filled his glass at the sink, gave it to the shaken man and encouraged him to continue the story with a simple, "And then what happened, Tom?"

Tom tried to explain what had happened, starting with his being awakened by the feeling of suffocating, a pair of strong hands wrapped around his throat. "I got him off me, somehow, then we were on the floor, and he was screaming, and I hit him with an ashtray until he stopped." Tom stopped talking. Beads of sweat broke out on his forehead. His right eye started twitching.

"Are you all right, Tom?" Jelly asked, leaning forward in his chair. He noticed Tom's left hand was contorted, sort of as if he were grasping a baseball. His thumb was locked out and extended.

"I think so, yes. It all happened so fast. And then there was a gun. And a second man. I shot him. I shot him in the chest, I think. Just like they taught us. Just like *you* taught us, Jelly. It was just like at the range, just like you said it would be. I stared at the man's chest just like you said and I fired the gun. He fell right down. But…"

"But what?"

"Well, I know it's strange, and it couldn't have happened this way, but when I shot the gun it made no noise. No noise at all. I could see the flash, and the man went down so I know it worked. I just remember thinking how odd that was."

"Was it your gun?"

"No, I didn't have a gun. Waterman said I wouldn't need one."

Jelly sighed sharply. He knew Waterman. Waterman was an idiot. One of the know nothing, do nothing types who routinely made rank despite their incompetence and ignorance. The Bureau had more than their share of these sorts it seemed. These were the guys who dismissed the value of training, who never took anything seriously except their own pleasure, career paths–and revenge on anyone who crossed them.

"So where did the gun come from?"

"It was his–the first man. The man who was strangling me." Again Tom's right eye began to twitch in jerky random patterns.

"Maybe it had a muffler on it?" Jelly asked, using a more accurate term than "silencer."

"No, no. It didn't."

"Are you sure?"

"I am. I carried that gun from that moment until…"

"Until when?"

Tom looked up at Jelly with a shocked expression. "Until yesterday. I had that gun yesterday. In El Paso."

* * *

Tom talked for another hour. He told Jelly about the soldier's pin on the man who'd tried to kill him; about his trek north, the train, the villages, the priest and Havier, the trucks and bus rides. He described the jungles and swarms of insects, the mountains, the giant snake he'd seen. He explained about calling his father and having money wired to him, about buying the new clothes and getting himself across the border using his fake identification and a good story. Finally, he told Jelly about getting jumped in El Paso, waking up on the street, and somehow getting to Jelly's house on the edge of the desert.

Jelly listened with minimal interruption, only asking for clarification on a few points during the tale. When Tom had finished, both men sat there quietly, thinking.

"It should have been suicide."

Jelly looked up at the comment. "What's that, Tom?"

"When that guy stuck the gun in my back, it should have been suicide, Jelly. But it wasn't. I screwed up bad."

Jelly smiled gently and shook his head. "Bullshit."

Tom's eyes locked on his. They were a little vacant.

Jelly sat up straight and looked back at Tom, a stony look coming into his gaze. Tom felt suddenly uncomfortable, as if he were staring into the hypnotizing eyes of a cobra moments before it spit its deadly venom.

"Now you listen to me, Tom, and you listen good. Do you hear me?"

Tom nodded.

"You were put into a fucked up situation from day one

of this assignment, and despite all the bullshit that was thrown at you, you not only survived but you fuckin' made it across a hostile continent by using your wits and your balls and you not only got yourself home, but all the fuckin' way to my doorstep. You did an amazing thing, Tom, and I can't think of many men in that situation who would have made it out alive, never mind get all the way back home in one piece. You need to be proud of yourself, here, mister. Heaven knows I'm proud of you. Do you hear me?"

Tom nodded halfheartedly, then shook his head and looked down at the floor.

"Hey!" Jelly said as he slammed his open palm on the table.

Tom, startled, looked up.

"Do you hear me, mister? You did a crackerjack job, and I am fucking proud of you. Couldn't be more proud of you if you were my own brother."

Tom smiled sadly, nodded. "But," he said meekly, "but Jelly…"

"What?" Jelly asked, gently now.

"But Jelly, I deserted my post. I abandoned my mission. I ran away."

Jelly grabbed the bottle of wine, filled Tom's empty water glass then poured the rest in his own.

"Drink that. Now. All of it." It was an order.

Tom picked up the glass and drained it. Jelly watched him for a long moment, took a drink from his own glass then put it on the table. Tom noticed Jelly kept his hand on the empty glass, almost as if making sure it was firmly planted before releasing it.

"I need your full attention, Tom. Do I have it?"

Tom looked up from Jelly's glass. His friend was staring at him. Tom nodded.

"What I am about to tell you is what happened. From

this moment until forever. Do you understand me?"

"Yes."

"Your mission went to shit in Peru. From what you've told me, the whole time you were there, you didn't develop one useful bit of information. That is correct, isn't it?"

"It is," Tom agreed. It was the truth. He'd seen nothing, heard nothing, done nothing of any value the whole time. It was an impossible situation from the first.

"And that's why I recalled you, Tom. I called you back. I gave you orders to exfiltrate. Do you understand? I called you back."

The words took a few moments to sink in through the haze of the wine and stress. Then they did. And once they had fully settled to the bottom of his mind, once the understanding passed from the human brain through to the animal brain and finally to the lizard with its little lizard hand or paw or whatever a lizard has resting on the adrenalin button, Tom felt as if an enormous weight was being lifted from him. He looked gratefully into Jelly's eyes; they were bright blue and shining, full of conviction and strength. They gave him courage and hope.

"But what if," he began weakly, the last remnant of fear and doubt bubbling to the surface.

Jelly instantly cut him off. "No buts. I called you back. I ordered you back. Now tell me that you understand."

"I understand," Tom replied. "Thank you, Jelly."

"From this moment until forever, Tom. And we will never discuss it again. Is that clear?"

Tom sat up a little straighter. He felt some of Jelly's strength and resolve seeping into his very soul. He nodded. "Yes, sir. It's clear, Boss."

CHAPTER THREE

Suicide

THE NEXT MORNING JELLY left Tom at the house and went in to the office. Tom was much better but still needed time to recuperate. Jelly made sure he had a good breakfast, cooking him more eggs, toast, and a big slab of ham. He'd told Tom he'd pick him up some blue jeans, a work shirt, and some socks and underwear on the way home that evening; then he told him to call his father to let him know he was all right. They didn't want Tom's dad calling the Bureau to find out what had happened to his son.

As Jelly drove, he thought about the conversation he'd had with Tom. It had been interesting on many levels.

Tom had a gun when he was jumped in town. Jelly was certain of the area it had happened in both because of the description Tom had provided and because the call trace Mrs. Stimson had run came back to the address of the Quality Coin and Loan. After stopping by his office and getting briefed on the status of several of the routine cases being investigated, Jelly had gotten the address from Mrs. Stimson and headed out to the store.

He spoke with the manager who'd been working that evening. The manager confirmed Tom's story but didn't know anything about what had happened after Tom had left.

Next, Jelly checked with a few of his trusted contacts on the El Paso Police Department and asked them to see if anything unusual had turned up the last few days that could be tied to a robbery. Specifically, he told them he was looking for anything involving a revolver–possibly loaded with only three rounds–a wallet with a Massachusetts driver's license, and a suspect or suspects who knew their way around a sap. The detective and patrolman he spoke with were good men. Jelly trusted them. That's why when they agreed to do this "off the books" as he requested, he knew they'd do just that.

The other part of the conversation with Tom that had stayed with Jelly had nothing to do with the words the injured agent had spoken. It was the non-verbal clues Tom had unconsciously provided that had caught his attention.

When Tom had described the fight in the hotel with the killer strangling the life out of him, he'd been unable to tell Jelly exactly what had happened. Jelly had seen this before when interviewing witnesses of violent crimes. It was very common for people to lose bits and pieces of violent events, especially if the witness had been the victim. Sometimes the bits of memory would come back later, sometimes never, and occasionally, the wrong bits of memory would replace the actual memory.

Not only did this phenomenon regularly result in witnesses giving the wrong descriptions of weapons and clothing, but it could also result in someone describing an innocent person's face as that of the person who'd assaulted them. It was like the brain couldn't stand the gap in memory, so it would pull some other memory from a recent event and plug it into the hole.

When this happened it could really get fucky–because in those instances, when a victim pointed to an innocent person and said, "He did it!", the victim *wasn't lying*. He or she was telling the truth as they honestly remembered it–even though they were dead wrong.

So Tom describing the fight moving from the bed to the floor with no recollection of how they'd made that transition wasn't surprising. It indicated to Jelly that something had happened during those moments that had been really traumatic for Tom–even more so than waking up in a death strangle.

For Tom to have displaced the killer from his superior mounted position meant that Tom had done something extraordinarily effective. The fact Tom couldn't recall it meant he probably hadn't thought his way through it, that he'd reacted on a more base, or subconscious level. And that's where the subconscious clues came in.

When describing those moments, Tom's right eye had started twitching. And the way he'd held his left hand, locked and contorted, with the thumb protruding, indicated to Jelly that Tom had probably jammed that thumb into the strangler's eye.

Jelly knew he was employing inductive reasoning, and that his theory was far from conclusive. But he believed it held water. The main reason he believed that was because of a story his old partner, H.V. Wilder, had told him years before.

*   *   *

H.V. had been a soldier in the first Great War and had seen a lot of brutal action. Occasionally, especially if they'd had a drink or two, H.V. would tell Jelly about different things he'd seen or experienced personally during the war. Usually, he would do this because the story related to something Jelly had asked him about, or a case they were working on.

One night, H.V. told Jelly about an assault he and his squad had made "over the top," meaning they'd climbed from their muddy, rat-infested trenches and run through sniper and machine gun fire in order to jump into the enemy's muddy, rat-infested trenches so they could kill each other face-to-face.

"It was always cold," H.V. said, eyes gazing off to the wall of his dining room. "We were always cold. Fuckin' trenches were always wet. So even though it was terrifying, running across that bloody ground and going hand-to-hand was at least a momentary break from freezing. Your heart pumped blood and the adrenalin made you forget the pain. Then there you are, facing some other freezing, suffering bastards, and the fight is on."

H.V. had stopped talking for a moment, listening to make sure his wife, Vivian, was still in their bedroom asleep. The men had been talking for hours after dinner.

"Any way, this day, we all actually made it the few yards across no-man's land into the Bosch's trench line, and as we're chopping our way through the men we found there, I happen to look over and see one of my boys, Milligan, a strappin' lad of twenty, shoot a round from his Springfield rifle into the body of a miserable, scared looking Kraut. The Hun falls back, dropping his Mauser, and lands with his back, you know, against the trench wall."

H.V. looked at Jelly and held his hand up, palm out– "Then he holds his hand up, like this, like trying to hold Milligan off him. But Milligan doesn't hesitate, doesn't even try to work the bolt on his rifle to reload, he just moves forward with the bayonet on the end of his barrel looking to finish the job, and the Hun, he sees this, he knows what's coming, and he opens his mouth to scream out, and Milligan drives that bayonet right into the Hun's mouth and through the other side, pinning the Kraut to the wall for a moment, then pulls out and starts to turn when our eyes meet and I can see that his eyes are crazy with the fever, the killin' fever; he's in the blood, he's in deep."

H.V. took a drink from his glass, and Jelly could see a thin bead of sweat on his forehead. H.V. felt it and wiped his forehead with his sleeve, then continued. "Well, just for a moment I thought Milligan was going to move on *me*, so I yelled out, 'Are you okay, Milligan!?' and he looks harder at me, nods and then moves on down the trench line."

H.V. took another drink from his glass, the amber-colored whiskey almost gone.

Though he usually tried to keep from asking questions, letting H.V. just tell what he wanted, this time Jelly'd asked, "So what happened to Milligan?"

H.V. looked at Jelly, reached over and took the cap off the whiskey bottle and poured another splash into both their glasses. Then he set the bottle down and continued talking.

"Well, we all made it back that day, too. It was almost a miracle, because usually you'd lose at least a few wounded or killed when you went over the top. But we all got back. Then later, I noticed Milligan was missing, and when I asked, my corpsman told me he'd been sent back to the rear; something was wrong with him, so the skipper had sent him back."

He paused for another sip of whiskey.

"About a week later, I took some shrapnel in my leg, and they sent me back to get patched up. Nothing to brag about, mind you, but it was too deep to pull out myself, stickin' out just enough to keep the wound open and bleeding. So I went back. It was always nice to see the occasional pretty nurse too, you know?" H.V. smiled, but it was forced. He was trying to keep it light, but this story was anything but for him.

"So as I'm limping through the casualty clearing station–just a bunch of tents really–I see Milligan sitting on a cot in a tent. Just sitting there, his back to me, but I knew all my men like family and immediately recognized him, so I say, 'Hey, Milligan!' and he turns around and looks at me, and his mouth is wide the fuck open, but not in a normal way, it's just like, wide open. And his tongue is dried and his lips are cracked and I'm trying to figure out how he's wounded but he looks fine except for his mouth. So I go over to him and try to talk to him but he can't talk, he's just looking at me. Then a nurse comes over and tells me he's being sent back to a hospital ship that very day, that he's been like that since he got there."

H.V. stared off at the wall again for a moment, then looked back at Jelly.

"So naturally I ask her, 'What's wrong with him? Does he have the lockjaw?' and she shakes her head no, says it's not lockjaw. So I ask again, 'Well what is it then?' and she says they don't know, they think it's a hysterical response to something that happened to him, and she asks me if I have any idea, and right away I remember the Hun and the bayonet so I tell her and she nods like it makes perfect sense. 'We see it all the time,' she said matter-of-factly. 'The mind can only deal with so much,' she says. 'Sometime the things we do affect us as much as the things that are done to us.' " H.V. shivered.

"I never forgot that, Delf." H.V. had said as he finished the story. "Sometimes the things we do affect us as much as the things done to us. You'd do well to remember it too, little brother."

*   *   *

Jelly did remember–vividly–both the story and the warning.

That's why his theory seemed to make sense. If Tom had drilled his thumb into the killer's eye hard and deep enough to send the man to the floor, it might have messed with Tom's mind. Jelly had always known Tom wasn't a hard sort. Tom had confided in him during the FBI School that he'd never even been in a fistfight as a kid. So for him to do something like that, it may have been hard for his mind to accept.

"Hard to accept." Jelly said the words out loud as he drove back to the house with the packages from the clothing store in the front seat. He'd had to deal with "hard to accept" quite a bit the past years.

Like the firearms training Tom had referred to. The training Jelly had been tasked by Hoover to design for the Bureau. A lot of what he'd brought to the Bureau had been hard to accept for a lot of the other instructors. Many of the other agents assigned to the training school had previous experience with firearms. Quite a few had military backgrounds, and a few others had considerable competitive experience as well. Surprisingly, they all shared a similar belief about training men to use pistols for fighting. Their idea of pistol training was to have the agents stand up ramrod straight, body bladed to the target, one hand on their hip or in a pocket, the other holding the pistol out straight so they could align the sights with each other, their dominant eye, and the bullseye target. They'd then admonish their students to "breathe in deeply, exhale slightly, then pause breathing, keep your eye on the front sight, and gently squeeze the trigger directly to the rear." And it *was* an excellent method to deliver precision sighted rounds to the target.

The only problem was, it generally only worked when the target wasn't trying to kill your ass.

"People don't respond to an immediate threat like that," Jelly had calmly explained at the range when first assigned to the training school as an instructor. "They crouch." He demonstrated as he spoke. "The body is usually squared up, facing the threat, like this. Their eyes–both eyes–open wide, trying to take in as much information as possible about the threat they're facing. Usually, if armed with a handgun, most men will stick the pistol out straight with one hand, but not like you fellas are teaching them. There is no 'squeezing the trigger gently to the rear.' Your hand will clench around the gun, convulse almost, as the trigger is worked."

Jelly held his empty fist out straight in front of him, simulating the convulsive grip. "And forget the sights. The sights are good when you have the luxury of using them. That's why you can use them on a range to such great effect. But our men won't be facing bullseyes out there in the world, gentlemen. They'll be facing other men. Men who won't hesitate to pour lead their way. Men who–for many of them anyway–have fought this way before and won, so they'll be calmer and more focused than our boys. Men who won't hesitate to murder because they settled that problem for themselves long ago. Not like our boys, most of whom probably haven't ever even been in a fistfight in school, or who've been taught all their lives that killing is a sin, and they'll go to Hell for it. These things cause hesitation and doubt. A big part of our job is to remove that."

In response to Jelly's words, most of the other instructors simply stared at him disbelievingly. Despite the fact Jelly had been in numerous gunfights and killed many an armed bad man in actual combat, several of the instructors actually argued with him at first.

"But if they don't use the sights, how can they expect to hit the target?"

"We'll teach them how to. It's really not all that difficult," Jelly had answered honestly, expecting the instructors to listen to his explanation and then evaluate the techniques for themselves as they learned.

Then one of them, a veteran agent named Bob Washington said, "I'm sorry, but you sound a little pompous to me. Everyone knows you have to use the sights to hit with any accuracy. You're talking about that whole 'instinctive shooting' business. I'm not a believer. I've tried it myself and it just doesn't work."

Jelly looked at Washington. He could see in the man's eyes that he was sure of his position. "Have you ever been in a gunfight?" he asked.

Washington smirked. "Well, no, but one doesn't need to have been in a gunfight to understand how to shoot properly, Agent Bryce. I realize you have a lot of experience on the streets of Oklahoma, but I have won nearly seventeen matches over the past four years alone, three on the national level. Surely, that counts for something."

Jelly was incredulous. The man was serious. "Can you hit that target behind you?" Jelly asked, indicating a bulls-eye target set up on the range about twenty yards away.

Washington looked at it and smirked again. "I should hope so." He laughed and looked around at the other instructors standing there.

"Okay, how 'bout this," Jelly said. "Let's do a test. When I say 'go' you turn around, draw your pistol and hit that target with six rounds, fast as you can. If you can do that, if you can land all six on target, we'll train the men your way."

Again Washington smiled confidently. "Fine. When you say go."

Jelly stepped back a few paces from the man, then motioned for the others to move back and away from the line as well. "Are you ready?"

Washington took a deep breath, blew it out and nodded, eyes staring at Jelly's, waiting for the signal to begin. *'This will put an end to the man's nonsense,'* he thought confidently. As he watched, Jelly's eyes changed. They hardened somehow, his face setting differently. Suddenly bright flashes of flaming light were leaping toward him, a terrible sound of explosions ringing out; hard, sharp needles hit his face, like being pelted by tiny buckshot, just missing his eyes and causing his eyelids to slam shut in response. Something powerful snapped by his head on both sides, inches away, zipping past like angry supersonic wasps. Startled to his core, Washington's eyes opened wide as he dropped into a low crouch, so low he split the seam of his trousers at the crotch even before consciously realizing Jelly had drawn his Registered Magnum and was shooting at him. *Shooting at him!*

What Washington didn't realize was the first three rounds had been directed down into the ground directly in front of him, causing dirt and rocks to fly up at his face. The last two rounds had zipped past his head, one on either side. Frozen now in place, hands held up, palms forward, the terrified man watched in horror as Jelly strode directly toward him, big magnum still in his hand.

Stopping less than a foot from Washington, Jelly calmly and quietly said, "Go."

"What are…?! *What are..?!*" Washington stammered unintelligibly, to which Jelly responded by bending down and aggressively barking in the instructor's face, *"GO!"*

Washington, hands shaking, reached for his holstered pistol with his right hand. Jelly let him get it up and out of the holster before he clamped his left hand on the man's wrist and twisted. Washington cried out in pain as he was turned and driven to his knees, now facing the target. He dropped his pistol onto the ground.

"Goddammit, pick up that gun and shoot that fucking target!" Jelly commanded, shoving Washington forward and down; then, leaning in and speaking quietly so only Washington could hear, "Shoot that target you pompous motherfucker, or my last round goes in your fucking ear."

Washington blanched, picked up his revolver, fired off

six shots down range toward the target and collapsed in a heap, his empty revolver falling from his shaking hand as his lungs began sucking air in gasping uneven gulps.

"Jesus," one of the instructors said from behind Jelly. None of the five had moved. It had happened so incredibly fast, and was so shockingly unbelievable that their minds hadn't been able to process what they were witnessing. It looked like Bryce had shot Washington to the ground. None of them dared twitch a muscle.

Jelly looked back at the instructors, holstered his pistol, then turned and walked to the target. He unceremoniously pulled the wooden frame and all up out of the stand and walked it back to the group of horrified agents. He held it up so they could see it. There wasn't a mark anywhere on the large bullseye or the surrounding paper.

"*That's* what your seventeen matches count for," Jelly said, dropping the target in front of Washington who was still lying on the ground. Turning back to the others, he said, "I'll listen to anything, gentlemen. I'll entertain any idea or notion. But I won't abide bullshit or ego. If you have something that will work in the real world, under the actual kinds of conditions our boys will be facing, I want to hear it. But before you teach a man how to keep himself alive on the streets when facing killers, you goddamned better be sure you're right. Cause if you're wrong, you own that agent's death as much as the piece of garbage that took his life from him. *This is no fuckin' game.* Am I clear?"

The agents nodded. Jelly turned to Washington, leaned over and held out his hand. Quietly he asked, "Am I clear, Bob?" Washington looked up into Jelly's eyes and saw a sincere look of concern had replaced the terrifying visage he'd faced just moments before. Relieved deeply in a way he couldn't express, he nodded and reached up toward Jelly's extended hand. They clasped hands and Jelly pulled him to his feet; then he bent down and picked up the empty revolver. As Washington gathered himself, hands on his hips, head looking down at the ground, Jelly brushed some dirt off the gun, opened the cylinder and held it out to the shaken instructor, grips first.

Washington raised his head, looked at the gun, then nodded at Jelly and took his pistol back.

Scanning all the gathered men, looking each in the eye one at a time, Jelly said, "Okay, gentlemen. Now let's get to work."

* * *

That hadn't been the first time Jelly's methods and approach differed somewhat from those of the more conventional agents assigned to training. His first run-in had actually occurred while he was going through the Bureau's Training School back in '34.

He'd been seated next to Tom in the audience that day while an instructor up on stage was explaining the new laws that applied to federal agents. The instructor had asked one of the trainees to come up on stage to demonstrate a point. Handing the young student an empty training revolver, the instructor turned his back to the student and told him to point the gun at him. "Closer," the instructor directed, until the student had the muzzle of the pistol right against the senior agent's spine.

"Now," the instructor said, looking at the audience and raising his hands in surrender, "Let's say you're in an alley and a criminal comes up behind you and gets the drop on you like this. Then he takes your gun and your wallet with your FBI identification. How would you report this incident to your supervisor?"

Before anyone else had a chance to say anything, Jelly

had called out, "A suicide."

A few men in the audience chuckled. The instructor had not been amused. Looking into the crowd he'd asked, "Excuse me? Who said that?"

Jelly had smiled and stood up. "Trainee Bryce, sir."

Recognizing Bryce, the agent had assumed a more respectful tone and then asked him to come up to the stage to explain. Jelly walked up confidently, smiled at the instructor and the student with the revolver, then turned to the class.

"If a man comes at you with a gun like this," indicating the student on stage who was still holding the pistol at the instructor's back, "from the front or rear, and he isn't pulling the trigger, then you've got a chance. If he's foolish enough to get within touching distance like here," again pointing at the demonstrators, "then he's a dead man. Because a man can act much quicker than another man can react."

Looking at the instructor, Jelly respectfully asked, "Would you like me to demonstrate, sir?"

The instructor nodded and stepped aside as Jelly jumped up onto the stage. Jelly then told the student to assume the same position with him this time. With his hands raised and facing away from the student, Jelly turned his head to the side, and speaking loudly enough to be heard at the back of the classroom, said, "When I move, you pull the trigger as fast and as many times as you can, okay?"

The student nodded and stepped closer, sticking the barrel against Jelly's spine.

"Are you ready?" Jelly asked.

"Yes."

No sooner had the student uttered the word than Jelly had spun around, clearing the gun arm away to the side and taking the pistol from the student's hand. The student hadn't been able to press the trigger even one time. The audience members were astounded at the speed and ease with which jelly had accomplished the maneuver. As they watched, Jelly stood there, red-handled training gun in his fist, muzzle pointed straight up under the student's chin.

"See?" he asked, the hard look in his eyes as he stared at the bewildered student; then he turned toward the audience, smiled, and said "*Suicide.*"

Everyone laughed, including the student, breaking the tension and the instructor's focus for the rest of the day. He thanked Jelly for the demonstration then declared the class dismissed.

That was what Tom had meant the night before when he'd said, "It should have been suicide."

Jelly nodded to himself, thinking about his two friends on the El Paso PD who were quietly working this case for him. They were good cops. If anyone could get a line on the mutts who'd bushwhacked Tom, they could.

"Suicide," Jelly said aloud as he turned down his driveway heading for the house. "It may still turn out to be just exactly that."

CHAPTER FOUR

A Slight Change of Plans
20 June 1941

JELLY LEFT TOM ALONE at the house for the next two days. The change in his young friend had been remarkable. Tom had been eating up a storm and had started talking about the Bureau and his work with growing interest and enthusiasm again. Jelly had convinced him he shouldn't make any quick decisions about his future until he'd had time to process his past.

The mind was funny like that. One day you could be convinced your whole world had ended, then a few days later your outlook could be completely different. Jelly knew this. Like most people he'd experienced it more than a few times in his life. That was one of the reasons he'd never understood suicides.

'Maybe,' he'd considered, *'if you were suffering from a horrendous illness with no chance of hope; or you'd committed such a heinous act you couldn't stand the thought of living with yourself for another moment...'* But in a lot of the suicide cases he'd investigated these weren't the facts.

"Why end your life if there's even a chance of things getting better?"

He couldn't grasp it. Even though once, when he was very young, he'd thought about it.

It had been right after his mother had died. Jelly had never been so distraught or in so much pain. It had been brutal. He'd not only missed her more than air, but he'd also felt guilty. He hadn't gone for the doctor soon enough. The idea that he should go had occurred to him, but she'd said no again and again. *'Why did I listen?'* The thought came to him as he lay in bed the night before the funeral. An image of a rope around his neck played over and over. The idea of using a gun had never occurred to him. He'd never do that. For some reason the rope was the way. Even though he never truly considered going through with it, the image kept returning.

"Never a gun," Jelly said aloud whenever he thought about that time in his life. It was actually a gun that had saved him. Then and many times afterward. Guns were things of life.

"God, guns and good luck." He'd told that to people for years. "The three things that have always kept me alive." And he'd meant it.

* * *

Whistling as he walked into the four-story storage building in downtown El Paso, Jelly took the stairs to the third floor and walked down the hallway, big wooden floorboards solid beneath his feet. Stopping at the unit the Bureau had secretly leased, he slid his key into the padlock, opened it, and slipped it from the hasp. Holding the padlock up so he could see into the key slot, Jelly grimaced and shook his head. This lock would take about 30 seconds to bypass, if that. *'And this is what they're using to secure high level secret shit,'* he thought incredulously. He didn't even want to think about how easy the hasp itself would be to cut if the intruder wasn't concerned about detection.

Pushing open the door, Jelly paused to look up and down the hallway. Then he just stood there for a few moments, listening. Nothing. He went into the small room and closed the door behind him.

A matched set of green, four-drawer file cabinets stood against the wall to his left. A gray metal desk and wooden chair were placed against the opposite wall, and stacked against the wall directly to his front were several metal foot lockers and cardboard boxes. An industrial-looking table lamp sat squat and lonely on top of the desk.

Jelly walked to the desk, placed the padlock on top, then pulled the little metal chain hanging from the lamp. The bulb lit up, bathing the room in pale yellow light. It was warm and stuffy in the windowless room. Jelly took off his suitcoat and draped it over the chair, loosened his tie and unbuttoned his collar. Turning to the cabinets, he pulled open the second drawer of the second cabinet and started thumbing through the tightly-packed files. He'd been going through each folder, each piece of paper, slowly and methodically since being informed about the room by Hoover. This was the SIS file room. Information for all the operations being run out of El Paso was maintained here, in this innocuous storage closet buried in an industrial building. The plan, Hoover had told Jelly, was to eventually relocate all the files to a dedicated, anonymous secure facility. The SIS was still in its infancy, however, so things were being done on the fly.

"Sometimes, Jelly," Hoover had told him as he'd draped his arm over Jelly's shoulder in a rare show of affection during the initial SIS briefing, "you've got to jump off the cliff and build your wings on the way down."

Jelly had smiled and nodded at the remark. But the unsettling image of crashing into the ground with his wings only half-finished had occurred to him at the time. Seeing Tom Wilson's bruised and bloody face the night he'd showed up at Jelly's house and collapsed on the driveway brought that image right back to him. Jelly hoped that

Tom's hitting the ground wasn't a harbinger of things to come for the entire SIS project.

Skimming through the files, Jelly kept looking until he found one with information about the Peru mission. How the files were organized was something of a mystery. Jelly was sure Hoover had no direct control over them, because Hoover couldn't stand to see anything done like this. The man had personally developed the FBI's filing system, a system so unique it was used as a model for the entire United States government.

Hoover's initial approach required all files be indexed as they were created. Then he'd reached back to his experiences as a clerk at the Library of Congress and added extensive cross-references within the indexed file cards. That meant that accessing one file would lead you back to connected information in all files included in the system. Hoover had figured out how to synthesize the information in all the files so a single piece of the puzzle could easily lead you to the rest.

'But this,' Jelly thought as he finally pulled the file he needed from the folder, *'this is a clusterfuck.'*

The one saving grace of the SIS filing system was each report was written in a coded format. Jelly had the code book with him, but as he read through the Peru file he realized he wouldn't need it. Much of the information was written in a way that could be easily deciphered.

"Lazy bastards," Jelly muttered as he shook his head.

From what he found about the Peru mission, Jelly could only conclude it had been haphazardly conceived and organized. "Agent Shilo" as Tom was identified, had been dispatched to Lima to establish contacts and set up an observation post of sorts. The mission requirements included him making regular transmissions to a receiving station in Mexico City using a special shortwave radio.

Transmissions were supposed to be made either daily or weekly. It was hard to tell which from the information in the file.

Jelly looked through the code book and found the telephone number for the Mexico City station. He sat down in the chair, took out a key and unlocked the bottom drawer of the desk. Pulling it open he reached inside and picked up the receiver of the telephone kept there.

"They keep secret files in unlocked drawers but the fuckin' phone they secure," he said quietly with disgust as he dialed the number.

The dialing tone rang twice in his ear. Someone picked up, but said nothing. Jelly said, "Station five. Romeo, bravo, one, seven, seven, alpha." Then he waited. He could imagine the agent on the other end of the line flipping through his own copy of the code book to confirm Jelly's identity.

"Station nineteen. Zulu, Charlie, eight, one, six, delta," came the response. Jelly followed along with the reply code in his book, holding his finger beneath each letter and number as given. It was correct.

"Roger, station nineteen. I need direct with comcon."

The line went silent for a few moments, then someone picked up. "This is comcon."

Using the stilted language of the code book, Jelly advised the anonymous man on the other end of the phone he wanted a situation report on the Lima station. The man placed his hand over the mouthpiece and spoke to someone else. A few minutes later he reported the Lima station had been making regular transmissions for approximately two months–but had apparently stopped about two weeks ago. The man sounded surprised by his own report.

"How is that?" Jelly asked pointedly.

"Well, sir, it appears"–papers being turned in the background– "it appears, that transmissions, ceased, and…"

Jelly waited.

"I'm not sure why, station five. They seem to have stopped around 23 May. As you know, I've only been on station for a week…"

Jelly held his breath for a moment. He'd been worried that Tom's disappearance had triggered an investigation, or worse, that agents had been dispatched to Lima to find him. Instead, no one had even realized the transmissions had stopped, much less that one of their own was in the wind. Jelly was simultaneously relieved and horrified. He shifted gears. Turning to the code book, he instructed the head of the Mexico City station to pull the Peru file and send it to him by special courier.

"And station twenty-two?" the man asked, using the code for Lima.

"Shut down until further notice. Is that clear, station nineteen?"

"Clear, station five."

"Five out," Jelly said, then hung up the receiver. He sat there thinking for a few minutes. Then he stood up, closed all the drawers, locked the phone up, grabbed the Peru file and left, snapping the padlock back on the hasp before quietly making his exit from the building.

*   *   *

Back at the El Paso office, Jelly caught up on the activities of the Bureau agents under his command. The cut and dried investigations and administrative duties that consumed the members of the FBI made so much more sense to him than the chaotic cloak and dagger operations of the Special Intelligence Service.

After meeting briefly with his men and talking to his

secretary, Jelly poured himself a cup of coffee and walked into his office, closing the door behind him. He looked around the room for a moment, seeing nothing but collecting his thoughts. Then he sat down at his desk, picked up the telephone, and dialed a memorized number.

"Hey, Hoover," he said with a smile on his face. The number was Hoover's private line.

Seated at his own desk in his inner sanctum office in Washington, the Director of the FBI smiled at the greeting and pushed aside a report he'd been reviewing. "So, how goes it there?"

"Well, sir, it certainly is interesting if nothing else."

Hoover lost the smile. He knew how Jelly talked. "Interesting" usually meant something was either dangerous or completely screwed up. "Tell me."

Without going into detail on the telephone, Jelly told his boss he'd pulled an asset back from a southern station, and that a full report would be mailed to DC. He then told Hoover he'd also run into an old colleague in El Paso, former Agent Tom Wilson, class of 1934, and that Wilson was interested in coming back on board with the Bureau.

"You want Wilson working for you in El Paso?" Hoover asked.

"Yes, sir. I think it would be wise."

"I don't have any problem with that. Just make sure all his paperwork is submitted through Miss Gandy. She'll know what to do."

"Thanks, Boss man," Jelly said sincerely.

Hoover nodded, thinking, receiver pressed to his ear. "Oh, and Jelly," he said, as if an afterthought, "we need to make sure that all of the asset's affairs are in order. We don't want any loose ends."

"I understand, sir. I'll take care of it."

"Very well. Stay in touch." Hoover hung up.

'Loose ends,' Jelly thought. *'Papers, contacts'*–his eyes widened. "Shit, the fuckin' radio."

*   *   *

Back at the house Jelly sat Tom down and debriefed him again, this time focusing on the operational aspects of the mission. Tom assured him all paperwork had been carefully destroyed after each transmission, and that the radio was securely hidden in a compartment beneath the floorboards of a safe house he'd been using. "Unless Waterman's contact is a double, it should be okay there."

Once Jelly was satisfied there was nothing else to be done right then, he told Tom the good news. Tom was free and clear of the Peru assignment. He was back–or would shortly be back–on the regular FBI payroll and roster. "Like none of it ever happened," he said looking Tom square in the eyes.

Tom seemed to be starting to smile, then didn't. He just nodded instead. "Okay, Jelly. Thank you so much, my friend."

*   *   *

A week later, Jelly got a call from Hoover. After exchanging pleasantries, Hoover came to the point and ordered Jelly to fly out to the Seat of Government for a meeting. This was unusual. Hoover usually had Miss Gandy or someone else make these types of routine notifications.

"Am I in the shit, Boss?" Jelly asked directly.

"No, Jelly. Not at all."

The following day Jelly reported to Hoover.

"Have a seat," Hoover said after ushering Jelly from his large formal office into the inner sanctum.

Jelly sat up ramrod straight. Hoover had something of importance to tell him. There were none of the niceties, offers of coffee or small talk that usually preceded their conversations.

"Jelly, I want you to know that I am very happy with you and the job you've done for me since coming on board with the Bureau. You've never let me down. There are only a few people I've ever known I can truly say that about."

Jelly nodded. "Thank you, Boss. That means a lot to me coming from you."

Hoover smiled and nodded in return. Then he continued. "What I need to discuss with you today is the S.I.S. and your part in it. And, again, please understand this has nothing to do with you, or your capabilities, or the job you've done so far down there. But there has been a slight change of plans."

Jelly sat back, listening.

Hoover explained that Jelly was going to remain in El Paso as the SAC, but another agent would be taking over SIS. The entire SIS command and control was going to be centralized and moved to New York City. The operation was both growing and going completely covert, and could no longer be run as a double-duty assignment.

"I would have offered you the S.I.S. command assignment, Jelly, but I have come to know you, my friend. And I know that if you thought I needed you to do it, you would. Without a moment's hesitation. Am I not correct?"

"Of course, Boss. You know I'll go wherever you send me and do whatever you tell me."

"I do. That's why I'm going to keep you in El Paso. I know you're happy there. And I know New York isn't your cup of tea." Hoover looked sideways at Jelly and added, "It's not mine either, frankly. But that's where S.I.S. must be based now. There have been some, developments. I won't bore you with the details right now. That's a conversation for another time."

"I understand. I'm fine with that, Boss."

"Good. I'm glad. But so there's no mistake, even though your primary responsibility will be running the El Paso office, I will still be calling on you from time to time to take on certain specialized missions."

Jelly nodded.

"Think of yourself as a sort of one man flying squad, Jelly." Hoover stood up and extended his hand. Jelly stood as well and took Hoover's outstretched hand. As they shook, Hoover finished, "That's how I think of you, my friend. You have my complete confidence. You always have."

Jelly smiled at his boss and friend. But he wondered: was Hoover telling him the truth? Had Hoover heard about Lima? Two dead men in a hotel would most likely cause a ripple, even down there. Before turning for the door Jelly searched the Director's eyes for a tell, some hint that Hoover knew Jelly had moved a few pieces on the chessboard to get Tom out of the glue and back into the Bureau. Hoover returned the stare. If he knew anything, he wasn't giving it away.

Jelly nodded and left the inner sanctum.

For his part, Jelly didn't feel he was deceiving Hoover. Hoover had given him the ground rules on this game years before. There were some things you wanted to know, other things you didn't want to know. As a result, sometimes many things were left unsaid, assumptions blindly made, the facts left to mingle and occasionally get lost or distorted in the shadows.

Nowhere was this truer than with the SIS. Of all the covert operations Hoover had initiated during his tenure as Director, the SIS was now heading full tilt down the deepest and darkest rabbit hole in the Bureau's history.

CHAPTER FIVE

The S.I.S.

IT HAD BEEN MORE than two years since the President of the United States had planted the seed for the Special Intelligence Service, or "S.I.S."

The initial meeting that led to the creation of the first U.S. Intelligence agency had taken place on October 14, 1938, when Franklin D. Roosevelt summoned J. Edgar Hoover to the White House.

That was the day Hoover had laid out his ambitious plan to create an entirely new government entity that would be responsible for all intelligence activities both in the homeland and overseas. Roosevelt had ostensibly approved the plan, but only after substantially paring it down in scope and size. Hoover had asked for five thousand men to staff the new agency, an agency which would be responsible for everything from passport and visa control to overseeing the Federal Communications Commission and, of course, investigating anyone suspected of being a foreign agent.

What Roosevelt provided was six hundred thousand dollars in "off the books" money, enough to hire approximately 140 new FBI agents who'd be assigned to intelligence work.

Hoover, disheartened over the decision, still had reverential respect for the presidency; he did what he could with what he was given.

The following year, while Hoover was simultaneously running the Bureau, working on developing intelligence assets, and breaking in Frank Murphy, the eighth attorney general he'd served under, the President directed the establishment of the "Interdepartmental Intelligence Conference." This new body, chaired by J. Edgar and meeting at FBI Headquarters in DC, was comprised of members from the FBI, Army and Navy Intelligence and the State Department. They were tasked to meet weekly in order to coordinate all activities involving espionage, counter-espionage, and sabotage investigations.

They met at the Seat of Government and Hoover relished his position as the de facto American intelligence czar as war enveloped Europe and the Communist threat expanded at home.

On September 1, 1939, Hitler invaded Poland. Two days later France and Great Britain declared war on Germany. Hitler and Stalin signed a non-aggression pact, meaning the Communists had made peace with the Nazis. US liberals and leftists were shocked and dismayed. This wasn't the communism they'd been sold.

Events continued to unfold quickly and violently on the world stage. Japan tore through China and expanded into the Pacific.

FDR declared US neutrality but aided the British with warships and intelligence to counter Axis spying and subversion in the US.

Understanding the value of clandestine intelligence, the President also issued a public statement on September 6, 1939, acknowledging the "FBI would take charge of investigative work in matters relating to espionage." He further ordered every law enforcement officer in the country to provide "any information obtained by them relating to espionage, counter espionage, sabotage, subversive activities and violations of neutrality law" to the Bureau.

FDR and Hoover remembered the Black Tom Island munitions explosion of 1916. The new Attorney General remembered the "red raids" of 1920. Frank Murphy assured the people that while everything possible would be done to keep them safe, civil liberties would be preserved by the FBI.

Hoover publicly agreed with Murphy but privately pushed for stronger laws against subversion. The Smith, or Alien Registration, Act included the toughest federal restrictions on free speech in American history. It outlawed "words and thoughts" aimed at overthrowing the government, and membership in any organization with that intent was deemed a crime.

Hoover, who'd long maintained an "enemies list," expanded it. On December 6, 1939, personal and confidential orders were sent to every FBI agent. "Internal Security" ordered them to prepare lists of people–Americans and aliens–who should be locked up in the name of national security should it be necessary. This operation was referred to as the "Custodial Detention Program."

A crucial component of his Intelligence apparatus as Hoover saw it was the ability to wiretap at will. Not everyone agreed. On December 11, 1939, the US Supreme Court, reversing an earlier ruling, said government wiretapping was illegal. Justice Felix Frankfurter, a liberal club lawyer from Harvard, made it clear in his opinion that "wiretapping was inconsistent with ethical standards and destructive of personal liberty."

Hoover again publicly nodded his understanding, but in house instructed his agents nothing had changed. According to the Director, as long as he and he alone approved the taps in secret, the work was done in the name of Intelligence, and no evidence was introduced in court from the wire, it was fine.

On January 18, 1940, Attorney General Murphy was himself appointed to the Supreme Court. The ninth AG Hoover would serve under, Robert Jackson, quickly and publicly declared that the Justice Department–to include its shining star, the FBI–had completely abandoned wiretapping. He went so far as to institute a formal ban.

Jackson didn't realize he'd stepped onto Hoover's chessboard completely unprepared and inexperienced. He didn't even realize that the "great game" was in play, though he would learn in short order.

Hoover leaked stories to his many contacts in the press. The basic narrative was that the Bureau was being handcuffed in its war against spies and saboteurs. Hoover sought support from his allies in the State and War departments. He warned that the very fate of the nation rested on wiretaps and bugs. His opponents raised the first open comparisons of the FBI to the Gestapo.

Meanwhile, the *actual* Gestapo was busy in the US as well, orchestrating a complex banking scheme to fund anti-American activities and recruit German-American spies. The "revenue stream" for these activities ran red with blood. The monies were derived from victimized Jews back in Europe.

Tens of thousands of these dollars were funneled to political opponents of FDR, including one Father Charles Coughlin, a notorious right-wing radio preacher who vehemently spouted hate and derision for both Roosevelt and his "Jew Deal."

Another recipient of funding was none other than Charles Lindbergh, American icon, hero aviator, and victim of a kidnapping during which his baby boy was stolen from his home and murdered. Lindbergh, himself a potential Republican presidential candidate in 1940, was also an ardent supporter of the Nazi party.

In discussions with the President, Hoover, aided by Treasury Secretary Henry Morgenthau, convinced FDR that the Nazi intelligence services had a network of money and information running through the American banking system. "And we, Mister President," the Director declared, "have no way of wiretapping them to put a stop to it!"

In response to Hoover's convincing and distressing presentation, the President decided it only made practical sense that in time of war, the Supreme Court decision about wiretapping could be disregarded as far as national security matters were concerned. He officially authorized the Bureau to use "listening devices against persons suspected of subversive activities against the government of the US, including suspected spies."

This order would stand for the next 25 years.

The key to his rationalization was found in the structure and implementation of the SIS. Roosevelt had, in effect, signed off on the creation of a covert, Presidential Intelligence service–not an investigative service.

Intelligence activities are not conducted with the intent of indicting criminals for crimes they have committed. They are conducted in order to stop spies and saboteurs before they strike.

The SIS, therefore, even though part of the FBI, was not actually working for the Attorney General or even the Department of Justice. SIS was working directly for the President of the United States.

Through this audacious maneuver Hoover finally achieved autonomy. It would have a lasting effect. For the next two decades he would only tell his ersatz boss, the Attorney General, what he wanted him to know.

As far as wiretapping went, it was still an incredibly powerful tool, even though evidence it produced couldn't be used in court. And J. Edgar Hoover–the President's Intelligence chief–was the man in control of it. Thousands of wiretaps and bugs were employed during the war years alone.

But what of the Special Intelligence Service? What was its true nature and value, beyond its use as a means of achieving greater power and control for Edgar Hoover?

* * *

In 1940 the Bureau ran its first textbook intelligence operation against the Nazis. An Abwehr spy in New York was actively sending Morse code messages by shortwave radio across the Atlantic to a receiving office in Hamburg. The Nazi agents in Hamburg thought they had scored a tremendous asset. Their spy in New York was capable, reliable, and effective. Unfortunately for them, he was also one of Hoover's men.

The Hamburg control officers sent detailed mission instructions to their man in New York; they revealed the identity of a real spy within the American defense structure, and they provided him with numerous other bits of intelligence that would prove devastating to the Nazi operation.

During this maiden operation the Bureau exercised all the tools it would eventually become expert at, including setting up dummy corporations, employing sophisticated wiretaps and hidden cameras, and opening mail in diplomatic pouches. As a result of this one operation, a number of Abwehr agents in the US and Mexico were arrested and their networks smashed. Other Nazi spy networks were also identified in Brazil and Peru.

Shortly after receiving a briefing on this enormous success from a beaming Edgar Hoover, the President made a speech on the radio. On May 26, 1940, his voice wavering with pride and emotion, the President declared that, "Today's threat to our national security is not a matter of military weapons alone. We know of other methods, new methods of attack. *The Trojan Horse*. The Fifth Column that betrays a nation unprepared for treachery. Spies, saboteurs and traitors are actors in this new strategy. With all of these we will deal vigorously."

FDR first directed Hoover to structure the SIS as a compartmentalized, completely covert spy agency. Its existence would not be acknowledged. This was done for a number of reasons, chief among them the desire to avoid the charge of having birthed an American Gestapo.

The initial plan was that SIS would establish branches throughout the world. Agents would be assigned missions, gather intelligence and report back. The problems surfaced immediately. The other members of the Interdepartmental Intelligence Conference Hoover worked with were neither stupid nor uninformed. They all had their own moles and spies throughout the government, and word of Hoover's SIS quickly spread despite the President's and Hoover's best efforts. Hoover knew the game better than all of them and wasn't surprised by this. He also knew all the members of the other intelligence agencies zealously protected their individual interests and that no one truly trusted anyone else.

What did surprise him was how quickly the President caved to their pressuring. On June 24, 1940, FDR amended the original SIS plan. Instead of having the whole pie, the SIS would only be responsible for foreign intelligence in the Western Hemisphere, from the Texas border down to Tierra del Fuego. Army and Naval Intelligence would carve up the rest of world. In an effort to appease too many people, the President had fractured his American Intelligence apparatus at its inception.

Again, Hoover had been disappointed by his President–betrayed, even, as he saw it.

The initial downsized operations of the SIS were handled by agents picked by Hoover. Bob Waterman was the first. He would prove more adept at schmoozing the

Director and blustering his way through meetings and debriefings than at spycraft. His work product was anything but impressive. He dispatched a number of agents to different countries in a haphazard manner. Waterman's organizational skills and approach to operations were also less than stellar.

Even as SIS grew to nearly 600 agents its effectiveness was marginal at best. Under Waterman's direction, FBI agents recruited to SIS were required to resign from the Bureau. Once on the rolls of the SIS, they were required to go through a truncated training program, even more truncated than the original FBI Training School had been. Few of the men knew foreign languages. Fewer still had any experience in foreign countries. The vast majority of men brought into SIS couldn't adapt to the work or environment. Only a rare few could perform effectively under cover. No training relating to the realities of this new occupation was provided, primarily because none was available in the US.

Most of this went unnoticed and unknown by Hoover or anyone else above Waterman. The SIS chief had instituted a new system of record keeping within SIS, known as the "do not file" files. It was exactly as it sounded. He set up "secure depositaries" and safe houses in a number of obscure locations where any files or records generated were stashed. Only the team leaders for any specific area were aware of where these records were kept. "Compartmentalization is the key to success!" Waterman would say with conviction and vigor whenever asked about the lack of coordination and control.

While this was going on, Roosevelt had started calling the Director of the FBI more frequently for information and updates. Everyone knew the US was going to become involved in the war. The plans being prepared were all based upon the US immediately going after Germany as soon as war was declared. In order to pull this off successfully, the Americans would need to work closely with Great Britain, and possess the ability to exchange intelligence and assets with her other allies in very short order. Time was running out.

After each call from the President, Hoover would in turn call the head of his SIS and request an update. Waterman's song and dance soon became stale. Though he didn't want to acknowledge it, Hoover knew he'd put the wrong man in charge. The SIS was quickly devolving into a failure of major proportions.

That was when he'd called in Jelly Bryce. Bryce was loyal to a fault. More than that, he was smart, honest, and direct. Bryce knew the territory the SIS was based out of, down on the border. He was of that part of the country, tough and shrewd and not known for putting up with any nonsense. Hoover would replace that fool Waterman with Bryce; make Bryce the SAC of El Paso and give him the SIS. See what he could do with it. Hoover didn't know what else to do.

If the SIS tanked, if it continued to be the disaster it was shaping up to be, Hoover's career and reputation would go down with it. As far as the Director was concerned, that was bullshit. That was unacceptable. His original plan had been solid. Even the bastardized form of the plan the President had originally approved had been workable. But once that fool Roosevelt had scuttled the integrity of the organization, broken it up to appease the other dull-witted arrogant heads of Army and Naval Intelligence, he'd doomed it to failure. And J. Edgar knew only too well that while success had many fathers, failure would usually only have one. And he was in position to have the entire unholy mess pinned on him with a dagger stuck squarely in the middle of his back.

On top of this pile of shit, the spread of Soviet

Communism in the US was still a very real threat. The FBI had just finished investigating Soviet offices in New York only to discover an espionage ring the Brits had first detected in London. Gaik Baladovich Ovakimian, a 42-year-old chemical engineer working in New York, turned out to also be a seasoned espionage agent and spymaster. Among his many achievements, he'd run a spy network headed by Jacob Golos, one of the founding members of the Communist Party of the United States of America; he was believed to have arranged the assassination of Leon Trotsky in Mexico, and he'd recruited Julius and Ethel Rosenberg in 1938–a married couple that would later be executed by the United States for conspiracy to commit espionage.

Ovakimian was arrested during a meeting on May 5, 1941. A Soviet agent who'd been turned by the FBI had given him up. Before the FBI could interrogate the spymaster, however, the Germans broke their treaty with the Soviets and invaded Russia. In an effort to foster good will with the Soviets, a deal was struck. Ovakimian was traded back to Moscow in return for several Americans.

That same month the Bureau arrested 29 German military intelligence agents in a move believed to have all but crippled the Abwehr's clandestine intelligence operations in the United States. Still, a message was delivered by a German agent to the Japanese ambassador in the US, telling him the Americans were reading his messages. At that time Japan was actively working on the creation of their own intelligence networks in Mexico, Brazil, Argentina, Chile and Peru.

On the American side of the chessboard it was different. No one was communicating. Army Intelligence refused to talk to Naval Intelligence and vice versa. Neither would share any information with the FBI or State Department. Despite the lack of coordination and information sharing, the general consensus in the United States was that a Nazi attack on America was imminent.

The SIS with its substantial assets sprinkled throughout the Western Hemisphere was incapable of providing anything of value to fill the intelligence vacuum. Waterman's poorly trained agents bumbled through their assignments, constantly being taken in by con men, reporting mostly rumor and false information.

Shortly after making Bryce the SIS coordinator, Hoover realized the curtain was coming down on his intelligence agency. He wouldn't let Jelly take the fall. Not only was Jelly a valuable asset, but Hoover had developed a true fondness for the man. He was unlike anyone Hoover had ever known. Deep down the Director of the FBI also realized he was a little afraid of Bryce, and what might happen if the Oklahoma gunslinger felt he'd been betrayed. But that wasn't going to happen.

"We certainly picked some fine lemons in our original selection for SIS," he confided in the Assistant Director, Clyde Tolson, at dinner the night before he met with Jelly to relieve him of SIS command. "But Bryce isn't one of them. I won't let him fall when this fiasco crashes and burns."

What Hoover did instead was assign the SAC of the New York office as the new head of the SIS. Stew Wallace was instructed to resign from the FBI and set up shop at 30 Rockefeller Plaza. He would now be the president of the Importers and Exporters Service Company.

His actual job of course, was to create an undercover clearinghouse for covert SIS operations. Wallace was much better at this than Waterman or Jelly. He took to the assignment and brought a greater sense of sophistication and purpose to it. Reaching out to his many New York contacts, he arranged to have his agents pose as reporters for Newsweek magazine, stockbrokers for Merrill Lynch, executives of ATT, US Steel, and a number of other companies and corporations. He also started to design a viable training program for his men, as well as figure out better ways to identify and recruit suitable agents.

Unfortunately, it would all turn out to be too little, too late.

CHAPTER SIX

The Boss Wants to See You
24 August 1941

DONNELLY STOOD IN THE darkened doorway of a haberdashery on Third Street in downtown El Paso. He'd been there for close to an hour just watching and waiting. He checked his wristwatch, noted the time as 9:00 p.m., took a deep breath and rolled his head from side to side in an effort to loosen his neck muscles. Surveillance was tiring work, especially when working alone.

He'd arrived in town a week before and had been carefully tailing his target since. Prior to landing in El Paso, he'd spent some time in Oklahoma developing a background profile on the man as well. The Boss had ordered it and the Boss liked things done a certain way.

As Donnelly expected, his target arrived a few minutes later, pulling up to the curb across the street in his car. It was impossible to miss the man he'd been shadowing. Not only was Agent Bryce a fancy dresser, but he now drove a large pink Cadillac sedan.

Bryce's entire method and manner amused Donnelly. Not that he thought Bryce was anything other than an extremely dangerous and intelligent man. It was just that his flamboyant style went against everything that was considered "normal" in the Bureau.

'Why does Hoover let you get away with that car?' Donnelly thought to himself as Bryce stepped out of his new "tits pink Caddy." Donnelly smiled in the dark remembering the description of the car given to him by one of his

El Paso police contacts. It was accurate.

Donnelly watched from the concealment of the shadows as Bryce calmly glanced around before closing the Caddy's heavy door. As Bryce's gaze passed his location Donnelly held his breath for a moment, feeling strangely certain Bryce had seen him even though the FBI Agent had given no indication of it.

'No way he saw me here,' thought Donnelly, hardly a novice when it came to this game.

Then Bryce put his snap brim hat on his head and started walking away from the car toward the diner around the corner as Donnelly had expected. Bryce had a meeting arranged with a local informant for 9:30 at a shit-hole called Jimmy's. Donnelly knew this because he'd had Bryce's telephone lines tapped. He also knew Bryce would show up at least half an hour early to scope out the area before the meet because the man was cautious. Prudently so. Far from indicating paranoia, this habit indicated good survival skills on Bryce's part. The only thing that surprised Donnelly was that Bryce hadn't shown up an hour earlier. Donnelly would have. Donnelly actually had.

Just before Bryce reached the corner, Donnelly stepped soundlessly from the shadows and began to move down the street, staying on the opposite sidewalk. He saw Bryce turn the corner, staying close to the wall of the four-story brick building located there. Donnelly crossed the street, keeping Bryce's shadow in view as well as watching his reflection in the windows of the building across the street and the cars parked on both sides. The light from the street lamps and storefronts created a patchwork of telling shadows, and the windows of the storefronts and cars served as mirrors for one practiced in their use.

Donnelly slowed his pace, letting the distance between them grow more than he normally would. He allowed this because he knew where his target was heading, and also because there were only a few people out on the streets. While not unusual at this hour in this area, the lack of pedestrian traffic was problematic: it made it much more difficult to hide in plain sight.

Crossing the street, Donnelly paused at the corner for a moment, listening. Hearing a door close somewhere ahead, he nonchalantly strode forward and turned the corner, expecting to see Bryce about half a block up near the diner. What he saw instead was a deserted street.

Donnelly neither paused nor swiveled his head around in an effort to locate his target. He simply kept walking with a natural, easy gait. He'd lost men before doing this type of work, but not for quite a while. It was extremely difficult to tail a person without either losing them or getting burned in the process. And doing this alone, in this environment, certainly made it much harder.

'But still,' he thought, *'what the fuck? Where are you, you cocksucker...?'*

"Hey," said the voice behind him as he felt a steely grip on his right wrist and another on his neck just before he was spun around, his head slamming into the door of a car parked next to the curb. Donnelly was a good-sized man and had been thoroughly trained in hand-to-hand combat, but he was tossed through the air like a child and landed hard on his hip, blinding white pain shooting through him. Then Bryce–he was sure it had to be Bryce–had a knee jammed into his side, left hand around his throat and Donnelly's own .45 in his right hand.

Donnelly's eyes focused on the gun which Bryce held by the slide so the butt of the handle protruded forward like the head of a hammer. Donnelly hadn't felt his pistol being stripped from the holster on his hip, but there it was. As he struggled to catch his breath, Donnelly saw Bryce cock his arm back: Donnelly was apparently about to have his head caved in with his own gun.

"Waitwaitwait!" Donnelly whispered forcefully, not struggling at all now.

Bryce's eyes practically glowed in the dark. Donnelly could feel the heat and intensity coming in waves off the man above him as Bryce's steel cord-like fingers wrapped tighter around his neck. On a gut level Donnelly knew he was about to die, right there, right then, on a deserted El Paso sidewalk. Just as his bladder and bowels were about to release, he felt something change. The grip around his throat eased just slightly.

*   *   *

"You," said Jelly, curiously, but with a hard edge to his voice. "I remember you–Holloway." The first and last time Jelly had seen the man beneath him had been six years before, when he'd given Jelly a small canvas bag containing a machine pistol, cash, and a car key. At the time, Jelly had thought Holloway was FBI. Turned out he wasn't. Jelly'd never been able to figure out who he was or who he worked for.

Donnelly nodded, unable to produce any words.

"Well what the fuck, Holloway?" Jelly growled, "What game are you playing at now?"

With that Jelly spun the .45 in his hand so it was held normally, pressed the magazine release button with his thumb and snapped his wrist sideways, expelling the magazine from the grip of the pistol. The narrow magazine bounced on the sidewalk, two fat .45 rounds falling free.

Keeping his grip around Donnelly's neck, Jelly hooked the pistol's tiny rear sight on the heel of his shoe and pressed the gun down, racking the slide back. The chambered round was extracted and ejected and fell to the ground, rolling into the gutter. Jelly tossed the Colt down next to it.

Still holding his catch by the throat, Jelly stood and scanned around, looking for possible accomplices or witnesses. Spotting no one, he dragged Donnelly across the sidewalk into one of the storefronts' darkened vestibules. Keeping him on the ground, Jelly slammed the man he knew as FBI Special Agent Gerard Holloway against the door and expertly frisked him. Donnelly coughed and spit some blood as Jelly removed a strange, metal, spike-like weapon from a sheath strapped to his left forearm and threw it aside. Then he took a wallet from Donnelly's inside suit coat pocket and opened it: pulled out a few hundred dollars in cash, tossed that to the ground, and then found what he was looking for–a photo identification card.

Jelly let go of Donnelly's throat and moved back slightly. He held up the ID card so he could read it in the light from the streetlamp behind him on the sidewalk. "Sean A. Donnelly," he read aloud. "Washington Post press credentials." Jelly looked at the photograph on the ID and compared it to the man on the ground before him. It was him. Jelly shook his head and smiled.

Donnelly struggled to sit up and rubbed his neck. "Jesus Christ," he said hoarsely. Then he looked at Jelly's face and realized only Jelly's mouth was smiling. His eyes were still on fire, staring at him intently, watching every move he made. Donnelly realized he was still in great danger. "Bryce," he said, trying to regain some ground, "for Christ's sake, do you know what you're doing?"

"I do," Jelly said with a nod. "I'm deciding on whether you walk away from this in cuffs or are carried out feet first, Holloway. Or Donnelly. Or whoever the fuck you are. Now start talkin'. And start with who's with you–and don't fuckin' lie to me. If anyone else shows up, I'll finish you first, no questions asked."

Donnelly stared at Jelly. He made himself breathe slowly. His composure came back to him. "All right. Listen to me. You know who I am. Here's the thing. The Boss wants to see you."

Jelly's eyes narrowed. "What do you mean, the Boss wants to see me?"

"He's here," replied Donnelly evenly. "No one knows about this. It's like that other thing, you know, the last time we met. He's arranged to meet you now, tonight."

"You're full of shit!" Jelly snapped at him as he picked up the pencil-length metal spike from the ground. "You were on me from the moment I parked, hiding in your blind across the street."

Jesus, he had seen me,' thought Donnelly, more than a little rattled by this. *'Not possible...'*

"Then you tracked me, and you're carrying this," holding up the odd triangular-bladed weapon. "What the fuck is this?" he demanded. "And why the fake credentials?"

"Why the fuck do you think?!" said Donnelly, becoming bolder now. "You know what I do for the Boss. You've done the same kind of jobs for him. This isn't about you, Bryce. For Christ's sake, if you were the target, don't you think I would have found a cleaner way to do this?"

Jelly thought for a moment, considering that. "How do I know you don't just suck at your job?"

Donnelly thought for a long moment, then sighed and said resignedly, "I don't know Bryce. Maybe I do. I mean, it *is* me laying here with my ass kicked and my shit thrown all over the sidewalk."

Jelly dialed it down just a bit. "Why didn't you just call me?"

"You know it doesn't work like that. Your telephone

lines are all tapped. Hell, for all I know, so are mine. This is a completely off-the-books meeting, Bryce. Only the three of us know about it."

"Three of us?"

"Yeah. You, me, and the Boss," Donnelly replied, then took a chance and added, "Who's waiting, by the way."

Jelly stared at Donnelly for a few seconds more before asking, "Where?"

* * *

The two men walked deeper into the industrial area, moving a block beyond Jimmy's Diner. Donnelly led the way. Jelly kept pace close behind, his .357 Magnum in his hand, held low against the side of his leg. He also had Donnelly's reloaded .45 tucked in his belt; the strange metal spike-like weapon rode in his pocket with Donnelly's wallet and ID.

They had crossed the street as they'd approached the diner so as not to be seen by Jelly's informant seated in the back booth, waiting. Though it was extremely unusual for Jelly to miss an appointment, the informant would leave after fifteen minutes. Jelly was known for being punctual in an unpunctual world, and had trained everyone he dealt with to be on time. He'd also made sure they knew what to do should he not show up for any reason. This applied to family, friends, co-workers and even members of the underworld he dealt with.

Donnelly abruptly stopped in front of an eight-story warehouse. "Here."

Jelly looked around and shifted his grip on his revolver. This made sense. It was similar to the SIS file room set up. Isolated location. Non-descript.

"Go ahead."

Donnelly turned down an alley on the side of the building. Jelly stayed close enough behind so he could reach out and grab him but not so close Donnelly could spin on him. The way Donnelly was limping, and from the size of the goose egg on his forehead, Jelly didn't think that would be a problem. Donnelly wasn't showing it now, but he was still in a lot of pain. Plus, he was afraid of Jelly. Jelly took no real pleasure in this. It was just the way it was. It was the mortal truth of the situation.

Donnelly stopped again, this time in front of a side entrance into the building. He indicated the door with a toss of his head. "There."

Jelly nodded, indicating with the barrel of his revolver Donnelly should lead the way in.

Donnelly climbed the two steps to the small platform in front of the green metal door. He knocked twice, paused, knocked twice more, then once again.

"Seriously?" Jelly asked quietly. Donnelly shrugged in response.

From somewhere inside the building the men heard two knocks in reply. Donnelly looked at Bryce for permission, then slowly turned the knob and pushed the door open once Jelly nodded.

Jelly flattened out against the wall of the building next to the door, muzzle of his gun on Donnelly and the doorway. Donnelly saw this and paused, then opened the door all the way. "It's okay, I swear on my mother," he said. "It's just the Boss up there, no one else."

The staircase was dimly lit by a single bulb on the upper landing.

Jelly nodded again. As Donnelly entered the doorway, Jelly slid smoothly in behind him and grabbed Donnelly's shirt collar with his left hand. Donnelly could feel the muzzle of the revolver against his spine. "That's fine,"

Donnelly whispered reassuringly. "Nice and easy now, Bryce."

Jelly kicked the door closed behind them; the men started to climb the stairs. As they stealthily ascended the staircase, Donnelly could hear Jelly breathing slowly and deeply, each step, each movement calm and measured. Jelly was also reading Donnelly's physical reactions, waiting for the slightest sign of deception or tenseness.

At the top of the staircase was a hallway lined with closed doors. The hallway was also dimly lit with wall-mounted light fixtures, only a few of which were illuminated.

Without warning an image of the hallway of the Wren Hotel appeared before Jelly's eyes. The entire sequence of events of the day he'd stepped into that small room where the gangster, Ray O'Donnell, waited with his .45 cocked and pointed at him flashed through his mind in an instant. Jelly heard the shots from his lucky gun, saw O'Donnell's face coming apart, heard the muffled screams of the woman who was somewhere in the room, smelled the burnt gunpowder in his nostrils.

His heart started to pound. Jelly's body hesitated in El Paso as his mind relived the long-ago event in Oklahoma City.

"You all right, Bryce?"

Donnelley's voice brought him back. Jelly scanned the hallway, then the staircase behind him and the staircase in front of them which led to the next floor. "Which way?"

Donnelly pointed to a door halfway down the hall. Each door had a brass number fixed to it. "Twenty-three."

They moved slowly down the hall toward number twenty-three. At the door, Jelly kept one hand wrapped around Donnelly's collar and the other around his gun as he stood to the side of the doorway against the wall. He put Donnelly directly in front of the door. If any rounds were going to come through that door, Donnelly would be catching them, not him. A vivid image of Agent Tom Spenser's shotgun-blasted face flashed in Jelly's mind, as fresh and horrifyingly real as the moment it had happened while he'd stood outside another door back in 1935.

Jelly shook his head and forcefully whispered, "Cut it out." Spenser's pitifully-shredded face vanished.

Donnelly looked questioningly at Jelly. "What?" he whispered back. The wound-up man pointing a gun at him was really making him anxious now.

Jelly nodded toward the door.

Donnelly knocked twice. "It's me, Boss," he said quietly.

"Okay," replied a voice from inside the room.

Jelly couldn't be sure if it was Hoover's voice or not. He did know this type of solitary clandestine meeting was definitely not Hoover's style. Hoover liked to have his people with him anytime he was outside the sanctuary of his home or office.

As Donnelly turned the doorknob, Jelly pushed him explosively through the doorway using him as a human shield and quickly scanned the room. It was nearly identical to the SIS file room: a small windowless office with a table and a few chairs, a file cabinet and not much else. A single bulb burned in the lamp on the table; a lone man sat in one of the chairs next to the table, hands folded together on his lap. It wasn't Hoover.

"Don't fuckin' move, either of you," ordered Jelly, the muzzle of his Registered Magnum pointed at the seated man through Donnelly's spine. "What is this?"

The man, dressed in nondescript street clothes, looked to be in his late fifties. In the glow of the lamp Jelly could see he had short, graying hair and watery blue eyes. Far from being startled or alarmed at the sight before him, the old man appeared... *'amused,'* thought Jelly. The man smiled but said nothing.

"Again, and for the last time," Jelly said, his voice going

flat, "what the fuck is this?"

"I take it this is Agent Bryce, Mister Palmer?" the man said, looking at Donnelly and speaking calmly. Jelly could see the old man was being careful to sit quietly and make no sudden movements.

"Yes, sir," replied Donnelly, adding, "I'm sorry, Boss. Things kind of got away from me."

"So I gather," replied the man. Then he smiled again, easily, naturally, at Jelly. "Agent Bryce," he said, still speaking calmly, almost soothingly, "I apologize if this situation makes you uncomfortable. Please believe me when I tell you that was not my intent."

As the man spoke, Jelly realized he looked and sounded familiar. Not that he'd met him before, but if he was right, he had seen him many times in newspapers and in newsreels; he'd also heard that distinctive voice more than once on the radio.

"Holy shit," Jelly said quietly.

The old man heard it and his smile grew. His eyes actually appeared to twinkle.

Donnelly straightened a bit and said, quite formally given the circumstances, "Agent Bryce, may I introduce you to Colonel William J. Donovan."

"*Wild Bill*," said Jelly, somewhat in awe. The old man sitting before him was "Wild Bill" Donovan, a true American hero. Donovan had commanded the famous "Fighting 69th Infantry" during the first Great War and been awarded the Medal of Honor and a fistful of other decorations. Hollywood had just released a hit movie called *The Fighting 69th* that recounted his wartime exploits. But that was far from all that made Donovan so easily recognizable. He'd had a long, successful career as a Wall Street lawyer and had dabbled quite a bit in politics. Many people believed he was destined to run for the White House on the

Republican ticket–and would probably win given his name recognition and popularity.

"Nice to finally meet you, *Jelly*," Donovan said as he slowly stood up. "Now if you'd be so kind as to release Mister Palmer, there, I'd appreciate it if you'd have a seat," indicating the chair opposite his. "We have a lot to discuss and I'm afraid my time is limited."

Jelly, left fist full of Donnelly's collar, slowly pushed his human shield away from him as he simultaneously moved backwards against the wall opposite Donovan. Once his left arm was at full extension, he released his hold on the silent man and lowered the muzzle of his pistol.

Donovan smiled again. "Thank you, Jelly." Looking at Donnelly he said, "Would you mind, Mister Palmer?"

"No, sir," Donnelly replied instantly. He didn't appear offended at the implied order to step out of the room. Donovan looked back at Jelly and added, "If that's all right with you, naturally."

Jelly nodded, glanced at Donnelly and said quietly, "Your gear will be here when I leave."

Donnelly rubbed the back of his neck, nodded at Donovan and stepped quietly out of the room, closing the door behind him.

"Please," Donovan said, indicating the chair across from him.

Jelly holstered his pistol, then slid the chair back a bit, angling it so it faced the door. He stood, waiting. Donovan sat down again. Jelly followed suit.

For a few heartbeats both men sat looking at each other. It appeared Donovan expected Jelly to talk, to ask a question. He didn't.

Donovan, keeping both hands flat on the tabletop, leaned in slightly and said, "Are you familiar with the Samurai, Jelly?"

Jelly's eyes narrowed. "I've heard of them. Jap soldiers from the olden days. Yes?"

Donovan's expression didn't change. "Yes. But they were more than that. They were men who practiced a severe code of honor. Bushido, it was called. A Samurai lived according to the code, or he wasn't a Samurai at all. Do you know anything about this code?"

Jelly looked questioningly at Donovan. His impulse was to ask what the fuck this was all about. Had Donovan arranged this clandestine meeting in order to give him a fucking history lesson? But something about Donovan's manner intrigued Jelly. In some ways it felt like he was sitting with Hoover. Hoover liked to discuss things like this. *'What the hell,'* he thought. "No. I'm not familiar with it, Colonel."

Donovan smiled. He could see Jelly was keeping himself under control, putting up with the ramblings of an old man.

"If you don't mind, I'd like to tell you about it, just for a few minutes. Won't take long. And I assure you, there is a point to all this."

Jelly nodded again. "Fire away, sir."

"The Samurai were raised believing that a life lived without honor was a disgrace to one's self and family. But their sense of honor was different than what many people think of today. Today, if a man is relatively honest, tells the truth, works hard, and doesn't let anyone hurt or insult him or his family, he figures he's living an honorable life." Donovan raised his eyebrows and grinned, then said, "I see a lot of soldiers sporting a tattoo, one that says *'death before dishonor.'* Have you seen tattoos like that?"

Jelly nodded, feeling uncomfortably certain Donovan somehow knew about his tattoos. His mind instantly dismissed the thought, internally whispering the words,

'Getting paranoid.'

"See, for the Samurai, Jelly, honor was a specific thing. I would imagine that for most of the men with *'death before dishonor'* cut into their flesh, it means they will not tolerate any insult or injustice to their person. That sort of thing. But you see, for the Samurai, that is a matter of *'face.'* Of being insulted, or shamed by another. That actually has nothing to do with the code of honor. A Samurai could *'lose face'* as they called it, but still maintain his personal honor. The way it works is like this..."

Jelly could see Donovan wasn't just talking about this in an abstract manner. He was enthused in the telling; was explaining it as if trying to convert Jelly to his religion.

"Honor has three basic components. The code itself is actually quite simple in design. It's living up to it that's difficult." Donovan smiled again; a kind, genuine smile, Jelly thought.

"The first part is *responsibility*. A man has got to understand and acknowledge his responsibilities to others. What it boils down to is this: if someone does you a service in this world, you owe them in kind. The greater the service, the greater the debt. Makes sense, yes?"

"Of course."

"Usually in this world, the people we owe the most are our parents. They give us life, take care of us, teach us, prepare us for the world. So we owe them a great debt. Honor thy mother and father, that sort of thing. We also owe a great debt to our friends and family members–those who do right by us–and we owe a debt to our employers, because they provide us a way to make a living and take care of our own families. Yes?"

"Yes."

"And finally, we owe a debt to our countrymen and our leaders. But again–and this is important–only if they act honorably as well. And the way we determine if they are doing that is by using the code."

Jelly's eyes narrowed again. He nodded, listening.

"That brings us to the second part of the code: *justice*. What justice means in this case is simply doing the right thing to repay the debt we owe to others. Now some people today will argue that *the right thing* is purely subjective, that there is no right or wrong, but that's just bullshit. Unless you're a fool or mentally defective, you know what's right and what's wrong. Aristotle perhaps summed it up best when he said that if people wish to be happy, they must act in accordance with reason. If someone acts against reason, they are not doing the right thing." Donovan stopped talking, cocked his head slightly, then asked, "Does that sound right to you?"

"If I say 'no' does that make me unreasonable?" Jelly asked with a straight face.

Donovan squinted, thinking for a moment he had misjudged the man sitting before him. Then Jelly smiled.

Donovan smiled back. "I suppose it would, at least according to Aristotle."

Jelly nodded. "I'm with you, sir."

"Okay," Donovan said, folding his hands on the table and leaning forward. "So what we have then is this: to follow the code of honor, one must first recognize his debts to others and then do the right thing to repay those debts."

Jelly nodded.

"Like I said, simple enough. And that brings us to the third part of the code. And this part, Jelly, is the most difficult. For the last piece of the code is *courage*. One must have–*or find*–the courage to do the right thing in order to repay the debt. This is the most difficult part, for while most reasonable people can recognize when they owe a debt, and will know what the right thing to do to repay it is, most people, Jelly, can't find the courage to *do* the right thing. That's the piece that's most often lacking."

Jelly thought about this for a moment. He thought about all the hard things he'd had to do over the years, the direct actions he'd taken because he'd believed them right and necessary, but which he'd often had to do alone–frequently while fighting off the efforts of others who'd tried to stop him.

His old partner, H.V. Wilder, had once said something that had stuck with Jelly–something Jelly had often repeated to others over the years: "The right thing to do is very rarely the easy thing to do," Wilder had said. "But, that makes it no less the *right thing* to do."

Jelly looked squarely into Donovan's eyes. For a moment he felt as if he were looking in a mirror, seeing himself twenty years in the future. "I understand."

Donovan sat back a bit and returned the gaze. "I know you do. That's why you're here."

"So what is it you want from me, sir?"

"What I would like you to do, Jelly, is consider this: we will not be facing Samurai in this coming war. Do you know why?"

"Because the Samurai no longer exist, I would imagine."

"Correct. They no longer exist. They no longer exist because they were defeated, destroyed. And do you know who destroyed them?"

Jelly shook his head.

"The Japanese government destroyed them. The same Japanese government which is now intent on destroying the United States and anyone else who opposes them. They did this, my friend, because governments and bureaucrats have a natural disdain for men of honor. Bureaucrats and men of honor are natural enemies, for the most part. That's why I find it so interesting that you are so loyal to Edgar Hoover."

This caught Jelly by surprise. If anything, he considered Donovan and Hoover cut from the same cloth. While his first instinct was to shut down and defend his boss, his years of training, experience and self-discipline caused him instead to remain silent, poker face intact. He would let Donovan keep talking, see where this was going.

From the other side of the table Donovan studied Jelly's face. He knew how close Jelly and Hoover had become over the years. He was expecting a reaction, even a well-hidden reaction to his comment, but there was none. The FBI agent in front of him was as good as he'd been led to believe. Now he was certain he'd made the right call.

"Before I go on, I want you to know I realize how loyal you are to Edgar, and I appreciate that. I also know he's been watching out for you for many years, and that your own innate sense of honor requires you to repay that debt by maintaining your loyalty to him. Please believe me, Jelly, I'm not here to try and alienate you from Edgar or the Bureau. On the contrary, I am here because I believe you're the type of man that can be trusted to remain loyal once you have decided that is the right course of action. What I am proposing to you, is the idea that you could be loyal to two bosses, simultaneously, so long as they were both serving the greater good."

"Whose greater good?" Jelly asked.

"The Nation's. America's greater good."

Jelly took a deep, slow breath as he considered this. It wasn't just the words that Donovan was speaking; it was the way he spoke them.

Over the past thirteen years Jelly had gotten very good at evaluating people. He'd sat through numerous interviews and interrogations with all types, from thugs to politicians, psychopaths to clergymen. Practically every one of them had lied to him at some point or another. Big lies or small, with only one exception–that being his second ex-wife, Vera–Jelly had unfailingly known when he was being deceived.

    Based on his years of proven experience, he'd come to trust his ability to correctly read people and situations. That's how he knew the man seated before him was a rare bird. Though he'd only been speaking with him a short time, Jelly had the overwhelming sense that Colonel Wild Bill Donovan was a man who could be trusted.

    In a respectful tone, he told all this to Donovan with three words: "I'm listening, Colonel."

CHAPTER SEVEN

Wild Bill Donovan

WILLIAM JOSEPH DONOVAN WAS indeed a rare bird.

Born to immigrant parents on New Year's Day, 1883, in New York's clannish First Ward, Donovan had exhibited from an early age the traits he would be both revered and hated for till the end of his life.

A tough, proud kid growing up in a rough Buffalo neighborhood, young Bill Donovan quickly learned to use both his fists and his brain. His parents, Timothy and Mary, encouraged their children to read and study, sending them to Catholic schools as soon as they were of age. All through his school years Bill excelled, especially when taking part in debating and athletics.

After high school he attended Niagara University, initially with the thought of entering the priesthood, but both he and his teachers soon realized that was not his calling. The law beckoned, and Bill pursued a legal education, first at Columbia College in New York City where he graduated in 1905, then on to Columbia Law School where he graduated two years later. A standout athlete and scholar all through college, the blue-eyed Donovan was also extremely handsome, charming and very popular with the ladies. His intelligence and calm, measured manner were noticed by many, including one of his teachers, respected New York lawyer Harlan Fisk Stone, who would later play an important role in Donovan's life.

Not everyone was enamored of Donovan, however. One of his classmates–future president of the United States,

Franklin Delano Roosevelt–had no interest in the rough Irish kid from the wrong side of the tracks. For his part, Donovan considered Roosevelt a wealthy "Beau Brummel" or "fancy Dan," so the two largely ignored each other all through college.

Once out of school, Donovan took a little time to figure out what he wanted to do with his education, then joined a law firm. Two years later he formed his own firm with a classmate, and they enjoyed such success that within three years they were merged into a powerfully-connected firm, Goodyear and O'Brien. The connections he made opened doors for him into New York's wealthy and influential high society.

Always full of energy and looking for adventure, in 1912 Donovan helped organize an Army National Guard cavalry unit. He was named Captain. Like he did with all his endeavors, Donovan threw himself fully into this new venture, studying military strategy and tactics, and organizing drills that both educated and pushed the men in his command far beyond what anyone expected.

Never shy around women but always a discreet gentleman, Donovan eventually married wealthy socialite Ruth Rumsey in 1914.

An inveterate traveler all his adult life, Donovan was in Berlin when orders came from the State Department activating his National Guard unit for immediate deployment to the Texas border. It was 1916 and General John "Black Jack" Pershing's expeditionary army was on the hunt for the Mexican revolutionary, Pancho Villa. Donovan's cavalry "Troop I" was to assist. A new father, he proceeded directly from Europe to Texas: duty had called, and Donovan responded without hesitation as he would for the rest of his life.

Promoted to Major, Donovan continued to drill his

troops relentlessly while deployed, understanding that preparation would be the key to success and survival.

Within a year, Major Donovan would be back in Buffalo, but instead of returning to his law practice he joined the 69th "Irish" Regiment of New York City. His travels to Europe had convinced him war was coming and he believed the US would end up in the fight. He also believed his men would be chewed up in battle unless they toughened up considerably. In addition to the regular cavalry drills he put them through, he started leading his men on daily three mile runs, after which they would strip to the waist and engage in hand-to-hand combat until bloodied. Many of the men under his command hated his guts for the way he drove them. But because Donovan led from the front and participated in all the drills, they also respected and followed him without question or hesitation.

One day, during a particularly arduous run while wearing full packs, many of the men, much younger than Donovan, fell out exhausted. Donovan stood there shaking his head, and yelled out, "What the hell's the matter with you guys? I haven't lost *my* breath!" A soldier called out in reply, "But hell, we aren't as wild as you are, Bill." It was that moment that christened Donovan, "Wild Bill."

As Donovan had predicted, all the training would prove crucial during the Great War. Unlike any conflict before it, the war in Europe was brutal beyond description. The weapons of the modern age–most notably the machine gun and poison gas–produced staggering carnage. The effectiveness of these weapons was compounded as many of the military leaders on both sides were still employing strategies and tactics used during the last war.

Donovan, promoted to lieutenant colonel, found his true-most self on the battlefields of France. Modern warfare was an element he thrived in, despite being wounded on several occasions and seeing more than half his regiment decimated in the muddy and bloody trench fighting. Time and again Donovan stood up in battle and rallied his men to follow him as he charged into the enemy's lines. On one of those occasions, his soldiers, pinned down by machine gun fire, watched their leader stand up, eyes ablaze as rounds snapped past his head, and rail at them, "What, do you want to live forever?!" Inspired by his heroic madness, they followed him over the top, out of certain death and on to victory.

Donovan repeatedly proved himself a smart and fearless leader dedicated both to the mission and to the welfare of his men. Though some considered him a bit reckless for his aggressive tactics, everyone acknowledged he was an extremely courageous, capable officer.

Wild Bill's reputation grew, soon morphing into legend both throughout the American Expeditionary Force then back in the States. His wife, Ruth, home after having given birth to a second child, sent edited copies of her husband's descriptive letters of the war and foreign lands to the New York papers. They were widely published and read by an admiring audience. Talk of a run for governor once Donovan returned started in influential social and political circles.

Still in Europe, Donovan was made chief of staff of the 165th Regiment, an assignment he accepted primarily because it put him in position to be the forward ground commander in an upcoming battle which would prove to be the final American offensive of the war–the battle of the Meuse-Argonne. More than a million American soldiers would participate in the battle that stretched along the entire Western Front and would last for 47 days.

As ambitious as the undertaking was, many of the overall US commanders would unfortunately prove to be inexperienced, indecisive, incompetent, or a combination of all three.

The offensive quickly stalled. Men were ground up in belts of barbed wire, minefields, machine gun and artillery fire. Donovan stayed at the front with his troops, many of them green, poorly trained replacements. On the second day of the battle, pinned down by fire, Donovan was struck by a fast-moving machine gun round that punched a hole through his tibia just below his knee. Though in excruciating pain, he refused evacuation; instead, he continued directing the attack by way of a field telephone and messengers. At one point he had soldiers help him move across ground from foxhole to foxhole so he could speak with his men and keep their morale up. He finally agreed to evacuation and medical care only after his men had been pulled back to a better defensive position on his orders.

By the time the battle ended with the signing of the Armistice on 11 November 1918, more than twenty-six thousand men were dead, close to one hundred thousand wounded.

For his actions in France, Donovan was eventually awarded the Medal of Honor, the distinguished Service Cross, three Army Distinguished Service Medals, the Silver Star and two Purple Hearts. In addition, he received the *Légion d'Honneur*, the Order of the British Empire, the *Croce di Guerra*, the Order of Leopold, the Order of Polonia Restituta, and a *Croix de Guerre* with Palm.

Before coming home and while still recuperating, the tireless Donovan helped form a new organization, the American Legion. The idea was to create an entity which could lobby for veteran's benefits and advocate for a strong national defense.

Despite all his successes and accomplishments, Donovan was haunted by the loss of the men he'd trained and led. More than half the men who'd sailed with him to France had not returned. He would never forget them.

Once back home, Donovan tried to settle into a normal life but this was short-lived. Public service called. In 1922 he accepted an appointment as United States attorney for western New York. He also took his first run at politics that year, throwing his hat in the ring for lieutenant governor of New York. He lost, but his appetite had been whetted.

Believing his duty as US attorney superseded social and personal interests, and in compliance with the law under Prohibition, Donovan ordered a raid on a speakeasy frequented by powerful and wealthy socialites–many whom he knew. It was not a popular decision and cost him dearly in terms of reputation and finances. But he never wavered or regretted the decision. It became apparent to all, including his detractors, that he was committed to doing the right thing.

This was when his old law-school professor, Harlan Fiske Stone, re-entered his life. Stone, recently appointed Attorney General by President Calvin Coolidge, brought Donovan into the criminal division of the Justice Department as an assistant attorney general.

It was while serving in this position that Wild Bill Donovan and J. Edgar Hoover first met. Immediately recognizing each other as natural enemies, the two would hate one another for the rest of their lives. Donovan, believing Hoover to be an untrustworthy, power-seeking bureaucrat, tried to have the newly-appointed, temporary director of the Bureau of Investigation fired.

Hoover, meanwhile, perceived the highly-decorated war hero as a dangerous, reckless threat and potential political adversary, and used the tools at his disposal to open a secret file on Donovan. For years the Bureau would collect all sorts of information on Wild Bill.

Their initial engagement ended with Hoover the victor: Donovan was passed over for the position of Attorney General when Stone was named to the Supreme Court in 1925. Many believed this was the greatest disappointment of Wild Bill's life–and one of Hoover's most treasured successes.

Donovan withdrew from public life after that and set up a new law practice, this time on Wall Street. He made a fortune. But money was not what made him tick. In 1932 he ran for Governor on the Republican ticket against Herbert Lehman, an FDR Democrat. Lehman easily won. Again Wild Bill returned to Wall Street and ran his law office.

Restless and curious by nature, he resumed travelling internationally throughout the 1930s, ostensibly cultivating business contacts, but in reality he was gathering information. After a while, his information was proven solid and detailed enough to be considered intelligence. Donovan relayed this intelligence back to Washington through his contacts where it was gratefully received, for they had no mechanisms in place to generate it themselves. Many in the US Government still considered "spying" a distasteful, unnecessary, and un-American activity.

Donovan, on the other hand, recognized the value and urgent need–he believed war was stirring again in Europe. He based this belief on first-hand observations as well as personal meetings with many of the leaders, to include dictators like Benito Mussolini and a wiry, nervous-looking Austrian named Hitler.

By 1940 the world stage was set for a second "great war."

Republicans and Democrats began to put aside some of their ideological differences in order to prepare the Nation for what many saw as inevitable US involvement. Roosevelt had begun to look at those within his administration who refused to acknowledge this with skepticism and suspicion. His Ambassador to the Court of St. James, Joseph P. Kennedy, was a Nazi appeaser who made public statements proclaiming Great Britain had no chance against Hitler.

On 10 June 1941, Roosevelt's Secretary of War, Henry Stimson, brought Donovan to the White House for a private meeting with the President. With the release of Warner Brothers' movie, *"The Fighting 69th,"* Donovan's hero persona had been brought back into the public eye. The President appreciated this. He was trying to lead an unwilling nation into a second European war because he believed it was necessary and right, and needed all the help he could get. Donovan, nearing sixty years of age, still possessed immense charisma, charm and energy. In addition, he was a fount of creative, intelligent, and bold ideas. FDR wanted his "old Columbia Law School friend" on his team.

As Roosevelt listened, Donovan confidently delivered his proposal.

"The Nation desperately needs an international spy service," he began. "I can provide this for you, Mister President."

Donovan described his thoughts: his agency would oversee the intelligence gathering activities of the FBI, State Department, Army and Naval Intelligence. When Roosevelt expressed doubt about anyone's ability to bring all these agencies into compliance with such a plan, Donovan smiled and assured him, "I will mesh the machinery. I will make it work." FDR looked into the eyes of one of America's greatest living heroes and believed.

He believed in part because this had been no off-the-cuff meeting. FDR had previously sent Donovan to Great Britain as the President's personal emissary–a move that had enraged Kennedy and sent a strong message to Winston Churchill. During his time in London, Donovan and

Churchill had met on several occasions. Churchill, a storied veteran of several battles himself, saw in Donovan a kindred spirit. They recognized each other at once as members of the honorable, warrior class. They trusted one another.

Churchill opened wide all the secret doors for Donovan. He'd already paired up the visiting American hero with one of Britain's own–a spymaster whose code name was "Intrepid." Intrepid took Donovan under his wing and educated him in the ways of spycraft. He helped him form the plans for the proposed American Intelligence agency based on the British model–the very plans Donovan presented to the President.

One month later, on 11 July 1941, Roosevelt named Donovan the national Coordinator of Information, or C.O.I.

Wild Bill was given the authority to collect and analyze any and all intelligence bearing on national security.

Keeping close tabs on these developments from his inner sanctuary office at the Seat of Government, Edgar Hoover was enraged. Believing Donovan was plotting to have him removed, Hoover proclaimed to all who would listen, "This job doesn't mean that much to me. Anyone wants it they can have it. I'll wire my resignation tonight if that's how the president feels."

Roosevelt considered it. One of his closest advisors–his wife, Eleanor–had been recommending Hoover be fired for years. She hated the Director of the FBI almost as much as Donovan did.

After careful consideration Roosevelt decided to let both Hoover and Donovan command their own domains. The President was a man who understood and enjoyed the "great game" as much as anyone.

He knew that conflict among his subordinates could be useful.

* * *

Even before being officially appointed COI, Donovan had been actively recruiting people for the new organization he was building. One of them was seated before him now in this cramped little room in an El Paso warehouse.

The rather intense FBI agent had indeed turned out to be an interesting candidate.

Donovan had first been made aware of Agent Jelly Bryce by one of his closest and most trusted associates, Intrepid. Intrepid had met Bryce, spent some time with him, and seen something in the man that intrigued him, some quality beyond his remarkable ability with a gun.

"I believe he would be of immeasurable value, Bill," Intrepid had said when speaking of Jelly. "The key will be getting him to buy into the importance of the mission. Once you do that, once he commits, you'll have a loyal, valuable asset."

Keeping his friend's advice in mind while seated across from Jelly, Donovan had explained why he'd wanted to meet with him. He'd told him about the Coordinator of Information appointment, then had gone further, describing the next stage of the project: the creation of a wartime intelligence agency that would soon be sending agents out into the world on behalf of the United States of America.

"What would you think about being parachuted behind Japanese lines into the Philippines?" Donovan asked seriously. "Not a military operation. Just a few good men going in on a top secret mission, to get something done that desperately needed to get done."

Jelly's eyes opened a bit. A smile spread across his face. "I don't think it would be boring."

Donovan smiled back. "No. Boring's not something I'm a fan of either."

"So how would I do this—if I *were* to do this? Serve two bosses simultaneously?"

Donovan leaned forward. "That would be pretty much up to you. I told you I wasn't trying to alienate you from Edgar or the Bureau, but that doesn't mean I'm averse to stealing you." He smiled. "You could leave the Bureau and come work for me. That's one option. Quite a few of your colleagues are interested, though I'm not interested in many of them. I need a particular type of man."

"Like Donnelly?" Jelly asked, question dripping with disdain.

Donovan's face tightened. "The man you know as Donnelly is a good man, Jelly. He's loyal and skilled. He's been with me for a number of years. He started with the Bureau, too. Became disillusioned with the way Edgar ran things." Donovan sighed. "My intent was not to discuss Edgar with you tonight, Jelly. But I will tell you this: I know him. He worked for me once. I was not impressed. He fancies himself an intelligence expert. In my opinion he's inept at best. I know you've seen his S.I.S. up close. I'm sure you've formed your own opinions. Suffice to say, in the real Intelligence community, his efforts are looked upon as a joke."

Jelly, poker face intact, remained silent.

"If nothing else," Donovan continued, "consider this: Edgar Hoover, the man who wants to run a clandestine, international intelligence agency, has *never travelled* outside the continental United States—with the exception of a few jaunts across the border into Mexico for pleasure. Is that really the man you want to follow down this trail, son?"

Jelly was surprised at that bit of information. He'd always just assumed Hoover was well travelled.

Donovan could see the wheels turning behind Jelly's eyes. As if reading Jelly's mind, he said, "How can a man send other men into harm's way, off to foreign lands, if he's never walked that trail himself? I don't know, Jelly. But believe me, there are plenty of men in governments all over the world who have no problem doing just that. Sending other men–other people's sons–off to die, rifle in their hands, while those same men who send those sons to die remain in safety, far from the sounds of battle. Those are the bureaucrats. The natural enemies of honorable men."

Jelly had heard enough. He became uncomfortable. He felt conflicted. The things Donovan was saying had the crystal clear ring of truth, yet, if he accepted that truth, it meant that Edgar Hoover was so much less than he'd always believed him to be. It was too much to process. He needed to leave. He abruptly stood up. Donovan looked surprised.

"Colonel," Jelly began, "I appreciate you wanting to meet with me. I believe you're an honorable man, but I need to leave now. I need some time to think over what you've told me."

Donovan stood up, nodded. "Of course, son. I realize I've thrown a lot at you out of the blue. Normally I'd have done this more incrementally, but things are starting to move very fast and I don't have that luxury." Donovan took a small white card from his shirt pocket and held it out. It was blank save for a telephone number printed on one side. "You'll be able to get in touch with me at that number anytime over the next two weeks. There's always someone there to answer. After two weeks, the number won't be good anymore."

Jelly reached over the table and took the card, glanced at the number and slipped the card into his own shirt pocket. He nodded. "I understand." Before turning to leave, he took Donnelly's loaded .45 from his belt and placed it on the table, hammer down and muzzle pointing off to the side away from him and Donovan. From his right jacket pocket, he produced Donnelly's wallet, placing that next to the pistol, then reached into the other pocket and took out the spike-like blade and sheath. As he started to lower it to the table top, Donovan held out his hand, palm forward.

"I'd like it if you kept that, Jelly."

Jelly looked questioningly into the older man's eyes.

"Consider it a gift. A symbol. From one old Samurai to another."

Jelly hesitated.

"What do you think happens to us when we die, Jelly?"

The question caught Jelly off guard. Donovan was good at doing that. "I have no idea."

Donovan smiled again. "I believe that when I die, the world will come to an end."

Jelly's eyebrows raised.

Donovan's smile grew. "Do you remember what it was like before you were born? Do you remember that?"

Jelly shook his head, not sure where the Colonel was going with this. The whole conversation had been like that, both intriguing and disturbing.

"Me neither. See, I think that's what death is like. I think it will be just like before we were born–the great, silent nothing. This world, everything we perceive us and it to be, simply stops. That's what I believe. That's why I'm not really concerned about the afterlife. I don't worry myself with thoughts of Heaven or Hell, Jelly. All I want to be able to do is, at the end of my life, I want to be able to look at myself in the mirror, look myself straight in the eye, and know that I'd lived a good, honorable life. That I'd always done–or at least tried my best to do–the right thing."

As he looked into Wild Bill Donovan's watery blue eyes, Jelly felt as if he were standing before a priest instead of a highly-decorated combat veteran. He also had the overwhelming feeling he'd just experienced one of the most important moments of his life, meeting this man.

Jelly returned the sheathed blade to his pocket. Donovan extended his hand again and the two men shook.

Jelly turned and walked out of the room, silently opening and then closing the door behind him.

Donovan stood there for a moment, thinking. He liked Bryce, liked what he saw. Not surprisingly, Intrepid had been correct in his assessment. Both Intrepid and Donovan knew men.

Once you'd been in battle, you came to recognize different sorts of men. *Usually*–but not always–you could recognize the good ones right away. It was in the eyes. Fear and fighting had a similar effect on most men. Most men would prefer to avoid both if possible. But some men were different. Some men were drawn to the flame, found their souls there–if there were such things. Who was to say?

All Donovan was sure of was that he wanted to go back to the battlefield. Though he knew war for what it was, and hated it for what it produced, he also knew it was inevitable. Politicians always saw to that through their ineptness at preparing for it. And if there was to be a war, he wanted to be in it.

Truth be told, Donovan *did* hate war–but he was also damned good at it. It was the element he thrived in, felt most alive in; it fit him most perfectly.

The Coordinator of Information appointment was fine for now. It had been his ticket in. The big war was already raging. Once the United States joined in it would be the greatest war the Earth had ever seen. He would build the secret intelligence organization everyone wanted him to build. He would lead it and shape it, make it something both great and useful. He would do it because he was being asked to do it, but most of all he would do it because it was the best way he could think of to get what we he truly wanted–a battlefield command.

For unlike J. Edgar Hoover, William J. Donovan had no true burning desire to head American intelligence. He'd been steered into this assignment by a number of people who'd convinced him it was his duty to do so. None had been more helpful, encouraging or insistent that he do it than his very good friend many only knew by the code name, Intrepid.

Donovan never called him that, of course. He simply called him Bill. To the members of the American and British top commands, they were known as the "Two Bills Team" because they'd spent so much time together.

It was amusing actually. The enthusiastic, verbose American, "Wild Bill" Donovan and the "Quiet Canadian," William S. Stephenson–had become pretty much inseparable.

CHAPTER EIGHT

The Quiet Canadian

WILLIAM SAMUEL STEPHENSON WAS a natural man of secrets. Most people throughout his life would never even know that Stephenson was not his birth name.

Stephenson was born on 23 January 1897, in Point Douglas, Winnipeg, Manitoba to William and Sarah Stanger. After his father died in 1901, his mother was unable to care for him and his two siblings. An Icelandic family adopted him and raised young Bill as their own on the prairies of Western Canada. He took their surname and became William Stephenson.

An intelligent and curious boy, Stephenson's interests ranged from science and mechanics to literature and boxing. Described as "restless and inquisitive," he was known as a bookworm who had a vicious left hook. After graduating from high school in 1914, the reedy Stephenson enlisted in the Army, becoming a member of the Royal Canadian Engineers. Sent overseas directly into the fray of the Great War, he received a field commission as a lieutenant and was promoted to captain within a year. Fighting in the trenches for nearly twenty months, young Stephenson witnessed the unvarnished horrors of modern warfare. After his second exposure to poison gas, he was sent back to England with the classification, "disabled for life."

Stephenson didn't agree. Instead of accepting the surgeon's diagnosis, he wrangled a transfer to the Royal Flying Corps. Pilots were being killed at such an alarming rate that his "permanent injured" status and cadaverous appearance were overlooked. He received a total of five hours' flight instruction before being given a plane and a combat mission.

It was around this time Stephenson would meet an interesting American on the battlefield. The United States had not yet entered the war, but the American–a sharp-minded, successful attorney who'd been dispatched to the European theater to conduct a survey for the American War Relief Commission–immediately established a bond with the young Canadian soldier. As Stephenson explained his thoughts on the war, the American–William Donovan–listened. He was greatly impressed with the young man's insightful comments and analysis.

Later, Donovan would learn that Stephenson was both intelligent *and* fearless. The novice flyer would see aerial combat numerous times, shooting down twenty-six enemy aircraft and destroying a score of other ground targets. His heroism would be recognized by being awarded the Distinguished Flying Cross and the Military Cross. The thing that meant the most to him, however, was a line in one of the citations: *"He is always there when the troops need him."*

Shot down over Flanders on 28 July 1918, Stephenson was wounded and captured behind enemy lines. Sent to a prisoner of war camp, he attempted several unsuccessful escapes and was severely beaten for his efforts. Turning his analytical mind to the problem, he then spent several weeks convincing his captors he was too injured to attempt another escape.

Biding his time, he crafted a set of wire cutters and a crude compass from utensils stolen from the camp kitchen; gathered intelligence about the camp's location and the location of the Allied front many miles away. Then on an early pre-dawn morning, wearing a "borrowed" German

Army greatcoat, Stephenson slipped out of the prison camp and made good his escape. He reached Allied lines three days later. The detailed report he turned in about the prison camp and his escape caught the attention of Admiral Sir Reginald "Blinker" Hall.

Hall, who ran British intelligence operations out of an unassuming back office known only as "Room 40," recognized the potential in the young, accomplished aviator. He wanted him on his team. The only problem with Stephenson being adopted by the erstwhile "father" of modern British Intelligence was found in Stephenson's high profile, stellar reputation.

Stephenson's heroics in the RFC had resulted in additional awards, to include the French Legion of Honor and *Croix de Guerre* with Palm. On top of that, the plucky Canadian had pursued his interest in boxing while in the service, and won the interservice lightweight world boxing championship. Known wide and far as "Captain Machine Gun," Stephenson found himself in the limelight alongside the interservice heavyweight winner, US Marine Gene Tunney. The two men would form and maintain a lifelong friendship, even after Tunney turned pro and became the undefeated world champ.

After the war ended, Stephenson was assigned to test fly all captured enemy aircraft and make recommendations for improvements to British planes. He was working for Admiral Hall, though Blinker had faded from public view into the clandestine background as he continued directing British secret intelligence operations. The Admiral would do so for the next 25 years.

For his part, Stephenson kept busy both on behalf of the military and in personal business dealings. A prodigious inventor and entrepreneur, his quick mind and business acumen made him immediately successful. For a while, at least, he was able to leave the horrors of war behind and tried to build a new life. The rest of the world was largely doing the same. The unprecedented wholesale slaughter and devastation wrought during the Great War had left most people disenchanted and distrustful of military leaders and ventures. Such a war, the common sentiment seemed to be, could never happen again.

Less than two decades later the fallacy of this belief was evident.

Shortly after the second Great European War began, newly-elected Prime Minister Winston Churchill, acting on the advice of Admiral Hall, dispatched William Stephenson to the United States. Stephenson's initial posting was as "Passport Control Officer." His actual assignment was to covertly establish and direct British Security Coordination, or BSC, in New York City.

Arriving in June of 1940 he went to work, opening an office in Room 3603 Rockefeller Center. His operation grew quickly, and in a short period of time he was representing Britain's own Secret Intelligence Service–also known as Military Intelligence Section Six, or "MI-6"–and the Prime Minister. In this role he was given access to President Roosevelt, who in turn made the requisite introductions to the hierarchy of the poorly-functioning US Intelligence community.

One of the members of this hierarchy, J. Edgar Hoover, hadn't expressed much interest in meeting Stephenson, so Stephenson had done what he did best–he moved the levers behind the scenes. Rather than requesting assistance from Roosevelt in the matter, Stephenson instead orchestrated an introduction to Hoover by enlisting the aid of the Heavyweight Champion of the World, trusted old friend Gene Tunney. As anticipated, Hoover had fawned over the Champ and welcomed him and his odd British friend into the Seat of Government with much fanfare.

Having made his initial contacts in the States and gotten the lay of the political land, Stephenson carried on, quietly orchestrating British secret intelligence operations throughout North America, South America and the Caribbean from his New York office. Studying reports sent back from his operatives in the field, Stephenson quickly understood just how poorly J. Edgar Hoover's own Special Intelligence Service was faring.

Realizing coordinated US participation in the war was vital to Britain's survival, Stephenson formed a plan. He'd reconnected with his old American friend, Bill Donovan. Donovan's own exemplary military career and political savvy made him uniquely qualified and perfectly positioned to take the lead in a new American enterprise: the establishment and command of a US Intelligence organization the Brits could work with.

At Stephenson's suggestion, in mid-July 1940 Roosevelt sent Donovan to England to conduct a "brief survey and report on certain aspects of the British defense situation." It was during this trip Stephenson and Churchill evaluated Donovan and found him to be the perfect candidate to lead the American Intelligence counterpart to MI-6.

Donovan had been enthusiastic about the undertaking, though Stephenson knew his heart still lay with the infantry. "It's your duty, old boy," he'd said to Donovan many times during the trip. "Hitler's overrunning Europe and kicking at the gate to Great Britain, and your Yank State Department has all of eighteen chaps working in intelligence."

"I know it," Donovan would reply halfheartedly.

That's when Stephenson would unerringly throw petrol on the Intelligence flame he'd lit within Wild Bill by saying, "Well of course, I suppose Edgar Hoover is capable of getting better at running US Intelligence if we give him enough time…"

That's when Donovan would grimace and reply, "By the time that happens, we'll all be speaking Deutsch."

Donovan's appointment as Coordinator of Information was confirmed the following July.

CHAPTER NINE

Departures

FOUR MONTHS AFTER JELLY MET Wild Bill Donovan, the Imperial Japanese Navy launched a surprise military strike against the United States naval base at Pearl Harbor, Hawaii. Fighter planes, bombers and torpedo planes launched from six aircraft carriers succeeded in sinking four US battleships, three cruisers, three destroyers, and destroying nearly two hundred aircraft. More than 2,400 Americans were killed, another 1,100 wounded.

The attack was carried out on 7 December 1941 without a declaration of war and without warning. The American people solidified in response; President Roosevelt announced the United States declaration of war on Japan the next day. Within the week the US was also officially at war with Germany and Italy.

Jelly's immediate response to the sneak attack was similar to millions of Americans: he wanted to enlist in the Marine Corps and fight for his country. Hoover again convinced him he was needed most right where he was, doing what he was doing. "They'll be plenty of fighting right here, Jelly," Hoover told him. "I need you here with the Bureau, with me."

Jelly wasn't happy about it but he honored Hoover's request and continued on as the SAC of the El Paso Office. Though still occasionally pulled into SIS activities, he was mostly out of that and glad for it. The SIS had continued to have problems despite the new commander in New York, Stew Wallace. Jelly, holding no grudge or animosity toward

Wallace, was relieved to see some of the changes the former New York SAC had brought about. Agents were no longer being dispatched helter-skelter to foreign countries. Instead, Wallace had begun the Legal Attaché or Legat program, that had agents assigned to selected Latin and South American US embassies as legal attachés. This approach had come about in great part as a result of the newly-enforced cooperation between the US, British and Canadian Intelligence agencies, and the resultant more-cohesive efforts at countering German espionage and propaganda activities.

As far as Wallace was concerned, though he'd been less than thrilled when first told Jelly was in the mix, he was still politically astute and understood Hoover's affection for the "Oklahoma gunslinger" as some in the Bureau referred to Jelly.

What neither Wallace nor Hoover knew, however, was that the Oklahoma gunslinger had been adopted by a second "godfather" in the growing US Intelligence community.

With just two days left before the telephone number on the card Donovan had given him was set to be disconnected, Jelly had called the Colonel and told him that though he wanted to remain with the FBI, he would be available should Donovan require his assistance. He also explained there were two caveats with his offer: first, he would never do anything that would reflect badly on Hoover or the Bureau; and second, he would take assignments only from Donovan and only when it didn't compromise his work for Hoover. Assisting two bosses with work that benefitted the US was one thing; becoming a pawn in whatever long-term chess game Hoover and Donovan were engaged in was something else completely.

Donovan agreed to Jelly's stipulations and seemed genuinely happy to have the connection made. "I may never call on you, Jelly," he'd said during the brief telephone conversation, "but if I need to, I'm glad to know I can count on you."

* * *

A month after the meeting with Donovan, Jelly had settled fully into the SAC position in El Paso and was busy overseeing investigations and operations. Work consumed him. His social life had become nonexistent.

One Monday evening well after ten o'clock, while seated in his office poring over reports, Jelly looked up from his desk when he heard voices in the outer office. Three other agents were also working late, but the tone and volume of the conversation was unusual. Through the glass window of his door he saw one of his men, Jim Kennedy, standing while talking to a stranger near the entrance. The tall, heavyset visitor, dressed in an expensive dark business suit, was pointing his finger at Kennedy's face as he spoke. Jelly stood up, walked to his door and opened it.

"What's this about?" he asked sternly.

Kennedy, face red and eyes narrowed, looked at his boss and said, "This guy says he wants to see you, Mister Bryce. Won't say what it's about."

Jelly nodded at Kennedy and said to the tanned stranger, "You want to see me?"

The man looked at Jelly and nodded, wavering slightly. The way he stood and the glassy sheen of his eyes told Jelly the man had probably been drinking. While the man's gaze was shifted to Jelly, Kennedy looked at his boss, held up his fist, thumb and pinky finger extended straight out, thumb pointed down into his mouth indicating a liquor bottle.

"Come in." Jelly extended the invitation and stepped to the side, clearing the doorway so the man could enter.

The drunk gave Kennedy a victorious glance and walked into Jelly's office. Jelly followed him in, closing the door behind him. "Have a seat," Jelly said, indicating the chair in front of his desk. The man sat slowly, his hands on the edge of Jelly's desk to steady himself. Once he was seated, Jelly walked around to his own chair and sat down, hands folded on the desktop. "What can I do for you, Mister…?"

"Lorenz. Mister Peter Lorenz. And it's what I can do for you," the man replied belligerently. "I have some information I want you to relay to that jackal you work for."

Jelly's eyebrows raised in question. "Which jackal would that be?" he asked evenly.

Lorenz laughed, "Which jackal…you know which one. That son of a bitch Hoover. I want you to tell that son of a bitch–that queer, cock sucking son of a bitch–that he'd better lay off my business interests, because he doesn't know who he's dealing with. I know a lot of people in powerful positions, and I'm gonna–"

Jelly cut him off by holding up his hand, palm forward like a stop signal. "Hold up," he said strongly, "before this goes any further, I need you to calm down and knock off the derogatory comments. Now what exactly is this about, specifically."

The man glared at Jelly and inhaled through his nose, nostrils flaring. "That's what I'm trying to fuckin' tell you, you dumb son of a bitch. Now you just listen to me, because you need to make that queer, half-nigger bastard understand this. I know a lot of people in Washington…"

Jelly stood up. "Time for you to leave," he said, words clipped and menacing.

Lorenz's face turned crimson as he stood up explosively, chair propelled backward far and fast enough to hit the closed door. Kennedy and the other two agents who'd been keeping an eye on the situation through the door's window immediately stood and headed for the office.

Before they could reach it, Jelly stepped around his desk toward the larger man. As the man's balled up hands started to come up, Jelly simultaneously palm-heeled the man's right shoulder, grabbed a handful of cloth on his left shoulder and pulled, the double action causing Lorenz to spin around 270 degrees. No sooner had the man stopped spinning when Jelly reached up and put his open right hand on the back of Lorenz's head, shoving down and forward. The big man's head led like a bowling ball, pulling his body behind it, and smashed into and through the horsehair plaster wall next to Jelly's desk.

Kennedy arrived at the door first as Lorenz collapsed to the floor, blood smeared on the cracked open wall and all over the man's unconscious face. *'That was unfuckin' believable!'* he thought blithely as he opened the door to help his boss.

The second agent in the office, Tom Wilson, had a similar thought as he watched Jelly easily handle the "aggressive, drunken asshole" as he'd later describe the man to friends.

The third agent had a different take. Newly assigned to the El Paso office from Maryland, Alex Kokinos was horrified by what he'd seen. This was not what he understood the Bureau to be like. He'd gone through nearly eight years of college to become a lawyer, and then been referred to the FBI by one of his uncle's friends because he'd wanted to serve his country and the law. It also hadn't hurt that FBI agents were deferred from the draft, as Kokinos couldn't see any sense in his education and talents being wasted in the military. But *this*–this was too much.

He'd heard before being transferred to El Paso that his new SAC was a bit of a ruffian. "Uncouth" had been the word his uncle's friend had used–and now he'd seen that was an understatement. He'd waste no time calling his uncle in the morning to fill him in on this. This man Bryce was an animal.

His uncle's friend, Herbert Breyer, former head of the Oklahoma FBI office, had been right.

*   *   *

The next afternoon, new plaster drying on the wall of his office, Jelly called Tom Wilson in for a meeting. Tom had been doing okay, mostly. He'd found an apartment in El Paso and had been putting in almost as many hours as his boss, but Jelly had started to see some cracks in the younger man's personality. For one thing, Tom had started drinking. Not all the time, and never on duty, but more than a few times Jelly had talked to him on the telephone, or stopped by unexpectedly at Tom's apartment to check on him and found him a little "half seas over" as H.V. Wilder used to say.

It was unusual because it was Tom. Tom had always been "squeaky clean." Tom also didn't seem to have a social life as far as Jelly could see.

In an effort to truly give Tom a new start with the Bureau, Jelly had taken a page from Hoover's book and sent him to a special training school. After finishing the first, where he'd learned to surreptitiously open suitcase and luggage locks without leaving a trace, Jelly had sent him on to another: this one focused on analyzing secret recordings made from the numerous "bugs" and "wires" the Bureau continued to employ. Unlike Jelly who found this aspect of investigative work boring, Tom really took a shine to it. Jelly was glad.

"So are your ears bleeding yet?" he asked Tom with a smile as he settled into his chair.

Tom shook his head, smiling back as he replied, "Not at all. I don't know why, but I find it really relaxing listening to other's people's personal conversations. Does that make me a voyeur?"

Jelly shrugged. "I suppose it doesn't really matter, does it?"

Tom looked at the plastered hole in the wall and shook his head. "I'm not really sure."

"Want to know what I think?"

Tom looked soberly at his friend. "Always."

"I think you need to take a few days off, go somewhere nice, meet some nice women and get yourself laid. That's what I think. You've got a fuckin' hump in your back, mister."

Tom smiled. "What do you mean, a hump?"

"Sperm backup. You've got to get that out of your system. Have some fun for Christ's sake."

Tom nodded. "I hear you, Boss. I'll see what I can do. Maybe this weekend. Got any free time? Maybe you can show me your lady hunting technique."

Jelly smiled. "Now you're talkin'. I'm getting a little backed up myself. We'll figure something out. But first things first." Jelly's persona changed. Tom recognized it as Jelly slipping into work mode. He sat up a little straighter and listened closely.

"I have a mission for you."

Tom nodded, pulled his small pad from his jacket, uncapped his pen and prepared to take notes.

"I'm assigning you to liaison with our Navy counterparts for a few weeks. Give you a chance to see their operation, make some contacts. You'll be leaving tomorrow."

Tom nodded, happy for the change in scenery. "Okay."

"But that's the cover, Tom. Your real assignment is to locate a particular Bakelite disk and destroy it."

The Bureau and other US Intelligence agencies had

been using specially designed recording equipment for years. The primary media used to record out-of-country calls was 78 rpm Bakelite disks. The record cutter simply recorded whatever came over the wire, producing what looked like any other music or sound recorded flat disk you could buy in a store.

Tom leaned forward in his chair. "Destroy it? A Navy Intel recording?"

Jelly looked back, calmly assessing his friend's reaction. *'Still squeaky clean,'* he thought. He was partly relieved. "That's right. It appears one of our top brass in State called his office from Mexico City. He apparently made some indiscreet remarks about one of the people he was dealing with down there. He knows all out-of-country incoming calls are recorded. He sent an urgent request to DC that the recording be purged. We're complying."

"Why not just tell Navy to destroy it?"

Jelly took out a cigarette and lit it. "He didn't call them. Didn't want to for whatever reason. He called the Boss instead. Boss called me. I'm calling you."

Tom was disturbed by the thought of running an operation against another US Intelligence agency. It just didn't seem right. "But how am I supposed to get access to it and destroy it without them knowing? I'm assuming that's what you're asking me to do, isn't it?"

Jelly blew out a stream of smoke and nodded.

"But, Jelly–*Boss*–that's impossible!"

Jelly cocked his head slightly and looked steadily at Tom. He wanted Tom to do well in the Bureau. He'd done all he could to steer him back on course so he'd have a solid career and thrive. He still believed Tom had a lot to offer, that he'd make a good boss himself one day down the road. "Nothing is impossible."

Tom sat back into the seat. He looked stymied.

"You go down there, make your contacts. Spend a few days making nice, go out for a few beers, buy them dinner. You'll have an expense account. Figure out who is most taken with the Bureau, who has the greatest need to be liked. Get him–or her–talking. Get access to the recording we want. I'll have the classification code and the recording number for you. Be like looking up a book in the library. You get the disk, put it on the player, find our call. Then simply press down on the needle as it plays back. These disks mutilate easily. Then check it, make sure the conversation we're interested in is unintelligible, and put the disk back in the file. If anyone ever even actually listens to it, they'll just think it was a junk recording or that someone accidentally fucked it up."

Tom nodded. "You really think this is a good idea?"

Jelly crushed his cigarette out in the ashtray. "I think this is an order, Tom. Are you going to have a problem with this?"

Tom shook his head. "No. No, I'll take care of it."

"Good," Jelly replied. "Now get out of here and get some rest before you head out. You look like you haven't slept well lately. Have you?"

Tom sighed. "No, no, I'm fine. I'll get some sleep tonight."

Jelly nodded. "Okay, Tom. Now get the fuck out of my office." He smiled. Tom smiled back, stood up and left.

*   *   *

One week later Tom was back. The mission had been successful. But Tom was finished.

"I'm sorry, Jelly," he said sadly, "but I can't do this anymore."

"Do what, Tom?"

"This job. I'm just, it's just not for me. More and more,

it's just been bothering me. Keeps me awake at night. You know?"

Jelly looked across his desk at his friend with concern. "I understand, Tom. But are you sure there's nothing I can do to help you? Would you like to take some time off, get some rest maybe?"

Tom's eyes started to water. He quickly wiped away a tear. "No, no. It's just better I leave. I've really tried, Jelly. And I'll never forget what you've done for me. Never." He looked Jelly in the eyes. "You've been such a good, loyal friend to me. I'll never forget."

Jelly looked down and nodded. "You're a good man, Tom." Looking up he asked, "Any idea what you'll do?"

"Going home. Back to New England. Gonna work with my dad in the practice." Tom stood up, reached inside his jacket pocket and produced an envelope. Jelly knew it was his resignation. As Tom placed it on the desk, his voice caught. "I'm sorry I let you down."

Jelly stood up behind his desk, walked around it, held out his hand. Tom shook it firmly. "I'm just not like you, Jelly. This stuff–all this stuff–it bothers me. You're so strong. Like some kind of machine."

"You'll be fine, Tom," Jelly said sincerely. "You'll be a great attorney. Get married, have some kids. Live a normal life. Put all this behind you."

Tom smiled and nodded. He wanted to tell Jelly more, wanted to tell him about the nightmares and panic attacks he'd been having; tell him about how the occasional whiskey he'd been drinking to take the edge off had turned into a nightly routine, helping him fall into a deep sleep for a few hours until his racing heart would wake him and keep him awake the rest of the night. Tell him about the strange new feeling he'd been experiencing lately, a feeling of detachment, as if he weren't real, weren't part of the world even though he was still living in it. About the dizziness that would overtake him at the oddest times. About the persistent thought that maybe he and the world would be better off without one another.

"Goodbye, Jelly," was what he said instead. Then he turned and walked away from the Bureau for good.

*   *   *

Tom wasn't the only friend Jelly said goodbye to that year.

Charlie Winstead, his FBI mentor and compadre, had run into some trouble that couldn't be handled with his quick draw or quicker mind.

Shortly after Jelly had taken over the El Paso office, Winstead had been assigned as the Resident Agent in Albuquerque. That meant though he worked alone and largely self-supervised, he still reported to the El Paso SAC. While it had been slightly odd for both men given their relationship, they were both professionals as well as friends and made it work.

Jelly quickly discovered that serving as a friend's supervisor could present its problems. While he trusted Winstead and had the utmost respect for him, Charlie could be a stubborn cuss. He spoke from the heart and feared no one or anything. These were the traits Jelly loved about the Texan. They were also traits that made protecting him a bit of a chore. Jelly did his best, though.

One of his duties as supervisor was to write regular performance reviews of all the men under his command. Unlike a lot of supervisors who wrote as little as possible about their men in order to save themselves work, Jelly spent a lot of time and effort writing reviews. These evaluations became part of each agent's personnel file, and were used when decisions were being made regarding transfers, punishments and promotions. *They counted*, Jelly thought, and his men deserved credit for what they did. The reports were also critical in the process of removing unsuitable agents from the Bureau. As far as Hoover was concerned, if it wasn't written down and filed somewhere, it never happened.

Unfortunately for Winstead and many others, the opposite also occurred: if it was written down and filed somewhere, it was presumed to *have* happened–even if it actually hadn't, or had occurred differently than presented.

It would be a combination of these two elements–Winstead's direct, frank nature, and the Bureau's reliance on documentation to determine praise or censure–that would result in the FBI's loss of the man who'd killed Dillinger and solved numerous other problems for Edgar Hoover during his career.

The fearless Charles Batsell Winstead would never be taken down by gunfire or violence. His FBI Waterloo would arrive instead in the form of an attractive brunette reporter named Bertie O'Neil.

During a supposedly "off the record" interview at his favorite coffee shop, Winstead had shared with Miss O'Neil his belief that the Soviets were vicious despots who'd one day need to be put down like rabid dogs. "I've known some regular Russian folks," he'd told her with a smile, "and believe you me, they hate the commie bastards running the show as much as we do. They're just stuck right now cause the commies are pointing their guns at their backs while the Nazis are coming at them with bayonets attached from the front."

To Winstead's surprise, the nice, pretty reporter's hazel eyes had narrowed at the comment as she'd replied, "Perhaps you don't understand just how much the Communists are actually making the 'regular folks' lives so much better, Agent Winstead. I'm sure your leaders in the F.B.I. wouldn't agree with you. I know the President wouldn't."

"Lady," Winstead said, looking her straight in the eye, "I understand fine, believe me. I'm familiar with the way things have been '*improved*' in Russia. And I know these goddamned commie bastards would run *this* country into the ground same as their own if given a chance. Anyone with any sense knows that. Roosevelt just has to play nice with the Reds for now, until we put those other bastards, Hitler, Mussolini, and Hirohito in a hole. *Then*," he said decisively, "it will be Uncle Joe's turn," uttering Stalin's nickname with undisguised disdain.

"There are many people in this country who would disagree with your narrow view of the world, Agent Winstead. And with your derogatory remarks about one of our strongest allies."

Winstead's lips curled into a thin smile while his eyes burned like coals. "I'm sure there are, Miss O'Neil. I know there's a lot of so-called Americans sympathetic to the commie cause. I've met more than a few from your profession. And every one that I've ever met was absolutely certain they were right."

"Yes," she replied just as adamantly, "most educated people *do* tend to be certain about their positions on these matters."

Winstead laughed. "Funny thing about being certain, Miss. You can be absolutely certain, and absolutely wrong at the same time."

Miss O'Neil stood up at that remark and picked her purse up off the table. "You'd do well to remember that yourself, Mister Winstead."

As she'd walked briskly away from the table, Winstead had watched her swaying hips and listened to the clipping sound her high heels made on the linoleum. "Make no mistake," he'd said quietly to himself, paraphrasing a line from one of his favorite movies, "I shall regret the absence of your attractive body; unfortunately, it is inseparable from an extremely disturbing mind."

Three days later the reporter's well-written letter of complaint landed on Hoover's desk. The Director read it, rolling his eyes. He'd have filed it immediately but for the notation she'd included on the lower left side of the first page, indicating she'd sent copies to everyone imaginable, including the President *and* his wife.

"Fucking bitch," Hoover said, efficiently employing a single epithet for both the reporter and the deeply despised Eleanor Roosevelt.

In his carefully worded reply sent to everyone who'd received the complaint, Hoover noted he agreed "the Soviets were a subject best left to the State Department, not the misspoken words of an FBI agent," and advised that the agent in question would be censured.

When a copy of Hoover's letter landed on his own desk in El Paso, Jelly read it then immediately went to bat for Winstead, calling Hoover directly. Jelly told Hoover he'd called the newspaper and spoken to the reporter's editor. "Her own editor said she was a screwball," he told his boss. Hoover had laughed at that, then explained Winstead wasn't being disciplined for condemning Communism so much as for making comments in an official capacity about the Russians.

"*Boss.*" Jelly said the word in a way that let Hoover know he wasn't buying it.

That's when Hoover sighed and admitted in confidence he'd had no choice in the matter. "The President and Mrs. Roosevelt are very upset about this, if you can believe that. He said something like 'the Soviet situation is far above the paygrade of an FBI agent.' Believe me, Jelly, if it was anyone other than Winstead, he'd be history. This will just be a temporary disciplinary transfer."

"Can we at least keep him around here?" Jelly asked. "You know Charlie. He belongs to this part of the country. We're just asking for trouble if he lands anywhere else."

Hoover thought for a minute on the other end of the telephone. "How about Oklahoma?"

"That'll work, Boss," Jelly said happily.

Two days later Jelly sat down with Winstead in his office to explain the situation, ending with the good news about Oklahoma.

Winstead just stared at him for a long moment. Then he shook his head and said, "Fuck that, Amigo."

Jelly was surprised but not shocked. "Come on, now, Charlie. It's only Oklahoma, and only for a short while."

"Naw. You know what? I'm being disciplined because I said the truth about a tyrant. And now my own home-grown tyrant is giving me a shot in the tights–again." Winstead looked directly at Jelly and asked, "Do you even know what my last disciplinary transfer was over?"

Jelly shook his head.

"Look, Jelly, I know you don't want to hear this, but just listen for a minute, okay? I know–or I hope, anyway–that you'll believe me, but just so you know, everything I'm gonna tell you can be verified by a lot of other agents."

Jelly nodded. "Of course I'll believe you, Charlie."

"Okay then. Back when I was still working out of Orlando, I was up in Oklahoma running down a case when I got a call to get in my Buick and drive straight through to Miami. *Immediately*. What's the fuckin' emergency you may ask? Turns out Hoover was planning a trip to Miami, and had his favorite sedan being driven down there so he could go to the track in style. But the kid driving the car cracks it up down in Titusville or some fuckin' place, so Hoover needed another car. So since the car I had was the second best in Florida, it needed to get back to Miami before Hoover."

Jelly sighed. "I know he's like that sometime–"

Winstead cut him off. "Oh no, Amigo, that's not the end of this story." The Texan leaned forward in his chair and continued. "So, bein' a good soldier, I drive straight through, get the car down there the next fuckin' day and meet up with two agents who were assigned to wash and wax the car and take it to pick up Hoover. Somehow though, they get their signals crossed and take the car to the wrong airport, so when Hoover lands he's inconvenienced again. Has to wait an hour or so for them to get there."

Jelly started to say something.

"*Then!*" Winstead continued, "Then Hoover gets to his hotel and he's takin' a bubble bath or whatever the fuck he does down there, and the two agents driving him around are waiting in the lobby when one of them recognizes a fugitive right there in the fuckin' lobby. So naturally he makes the pinch, and they call for another agent to come to the hotel and take the guy out of there."

Jelly pulled a cigarette from his pack with his lips, held the pack out to Winstead who shook his head. As Jelly lit up, Winstead continued the story.

"So now, later, word gets out to the press that the fugitive was picked up in the lobby of the hotel the Director was staying at, and they run a nice piece about the arrest. *And this*, Jelly, this goes right up Hoover's ass sideways, and the agents who made the collar are censured. *Censured!* Do you know why?"

Jelly sighed again. His chest was getting tight. He shook his head as he blew twin streams of smoke through his nostrils.

"Because they hadn't told the press that Hoover had

recognized the fugitive and caused the arrest to be made. *Okay?*" Winstead was getting angrier as he told the story. "And then that cocksucker had both those agents transferred."

"I know Charlie, but–"

Winstead held up his hand, palm out. "Wait. Not done yet." Reaching across the desk with the same hand he picked up Jelly's pack of Lucky Strikes and pulled a cigarette out, tamping one end against the table top. Jelly flicked the top of his Zippo against his other hand and held the flame toward Winstead so he could light up.

Winstead took a drag then wiped a loose bit of tobacco off his lip before continuing. "One day later, I get called on the carpet again. This time, Jelly–and I shit you not–I'm in the glue because the car Hoover's fat ass is being carted around in–the car I drove down there for him–well, a wire from one of the dash lights somehow came unattached from under the dashboard and it fell against his holy highness's shoe. *Touched* his fuckin' shoe. And I was ordered to write a letter explaining how that wire came off the hook and touched his shoe." Now Winstead was seething. "*That's* the fuckin' guy you think walks on water, Delf. He's a fuckin' screwball. And I'm done with his nonsense."

Jelly had no response. He knew Winstead was telling the truth. He'd been hearing these types of stories more and more the past few years. The two men sat there smoking for a few minutes as Winstead slowed his breathing and made himself calm down.

"I know it's fucked up, Charlie," Jelly began, "but I mean, the pressure he's under has gotta be enormous."

Winstead looked at him. The storm clouds left his face. He smiled and shook his head. "You're a loyal man, Delf Bryce. And I've always known that. And I know you're as loyal to me as you are to him. I just hope he doesn't give you a fuckin' one day, Amigo." Winstead leaned forward and crushed his cigarette out in the ashtray next to the telephone. Then he stood up.

Jelly crushed his own smoke out and stood as well. "What'll you do, Charlie?"

"There's a real war to fight, my friend. I've still got plenty of contacts, been getting calls to do some things. I think I'm going to take the Army up on their offer. They want me back. Say they'll make me captain, give me a home in Intelligence." He smiled. "Who knows? Maybe I'll get a chance to do some Kraut or Jap hunting while I'm at it. I've always been better with a rifle than a search warrant anyways."

Jelly sighed deeply again. Part of him was disappointed at losing Winstead, another part envious of his friend's new path. "Good luck, Charlie," he said sincerely, holding out his hand. "Stay safe, my friend." The men shook warmly.

"Frankly, Amigo," Winstead said before turning to leave, "I'm more concerned about your hide than mine. Like I said, watch out for that fuckstick in DC. The only backside he's concerned about is his own." Then Winstead grinned, winked, and said, "More or less, anyways."

Jelly smiled back, shaking his head. "I'll see you down the road, brother."

"Count on it," the Texan replied. Pausing, he pulled a small, black-handled .44 caliber, single-shot derringer from his jacket pocket and held it out to Jelly, grips first. "A keepsake," he said quietly as Jelly solemnly accepted the gift. "Don't shoot your foot off with it."

Then he was gone.

*   *   *

One year after Winstead's resignation, Jelly stood outside the door to his office with a scowl on his face, the look directed at Agent Alex Kokinos. Kokinos had been a poor fit for El Paso and the agent in charge since arriving fifteen months earlier. Jelly was sure Kokinos had been feeding information about his activities to someone, because things kept surfacing back in DC that only someone in house at El Paso would know about. Jelly had bided his time, planting unique bits of information with each of the men under his command, waiting for that particular piece to float to the surface and reveal the leak. The technique had worked. Jelly had Kokinos cold.

"Who are you talking to?" The question was direct, Jelly's tone and demeanor indicating an answer was required.

Kokinos' eyes darted to the side, the question taking him by surprise. "What do you mean?"

Jelly stepped closer. Kokinos took a step back. "Look into my eyes, mister. I am not fucking around, and I'm not going to repeat myself."

Kokinos started to turn away when he felt Jelly's left hand grip his right upper arm. Jelly's left thumb drove into the bicep producing what felt like an electric shock. "Ouch!" he yelled out, panic starting to take root in the pit of his stomach. "I don't know what you're talking about!" Even though he was nearly thirty and had been an agent for three years, Kokinos had never been in an actual fight. His mind reeled with pain and fear. He looked around the empty office for help. They were alone.

Jelly kept his grip on the pudgy man's bicep as he drove the index and middle fingers of his right hand straight down behind Kokinos' clavicle, inducing sudden agony. The agent gasped and collapsed to the floor in a sitting position, legs splayed. "Jesus!" he shrieked when Jelly stopped pressing down, "You can't do this!"

"Alex," Jelly said in a fatherly tone, "I can put you in a world of pain for a long time without leaving a single mark. You're a smart man. No one will believe you if you make an accusation, and even if they did there's no proof. So make a decision. Talk or squeal."

Kokinos looked up into Jelly's emotionless face. The blank look was horrifying. The agent suddenly had the disconcerting feeling his boss was enjoying this. "Okay, okay, just stop!"

Jelly kept pressing on the bicep while he waited for an answer and dialed in on the next pressure point he'd work: the point right behind the ear where the jaw connected. He was just about to go for it when Kokinos broke and blurted, "I've only been talking to a friend of my father's, no one else. He's not even an agent anymore."

"Name."

"Herbert Breyer." Kokinos slumped his head forward.

Jelly released his grip and straightened up. His eyes narrowed. "Breyer? H.R. Breyer?"

Kokinos nodded.

Jelly hadn't seen or heard from Breyer in years. They'd only ever worked together one time, and that was back when Jelly was still with the Oklahoma City PD. Breyer had been the SAC for Oklahoma City then, and had been in charge of the Wilbur Underhill capture. He'd retired a few years back, was working as an investigator for an insurance company last Jelly'd heard.

"What have you been telling him, Alex?"

Kokinos stared at his feet as he rubbed his bicep with his left hand. "Just stuff about what goes on here. About you, mostly. He's interested in you." Kokinos looked up at Jelly and asked, "Can I please get off the floor now?"

Jelly nodded and the agent clumsily struggled to his feet. Jelly pointed to a chair near the water cooler. "Sit there. Drink some water."

Kokinos did as instructed. Jelly prodded him for more information and the agent talked. Breyer apparently had been nurturing a grudge against Jelly ever since the Underhill job. Blamed him somehow for the way Hoover had turned against him. Jelly was mystified. He'd never even given the man another thought.

After a few minutes of talking and the absence of pain the arrogance started to return to Kokinos' tone. "The bottom line is Breyer isn't a fan of yours, Mister Bryce. And to be honest, neither am I. So unless you plan on torturing me some more, you need to let me go. I'll request a transfer first thing tomorrow."

Jelly looked at the agent. He was immature for thirty. He'd also let himself be used. All the intelligence and education in the world couldn't counterbalance weakness of character. "No need. You're effectively transferred as of midnight tonight."

"How's that?"

Jelly smiled as he produced an envelope from his inside jacket pocket and held it up. "Oh yes. You'll be spending some time in Mississippi. At least until the war is over. Take this with you for your new SAC," he said handing the envelope over. "It's a copy of your orders. Now pack your trash and get moving."

Kokinos could have been fired for his indiscretion. Why he wasn't Jelly neither knew nor cared. That was Hoover's decision to make. The Director knew what had been going on. Hoover had actually been the first to tip Jelly about the leak. Someone had passed the story about Mister Lorenz's head busting a hole in Jelly's office wall to DC before Jelly'd had a chance to report the incident himself. Hoover told Jelly this when he'd called to thank him for the way he'd handled the matter. "I truly appreciate the way you dealt with this individual, Jelly," Hoover had said warmly over the phone. The Director had heard the whole story by that time, not just the parts Breyer had cherry-picked for distribution through his FBI backchannel contacts.

This type of intra-agency guerrilla fighting was actually pretty common. Agents occasionally launched career-busting torpedoes at one another, some using this covert style of attack more than others. If your launch was successful and blew up your target, you won that round. If it was less than a "fatal" career-ending blow, you could expect retaliation if you were revealed as the source. If your shot missed–as Kokinos' had–the torpedo you launched could boomerang back on you. The *real trick* then was to launch with no discoverable backtrack. That way, no matter if you hit or missed, you stayed clean and avoided retaliation.

Though Jelly typically avoided this game if possible, preferring to take a direct, in-your-face approach to resolving problems, he'd played once or twice out of necessity–always remembering the lesson he'd been taught years earlier, that "a good runner leaves no tracks."

CHAPTER TEN

Jelly's War

IN FEBRUARY OF 1944 Jelly became involved in another game that required stealth and cunning. The penalties for getting caught at this one were severe, especially during war time.

The game was treason. The potential penalty: death.

This game would be more complicated than most, however. Not only was Jelly's opponent another bright, college-educated man, he was an active duty member of the 620th Engineer General Service Company, a US Army unit based at Camp Hale, Colorado. What made the 620th special was the fact that it was comprised of pro-Nazi sympathizers. Incredibly, the Army had intentionally formed this unit because they felt it was better to keep these men–approximately 200 of them–all together and controlled rather than letting them run wild out in the world doing God only knew what. Members of the 620th were kept unarmed and assigned non-critical, make-work duties.

At Camp Hale, they were also billeted next to a detachment of an equal number of German prisoners of war.

Compounding the questionable judgment used to create a volunteer Army unit made up of men who openly desired to work against the American war effort was the way the plan was executed. Apparently perceiving the pairing of German PWs and active duty US Army pro-Nazi sympathizers on US soil as presenting no viable threat, the Army placed Camp Hale under the command of some of its "worst and dullest" officers. Their inept leadership and lack of control was a gift for the pro-Nazi residents of the camp interested in committing espionage and acts of guerrilla warfare against America.

Not only did the enemy not need to sneak into the US, they had easy access to US Army uniforms and equipment; the soldiers assigned to the 620th could get passes and leave the camp like any other soldiers; while on leave they could buy things like guns, cars and cameras, have fake identifications made, and conspire with other like-minded folks who weren't currently serving on active duty as they were.

This "unique" set of circumstances perfectly set the stage for the game. All that was required was an ambitious, capable man to serve as lead player for the pro-Nazi team.

US Army Private–and Harvard graduate–Dale Maple would take that role.

The rules in the treason game were simple: First, a charge of treason could only be levied during war time. Disloyal acts committed during peacetime are not considered treasonous under the Constitution. Since the US was at war, a charge of treason could be brought.

Second, only a US citizen or someone who otherwise "owes allegiance" to the United States could be charged with the crime. Twenty-four-year-old Dale Maple, born in San Diego, California and a member of the US Armed Forces met this requirement.

Finally, you have to personally "levy war" against the US or give "aid and comfort" to the enemy to be charged with treason. Aid and comfort could be defined as providing weapons, troops, transportation, shelter or classified information, or any other act that manifests a betrayal of allegiance to the United States.

Again, Private Dale Maple qualified–in spades.

Maple had developed into a self-described "political dissenter" as early as high school. In September 1936 he'd entered Harvard on a full scholarship to study history and chemistry, and became a member of the US Army Reserve Officer Training Corps (ROTC). Shortly after beginning school, the multilingual freshman changed his major to Germanic Language and Culture. His interest in all things German continued to grow during his four years at Harvard. He became the treasurer of the German Club and became enthralled with the tenets of Nazism. By his senior year Maple had become a self-described "proud and enthusiastic Nazi." As his enthusiasm grew so had his willingness to advertise it. He insisted on singing Nazi songs at school; he dressed up as Adolf Hitler for a costume party.

Eventually, the Harvard German Club relieved him as treasurer. In response, he resigned completely. Then the ROTC commander dismissed him. Desiring to express his opinions and beliefs to a wider audience, Maple sent a copy of his German Club resignation letter to *The Crimson*, Harvard's college newspaper. It was quite a letter. They published it. The local papers immediately picked up the story. How could they not? One of his quotes read, "Even a bad dictatorship is better than a good democracy." *Time* magazine sent a reporter to cover the tale of the Nazi at Harvard. The local papers dubbed him, "The Boston Nazi leader."

After the story broke nationally, Maple visited the German Consul in Boston and told him he "wanted to do something" to help the Nazi cause. The German government was interested. Plans were made to send Maple to Germany after he graduated from Harvard–*Phi Beta Kappa* and *Magna Cum Laude*, no less–in June 1941. These plans were scrapped a month later when diplomatic relations between the Americans and Germans were severed and the consuls recalled.

The newly-graduated Maple decided to go back to

California and apply for a job at Consolidated Aircraft Corporation. The FBI, aware of his flagrant pro-Nazi activities, intervened and the job was denied.

On December 7, 1941, when reports started coming in about the surprise Japanese attack on US forces in Hawaii, Maple called the German Embassy in Washington and pleaded to go with them back to Germany if war was declared with the US. The offer was declined. Maple would later write, "I was then left in the position of being in a country at war with The Country whose ideals I wished to uphold."

Two months later, on February 26, 1941, Dale Maple enlisted in the US Army as a private. First he was sent to Fort Bragg where he received training at the Field Artillery Replacement Center. Nine months later he was transferred to Fort Meade, Maryland and assigned to a task force which was to provide replacement troops in the Africa Campaign. While there he went to radio school and performed so well he was made an instructor. In January 1943, with orders for deployment to Africa in his hand, Maple was advised he would instead be transferred to the non-combatant 620th at Fort Meade, South Dakota.

Once he realized he was stationed with other like-minded, pro-Nazi sympathizers, Maple decided he would organize them and begin operations of his own–operations involving sabotage and espionage directed against the United States.

A short time later the 620th was transferred to Camp Hale, and Maple discovered they would be sharing the location with a German PW facility. His creative, intelligent mind quickly formed a plan: he would engineer and lead an escape of German PWs out of the camp and down to South America. Once there they would establish contact with German Intelligence agents so they could all return to

Germany and assist with the Nazi war effort.

The plan came together fairly effortlessly. The camp's sloppy security protocols enabled clandestine meetings between the Army soldiers and PWs even though it was strictly forbidden. Maple was even able to infiltrate the PW camp and live there disguised as a prisoner for three days while on leave from his Army unit.

The final stages of the plan required Maple to purchase a car, some women's clothing, and a .38 caliber Colt revolver. He got it all done. He also stole some Army officers' uniforms and insignia and forged furlough papers. Together with the five German PWs he'd selected for the mission, Maple gathered supplies and maps. The final details of the plan were soon set: two of the PWs would be disguised as civilians, one dressed as a woman. The other three would be disguised as US Army officers. Maple would also be disguised as an officer and serve as driver.

At noon on Valentine's Day 1942 they put the plan in action. When Maple pulled the '34 REO "Flying Cloud" sedan up next to the PW camp wire, he discovered only two of the prisoners had gotten out in time. They bundled in the car and left, headed south on Highway 285 to Santa Fe. Driving carefully, Maple piloted the car without incident all the way down to Columbus, New Mexico. About twelve miles from the Mexican border the car broke down. They deserted it and struck out on foot, travelling by night for three days. On the third day they were discovered on the road to Vado des Fusiles by Mexican customs officials. The dehydrated Nazi soldiers and their renegade American leader were captured without a fight.

It was at this point in the treason game the second player stepped to the table.

Jelly had received a call from one of his many contacts south of the border advising him of the odd group found hoofing it through the Mexican desert. The El Paso SAC was no stranger to the Mexican government, having travelled there on several occasions to meet with his law enforcement and intelligence counterparts. While there, at the request of both Hoover and Mexican officials, he'd put on entertaining shooting demonstrations that had wowed the crowds of spectators who'd watched, open mouthed, as the Yankee pistolero drilled holes in coins tossed high into the air among other feats of skill. His investment of time and effort, and his ability to make contacts on a personal as well as official level usually paid off. This time was no different.

In short order the three prisoners were shuttled back across the border, landing at the FBI office in El Paso. The German PWs' identities were quickly confessed. Only the tall, blond sunburned prisoner refused to talk. He simply sat, one wrist handcuffed to a pipe fixed to the wall, and stared smugly at his interrogators, revealing nothing. The two FBI agents asking the preliminary questions finally stood up, looked into a two-way mirror mounted on the wall and shook their heads. They left the room.

A few minutes later Jelly walked in, unlocked the handcuff around the prisoner's wrist and sat down. The game had begun in earnest.

"What's your name?" Jelly asked calmly, his hands flat on the table in front of him.

The question was met with silence accompanied by a bored expression as the prisoner rubbed his now-unshackled wrist.

"I know you speak English. You've followed all our instructions without a problem. Now follow this one and save yourself a boatload of trouble. Tell me your name."

The handsome, blue-eyed Maple stretched his arms out and yawned. Then he smiled at Jelly. The look was unmistakable. He was telling Jelly and the United States government to fuck off.

Jelly didn't show any obvious reaction, though if Maple had been paying attention he would have noticed his interrogator's thumbs slip off the table top against the edge, the nails on his fingers turning from pink to white as his grip tightened.

"Last time. What's your name?"

Maple's eyebrows raised for a moment, then he sighed deeply and looked away.

Jelly stared silently at the young man's face for a good five seconds. Then he exploded, springing forward off the chair, driving the table across the small room, pinning the seated Maple between it and the wall. The force of the table edge driven into Maple's stomach punched all the air from his lungs as his head snapped back and bounced off the cinderblock wall behind him. The next instant he felt the barrel of Jelly's .357 Registered Magnum under his chin and heard the guttural, menacing words, "Listen you son of a bitch, I'm fighting a war here. Now answer my fucking question! What's your name?"

Struggling to regain his breath, Maple looked into the crazed eyes of the man holding a gun under his chin and–*smiled*. Jelly grabbed a handful of Maple's uniform shirt then cocked the big pistol's hammer back, his finger on the trigger. The men, eyes locked, both breathing hard, waited for one of them to break.

As Jelly stared into Maple's eyes, a sudden feeling of recognition overtook him. He'd seen that look before. He was certain of it. It was a strange thing to look into a man's eyes, a man facing imminent death, and see absolutely no sign of fear. This was something that couldn't be faked. That's what he saw now. The last time he'd seen it so closely, so clearly, was while looking into the eyes of

Wilbur Underhill as the gangster lay on a bed in a furniture store shot to pieces, Jelly's lucky gun screwed in his ear. Jelly'd realized at that moment that Underhill truly didn't feel fear, not like normal men. Neither did this one.

Jelly blinked.

Standing up straight, he released his grip on Maple's shirt. He lowered his pistol and carefully decocked it, then placed it back in his holster under his suitcoat. As he slowed his breathing he pulled the table back across the room, keeping his eyes on Maple. Maple watched him closely as well, a mixture of superiority and curiosity evident on his face. Both men knew he'd won that round.

Jelly wiped his mouth with the back of his hand, turned and left the room. A few minutes later he came back in, closing the door behind him. He was carrying a paper cup full of water. He placed it down on the table on Maple's side, then sat back in the chair. After a few moments Maple stood up, carefully straightened his clothing, then slid his chair back to the table. After sitting down he picked up the cup, glanced inside, smiled at Jelly and drank it down.

"I know you," Jelly said with certainty after Maple placed the empty cup back on the table.

Maple's eyebrows raised.

"And soon I'll know your name and identity. We're just waiting to hear back from Army Intelligence."

Maple tilted his head to the side, eyes narrowing. "What do you mean, you *know* me?" he asked quietly.

"I mean I've known men like you before. Even though you haven't said anything, you've revealed quite a bit about yourself."

"Really," Maple said, drawing the word out and down to express disbelief.

Jelly nodded. "Really."

"All right then Mister FBI, why don't you just go ahead

and tell me about myself." Another smile, though Jelly could see he was truly interested in what Jelly had to say.

"I can see that you are very well disciplined. You have a lot of self-control–much more than most men."

Maple's eyebrows went up. He nodded slightly in agreement. "Go on."

"You don't fear for yourself. From the way you act, I'd bet you never did–even when you were a kid. You're more concerned with things bigger than yourself. Like a mission. You want to do things for the greater good, or a cause that has meaning to you. You're even willing to die for what you believe in." Jelly pulled a pack of cigarettes from his jacket pocket, took one and slid the pack across the table. Maple just glanced at it, then locked eyes with Jelly again.

"And," Jelly continued after lighting his smoke and placing the lighter on the table next to the cigarette pack, "If I had to guess, I would say you are extremely intelligent. Much more so than the average man–and frankly, you're probably much more intelligent than me."

Maple stared at Jelly for a few seconds, then his face relaxed and he smiled widely. "Very good, Agent…?"

"Bryce," Jelly replied.

"Bryce." Maple repeated. He picked up the pack of cigarettes, shook one out and lit it using Jelly's Zippo lighter.

Jelly reached out and slid the empty paper cup back toward the center of the table. Holding the burning end of his cigarette over the cup he asked, "Do you mind?"

Maple shook his head and Jelly flicked the ash from his cigarette into the cup.

"So what do we do now?" Maple asked. "Is this my last cigarette before you put me up against the wall and shoot me?"

Jelly smiled, shook his head. "No. It doesn't work that way. We'll just hold you here until the Army Intel boys come and pick you up. Then you're their problem."

Maple thought about that for a moment, then nodded and took another drag.

"Kind of a shame, though," Jelly offered.

"What's that?"

"Well, from everything I can gather, you have a really interesting tale to tell. I'm sure that a man like you doesn't do things haphazardly, or without cause."

"So?"

"So," Jelly said easily, "It's a shame no one will ever hear your story."

Maple smirked. "And why wouldn't they?" he asked. "I'm sure there are millions of people who'd be interested in what I did, and why."

Jelly nodded. "I know there are. Hell, I'm interested myself, and not just because it's my job. But once the Army gets hold of you, that'll be it. End of story. Surely, you know that?"

Maple's eyes narrowed. He couldn't see it yet.

Jelly took a long drag and blew the smoke out his nostrils. "Think about it," he said as he leaned forward. "Somehow, you masterminded a PW break from a secure Army base, if your two friends in the other room are to be believed. Got yourself and them all the way down across the border into Mexico." Jelly flicked his ashes into the cup again, then smiled. "Do you really think the United States Army will want that story known?"

Maples eyes widened.

"I'm not sayin' you'll be put up against that wall, friend. But at the least, I think you can count on being squirrelled away in a deep dark hole for a long, long time. At least until the incompetent dopes you outsmarted are long gone and retired. Wouldn't you agree?"

The blood drained out of Maple's face as his eyes

drifted to the cup on the table. Jelly saw it. *This* was what the man across from him feared. He feared being silenced. He feared not being able to tell the world about himself, not being allowed to show everyone just how smart he was.

"Of course," Jelly said reasonably, "there is another option."

Maple looked up at him. His shoulders were slumped more than they'd been since being brought in. He'd lost the confident gaze. "And what would that be?"

"You give me a statement. Explain about what you did and why. The whole story, however you want to tell it. Then I'll make sure the papers get it. You'll have your chance to be heard."

Maple looked disbelievingly at Jelly. "And how do I know you'll actually do that? It's not like it's unheard of for FBI men to lie."

Jelly looked back into his eyes. "I don't lie."

Maple was almost there. He wanted to talk, but didn't trust that Jelly would keep his word. Jelly could see it. All the man needed was one more gentle push over the edge. Jelly looked at the two-way mirror and loudly said, "Bill, come in here."

A minute later the lock on the door was turned and a short, dumpy, unshaven man dressed in a worn, cigar ash-marked suit walked in hesitatingly. "You want me in here?" he asked, looking nervously at Jelly.

Jelly nodded. "Tell this man who you are."

The man looked at Maple and stammered, "I'm Bill Fuller. I'm a reporter with the Associated Press."

"Baloney," Maple replied.

"Show him your credentials," Jelly instructed.

Fuller took out his press credentials and held them out so Maple could see them. Maple looked at them closely, but still had doubt in his eyes.

"Now look at the man holding those credentials," Jelly said. "And you tell me, is that an FBI agent standing there, looking like an unmade bed?"

"*Hey*," Fuller said halfheartedly.

Jelly smiled at Maple. Maple looked from Jelly's face to Fuller's and back again. "I get to tell it in my own words?" he asked.

"Hell," Jelly said, "you can type it up yourself. Take all the time you need."

The prisoner took another deep drag off the smoke. Then he flicked his ashes into the cup, looked at Jelly and said, "Maple."

"How's that?" Jelly asked, eyebrows raised.

"That's my name, Agent Bryce. Maple. Dale Maple. And I'll take that typewriter now. And plenty of paper."

Jelly nodded. He had a typewriter, paper, a pen, big pitcher of ice water, some coffee and sandwiches brought into the room. Then he and Bill Fuller sat there drinking coffee and watched as Dale Maple produced a four-page, single-spaced statement, detailing everything he'd done and why. When he'd finished, Maple signed and dated the document, then slid it across the table to Jelly.

Jelly nodded, read the entire statement out loud, then looked at Maple and smiled. "Thank you, Dale," he said sincerely. "This is really well written."

Game over.

Army Intelligence arrived a few hours later and took Maple and the PWs into custody.

As Jelly and the AP reporter watched the Military Police drive away with the prisoners, Fuller turned and smiled at Jelly. "That was pretty slick, the way you worked him. You'd make a good reporter."

Jelly grimaced. "If you're gonna insult me, why not just go all the way and say I should be an attorney."

Fuller laughed. "What do you think they'll do with the kid?"

"Maple?"

"Yeah. Maple."

"Hang him, I suppose." Jelly said the words with no emotion. It was the penalty for both desertion and treason.

Fuller took out a half-smoked stogie and clenched it between his teeth, then fished a pack of matches from a pocket. Jelly took out a cigarette and leaned in to light it off Fuller's match. As Fuller puffed the cigar to life he asked, "What do *you* think they oughta do with him?"

"If I had just fifty men like that," Jelly said quietly, "men I could train and direct, I could clean up this country in a New York minute."

"A New York minute?"

Jelly smiled. "Yeah, that's only like thirty seconds."

Fuller smiled. "Before you go on, *Mister FBI*, just let me remind you I'm a reporter."

"Yeah, I know," Jelly said. Then he turned and faced his friend, one of many he'd developed from members of the press, and fixed him with his gimlet stare. "Just remember who *I am*, mister reporter, or *you* may be goin' on sooner than you'd planned."

Fuller's eyebrows raised up as he turned his head to the side, eyes on Jelly. Then he laughed. "Come on," he said good naturedly. "That look don't work on me."

Jelly kept the death stare going for a few more seconds, just until he saw concern creeping into the corner of the reporter's eyes. Then he smiled and laughed too.

*   *   *

On 24 April 1944, after a secret court martial proceeding lasting three weeks, Private Dale Maple was found guilty on all counts of desertion and aiding the enemy. The signed statement typed by his own hands was the final, damning piece of evidence required.

The verdict gave Maple the dubious distinction of being the first American-born soldier in the history of the Army to be found guilty of treason as defined by the US Constitution. For his crimes, Maple was sentenced to be hanged by the neck until dead.

President Roosevelt later commuted the sentence to life imprisonment at hard labor. Maple applied himself and excelled at prison life, becoming a model prisoner at Leavenworth Federal Penitentiary. He taught classes, organized a choir, and wrote for the prison magazine.

After the war ended, his sentence was reduced from life to ten years. He was released in February 1951, and disappeared from public view. He would die of natural causes fifty years later.

CHAPTER ELEVEN

The World's War

THE WAR GROUND ON. Twenty-nine months after the Japanese attack on Pearl Harbor much of the world was still engaged in a death match, the likes of which had never been seen.

The Tripartite Pact of 1940 that bound Germany, Italy, and Japan into the Axis Powers was holding. The separate Nonaggression Pact Hitler and Communist dictator Joseph Stalin signed in August 1939 didn't fare as well. Ten months later, after Stalin stood by as secretly agreed and watched Hitler's "blitzkrieg" sweep through Poland, three million German troops invaded the Soviet Union. Three months later the Germans began the battle for Leningrad. It would rage for more than two years; more than half a million Russian people would die of starvation alone within the city.

Ferocious air attacks plagued London nearly every night through May 1941. "The Blitz" as the British people referred to it, killed more than 40,000 and reduced much of the city to rubble.

The Battle of the Atlantic raged, packs of German submarines stalking and sinking vessels of all kinds, including a half-dozen old destroyers the US had provided to England prior to entering the war. The destroyers hadn't been donated as Churchill had requested: due to political considerations prior to the US declaration of war, they were traded for 99-year leases on naval and air bases in the Western Hemisphere.

The Warsaw Ghetto was filled with nearly half a million

Polish Jews. Concentration camps, first established after Hitler became chancellor in 1933, multiplied and expanded. Italy invaded Greece, Hitler's troops supporting Mussolini's.

The Japanese attack on Pearl Harbor hadn't been an isolated maneuver. Japanese warplanes also swept down from the skies over the Philippines, Wake Island and Guam–all controlled by the US. Unlike Hawaii, these areas were captured by the Japanese and held throughout the war. The Japanese also invaded Malaya, Thailand, Burma and Hong Kong, and continued their vicious onslaught against China begun in 1937.

Horrors and atrocities abounded. From the rape of Nanking to the Bataan death march to the Warsaw ghettos and beyond, the Axis Powers consistently demonstrated their desire to conquer, at any cost, civilian casualties considered inconsequential.

To combat the Axis Powers, nearly twenty countries banded together. They became known as the Allied Powers, the "big four" being England, the United States, the Soviet Union and France. Regardless of the fact that the Soviets joined the Allied party only after being betrayed by Hitler and his Third Reich, their dictator was welcomed into the fold and generously courted. The Soviets possessed millions of troops, mountains of equipment, and controlled a huge land mass; they were considered vitally important to defeating the Axis.

To that end, Allied counter-offensives had begun worldwide. The first US bombing raid against the Japanese Home islands was carried out in 1942. Codebreakers were able to intercept and unravel Japanese messages, allowing the US to curtail an invasion of Midway and defeat the Japanese Navy there in a battle considered the turning point of the war. US Marines were unleashed in an "island hopping campaign" beginning with Japanese-held Guadalcanal in the Solomon Islands.

Jelly's friend Walter Walsh, who'd taken leave from the FBI to serve with the Marines, added to his growing legend while serving in the Pacific Theater during a number of widely-reported engagements. In one incident, he eliminated a treed sniper that had his unit pinned down from 90 yards away. Walter took out the sniper by standing up and firing one round–from his .45 Colt pistol.

By February 1943 things had really started to turn in the Allies' favor. The Soviets defeated the Germans at Stalingrad, and began their drive toward Berlin. The British and US air forces launched round-the-clock bombing raids on German targets. In September, Italy surrendered, though the Germans fought on, seizing Rome. US Marines took Tarawa in the Gilbert Islands.

The beginning of 1944 saw the Allies launch the first ground attack against Germans at Cassino, Italy, followed by the landing of two divisions of the US Fifth Army at Anzio, just 30 miles south of Rome. Soon thereafter the Allies launched the first major daylight air raid on Berlin. The Germans retreated from Anzio. In the Southeast Asian Theatre, Allied forces began an advance into northern Burma.

Then on 6 June, Operation Overlord was launched, establishing a beachhead on the French coastline at Normandy. More than 5,000 ships and 13,000 aircraft assisted in the delivery of 160,000 Allied troops along the heavily-fortified coast. The cost in lives was tremendous. More than 9,000 Allied soldiers were killed or wounded as they battled Hitler's best troops. By the end of the day, the beachhead had been established and the final battle for Europe was underway.

The fighting was still bloody and far from over, but the

projected outcome was more promising than it had ever been.

*   *   *

Back on the US Homefront the war held everyone's attention. Though no major military engagements had taken place on the US mainland, there had been a few significant minor ones that stoked the fears of invasion.

In September 1942, a small Japanese aircraft was launched from a submarine off the coast of Oregon. It dropped four 168-pound firebombs on forests in an attempt to spark a major fire and panic. Fortunately, it failed, as did an earlier submarine attack off the coast of California. In that incident, the Japanese crew fired shells from deck guns at an oil field. No significant damage was inflicted in either attack. But there was a response. Sentiments against all Japanese in the US were hardened. This was understandable but hardly necessary. The "Japanese problem" had been contained.

In April 1941 the US government forced thousands of Japanese-Americans to move from the West Coast to "relocation" camps in remote areas. The plan had come down from the President's office. Hoover hadn't agreed with it and let FDR know.

As usual, Hoover had his own plan. Prior to US entry into the war, he'd started compiling lists of German, Italian, and Japanese aliens he considered "dangerous" as a result of information his agents had gathered about them. The Director didn't think it wise to imprison people because of race, but for their allegiances. He was overruled. Instead of only the 3,800 people his agents had picked up days after Pearl Harbor, nearly 112,000 Japanese nationals and Japanese-Americans were indiscriminately rounded up and sent to the camps.

This was but one of Hoover's concerns. As the war effort had spun up so had the number of meetings, investigations, panels and committees he needed to attend to. His FBI had grown from 898 agents in 1940 to a whopping 4,591 agents backed by 7,400 staffers by 1943. The Seat of Government and all 54 field offices were operating on 24-hour schedules.

Hoover's people were everywhere. Members of the Bureau's Technical Laboratory were working with engineers, scientists, and cryptographers to unravel and defeat Axis communications systems while the SIS Legat program was siphoning off agents to South and Central America.

Sabotage and espionage investigations had to be handled along with all the other duties the Bureau was tasked with. And handled they were, some better than others.

Without doubt the greatest success was the smashing of the Frederick Duquesne Spy Ring, which had been operating in the US for years prior to the war. The case came about because of the bravery of one man–German native and naturalized US citizen William Sebold.

While visiting his mother in Germany, Sebold was approached by a Gestapo agent. The Nazis wanted him to spy on the US when he got home. They motivated him by threatening the lives of his mother and family living in Germany. Sebold agreed. Then he quietly made contact with the U.S. Consulate and told them his story, volunteering to serve as a double-agent for the US. The Bureau was contacted and the operation started. The Germans trained Sebold in espionage, micro-photography and message coding. Once back in the States he assumed the identity of "Harry Sawyer" and set up his double-agent operation in New York with the assistance of FBI agents.

Bureau technical experts put together an elaborate shortwave radio system for him, and for the next 16 months FBI agents posed as "Sawyer," sending and receiving nearly 500 messages; the American messages containing disinformation, German messages containing a wealth of accurate intelligence.

Sebold, in the guise of Sawyer, also met with German agents in his office, meetings recorded by Bureau agents from the next room and filmed through two-way mirrors. Once they had their evidence the Bureau pounced, arresting 33 spies and seizing bombs, espionage equipment, and files. This single operation broke up a major Nazi spy ring and undoubtedly prevented serious planned attacks on the Homeland.

All involved either confessed or were found guilty of espionage in a high-profile case that enhanced the Bureau's reputation and reassured Americans that J. Edgar Hoover and the G-Men were on the job keeping them safe.

Another high-profile case that hit the newspapers in 1942 had as many dramatic components as the Duquesne case; however, the story told was not exactly the story that had occurred.

This case began on June 13th when two German submarines delivered eight saboteurs to two locations simultaneously: four made their way to shore at Amagansett, Long Island, four others at Ponte Vedra Beach in Florida. All the men had lived in the US for years and spoke perfect English. They'd also been specially trained in guerilla tactics back in the Fatherland. Their mission now was to blend back into American society and carry out sabotage operations, spreading terror and fear on the US mainland.

They'd come ashore under cover of darkness equipped with everything from disguised explosives and fake identities to $180,000.00 in cash. One of the men, George Dasch, leader of the New York sapper team, also brought ashore something his German controllers had missed: divided loyalties.

Dasch had fought for Germany during the first Great War at the age of fourteen. At nineteen he'd stowed away on a steam ship, eventually landing in New York City. As soon as he got his bearings, he'd headed to an Army recruiting center and joined up, hoping to become a US citizen that way. After a year's service he applied for citizenship, returned to New York and married an American woman. Without citizen status, the only job he could find was working as a waiter. His unscrupulous manager kept half his wages. The subsequent resentment and struggle for money made him a prime recruiting target for agents from the German-American Bund working out of the city. Dasch signed up to become a well-paid saboteur, shipping back to Germany for training.

But then, months later, standing on the beach back in America, back in New York City, he'd had a change of heart.

No sooner had Dasch and his team dragged their inflatable boat ashore than a young Coastguardsman walked up on them smoking a cigarette. "What are you fellas doin'?" eighteen-year-old John Cullen asked innocently, not realizing what he'd just stumbled upon.

Unseen by Cullen, one of Dasch's men raised a Walther pistol and pointed it at the American's heart. Dasch saw, and pushed the pistol down before it had been fired.

"Leave here," Dasch ordered, the tone in his voice alerting Cullen he was in danger. Cullen fled for help, hearing confused shouts behind him–in German.

Dasch ordered his men to scuttle the raft and bury it in the sand along with all the equipment. He led his team to the train station, carrying only the suitcase filled with US currency. They rode into New York City, where Dash split the team into two-man groups. He gave the other team some money and told them to get a hotel room. They'd meet back at the train station in two days. Then he and his partner, a naturalized US citizen named Ernest Burger checked into their own room downtown.

Burger's story was a little different than Dasch's. He'd become a citizen in 1927, living in Milwaukee and working in a machine shop. The rise of Hitler and the Nazi Party drew him back to Germany where he served as a loyal Nazi until his competence threatened a superior. Burger was shipped off to a concentration camp where he languished for more than a year before talking his way into a special program for saboteurs. The assignment was considered a suicide mission. None of the men were expected to return from the US.

Sitting in the hotel room a world away from Germany and the Nazi machine, Dasch and Burger looked at each other and then the suitcase full of money. Burger wanted to split the cash and lam it. Dasch had a better idea–one that would not only get him the US citizenship he wanted, but would make them both American heroes to boot.

"We'll go to the FBI," he said, "Tell them we were forced to participate, but we're actually double-agents. We are here to help America. It will work, Ernest. I know it will. I used to read all the time about the FBI and Mister Hoover. He'll know what to do."

Burger wasn't convinced, but eventually agreed. It *did* make sense. Choose a side and get set up in the States, or go on the run from both the Americans and Nazis for the rest of their miserable lives. "Okay," he said. "Call the FBI."

Dasch smiled and picked up the telephone in his room. He asked the operator to connect him to the FBI office in New York City. An agent answered the phone and listened politely as Dasch told his story. Several times the agent asked Dasch to repeat parts of his tale, obviously making detailed notes. When Dasch had finished, the agent thanked him for the call and told him someone would be in touch. Dasch hung up and looked at Burger, greatly relieved.

At the FBI office, the agent who'd taken Dash's information opened a filing cabinet and placed the report in a manila folder. Then he slid the drawer closed and stared at the label someone had affixed to the front of it: "NUT BOX." The agent laughed and shook his head. "Third one tonight. Must be some kind of record."

Five days later things had gotten desperate in the hotel room. It had become like a prison cell with room service. Burger finally demanded half the cash, threatening to kill Dasch and take it all if he didn't agree. Dasch gave him $85,000.00. Burger stuffed it into a pillow case and left.

Dasch couldn't understand what had happened with the FBI. His subsequent calls were received rudely, the agent who answered finally simply hanging up when he recognized Dash's now-familiar voice.

Dasch'd had enough. He cleaned up, took the suitcase and jumped on a train to Washington, DC. He knew that was where FBI Headquarters and J. Edgar Hoover were. Walking off the elevator on the fifth floor of the Justice Department Building, Dasch approached the security officer behind the counter and demanded to speak with Hoover. Two agents came out front to see what was going on. Dasch began to panic: they weren't taking his story of landing by submarine on the beach in Long Island seriously. He bent over, unlatched the suitcase locks and dumped $82,000.00 cash on the floor. "Does that look like bullshit!?" he practically screamed.

That worked.

For the next eight days Dasch sang like a German Roller

canary. By 27 June 1942, all of the other saboteurs were under arrest, including an angry Ernest Burger.

Not surprisingly, the official recounting of the events leading up to the high-profile arrest of honest-to-God Nazi saboteurs in America was a bit different than the reality.

It would be so different, and the actions taken in its wake so impactful, that it would affect the conduct of US civil and military law for many decades to come.

First, Hoover changed the story. Dasch had been apprehended as a result of a highly-classified, secret FBI investigation. The telephone calls, visit to DC, attempted defection–none of that happened.

Then the President, his attorney general, Francis Biddle, and Edgar Hoover put their heads together and constructed a military tribunal that would be dissected by lawyers and historians well into the next century. The secret trial was held on the fifth floor of the Justice Department Building in the classroom where Jelly had given his action-reaction demonstration years before. The trial would prove just as stunning to those who witnessed the proceedings. At the time, however, the US was at war, so no one looked too closely, or questioned too loudly. The end result would be the immediate execution of six of the agents–excluding Dasch and Burger–in the electric chair on 8 August 1942. That was less than two months after the covert submarine landings.

The remaining two ambivalent saboteurs were sent to the federal penitentiary; Burger for life, Dasch for thirty years in solitary confinement–one of those "deep, dark holes" Jelly had alluded to while speaking with Dale Maple.

The newspapers ate the story up. It was a headline-worthy event for weeks. Hoover's version of the tale helped allay fears of Axis subversion and further bolstered Americans' faith in the FBI. There was talk of a Medal of

Honor award for Hoover himself, something he encouraged though it would never come to pass. That would prove a disappointment to him. It would have been nice to have that medal. Bill Donovan, his rival for control over US intelligence had one.

Hoover felt he deserved one just as much. After all, he'd just saved America from an invasion of the US homeland, practically single-handedly.

"It had to be true," he would say half-jokingly to Clyde Tolson over dinner. "It was in all the papers."

*   *   *

The naming of Wild Bill Donovan as Coordinator of Information had not been warmly received by most members of the US Intelligence community. When he'd first heard about it, Hoover had actually become nauseated. Edgar Hoover disliked many people, but he absolutely hated Donovan. Not only had Donovan belittled him and threatened his job on numerous occasions, but Hoover considered him dishonest, dangerous, and worst of all, a goddamned commie sympathizer.

"Who the fuck does this guy think he is," was the most common sentiment shared by Hoover and the other leaders of US Intelligence whenever Donovan was mentioned. They weren't impressed by his medals, money, or accomplishments. They believed him to be a dilettante when it came to Intelligence work, a poseur, and by his very presence he made a mockery of the work the others had been engaged in for decades. But they weren't making the decisions.

On 13 June 1942 Roosevelt decreed the Office of the Coordinator of Information would become the Office of Strategic Services (OSS), subordinate only to the Joint

Chiefs of Staff (JCS). Donovan was reactivated as a colonel in the U.S. Army and appointed to lead OSS. Within a year he was promoted to brigadier general. The JCS abolished the Joint Psychological Warfare Committee and turned its functions over to OSS.

Under Donovan's leadership the OSS would expand quickly in a number of unexpected directions–unexpected to everyone but Donovan. He had a far-ranging and ambitious vision for his organization, and was already planning for its post-war reorganization.

OSS personnel were drawn from all walks of life and societal strata. Donovan was only interested in the person he was dealing with; their backgrounds, education, and politics only told part of the story.

Donovan was looking for *character*. He wanted talented people who'd fight the good fight and do it well. Eventually, OSS would run a number of successful operations in Europe and parts of Asia, but the full potential of his organization would never be realized. Part of the reason was Roosevelt's desire to "avoid criticism or objections which might be raised to the expansion of the present structure of intelligence work." Roosevelt knew that espionage was still a repugnant word to Americans, and he downplayed much of what OSS was doing.

The President also insisted on "keeping the field divided." Because of this approach, OSS was further crippled. Hoover was allowed to keep his SIS operating in South America.

General Douglas MacArthur, commander of the Southwest Pacific Theatre, shared Hoover's disdain for Donovan and OSS: he, along with Admiral Chester Nimitz insisted both be barred from the Philippines.

Eventually, even Donovan's stalwart allies in the British Intelligence community started to back away from him. As early as 1943, the Brits started expressing concern over the way OSS was operating. Donovan marched to his own tune, sometimes taking risks with his very life and operational security that seemed excessive and irresponsible to his staid colleagues across the pond. This was compounded by the Brits' dawning realization that the post-war world would be significantly different. It became obvious to all the United States was emerging as the dominant power on the world stage, Russia close behind, leaving Britain a distant third at best.

Worse, the Brits had started to suspect Donovan was working behind the scenes to make it easier for the Soviets to take parts of Europe. While true, it wasn't Donovan's idea. He was following the instructions of his commander-in-chief, the President of the United States.

Roosevelt had become convinced Stalin was a friend. He directed Donovan–his soldier–accordingly.

Stateside, Jelly quietly kept tabs on Donovan's activities, both through news reports and through the FBI grapevine. A lot of information was passed through the unofficial backchannel system, most of it based on truth, some purely rumor and speculation, but all of it filtered through personal biases or intentionally altered for political reasons. The trick was to comb through it and see which strands could be connected, find the recurring bits of information that could be verified, and try to make sense of it all against the bigger, known picture.

It was a complicated mess. But still, Jelly kept at it. He had no choice. He was connected to Donovan. He believed in the man and wanted to be ready to assist him should he ever be called upon. As of mid-June 1944, he still hadn't been contacted.

That was about to change.

CHAPTER TWELVE

The Land of Enchantment
21 June 1944

JELLY WALKED BRISKLY DOWN the street, briefcase held in his left hand, newspaper under the same arm. He scanned the main street of Roswell, New Mexico, sun high overhead, beating down. The streets were busy with traffic and people.

He was glad he'd brought his Panama suit for this trip. The white straw fedora on his head also helped keep him cool, reflecting the sun's rays instead of absorbing them like his black fedora did.

He checked his wristwatch; a little before noon. He was early as usual.

He'd wanted to set up across the street from a meeting spot he'd arranged with a potential informant, watch the place–a small coffee shop–for an hour or so. Just to see. There was a bookstore across from the coffee shop. He'd checked it out the day before. They had some chairs and a table set up inside so you could read, pretty far back from the big plate-glass front window but in perfect alignment with the shop across the street. He couldn't have set it up better if he'd had to.

A block from the bookstore he stopped by a streetlamp, placed the briefcase down and took out a cigarette. They didn't allow smoking in the bookstore, which he thought was strange, *'But them's the rules'* he thought, remembering the way the clerk had explained it to him the day before.

After tamping one end of the Chesterfield against the

lamp, he placed the smoke in the corner of his mouth and took his Zippo out, using his cover snapping trick to spark the flame. Looking around before lighting the cigarette he spotted a tanned, raven-haired vision in a pale yellow dress walking on the opposite side of the street. She had a wide-brimmed, white braided paper hat fixed on the back of her head so it looked like a halo around her face and hair, top of the brim curving forward as if to shield her eyes from the sun's rays. In her right hand she carried a small, burgundy leather purse, same color as her high heels.

Even from a distance Jelly could clearly see the woman was absolutely beautiful. More than beautiful–*stunning*. He kept his eyes on her as he brought the flame to the cigarette and inhaled deeply. He snapped the cover closed, feeling the warm metal in his hand as he slipped the lighter back in his pocket.

He thought about the time again, and the coffee shop, and was glad he was always so early. He could wring a few minutes out of this operation for a social call.

Picking up his briefcase he stepped off the curb. Walking carefully in between traffic, Jelly navigated himself into an intercepting position just ahead and to the side of the young woman. She was heading right toward him. He took a last drag off the smoke and pitched the cigarette into the gutter as he stepped up onto the sidewalk and stopped. As she drew closer he gave her oncoming left hand a quick scan–no wedding or engagement ring. Then he discreetly scanned the rest of her. The closer she got, the more perfect she became. Though she barely wore any makeup, her natural features were movie star quality and her long, straight black hair was lustrous, with an almost blue tinge.

Then she was upon him and the light scent of her perfume reached his nostrils.

"Excuse me, Miss."

The woman, in her late twenties Jelly guessed, stopped abruptly, her crystal blue eyes locking on his. "Yes?"

'She's not afraid,' Jelly thought. But she wasn't happy about the intrusion either. "My name is Delf Bryce. I'm a federal agent here in town, on business."

That got her full attention. "A federal agent? Is anything wrong?"

"No, Miss, nothing is wrong at all," Jelly said reassuringly. "I just thought you should know something."

As he watched her face trying to read her reaction to him, he was surprised he couldn't. She didn't immediately respond either. Just looked him straight in the eye, waiting. Finally, she asked, "Yes?"

Jelly smiled his charming smile and said, "I just thought you should know that I'm the man you're going to marry."

The young woman appeared slightly taken aback, but amused. "Is that right, Mister Bryce?"

"Yes, Miss. I never lie."

She looked at him and smiled, then cast her blue eyes downward toward his feet.

For a moment Jelly thought of his Aunt Susan, who used to tell him the first thing a woman looked at when assessing a man was his shoes. He stole a quick glance at his shoes just to check. They were highly polished like the rest of him. When he looked back up her eyes were waiting for his.

"You know, Mister Bryce, I bet you don't. Lie that is."

Jelly smiled.

"So then tell me true, Mister Bryce..." she said, words spilling from her pretty mouth in an almost musical cadence.

"Anything," Jelly said, happy this was going so well. He'd already decided to ask her to dinner that evening. He knew a perfect place.

"Does this juvenile approach usually work with the women you meet on the street?"

Now it was Jelly's turn to be taken aback. His smile collapsed as he stammered, "No, no wait, you misunderstand..."

"No, Mister Bryce," she said directly. "I think I understand perfectly. The misunderstanding is all yours." With that she turned her eyes forward and resumed walking down the street.

Jelly watched her go, slowly shaking his head. Then he smiled and said quietly, "Now *there's* a woman."

Pulling out another smoke, he lit it, following her with his eyes until she disappeared around a corner.

"*Dammit.*" Having a strong urge to go after her and try again, he stood there for a few minutes thinking about the informant and his job. Work came first. *Always*. But this woman was something special. He could feel it in his bones. He checked his watch. Still plenty of time. But he never did this, he thought to himself, never put pleasure ahead of business. "What the fuck's wrong with me?" As the words left his lips he saw the woman driving slowly toward him on the opposite side of the street in a white Buick sedan. She was alone, the driver's side window down. As she passed, she slowed the car and said, "If you really are a federal agent, you should be able to get my telephone number yourself." Then she smiled, laughed, and drove off.

Jelly instantly memorized the car's registration plate number.

*   *   *

Five minutes later Jelly stood in front of the bookstore. As he took his last drag off the smoke the bespectacled clerk looked at him through the window and grimaced. Jelly smiled back at the middle-aged man, held up what was left of the Chesterfield and rolled the filterless cigarette between his fingers disintegrating it into a little shower of tobacco, orange embers and white paper. Opening the door, he stepped in and said, "I know, Mister Burgess, a filthy habit."

"Give you cancer, you know," the clerk replied, unconsciously touching his red striped bowtie. "Plus it stinks up the books."

Jelly smiled. "Some books just stink on their own," he quipped, waiting for the laugh. It didn't come.

Burgess looked hurt. "All books have value, you know. They mean different things to different people."

Jelly's eyebrows raised up. Burgess didn't get the joke. "I'm sure you're right. If you don't mind, I'm just gonna sit in here for a little bit. I won't be long."

"That's fine," the clerk said, then picked up a folded white cloth and started wiping down the bookshelves.

Jelly sat down on the chair facing the window and made sure he was in position to observe the coffee shop. He'd come to Roswell to meet a man named David Clark. Clark had reached out to Jelly through a mutual acquaintance, Freddie Schmeltzer. Schmeltzer was an oil man back in Oklahoma Jelly had helped out on a few occasions. Now he was trying to return the favor by hooking Jelly up with Clark. Clark supposedly had some information about a few prisoners of war currently interred in Roswell.

PW camps had sprung up all across the US holding prisoners shipped back from overseas. In the Roswell facility there was a high concentration of Germans, most from General Rommel's elite Afrika Korps. Jelly made the trip himself instead of sending one of his agents mostly because he was curious. All his men were also stretched thin as it was.

Opening the newspaper, Jelly sat back and pretended to read as he watched the coffee shop over the top. Clark wasn't due to show for at least 40 minutes. Jelly was watching for any unusual activity that might indicate surveillance of him, Clark, the location or all three.

"I'm surprised you don't just tear a little peephole through the paper." The voice came from directly behind him. Jelly's first thought was the clerk, but he could see Burgess in his peripheral vision across the shop still wiping shelves. The voice's owner was positioned so Jelly would have to turn all the way around in his chair to see him. He was at a complete tactical disadvantage. Realizing that, Jelly just sat still as a statue. If the man wanted to ice him he could have already done so.

"Do you mind?" the voice said as the man walked around the chair next to Jelly and sat down. It was Donnelly. Jelly took a breath and let it out slowly as he lowered the newspaper and folded it up. He looked at Donnelly. The OSS agent was dressed rather casually in an open collared blue shirt, chinos and brown leather soft soled shoes. A white cotton jacket covered the gun Jelly assumed he was wearing. His hair was cut short and he was smiling. He also had a cast on his left wrist and hand and a sutured scar running up from inside his shirt collar, along the left side of his face stopping just below the eye. "That a gift from the last guy you snuck up on?" Jelly asked, pointing to his own left cheek.

Donnelly laughed. "Got blowed up, actually. Courtesy of a Jap booby-trap in Burma. One of the perks of the job."

Jelly looked into Donnelly's eyes. They were steady and clear. There was more to this man than he'd previously thought. "You all done, then?"

Donnelly shook his head. "Nope. Just stateside for a little while, healin' up, then I'm off to somewhere's else.

World's an interesting place right now, Bryce. You oughta think about expanding your horizons."

Jelly could tell Donnelly wasn't insulting him. He was serious. "That an invitation?"

"Open. But I wouldn't wait too long. This war won't last much longer."

Jelly nodded. "Let's hope."

Donnelly smiled. "You don't mean that."

"So how's the General?" Jelly asked, changing the subject.

"The Boss is fine. Still alive and fightin' the good fight as always."

"Can I ask where he is now?"

Donnelly raised his right foot and used both hands to gingerly direct his ankle across his left knee, putting himself into a "figure four" seated position. "Last I heard, he was enjoying the beaches in France."

Jelly's eyebrows raised in surprise. "What the fuck would he be doing there?" Donnelly apparently meant the head of OSS had participated in the Normandy invasion, commonly referred to as D-Day by the press. That made no sense. Why would you risk the head of America's spy service being killed or captured during a major invasion? Who would have given that order? Or allowed it?

Donnelly smiled again. "The man does what he does. What I heard was he wrangled a spot on an observation ship off the coast after promising he wouldn't try to go ashore. Then naturally, he finds a way to leapfrog from ship to ship to boat to landing craft, all the while being dogged by some poor second lieutenant intelligence officer the brass had assigned to watch him and make sure he stayed out of trouble. Next thing the poor butterbar knows, they're on shore in a jeep, engaged in a fire fight."

"What the fuck?" Jelly repeated, raising his voice above the whisper they'd been talking in. The clerk stopped dusting and looked over, surprise registering on his face there were two men in his shop. He'd only been aware of the one.

"Yup," Donnelly said. "I heard that at one point they were actually surrounded, laying on their backs in a field taking fire, and the Boss told the lieutenant not to worry. Said if they were about to be captured, he'd shoot the L.T. and then himself so they wouldn't be taken."

Jelly was speechless.

"How can you not love a guy like that?" Donnelly asked, shaking his head and smiling.

"So what happened?" Jelly asked.

"It's the Boss. What do you think happened? They both came out of it fine. The man has a squad of guardian angels watching over him."

Jelly slowly shook his head. Donovan truly was larger than life.

"Anyway," Donnelly said, "as pleasant as it is catching up with you without having your pistol pressed into my kidney, there is a reason I'm here."

Jelly looked at the wounded man next to him. "Okay."

"The Boss has a mission for you."

*   *   *

Back in El Paso the next day, Jelly walked into his office and set his briefcase down in the corner. His secretary, Miss Stimson followed him in a moment later, carrying a cup of hot black coffee in one hand and his mail in her other. Jelly got a lot of mail. Miss Stimson carried the pile of envelopes and a nearly-shoebox-sized package wrapped in heavy brown paper under her arm like a running back carrying a football downfield. She'd stacked the envelopes on top of the box and wrapped a giant rubber band around the whole thing.

After placing the cup down on his desk she maneuvered the package into both hands and set it in front of him. "Good trip?" she asked seriously. She knew it had been all business. It always was with Agent Bryce.

"Yes and no," Jelly replied. That would be all she got. She knew it, so simply said, "Okay, sir, let me know if you need anything," then walked back to her own desk, closing his door behind her.

The trip to Roswell had been interesting even though the potential informant he'd met in the coffee shop had proved a bust. All the man had was unsubstantiated rumor and innuendo he'd picked up around town about goings on in the PW camp. After the Maple story had hit the newswires, everyone in America living within driving distance of a PW camp had begun seeing escaped Nazi, Jap and Italian soldiers everywhere they looked.

It had been worthwhile, though, to check in on the camp and get a look at how they ran things there. Again, in response to the Maple story, the Army had cleaned house stateside and gotten all the camps in order. Security looked good in Roswell. The prisoners were well-fed, clean and orderly. Not like the horrific way US GIs were being treated by the Krauts and Japs.

The PWs in Roswell were even allowed to make small crafts out of discarded cans and other metal items, things they could use to trade with the local population for cigarettes and chocolates, that kind of stuff. Most of the PWs Jelly saw seemed genuinely happy to be there. Most were taking classes learning English. The camp commander told Jelly many were petitioning to stay in America after the war, to become citizens. "I suppose getting captured is one way to emigrate," Jelly'd said in response to that interesting news.

Then of course, there was the woman. Francine Elizabeth Bleath. It had only taken a call to the New Mexico Motor Vehicle Division Headquarters in Santa Fe to get the listing for the bright yellow, five-digit plate. He'd had her name and address within an hour of making the request. The process of looking up the information was actually pretty quick, since people had been using the same, single metal plate for two years running in an effort to conserve steel for the war effort. Current registration status was indicated by a small colored paper sticker affixed inside the windshield, not the year stamped into the plate below the registration number.

Jelly smiled as he thought about the new logo stamped across the top of the plate in red-painted letters: *The Land of Enchantment*. It certainly was.

After getting the address he'd stopped by a florist and paid to have a nice bouquet delivered to her. On the card, in fancy script he'd written:

> *Dear Miss Bleath:*
> *I am, I did, and I apologize for being abrupt.*
> *Your beauty got the better of me. Please do*
> *me the honor of a second chance.*
> *Yours, respectfully,*
> *Delf Bryce.*

He attached a copy of his FBI business card, circling the telephone number. Even though he'd looked hers up in the phonebook, he'd let her decide if she wanted to grant his request.

And finally, there was Donnelly. Jelly had decided to just call him that, despite the fact he knew it was one of many aliases the man used. "Donnelly" fit him and he didn't object when Jelly called him by it.

Even though Jelly'd started to warm up slightly to the man, he still didn't trust him completely. That's why he was glad Donovan had included a note with the small canvas bag Donnelly gave him in the bookstore.

The "mission packet," Donnelly had called it. Seeing it reminded Jelly of the last mission packet Donnelly had given him, the one containing the Mauser for the New York job years before when Jelly thought Donnelly was FBI.

* * *

"So what is it this time?" Jelly asked as Donnelly indicated the small canvas bag in the corner of the bookstore with a nod of his head.

"There's a note with instructions inside. After you've memorized the information, just touch a match to the paper. Make sure you're not holding it when you do. It goes fast."

Jelly nodded. "What if I can't do it?"

Donnelly looked at him. "You can do it. The Boss is counting on you to do it. He said to tell you it doesn't conflict with your agreement, whatever that means."

Jelly nodded again. "Anything else?"

Donnelly scanned around the empty shop, locating the clerk. The man was seated in a padded chair behind the front desk, asleep. "Nice job," Donnelly said. "Apparently reading isn't big business in Roswell." He held his right foot, lifted it off the other knee and gently placed it back on the floor, making just the slightest sound to indicate discomfort.

"You all right there?" Jelly asked. Apparently, not all of Donnelly's wounds were visible.

Donnelly nodded and turned in the seat to face Jelly directly. "There's a plane leaving from an airfield in a week. The cargo on that plane must not arrive at its destination.

What you're going to do is to place the item in that bag," tilting his head toward the corner, "in one of the weight-lightening holes in the wall of the landing gear studs. Do you know what I mean?"

Jelly looked at him. "Studs?"

"The wheels are fixed. They don't retract. There are open spaces on the inside of each of the down struts. You'll see them. Just make sure the item is secure and out of sight, and that you pull out the metal pin before you leave it."

Jelly breathed in deeply through his nose, letting the air out slowly through his mouth. "How long do I have before it goes off? I mean, I'm assuming it's an explosive, yes?"

Donnelly nodded. "It's not on a timer. It's special. It only goes off once it gets above a certain altitude. That means you can place it any time before take-off. Just make sure—"

"To pull the pin," Jelly finished.

"Yeah," Donnelly said, "that too. What I was gonna say is make sure you put it on the right plane and that no one sees you. There can't be any trace back."

Jelly considered the mission. "Who's on the plane?"

Donnelly looked appraisingly at him for a moment. "Does that matter?"

"I suppose it does to the people on the plane."

"This did not come down lightly, Bryce," Donnelly said with certitude. "This matter is considered of grave importance. If this airplane doesn't come down in pieces, a lot of Americans are going to die."

Jelly looked at Donnelly, nodded his assent. "When and where?"

"One week from today."

Jelly's hand clenched. "I'm scheduled to be in Mexico next week at a conference for the Bureau. Hoover's already assigned me to represent him."

"I know. You'll be five miles from the airfield we're discussing."

Jelly was again impressed by the obvious quality of the intelligence Donovan had at his disposal. Jelly's trip south had just been assigned two days previously.

"Any other questions?" Donnelly asked, prepared to wrap up the surprise meeting.

"Not now. But one day, I would like to get the rest of the story on the New York thing."

Donnelly smiled knowingly. "Asking me to let the pigeon out of the barn?"

Jelly stared hard at Donnelly. "What the fuck does that mean?"

"Another time," Donnelly said as he slowly rose to his feet. "Good luck in Mexico." Donnelly threw Jelly a short hand salute and started to turn. "Oh, and Bryce…"

Jelly stood up and looked at him.

"Your guy went inside there a few minutes ago," indicating the shop across the street with a toss of his thumb. "Don't forget your bag."

Jelly looked out the window at the coffee shop. He'd been so caught up in the conversation he'd forgotten about the informant. He looked at Donnelly and nodded. "And don't you go pickin' up any more souvenirs in jungles."

Donnelly smiled and limped to the back of the store heading for the rear exit, apparently the way he'd gotten in.

* * *

After replaying the conversation with Donnelly over in his mind a few times, Jelly focused on the present. He picked up his coffee cup and took a sip. It had gone cold. Apparently he'd been lost in thought for a while. Pushing the intercom button on his desk, he asked Miss Stimson to get him a fresh cup. Then he thumbed through the stack of letters, all the mail he'd missed the past three days while away. Like a kid saving the best for last, he ignored the paper-wrapped box until he'd finished with the letters and Miss Stimson had delivered his coffee.

Picking up the box, he looked it over, the thought of bombs fresh on his mind since Roswell. Nothing leaking through the paper, no strange odors, nothing ticking–but it *was* heavy. He checked the return address: Boston, Massachusetts. His first thought, Tom Wilson, was confirmed by the name of the firm: *Wilson & Wilson, Attorneys at Law.*

Jelly smiled. He hadn't heard from Tom in a few years. They'd kept in touch pretty regularly after Tom had first resigned, but in short order Jelly'd been swamped with work and all the letters and calls he'd received from Tom had been positive. It seemed he'd adjusted fine to being a "rotten civilian" as he called himself with a chuckle, so Jelly had slowly but surely turned his attention to other people, other matters. Then years had suddenly gone by. Jelly shook his head considering just how quickly the time had passed. His father had been telling him that since he was a kid, that the clock sped up the older you got, and he'd been right on the money.

Jelly carefully sliced the paper wrapping on the outside of the cardboard box with his little blue-handled, combination bottle opener and single-bladed knife. He'd had the opener since the New York job he'd mentioned to Donnelly the day before. It brought back a lot of memories for him. He'd definitely covered a lot of ground in the intervening nine years.

Dropping the paper into the wastebasket next to his desk, he sliced through the brown paper tape running along the box's flap, then pulled the cover open. The something heavy inside was wrapped in multiple sheets of wrinkled newspaper. On top of the paper bundle was an envelope. Handwritten on the envelope were the words, "Agent D.A. Bryce / Personal"

Jelly took a breath and let it out slowly before opening the envelope. He had a bad feeling about this package. That wasn't Tom's handwriting.

Opening the envelope, he took out the two-page letter and unfolded it. It too was handwritten, on heavy parchment paper; the law firm's heading was embossed on the top center of the first page. The letter was dated June 11, 1944.

Dear Agent Bryce:

It is with a heavy heart that I write to you today.

There is no easy way to convey the news I must, but to simply tell you that our beloved son, Thomas, has passed away as the result of a terrible accident.

It happened a week ago, on Sunday evening, June 4th.

Thomas had apparently been cleaning his revolver when it somehow discharged, striking him in the chest. We know it was an accident because all of his gun cleaning equipment was out on the table where it happened. He had been happy working with the firm, and the last two years had been a joy to his mother and me.

I wanted to write to you personally to tell you, for I know how much Thomas thought of you. Both my wife, Karen, and I also wanted to thank you for being such a good friend to our boy for so long. He truly looked up to you and admired you greatly.

I hope you don't mind, but I have sent you his revolver. It has been cleaned by a friend of ours. I would appreciate it if you would do whatever you thought best with it. While my first instinct was to destroy it, I simply could not. Thomas had a great attachment to that old gun as I'm sure you know. He had it with him both day and night it seemed. Though he would never tell us the story behind it (I am sure it had something to do with his secret work for the government), I am also sure he would want you to have it.

He always told Karen and me that if he were ever in trouble, you would be the first person he would turn to for help. While a father would like to think he would be his son's first call, I understand that in the business you gentlemen shared, that sometime that is not the case.

So now, Agent Bryce, I am turning to you for help. If you would take care of this matter for me, it will put my mind to rest in no small way.

With the greatest regard and appreciation, I am most humbly yours,

Steven M. Wilson

Jelly folded the letter up and returned it to the envelope. He looked at the newspaper-wrapped item in the box for a long moment, then placed the envelope back on top of it and closed the box. Rolling his chair back a bit, Jelly reached down and pulled open the big sliding drawer in his gunmetal gray desk. He picked up the box and gently placed it in the drawer. Reaching deeper into the drawer he retrieved a green bottle of Jameson Whiskey, unscrewed the red cover and poured, the alcohol mixing with the hot coffee until the liquid reached the cup's brim.

Standing up, he walked to the door to his office and let the blinds down over the glass that had his name and position stenciled on it. Turning to his desk, he pushed the button on the intercom. "Miss Stimson," he said, his voice cracking slightly, "please hold all my calls till further notice."

*   *   *

Jelly knew what was inside the box.

It was a Model 1892 revolver. He'd tracked down some information on it back in '41 after his friends in the El Paso Police Department had found it for him. They'd tracked down the mutt who had it within a week by a simple process of elimination. Between the detective shaking his informants and the patrolman shaking the bushes on his beat, they'd soon had conversations with all the stickup men in town.

A lowlife named Manny Chavez won the jackpot when he was caught carrying the odd revolver loaded with three live rounds and three expended shell casings–just as Jelly had described. While it wasn't that unusual to grab up a criminal off the streets with a partially loaded gun, in this case the gun itself was unusual.

The Model 1892 was a French revolver produced by Manufacture d'armes de Saint-Étienne. It had been used by French military officers in the first Great War, and kept in use since. The El Paso copper who'd found it, Jelly's friend "Taco" McDonald, knew it wasn't just another junk foreign blaster as soon as he'd relieved Chavez of it during their "conversation" on the street. It was a well-made double-action pistol, mechanically tight and well finished inside and out. The ammo it was loaded with was unusual too, as it was chambered for an 8mm round, similar in appearance and effect to a .32 ACP.

After falling down the stairs at the police station for the second time, the clumsy Chavez confessed he'd taken the pistol from a businessman he'd spotted walking through the wrong part of town near the money exchange store.

A little more prodding produced a full confession, Chavez detailing how he'd had no gun of his own during the robbery, he'd just stuck a small piece of pipe he'd picked up from the ground into the mark's back, simulating the barrel of a pistol. Even though the mark hadn't seemed willing to fight him, Chavez had reverted to his normal business practice of clubbing his victims over the head with the leather sap he held in his other hand. He'd learned that beating his victims senseless made his job easier, with the added benefit of eliminating the problem of one of them identifying him later.

Chavez admitted he'd been pleasantly surprised when going through the unconscious victim's pockets after dragging him out of sight behind a small wall to find a pocketful of bills and a wallet containing more cash. He'd almost missed the pistol as it was stuck in the man's belt in front, since he'd dumped the mark face-first onto the ground. He only saw the handle protruding from the belt after he'd applied one more kick to the victim's ribcage for good measure, his booted foot peeling away the suitcoat that covered the gun.

"I thought eet was my looky day," Chavez said smiling up at his interrogators through bloody teeth, right before Taco McDonald threw his ass in the cell.

Jelly had arrived at the station a short time later. The

detective, Bill Goodman filled him in since Taco had been dispatched to a call. "Want to spend some time with Mister Chavez?" Goodman asked Jelly, motioning toward the cell block.

"I'm assuming you fellas have already spoken with him?" Jelly asked, all business.

Goodman nodded soberly. "We spoke with him quite a bit."

Jelly nodded. "I appreciate that, Bill. I'm sure you gentlemen already said everything that I'd say to him. If it's all the same to you, I'd like to let this go at this point."

"Understood, Jelly. Not a problem." The detective reached behind him and picked up a paper bag with the top rolled down, as if a sandwich was inside it. He held it out. "I'm assumin' you want this. I left it loaded just like we found it."

Later, back at the house, Jelly had unloaded and cleaned the gun. He'd never seen one like it. The cylinder swung out to the right instead of the left like most revolvers he was familiar with. It had a case-hardened loading gate on the right side of the frame that locked the cylinder closed. After fooling with it for a bit, Jelly also found that the left sideplate of the frame swung back on a hinge. This provided access to the gun's internal parts, presumably to make cleaning and oiling easier. It was a nice design, and the cylinder swinging out to the right meant it was perfect for a left-handed shooter–like Tom.

When he'd showed the pistol to Tom, the injured man's eyes had brightened and he'd actually smiled. "That's it!" he'd said, holding out his hand from the bed where he was lying in a semi-upright seated position. Jelly gave it to him grips first, and Tom had seemed to regain some of his confidence the moment he'd held it.

"But how?" Tom had asked.

"The fuckstick that took it from you has been repaid in kind, with interest. It wasn't personal. Just a fuckstick doing what they do. I'm thinking we consider the matter closed and move forward from this point. Agreed?"

Tom had nodded, then, keeping the revolver in his hand, closed his eyes and fallen back asleep.

Jelly learned more about the gun that afternoon by telephoning Elmer Keith, one of the most knowledgeable "gun guys" he knew. As soon as Jelly mentioned the fancy hand engraved inscription of "Mle 1892" on top of the barrel, Elmer had asked, "Got a lanyard ring, big flat hammer with a number "2" on the side?"

"It does."

"That's a Model 1892. Frog gun. Some folks call it a 'Lebel'. I'm not a fan of the cartridge. Too weak."

After filling Jelly in on more of the gun's history, Elmer had told him he'd send a box of cartridges for it. Two weeks later, the box arrived by mail. By that time, Tom was up and around, and he and Jelly spent some time out behind the house engaged in shooting practice. Tom was pretty good with the old French pistol. Jelly told him he should use it as his carry gun.

"But won't the Bureau mind? Shouldn't I use the duty .38?"

"A carry gun is a personal matter," Jelly had said. "The gun has gotta feel right in your hand. You should feel confident with it. I'm assuming you feel confident with that piece, seeing as how you've already used it to save your own life?"

Tom had nodded. "But," he'd then asked, "What about the caliber? Isn't it kinda small? And where am I gonna find ammo for it?"

"Thing with bullets is placement, mostly, Tom. Put the bullet in the right place and it will do what you need it to.

As far as caliber, while I prefer bigger, that'll work. Hoover himself carries a 3-inch Colt, .32 Pocket Positive. That's pretty much the same thing you've got there."

Tom considered this. "And ammo?" he'd asked again.

Jelly smiled. "I've got a case of it coming for you. Soon you'll be able to put that little frog round wherever you need to."

*   *   *

Sitting at his desk, Jelly looked into the coffee cup now filled only with whiskey and relived that conversation in his mind.

"Soon you'll be able to put that little frog round wherever you need to," he said aloud. "Jesus."

'Maybe,' he thought, *'maybe if I'd only called him more. I should have kept in touch. I could have done something, could have helped him.'* The guilt he was feeling was enormous. Jelly knew it hadn't been an accident. He'd been to more than half-a-dozen "accidental shootings" where officers or agents had died while "cleaning their guns." The cleaning equipment provided deniability.

It was a way to save their families from having to know or admit it had been suicide. It was a way to preserve the insurance benefits since suicide wasn't always covered.

"Jesus," Jelly said again, quietly so as to not be heard outside his office. Then he shook his head sadly. "I'm sorry, Tom. I'm so, so sorry."

CHAPTER THIRTEEN

The Charm
27 July 1944

JELLY AND FRANCINE KISSED. The crowd seated in the charming little church in Carrizozo, New Mexico erupted in applause.

As the newly-married couple turned from the minister and faced their families and friends, Jelly smiled, happier than he'd ever been. His bride was gorgeous inside and out. Though they'd only been courting for a month, both of them were certain they'd found their other.

The flowers and card Jelly had sent had produced a return phone call as he'd hoped. That had opened the door to a date in Roswell, at the nice restaurant Jelly had envisioned them in when he'd first spotted Francine walking toward him days before. That date had been unlike any other he'd ever had.

The recent death of his friend, Tom, had affected Jelly in a number of ways. Not only had it reinforced his innate feeling that precious time was slipping away at an accelerated rate, it also made him more willing to reveal his inner self to Francine. As they'd sat across from one another that first evening, the food was largely ignored. They talked for more than two hours straight, confessing things to each other they'd never shared with anyone.

Francine told Jelly all about herself: she was thirty years old, had never been married, had never even been with a man. She'd dated, of course. But the men who'd approached her had always been the wrong type. Though she thought she was attractive and she enjoyed dressing well, she'd never considered herself beautiful. She liked simple, honest things and people who were direct and could see–and accept her–for who she truly was. And a big part of who she was, was American Indian.

The fact she was more than three-quarters Indian often complicated her relationships with Caucasian men, for some were put off by it once they'd found out. Francine, fiercely proud of her heritage, never tried to hide her Indian ancestry, even though she'd been encouraged to many times while growing up in Chickasha, Oklahoma. One of her earliest memories, she'd confided to Jelly that night at dinner, was being told by a white lady at church that she was a beautiful little girl. Then the lady had said, "You're so lucky, sweetheart," as she'd gently touched Francine's cheek. "You don't look Indian at all."

Francine had been crushed by the offhanded comment. It had made her feel dirty somehow, ashamed. She swore to herself that day she would never pretend to be anything other than she was. She was a good person. She was Choctaw. She was French. She was an American. Anyone who couldn't accept her as she was could go straight to Hell.

Jelly had reached over the table and placed his hand on hers after she'd told him that story, the memory causing her eyes to tear even after all those years. At the moment their hands touched for the first time, they both felt something like an electric current running through their hands and up their arms. It wasn't a static shock; it was unlike anything either had ever felt.

"Did you feel that?" Jelly had asked her, and she'd nodded in response.

Then as she'd listened, Jelly told her all the things he'd always kept locked in his innermost vault. He told her about his mother's death, his failed marriages, his estranged son

Austin; he told her about the tattoos that covered his upper body, about how he'd been compelled to get them when he was younger, how they'd given him a feeling of self-control when he'd felt in danger of losing it. Without going into detail he'd also told her about the horrible, heartbreaking things he'd seen and dealt with over the years as a cop, about the friends he'd lost. Before he'd known it, he'd even started describing to her the terrible pressures of being the one expected to always know the answer, to do what was necessary, to face the dangers behind the door first.

"But who makes you do that, Delf?" she'd asked him bluntly. "Who makes you go through the door first?"

That's when Jelly'd told her his ultimate truth, the truth he'd finally started to realize. "I do," he'd said, without bluster. "It's just me. It's how I am. I don't know why."

*   *   *

The day after their first date Francine had brought Jelly to her home to meet her parents. They'd been immediately taken with him; Jelly had been charming, funny and respectful, bringing flowers and candy for both Francine and her lovely mother, the obvious source of her daughter's great physical beauty. At Jelly's request, Francine's dad and he even had a private conversation that first day, Jelly telling Mister Bleath his intentions were honorable, and he wanted permission from both of Francine's parents to court their only daughter. His respectful manner was appreciated. The fact he also had Indian blood was a comfort to them.

Later, while eating dinner at the Bleath table, Jelly had told Francine's parents about his two prior marriages, explaining about his son, even going so far as to admit he wasn't proud or happy about the way he'd failed to establish a relationship with his boy, but he planned to do just that in the future.

The Bleaths listened closely, hearing not just his words, but the clear, open, natural way he expressed them.

When Jelly'd finished talking, Francine's mom said quietly, "*Two* wives, is that right?"

Jelly didn't disturb the heavy silence that descended on the table with her question–he simply looked straight into her eyes and nodded.

"Well," she said, looking first at her husband, then her daughter, "don't they say the third time is the charm?"

Francine threw her arms around her mother as they all smiled, the sound of laughter, joy and relief filling the house.

* * *

One week later Jelly and Francine sat at the Bryce family's table in Mountain View, sharing another meal. Jelly had taken a few days off, the extraordinary occurrence drawing the interest of everyone he worked with at the office in El Paso. Word had already started going around about the mysterious, exotic woman he'd been seeing, some passing along rumors they'd heard she was an Indian princess, a model, a spy, or all the above.

Jelly's family in Mountain View were just as impressed with the stunning woman Jelly had brought home. Francine was warm, lovely and sweet, and fit right in with Jelly's dad, Fel, stepmom Winnie, and sisters and brother. Jelly's sister, Lila, who Jelly hoped above all others would like and accept Francine, fell in love with her almost as quickly as Jelly had. They instantly became bonded as sisters, Lila wasting no time spilling the beans about all of Jelly's brotherly faults and childhood secrets.

* * *

Just a few weeks later, both families had made the trek to New Mexico for the wedding. It was the first wedding of Jelly's any of his family members had attended. The change they saw in him had filled them all with great hope for his future and happiness.

That night, after all the guests had eaten dinner, after Jelly and Francine had danced their first dance as man and wife, after the toast had been made by Jelly's best man, H.V. Wilder, and after Jelly had whisked his new bride away to their honeymoon suite in his shiny, pink Cadillac, Jelly and Francine Bryce celebrated their new start in life as a couple in each other's arms.

While it was Francine's first experience, for Jelly it was something foreign as well. They fit together like pieces of a puzzle.

Sometimes while making love to her, he wasn't able to tell where he ended and she began. He'd never experienced anything like it before.

After their first time together that night, he'd looked at her and said, "Now I get it." She'd looked back at him with her half-closed, dreamy eyes, smiled at him and didn't say a thing. She didn't need to. He could see she understood completely.

CHAPTER FOURTEEN

The Blessing
22 August 1945

A LITTLE OVER A year after their wedding, Jelly and Francine were awaiting the arrival of their child.

Hoover had given the Bryces an early baby gift four months earlier by transferring Jelly back to Oklahoma City. This time he would be in charge. Jelly found a nice house to rent in an upscale part of the city and quickly settled his wife in the new neighborhood. Having grown up less than forty miles away in Chickasha, Francine couldn't have been happier. Though further from her parents, she'd have plenty of friends and relatives nearby to visit with and help with the baby.

Though two weeks overdue, Francine had been carrying the baby without complaint, finding the joy in every new feeling and experience–even the less than pleasant ones. Backaches, swelling feet, constipation, difficulty sleeping, fatigue: she'd endured them all. Fortunately, morning sickness and mood swings hadn't joined the party for whatever lucky reason.

When the first contraction started that morning she'd been both scared and greatly relieved, and found herself looking forward to the hospital in a way that surprised her. She'd originally wanted to have the baby at home with the assistance of a midwife, but Jelly had talked her out of that. The experience with his mother so long ago, when the immediate presence of a doctor could have saved her, had made the idea of his wife delivering their child without a doctor present unacceptable.

Jelly had also treasured the past months watching his wife's belly and breasts grow; the first time she'd told him to put his hands on her so he could feel the baby moving had been momentous. It truly was a miracle. The cycle of birth and life, illness, old age and death were known quantities for him, having grown up taking care of animals since he was a child, then having seen both human life and death in its unvarnished state as a policeman. He understood the way it worked, from inception to interment. That's why he'd been able to stay so calm and levelheaded throughout the pregnancy, even though his wife and unborn child meant more to him than anything in the world.

"Delf?" Francine said calmly after the second contraction ended. They were still pretty far apart, but she knew this was it.

"Hold on a minute, honey," Jelly replied. He was listening to the radio. The news reporter had just issued a warning for a special announcement. The last time he'd heard a similar warning a month earlier, the report had been the unexpected death of President Franklin D. Roosevelt.

The war was now heading to a final end. Germany had surrendered in May. The Allies had crushed the Axis Powers both in Europe and in the Pacific. Hitler was dead. Mussolini was dead. Just a few weeks earlier the new American president, Harry Truman, had ordered the US Air Force to drop two atomic bombs on targets in Japan, unleashing devastation that shocked the world and finally convinced the Japanese to agree to unconditional surrender.

"But honey," Francine said, still calm, no urgency in her voice.

Jelly held up his index finger to his wife, eyes on the radio. "Just one minute, please, Franny."

The announcer's voice boomed out of the speaker, "The

Soviet Union has just declared three major cities in northeastern China have been taken and secured. These cities, Mukden, Changchun, and Qiqihar were taken as a result of a surprise attack launched by the Soviets through the Greater Khingan mountain range, which was believed to be impassable. Some Japanese forces are still fighting on despite Emperor Showa's edict to surrender."

"That is well," Jelly said enthusiastically. The Russians had brutally torn up the Germans in Berlin and now they were spilling into China to tear up what was left of the Japanese. Better to let the Reds go in than Americans. The Americans had already lost way too many boys in this war.

"This war won't last much longer, honey."

"I'm sure," said Francine. "But Delf honey, we've gotta go now."

Jelly turned around in his chair and saw his wife standing in the doorway, her hand on the doorframe. She looked a little pale. He sprang to his feet. "Are you all right?!"

Francine smiled. "I'm fine, sweetheart. But I think it's time."

Jelly looked at her. "Time? You mean time for the baby?"

Francine nodded.

"Okay!" Jelly said. He'd been staying home the past week in anticipation of this, keeping in touch with the office by telephone and having paperwork shuttled back and forth to the office by his agents. That morning he'd just finished exercising when the radio report had come on, so he was wearing shorts and a t-shirt. "Do I have time to get dressed?" he asked, moving toward his wife. "Is there anything I can do? Do you need anything?"

Francine smiled again. "No, I think we have plenty of time still, Delf. If you can get dressed and we can get to the hospital, I think we'll be good."

"Okay, honey," Delf said steadily. "I'll make this quick. Just give me a minute to get dressed and we can get to the hospital."

Francine smiled. "That sounds good."

"Do you have your bag?" Jelly asked.

"Right there," Francine replied, pointing to her small suitcase by the front door.

Jelly nodded then went into their bedroom, stopping at the doorway to call out, "Do you think I have time to take a quick shower?" As soon as he asked the question he regretted it. Of course there was no time. He had to get her to the hospital.

"I think we might want to go to the hospital first," she said. "You can come back and take a shower after you drop me off."

"Drop you off?!" Jelly said, "I'm not gonna drop you off! We're not getting laundry done. I'll be staying at the hospital till this mission's complete. Just let me get dressed, will ya?"

Jelly grabbed a pair of socks out of the drawer and sat on the edge of the bed. He couldn't believe how calm he was. He'd thought he'd be more nervous. Then again, he was always calm. As he started to pull on the first sock, holding the top edges with his hands and sliding his foot inside, he was startled to watch his foot go into the sock and come clean out the other end.

"What the hell?" he asked quietly, trying to figure out what had happened. Somehow he'd driven his foot clean through the material at the toe end. "You won't believe this," he started to call out to his wife, then changed his mind and grabbed another pair of socks. He managed to get them both on without incident.

* * *

Five hours later the nurse came into the waiting room. The four fathers-to-be gathered there all raised their heads, squinting at her through the cloud of cigarette smoke, looking for a sign. "Mister Bryce?" she said pleasantly.

Jelly stood up. "I'm Bryce."

The nurse smiled. "Would you like to come with me, please?"

Jelly, dressed in a blue suit with matching tie loosened and shirt collar unbuttoned, nodded and fell in behind the young woman. "Is everything all right?" he asked.

She turned as she walked and looked at him, smiled again and said, "Everything is just fine, Mister Bryce."

Jelly buttoned his shirt and fixed his tie as they turned the corner. He followed the nurse through a doorway into a private room. Francine was lying in a bed against two big white pillows, covered with white sheets and a blanket, holding a baby wrapped in its own little blue blanket next to her. His wife looked sleepy and beautiful; the Spanish bluebells in the flower arrangement on the table next to her matched the blue in her eyes.

Jelly stopped and took in the scene for a moment, then smiled at his wife and moved to the bed to meet his son. "A boy, yes?" he asked.

Francine nodded and smiled.

"The blanket was a clue," Jelly said, smiling. "I did used to be a detective." Then he carefully peeled the edges of the blanket back to see his new son. The baby looked like an angry little alien that had been worked over, face all red and blotchy, big mound of crazy black hair on its head. For a moment Jelly was shocked; then the baby opened its eyes and looked at him, these two clear, crystal blue eyes just like his mother had, and Jelly was done.

"So, how do you like him?" Francine asked quietly, still shaking off the effects of the drugs they'd given her to knock her out while she'd delivered the baby.

    Jelly just stared at the little face and smiled. "He needs a haircut," was all he said, then bent down and kissed his wife gently on the mouth.

CHAPTER FIFTEEN

LIFE
October 1945

IT WAS A QUIET Sunday afternoon. Jelly was sitting at home on the couch reading the newspaper, baby asleep in the basinet across the living room, when the telephone on the table rang. He jumped up to answer. The baby was napping and Francine was in the bedroom passed out cold. He wanted to let them both sleep. They needed it, and he was enjoying the rare spell of quiet.

He picked up the receiver with his right hand and telephone base with his left, quickly carrying them both out to the kitchen. He'd attached an extra-long cord to it for just this purpose.

"Yes," he said into the receiver, expecting it to be the office, surprised and happy to hear Hoover's voice instead.

"Hey, Hoover," Jelly said, placing the base on the small pine kitchen table and settling into a chair.

"Are you sitting down, Jelly?" Hoover asked.

"Of course not, sir, I'm standing at the position of attention."

Hoover chuckled. "Well, at ease then, mister, and have a seat."

Jelly smiled. "All set, Boss. What's going on?"

"Well, first things first. How is that lovely bride of yours, and the junior G-Man? Both good I hope?"

Jelly smiled. "Yes, sir. Both fine thank you. And thank you for the nice flowers by the way. Franny really appreciated them. She'd tell you herself, but she's catching a few Zs while she has a chance. Little Jimmy's nocturnal still, keeps her up all night."

"My pleasure, my pleasure," Hoover said. "I'm glad to hear everything is going well at home. And the office?"

Jelly became alert at the question. Hoover kept tabs on pretty much everything. He knew how things were going at the office. That harmless sounding question could signal a pending shakeup, even a transfer. It wasn't unheard of to be shipped somewhere else even after just a few months. Jelly and Francine were happy in Oklahoma City. They had a nice place and Francine's mother came and stayed with them pretty often, easing the load on Francine and letting Jelly attend to work without worry. He was still active, needing to go away on frequent trips to take care of Bureau business.

"It's all good there too, Boss man," Jelly said, then asked, "Why? What are you hearing?"

Hoover chuckled. "Nothing bad at all." Then he added, "Don't worry. You're not going anywhere for a while." Hoover knew the effect he had on his agents.

Jelly quietly breathed a sigh of relief. Then Hoover said, "But I do have a mission for you. Something different. And you might not like it, but I need you to do this for me."

Jelly turned in the chair and picked up a small notebook from the table. Flipping the cover open to the first blank page he grabbed a pencil and hunched over the pad, pressing the telephone receiver to his right ear with his shoulder, elbow braced on the table. "Ready, Boss."

"I need you to fly to New York. You'll be meeting a man named Gjon Mili." Hoover pronounced the first name, 'Gin'. "He's an engineer out of M.I.T. Him and another egghead, Doc Edgerton, have come up with a new method of photography. Pretty nifty actually. They use an incredibly bright flash of light; *strobe light* they call it. We used it during the war. Unbelievably effective, Jelly. They were taking aerial photographs from a mile up at night using these things and they would get pictures as clear as daylight. They even took pictures of Normandy the night before D-Day."

Intrigued, Jelly asked, "Okay, so what's the mission? Am I bringing back one of the strobe lights, one of the eggheads, or both?"

Hoover chuckled again. "None of the above. This time, Jelly, *you* are the mission, actually."

Hoover explained that he'd arranged a photo shoot with *LIFE* Magazine, and that Mili was going to be the photographer. The purpose of the shoot was to capture Jelly's draw.

"Say that again?"

"This guy Mili is going to take a series of photographs of you drawing your pistol, Jelly, using the strobe light. They tell me they can show each moment of it. They'll actually be able to time you down to a fifth of a second. Now tell me that doesn't sound interesting to you?"

Jelly couldn't. *It did*. "What's the purpose, Boss? Are we going to use this for training?"

"Hmm," Hoover said over the line. He hadn't considered that. "That may be a possibility. But the primary purpose, Jelly, is to have the photographs published in the magazine. You're going international, my friend. We're going to make you famous."

"I'm gonna be in *LIFE* Magazine?"

"Correct."

"No thank you."

Hoover sat up in his chair. "I'm not asking. This is a direct order."

Jelly was torn. The idea of being in LIFE was both exciting and disturbing. His instincts were screaming 'No no no' but his ego was thinking, *'Maybe?'* "But, Boss," he began when Hoover cut him off.

"Listen; I knew you wouldn't be thrilled with this idea, at least not initially, but just hear me out, Jelly. If we get your pictures in the magazine, identified as *Agent* Jelly Bryce, FBI, and people can see just how fast you are, how good you are, then that translates–in the public mind–that *all* our agents are that fast, that good. Do you see? It's a win, win, win. You get some recognition, the Bureau's reputation gets enhanced, people get to see what an honest-to-God G-man gunfighter looks like up close and personal." Hoover let that sink in for a moment before finishing with, "I really need you to do this for me, Jelly. You're the only man who can get this done."

Silence on the line.

"Can't you see?" Hoover continued, "I'm asking you to be the face of the Bureau, my friend. The face and the gun. This is no public relations gambit. This is shaping the public's perception of the Bureau, right down to the very fabric. They get a look at you wielding your blaster like nobody's business, and the message is clear: The Bureau protects the good folks by having the ability to eradicate the bad guys."

"Loved and feared," Jelly said in response.

Hoover sat back in his chair in the inner sanctum office and smiled. "Exactly."

*   *   *

The photo shoot went perfectly. It turned out to be a lot of work and took twice as long as originally estimated, but Jelly hadn't minded–he'd been fascinated by the process. The photographer, Gjon Mili, was a decent guy. Jelly hadn't really known what to expect since he hadn't spent a lot of time around bona fide geniuses, which is what he assumed Mili was. What he found was a funny, intense guy with a moustache who chain-smoked Camels and was obsessed with his work. Originally from Romania, Mili had emigrated to the US as a kid and had been living an interesting life ever since.

The idea was to take a series of photographs using the strobe light equipment to "freeze a moment in time in the image," as Mili put it. He'd been experimenting with the technique, and thought Jelly would be an interesting subject.

He started by taking some still images of Jelly so he could get used to the strobe. One of the strange things about the process was the studio lights were shut off just before the pictures were taken, plunging everything into blackness. The camera's shutter was then opened, and the strobe fired, capturing the image on the film.

Once they were set, Mili had Jelly draw his pistol nearly fifty times before he felt they'd captured the right sequence of images. When they were finally finished, Jelly felt like he'd just spent six hours at the gym; unlike his usual practice sessions where he "stepped into" the draw, the photo shoot required him to stay in his forward squatting position for five or more minutes at a time before drawing.

"Of course," Mili told him at the end, "if the images are no good once I develop them, we'll have to do this all again."

Jelly had smiled before he realized Mili was serious. "Not a problem," he said once he realized he was.

Before Jelly left, Mili asked him if he'd look at something for him. He showed Jelly an image in slide format; a little two-inch square card with a transparent image in the center. Holding it up to the light you could make it out. In this particular photo a bullet had been clearly captured in flight. It hung, suspended in the center of the image, about to strike an apple.

"Is that real?" Jelly asked.

"Oh yes," Mili answered, handing Jelly a jeweler's loupe to examine the image under magnification. "But there is a problem. My associate, Doc Edgerton took this photograph at M.I.T. But he is messing with me. He bet me I couldn't tell him which way the image went; in other words, was the bullet traveling from right to left, or left to right? Do you see?"

Jelly looked at the slide again. By flipping it over the image was reversed. To the untrained eye, nothing in the photograph could be used to determine the actual direction of flight. "Any idea what type of gun he fired this from?"

"Yes, actually," Mili replied. "He has an old rifle he uses for these bullet pictures. I believe it is called a 1903, a Springfield. It uses the bolt, you know? Does that make sense?"

Jelly smiled. "If that's the rifle he used, you just won your bet."

Mili looked at him soberly. "How so?"

"The bullet," Jelly replied, holding the little slide up to the light, "was traveling from left to right in front of the camera."

Mili squinted at the image. "But how could you know this? There is no key there, nothing to substantiate that."

"It's the marks on the bullet itself that tell you, my friend. That rifle has a right hand twist in the bore. See these little grooves on the side of the bullet?" He pointed with a pencil. The light marks were nearly invisible due to the small size of the image. "Those tell you which way the bullet was spinning in flight. The rifle has a right hand twist. This bullet was spinning to the right. That means the rifle was to the left of the apple when he fired this round."

Mili peered at it closely. "That is amazing!" He smiled at Jelly. "I hadn't even noticed those marks." He shook Jelly's hand, then asked, "And you're sure?"

"Sure as shootin'." Jelly smiled.

Mili laughed. "Wait 'till I tell Doc the answer. I'm going to enjoy this. He always likes to be the smartest guy in the room, you know? Well this time, I've got him. Thanks to you, my friend!"

"What do you win?" Jelly asked.

"Win?" Mili looked confused. "Oh, you mean the bet. I don't win anything. It's just the satisfaction of being right."

As they packed up their gear and Jelly was ready to go, Mili asked him if he had plans for the rest of the evening. Jelly shook his head. "Just heading to the hotel. I figured I'd get on a plane in the morning but now you're telling me we might not be done, right?"

"Yes," Mili said, "right. I'll be able to let you know around ten o'clock in the morning. Will that be all right?"

Jelly nodded. "My orders are to do whatever you need me to so we can get this done."

"Good," said Mili. "So then, if you don't have to get up early, how about coming to my loft? I have some people coming over tonight to play some music. You like Duke Ellington?"

Jelly nodded because he did, but he really didn't feel like going to an apartment and listening to records with a bunch of New York artist types. He was about to graciously decline the invitation when Mili said, "Oh good. He'll be there. Dizzy and Mezz are supposed to be coming too."

"Duke Ellington?" Jelly asked incredulously. "He'll be there at your loft? Playing?"

"Sure. And Dizzy Gillespie and some other guys. It will be good. We jam until the sun comes up or the booze runs out. You'll come, yes?"

Jelly thought about it for a New York minute. It was one of the most memorable nights of his life.

*   *   *

The story featuring Jelly along with Mili's dramatic photographs of him was published on November 12, 1945.

In the images, the strobe lights captured him moment by moment as he drew his Registered Magnum from his holster to firing position. The movement was timed at two-fifths of a second, the caption below describing it as "faster than the human eye can follow."

Jelly's friends and family were incredibly proud when the issue came out.

The law abiding public was thoroughly impressed with the G-Man's prowess, as was the criminal element–who were also made uneasy. "Don't fuck with the G-Men," became a common sentiment among them all, inspired in no small part by the layout in the popular magazine.

Hoover, above all, was pleased. It had gone just as he'd hoped. "I want that gun and those unnerving eyes to be the gun and the eyes of the United States Federal Bureau of Investigation," he'd declared back in 1934 while trying to recruit Jelly into the ranks of his Bureau. And now he had his wish. He especially loved the wrinkle Jelly had added to the photoshoot, by including a coin. In several of the pictures, the strobe caught Jelly releasing a coin from shoulder height, then drawing his pistol with the same hand and getting the gun out and pointed before the coin fell to that height. Hoover knew there were people all over the globe who were going to try and replicate that, and fail miserably. It warmed his heart to think about it: *"Two-fifths of a second, faster than the human eye can follow."*

Jelly wasn't disappointed with the article either. It

served its purpose as well as being a hoot for him, having his picture in *LIFE* Magazine and all. But Jelly also knew the caption about his draw being "faster than the human can follow" was a lie–at least as far as he was concerned.

His eyes could follow it. His eyes could see and track a moving bullet.

*   *   *

Jelly never realized there was anything unusual about his eyesight until he was twelve. He'd always taken for granted that everyone saw things the same way. Then one day while fooling around with the old .38 Smith & Wesson revolver his grandfather had given him, Jelly had his cousin Jimmy throw a tin can high into the air. Not only did Jelly hit it, but to his cousin's amazement, he hit it six times in one go, several of the impacts propelling the can back into the air in the process.

When the can landed in the field Jelly had looked at his cousin with a thrilled expression. It was the first time he'd ever attempted the trick.

"Let me try that!" Jimmy had said. After all, if his younger cousin could do that on the first attempt, how hard could it be? Eighteen rounds later he'd found out. Three times he'd loaded the pistol, and eighteen times he'd launched rounds at that can without once having them meet.

Jelly, arm tired from throwing the can, had squinted at his older cousin and said, "You're still shootin' too low. Your bullets are goin' under the can most every time."

Jimmy'd looked at him. "How could you possibly know where the bullets are going, kid?"

Jelly, exasperated, had sighed loudly. "Geez," he'd said, "aren't you even watching?"

"Watching *what*?"

Jelly'd slapped his palms against his thighs. "The gosh danged bullets, what else?"

Jimmy had given his cousin a withering look. "You don't need to be a wiseass, Delf. Ain't nobody in this whole world can see a bullet once it comes out the barrel. You know that."

This had mystified Jelly. Surely his cousin was messing with him. Jelly had always been able to easily track bullets, birds, insects, whatever, with his eyes. That's why he was always able to hit the things he shot at. To *his* eyes, the birds and rabbits moved like molasses compared to the bullets–even when running full tilt. Once he'd gotten used to the velocity of a particular bullet out of a specific gun, he could figure the lead instantly and easily. To top it off, there was plenty of room for error.

Take the jackrabbit for example. It's incredibly strong legs and tightly-wound muscles allowed an adult to reach a top speed of around 45 miles per hour–as fast as the early Model T Fords could go, throttle wide-opened.

But the little .22 caliber bullet he fired from his hunting rifle, well that was travelling at about 1,100 feet per second–or a whopping 750 miles per hour! So once Jelly was dialed in on his moving target, he'd intuitively lead it just enough so the bullet and bunny would arrive at the same spot at the same moment. Because the bullet was travelling so much faster, if there was any deviation on Jelly's part, such as breaking the shot a millisecond too soon or late, or miscalculating the lead by an inch or so, it usually made no difference. That rabbit's head was going to catch that bullet, and a headshot was a headshot.

Jelly's unusual eyesight was one of the reasons he'd become such a successful man hunter. Not only could he deliver his rounds with unerring accuracy on the much larger and normally slower human target, but when a gunman made an aggressive move for his pistol or other weapon, he moved dramatically slower than a startled bunny or bird.

As he'd become more experienced, Jelly'd also learned to look for his opponent's hand and forearm muscles flexing as the movement was initiated to access or fire their weapon. In response, he'd then initiate his own highly-practiced and conditioned movement, which, being so much faster, gave him the advantage. *Every time.*

It was a gift he filed under "God" in his "God, guns, and good luck" saying.

CHAPTER SIXTEEN

Austin
June 1946

THE YOUNG MAN, ALL of nineteen years old, walked confidently into the Oklahoma City FBI office and smiled at the secretary seated outside Jelly's office. "Hello," he said politely. "I'd like to talk to Agent Bryce."

"Your name?" she asked in reply, looking up at his handsome face, her eyes then scanning his suit and tie. *'Nice,'* she thought.

"Austin Delf Bryce."

"Oh, are you a relative?" she asked sweetly.

"Yes, ma'am. I'm his son."

The secretary couldn't conceal her surprise at that bit of information. Motioning her head toward the office behind her she asked, "*His* son?"

Austin looked back at her and calmly stated, "Yes."

The secretary, a young strawberry blonde named Marjorie Peel, squinted up at him, then smiled and said, "Oh yes, I can definitely see it."

Austin smiled back. "Is that a good thing or a bad thing?"

She laughed and replied, "A good thing. Definitely." Pressing the button on the intercom set on the left edge of her desk, she announced, "Mister Bryce, your son is here to see you."

Seconds later the door opened and Jelly appeared, big smile on his face. Austin hadn't seen his father in years, and wondered how he'd be greeted. He was pleasantly surprised. A moment later he was unpleasantly surprised when Jelly's face fell, smile vanishing as he locked eyes on Austin.

"Austin?"

"Yes, sir. Sorry I didn't phone ahead. I just hoped to catch you at the office."

Jelly hesitated, then motioned Austin into the office. "Miss Peel, please hold my calls for the next fifteen minutes."

Inside the office Jelly walked behind his desk and stood there, looking Austin over. "You look well," he said, then pointed to a chair in front of his desk. Austin walked toward the chair, but instead of sitting extended his hand.

Jelly nodded, extended his own and the men shook. Then they both sat down and stared at one another for a few uncomfortable moments. Jelly finally asked, "So, how's your mother?"

"Mom's fine, I guess, sir. As good as can be expected, I suppose."

Another nod from Jelly. Keeping his gaze on Austin, he picked up a pack of Lucky Strike cigarettes from the table and gave it a shake, a few white butts protruding from the small square opening. He held out the pack toward his son. Austin shook his head as the thought occurred to him how much the logo on the pack looked like a bullseye. "Never acquired the habit."

Jelly cocked his head, looked as if he was going to speak, then looked down and pulled a cigarette from the pack, tamped the end on the table and stuck it in the corner of his mouth. Cigarette dangling from his lips, he put down the pack and grabbed his lighter. Holding it in one hand, he slapped the top against his other, pressing the Zippo down then up, causing the cover to open and wheel to spin against his skin, lighting the flame. Holding the flame to the end of the cigarette he inhaled deeply, snapped the lighter's cover closed and placed it carefully on the desk again, next to the cigarettes. "So," he said as he exhaled a long stream of smoke toward Austin, "what brings you here?"

Austin cleared his throat. He'd rehearsed what he was about to say many times the past few weeks. "Well, sir, as you know, I've done really well all through high school. And now I'd like to go to college." He cleared his throat again. "And what I was hoping, was that maybe you'd be able to help me with that."

Jelly kept his eyes on Austin's as he took another drag off the smoke. "You want me to give you money for school, is that it?"

Austin nodded. "Yes, sir. Mom thought–"

Jelly interrupted him. "I'm not really concerned with what your mother thinks Austin. This is between you and me. I'm more concerned with what you think."

Austin swallowed. Nodded. "Okay."

"Now, you say I know you've done well in school? Well, the only reason I know that is because your mother has kept me informed about your progress. I've never heard a word from you about it, though, have I." It wasn't a question. "And so now, after years of not hearing back from you when I call or write, you show up here looking for money for college?"

Austin looked directly at his father and nodded. "That's what I'm doing, yes."

Jelly's eyebrows raised. He sat back into his chair. "You do know I never went to college, right?"

Austin nodded again.

"What exactly do you want to go to college for?"

Austin sat up straighter, cleared his throat once again and clearly stated, "I want to study law."

Jelly cocked his head slightly again, took another drag

and blew the smoke out through his nostrils. "Are you thinking about law enforcement? The Bureau?"

Austin's face set. A hardness came into his eyes. Jelly was surprised by this.

"No, sir. I don't want that life for myself or my family. I want to be a lawyer."

"What family?" Jelly asked.

"The family I plan to have one day. *That* family." Austin felt himself getting flushed. His eyes got a little wet. He was getting angry but it was trying to work its way out through his tear ducts.

"Jesus," Jelly said, "Please don't tell me you're gonna cry." Jelly crushed his cigarette out in the ashtray next to the telephone. "You know, Austin, I know you got a raw deal when you were a kid. And I know that a big piece of that was my fault. I do. I really do. And I feel bad about that. But this is a hard world, mister. You've gotta be tough and hard yourself or the world will chew you up and spit you out."

Austin's fists balled up tight. He pressed them into his thighs to keep them there. He wanted to yell at his father, scream all the things he'd held in for so many years; wanted to grab him by the lapels and slam him into the wall, pound his fists into his face, make him understand just what he'd put his son through all the days of his life. But most of all he wanted to ask, "What the hell is wrong with you?! How can you be like this?" Instead he sat there and stared at the man he knew as Delf Bryce. His father. The man he secretly always referred to as "Dad." For deep down, and with no true understanding of why, Austin loved Delf.

In many ways, he pitied him. His father didn't seem to understand what he'd missed, what he was missing. Austin didn't have an unrealistic view of himself–but he knew he was a good kid–*a good man*. He'd always been good. And the one person he needed to see that, to acknowledge it, just either couldn't–or wouldn't.

"Maybe you oughta think about going into the service," his father was saying now. "Join the Marines. They'll make a man of you. Give you some experience. Then once you get out, you'll have the G.I. Bill. Go to college, get your degree then, figure out what you want to do." Jelly stopped talking and looked at his oldest son. "Are you listening to me?"

Austin stood up, wiped his eyes with the heels of his hands and looked down at his father's face for the last time. He took a deep breath and slowly exhaled. A calmness came over the young man. Jelly could see it. "Oh, yes, sir. I hear you. I hear you loud and clear."

Austin turned, strode confidently to the door, opened it and walked through the doorway leaving it open behind him. Jelly watched as he walked straight through to the outer office exit and left. He never looked back.

* * *

Jelly's relationship with his first wife, Darlene, and the son they'd had together had always been complicated. After they'd first split up in late 1927 Jelly had gone back to Mountain View to figure things out. During that time, he'd managed to scrape together twenty-five dollars a month and sent it to Darlene for her and the boy she'd named Austin. After nearly a year of this and soon after he'd been hired by Oklahoma City PD, Darlene sent Jelly divorce papers.

He'd signed them. And though there was no alimony stipulation, he continued to send her money each month, his new police salary allowing him to up the ante to forty dollars.

After a few months of silence, Jelly called his now ex-wife on the telephone and asked her how she was doing for money. She'd angrily replied she didn't want or need any money from him, and then told him she was seeing a man– *'a real man'*–who was going to marry her and take care of her and Austin right.

Jelly had been a bit dumbfounded by her response, but took it in stride. Darlene had always been unpredictable and hard to understand. Before he could ask her if she really wanted him to stop sending her money each month she'd hung up the phone on him. He took that as her answer. Only years later did he learn that all the money he'd been sending her had been intercepted by her Aunt Florrie. Florrie had been letting Darlene and Austin stay with her since the split. Whenever one of Jelly's letters had arrived, she'd taken out the cash, thrown the letter away, and then given some or all of the money to Darlene, telling her it was a gift from her, since her niece had married a "no account" from Mountain View.

When Darlene told this to Jelly more than eight years later, he'd shaken his head, first angry, then simply disgusted. Florrie had always been a miserable, interfering pain in the ass of a woman. Darlene agreed when Jelly said that out loud during their first post-divorce meeting in 1936. Then she apologized to Jelly for all the awful things she'd thought and said about him for all those years. She'd felt abandoned by him, she'd tearfully told him, never learning the truth until Aunt Florrie lay on her death bed and confessed her deception.

"I just have to believe she meant well," she'd said to Jelly sadly.

Jelly'd nodded. "I suppose. But at least we know where she ended up."

Darlene'd raised her eyebrows in question at the remark.

"The road to Hell is paved with good intentions. I'm sure she's right at home."

Darlene had looked down, then smiled and nodded herself. "You're probably right, Delf."

That simple comment had helped reestablish a civil relationship between them. Darlene had never before taken Jelly's part in any way with any type of conflict between him and her blood relatives.

The day after that initial visit Darlene brought nine-year-old Austin to meet his father for the first time. Even though Austin had been raised by his mother's second husband, a banker named Richard Snow, he'd always known that Delf Bryce was his natural father. Darlene had chosen to never lie to the boy from the time he was born–with one exception.

Starting when Austin was around four or five years old, when she'd had a few drinks she'd tell him about his dad; tell him the stories of the wild shootouts and police work; about his superhuman prowess with firearms; and how she and his dad had a storybook romance but an unhappy marriage. Austin listened to the tales about his father, creating a picture in his mind of a man seven feet tall wearing a white Stetson and gunbelt festooned with shiny cartridges held in leather loops, drawing a revolver faster than any of the pistoleros he read about in the dime novels his mother bought him at the drug store. *His father*. His natural born father was a hero like you read about, like he saw in the serials at the theater in town. It was heady stuff.

Then one afternoon, when Darlene had a few more drinks than usual, she'd told Austin a story not based on fact like the others. She'd told him his father was going to come for him–come for them both and take them away. Darlene didn't know why she told Austin that. Later she'd confess to herself it was a combination of wishful thinking and alcohol. The alcohol had been pretty much a constant for a long while. The wishful thinking had started the second year into her second marriage to the banker.

Dick, as everyone called the banker, was a good provider. But he was a bit of a drinker himself. On top of that, he was insanely jealous of his wife's first husband, the copper. Over time, Dick's emotional cocktail of choice became a mixture of alcohol, insecurity, and anger, with a twist of cruelty directed at the only part of Delf Bryce he had the courage to confront directly–Austin.

"Your father's never coming for you," he'd sneer at the little boy. "It's been years since he abandoned you. If he was coming, don't you think he'd have been here by now? *Don't you?* Like it or not, I'm what you've got, kid. And believe you me–you and your mother will be lucky if I stick around."

Afraid, Austin wouldn't answer, but in his mind he pictured it often: the Hero with the white Stetson, pearl-handled pistol spinning on his trigger finger like a propeller, kicking in the door to their house, throttling the terrified banker with his left hand while he knocked him over the head with the butt of the gun in his right. *He'd* show him. His real father would show him and set things right. Then he'd scoop up Austin and his mom and take them away from this place, take them back to his cabin high up in the mountains where they'd live forever.

But the Hero never did come. For four long years Austin waited, listening to the banker's threats, feeling his open-palmed slaps to the back of his head, witnessing his cruelty to his mom and him, especially when the bottle was open on Friday and Saturday night.

Then, one spring Sunday morning, Austin's mom gently shook him awake, greeting his sleepy stare with her index finger to her lips. Whispering, she instructed her son to get up and get dressed. She pushed him into the bathroom with his toothbrush already covered in brushing powder and combed his hair as he scrubbed his teeth.

As they left the house, him trailing behind his mother as she pulled him along by the hand, she turned and smiled at him. "I have a surprise for you, honey."

Climbing into the backseat of their car, Austin stood up on the floor, hands draped over the front seat and repeatedly asked what the surprise was.

"You'll see," was all Darlene would say as she stepped on the gas pedal, propelling Austin backward into the big cushioned seat as she turned out of the driveway and down the street toward town.

When their car stopped in front of the drugstore, Austin got excited. The Veazy Drug Company not only provided medications, milkshakes, and hamburgers, but they maintained an inventory of toys and colorful knickknacks as well as shelves full of comic books and dime novels.

Darlene shut off the motor and turned in her seat. "Austin," she said seriously, reaching over and taking his hands in hers. "I'm going to introduce you to someone today, right now in fact."

Austin looked at her, disappointment in his eyes. "Can't I get a toy?"

Darlene smiled. "Of course, honey. But you need to listen to me now, this is very important. Okay?"

In response to his silent nod, Darlene said, "You're going to meet your father, Austin. Your real father. I want you to make a good impression now, okay honey? You look him right in the eye when you meet, shake his hand like a big boy, and say hello nice and loud. Can you do that?"

Austin didn't know what to say. He'd given up on the Hero. And now the Hero was here to come get him and take him away. His heart fluttered in his little chest. He smiled and nodded excitedly. This was like a dream, he thought. He'd never have to see the banker again.

Out of the car and into the drugstore, they wound their way to the back of the long narrow building, where two men dressed in dark suits were seated at a table. They both stood when they saw Darlene and Austin approaching.

At first Austin didn't understand why two men were there. Which was his father? The taller of the two men smiled when he saw the boy. Austin's first thought was, *'There he is!'* Then his mother directed him to the second man, smaller than the first, but as soon as Austin looked him in the face he knew.

Austin shyly looked into the man's eyes, extended his hand and said, "Hello, sir," with as much strength and conviction as he could muster.

*   *   *

Seeing his son for the first time in nearly nine years was a bit of a shock for Jelly. The young boy was unmistakably his. Though Darlene had sent him a few snapshots and told him about Austin, Jelly suddenly realized he wasn't prepared to meet him. It was all too real. The thought that he'd abandoned his son–a thought he'd suppressed and rationalized away–wriggled awake deep inside his chest and came tearing out, all teeth and claws. Jelly felt a warm surge of blood travel up through his chest, into his neck and across his face. He wondered if it showed as he reached out and grasped his son's extended hand for the first time since the boy was an infant.

"Hello, Austin," Jelly said formally in reply to the boy's own formal greeting. "I'm Delf."

The boy nodded up at him as Jelly released his hand.

"Would you like to sit down?" Jelly asked, motioning to one of the four chairs around the small round table. "Are you hungry?"

Austin shook his head, then looked at the other, taller man. Jelly glanced at the man and said, "This is Special Agent Lane. He's an FBI man like me, Austin. He took a ride with me today to meet you and your mom."

Darlene, who'd remained silent until this moment, placed her hand on Austin's shoulder and steered him into the seat. She'd hoped Jelly wouldn't feel the need to bring along a witness for this second meeting of theirs. But apparently he had. "Your dad's always been a cautious man, honey," she said, nodding at the tall, silent agent. "But maybe Mister Lane could sit at another table, close by?"

Jelly looked at Lane and nodded. The man stood and glanced around at the several other tables and booths.

"Not too far," Jelly said quietly.

Lane nodded and walked to a nearby booth, sat down and folded his hands on the table. Though he wasn't looking at them directly, both Jelly and Darlene knew he was listening and watching them in his peripheral vision.

Jelly and Darlene sat down opposite one another, Austin in between.

"So, Austin," Jelly began. "How do you like school?"

* * *

As soon as Austin heard the question, he knew in his heart the Hero wasn't there to take them away. He just knew. The banker had been right all these years. The boy's eyes filled with tears and he dropped his head into the crook of his elbow, arms folded across the table.

* * *

Over the next few years Jelly would stop by and visit

with Darlene and Austin using the same routine. Always in a public place; always in the company of a fellow agent who would serve as witness and discourage any mistakes or accusations.

During these short visits Jelly tried to establish some type of rapport with his son, but he found it difficult. The boy just didn't seem to like him very much. Jelly understood it. He was a stranger to the kid. Darlene's husband had actually raised him. He was the boy's true father.

When talking didn't work to open up a dialogue, Jelly tried other approaches. At the end of one visit at the Veazy Drug Company, Jelly placed his hand on Austin's shoulder, and with his other hand pointed to the shelves of toys in the back of the store. "Go pick something out, Austin," he said. "I'll buy you anything you want."

Austin looked up at Jelly, then back at his mother. Darlene smiled at him and nodded encouragingly. Austin walked toward the toy section, Jelly trailing close behind. The boy looked at everything, eyes and head moving up and down, back and forth. Finally, he pointed at the biggest item on the shelves, a backyard croquet set in a large, white cardboard box.

Jelly asked, "Are you sure?"

Austin nodded.

"Do you like croquet?"

The boy shrugged.

Jelly looked at Darlene. She shrugged as well.

"Okay, son." Jelly said as he pulled the box from the shelf.

Austin's eyes filled with tears. He turned away, his face in his hands, moved to his mother and pressed himself against her. Darlene wrapped her arms around him and looked at Jelly, dismayed.

Jelly watched this, horrified. His heart started pounding.

He had no idea what was wrong with Austin. The boy would cry at the drop of a hat for no apparent reason.

But there was a reason, though neither Jelly nor Darlene had caught it.

That had been the first time Jelly'd ever called Austin son.

* * *

On another occasion, with Darlene's permission, Jelly deviated from the normal visitation protocol and took Austin to a nearby shooting range. Just he and his son made that trip. At the range, Jelly laid out a few of his trick-shot props on a wooden table, tacked up a paper bullseye target to the wood-framed carrier ten yards away, and put on a performance for the boy.

First he shot the target rapid fire from hip level, delivering six rounds into a one, ragged hole group. Then he reloaded, and, keeping the pistol pointed downrange but holding his body sideways to the target, got himself into position for the next trick. As he did, it became apparent to Austin his father wasn't looking at the target or the pistol's sights–rather, he was staring at a diamond ring he wore on his left hand, holding the hand up next to the pistol. Jelly glanced at Austin and smiled. No response. "I'm using the reflection of the pistol's sights and target in the diamond, Austin. To aim the shot." Again nothing.

Jelly shot another tight group while staring at the brilliant stone. When he'd finished, he asked Austin what he thought. "That's a big diamond," the boy stated. "Why do you wear that?"

Jelly thought about that for a moment, then answered truthfully, "I saw it, I liked it, I had the money so I bought it."

Austin just looked away, blank expression painted on

his face.

Jelly chewed the inside of his cheek as he stared at the boy. "Okay, kid," he said a moment later, "Let's see how you like this, then." He walked to the table, placed the Registered Magnum down and unzipped a brown leather pistol case. Picking up the nickel-plated revolver within, he swung open the cylinder and showed Austin the chambers were empty. He held out the pistol to Austin. "Want to look at her?"

Austin squinted at the revolver. It was ornately engraved and had white grips. On one side was a steer's head with little red jeweled eyes. He reached out and accepted the gun, his hand dipping once the weight was completely under his control. "It's heavy," he said.

"It is."

Austin turned the gun over, looking at the other side of the grips. On that panel a number "13" had been cut in and colored black; something else was engraved below it. "What's that?" he asked, pointing at the black figure.

"That's a black cat. You know, like bad luck. Like the number thirteen. I call her my lucky gun." Jelly smiled again.

Austin looked up and said, "Doesn't look like a cat. Or maybe a cat that got run over by a truck or somethin'."

Jelly inwardly sighed. "Yeah, well," he began, reaching out for the gun, "maybe that's why the cat was unlucky–gettin' run over and such."

Opening a cardboard box filled with .44 special cartridges, Jelly pulled four out and slipped them into the revolver's chambers. Then he fished out a coin from his pants pocket and held it up for Austin to see. "Mexican peso."

The boy nodded.

"I use these because it's against the law to damage or

destroy US currency."

Jelly turned and took a few steps away from the table. Then he stopped, looked at Austin and said, "Now watch closely, Austin. The idea is I throw the coin up in the air and shoot it. If I hit it, it's going to fly a long way. Let's try and see if we can find it after, okay?"

Austin nodded. Jelly tossed the coin high up in the air, raised his lucky gun and fired one round. There was a distinctive sound as the bullet hit the coin. The coin immediately disappeared from view. Jelly seemed to be watching it, but Austin had no idea where it went. "Could you see it?" Jelly asked after a bit, looking into his son's hazel eyes.

Austin shook his head.

"Well, maybe the sun was in your eyes," Jelly offered. He'd been curious to see if his son had inherited his extraordinary vision. "So, what'd ya think?"

"It was all right," Austin said glumly.

Not understanding the boy's tepid responses, Jelly walked across the field to where he'd seen the coin land, scanned the ground for a few seconds, then bent over and picked up the peso. It had a hole clean through it, close to the edge. He turned and brought the coin to Austin and handed it to him. "That's for you, if you'd like it."

Austin stared at the coin and nodded, then slipped it in his pocket.

Jelly opened the lucky gun's cylinder and emptied out the three remaining live rounds and single spent casing. Placing the big revolver carefully down on the table, he leaned back against the edge of the table and folded his arms across his chest.

"Austin," he asked gently, looking down at the boy, "is everything all right?"

Austin shrugged. Jelly was stymied. Since their first

meeting when the boy had burst into tears for no apparent reason, Jelly had found it hard to relate to his son.

"Austin," he said, more sternly than intended, "is there anything wrong? Do you want to ask me anything? Or tell me anything? Is everything all right at home?"

The boy looked vacantly back at him and shook his head. Then he spoke. "Momma says you're fast on the draw like Tom Mix."

Jelly chewed the inside of his cheek again as he looked at the boy, trying to read him. He nodded. "I'm fast enough, I guess. Why? Do you like that? The fast draw stuff?"

Austin nodded.

"Would you like to see me draw?"

Another nod.

Jelly said, "Okay, sure," then picked Austin up under his armpits and set him on top of the wooden table. Austin sat there looking at him, legs swinging over the edge, hands flat on the planked table top.

Jelly picked up the unloaded Registered Magnum and slipped it into his holster, letting his suitcoat cover it.

Stepping back a little and turning his right side toward his audience of one, Jelly smiled at Austin, settled himself by taking a few slow breaths, then became completely still. Focusing on something off in the distance, Jelly executed the draw he'd practiced an uncountable number of times. The gun appeared as if by magic in his right hand at hip level. Holding the position for a moment, he came out of his trancelike state and lowered the pistol. Looking at Austin expecting to see the usual disbelief, joy, or excitement his drawing demonstration usually elicited, he saw instead the same bored look the boy always seemed to have. Jelly raised his eyebrows in question. "How was that?"

"Weren't so fast," the boy replied evenly, no trace of sarcasm or satire in his voice.

'Fuckin' kid is inscrutable,' Jelly thought. *'Like a Chinaman.'*

"You, Mister Austin," Jelly said, "are one tough audience. All right, let's try something else. This I know you're gonna like."

Jelly started walking back toward his sedan. Austin scrambled off the table and landed flatfooted on the soft earth, then started following Jelly toward the car.

Reaching into the trunk, Jelly pulled out a black case, placed it on the ground and opened it. Inside sat a Thompson Submachine Gun, all gleaming blue steel and polished wood. Out of the corner of his eye he could see a look of awe spread over the boy's face. *'Finally,'* he thought. "Do you know what that is?"

"Tommy gun!" Austin answered excitedly. "Is that a *real* Tommy gun?"

"It is," Jelly replied, looking at the quickly setting late afternoon sun. "This is an M1928A1 Thompson Submachine Gun, Austin. And in just a little bit, I'll show you how it works."

Austin kneeled down on the ground staring at the gun in its case as Jelly reached into the back seat of the sedan, opened a small cooler and took out a paper-wrapped bologna and cheese sandwich and a bottle of pop.

"Hey," Jelly said.

Austin tore his eyes away from the gun and looked up. Jelly handed the sandwich to him, then took the cap off the bottle with his small, blue-handled opener and gave the boy the soda as well. Leaning back against the car, Jelly shook a cigarette from his pack and lit it, gazing off across the field. He'd taken a second drag off the smoke before he realized Austin was just looking up at him, sandwich and pop in his hands.

"Eat," Jelly said.

The boy sat down cross-legged on the ground next to the case and ate as he stared at the deadly machine he'd previously only seen in movies and magazines. It was awesome.

* * *

Half an hour after Austin had wolfed down the sandwich and finished the pop it had grown dark enough for what Jelly had planned. As Austin watched, Jelly pulled back the cocking handle on top of the Tommy Gun's receiver, then slid a 50-round drum magazine sideways into the submachine gun.

"The stick magazines are easier to work with," he said as he fiddled the drum into place, "but they only hold twenty rounds. Won't work for what I'm gonna show you."

Jelly checked the selector and safety levers, then took a few long steps away from his son. He planted his feet in a wide stance, looked over his shoulder, smiled and said, "You might want to put your fingers in your ears. This'll be loud."

Austin was confused. It was too dark to make out any more than the silhouettes of the target frames across the range. He had no idea what type of trick shooting could be done in the dark.

Then Jelly leaned back, pointing the muzzle up at the night sky. Austin had barely gotten his index fingers planted in his ear holes when a tremendous, jackhammering noise began, the Thompson's heavy steel bolt slamming back and forth at a cyclic rate of nearly 700 rounds a minute.

Austin's eyes were first locked on the gun, for each time it fired a round the bolt snapped back and forth and a strobe-like flame leaped from the end of the muzzle. Then his eyes were drawn to a strange series of little flaming lights leaping into the sky. Jelly was firing a magazine full of tracer rounds. The ammunition contained a small pyrotechnic charge in the base. When each round was fired, the pyrotechnic composition burned very brightly, making it possible for normal humans to follow the trajectory of the bullet with the naked eye.

Jelly was using the gun to show his son one of the tricks he used in his shooting demonstrations. By moving the gun while shooting the tracers it was possible to spell out letters in the night sky. The burning phosphorous left a visible trail that hung in the air for a moment, long after the bullets themselves had dropped back to Earth. It was a neat effect.

As Austin watched the light show, Jelly spelled out "FBI," then put a period after each letter before the first tracers had burned out.

Austin smiled and laughed unselfconsciously as Jelly lowered the subgun and looked back at him. Then Jelly removed the nearly empty drum magazine, placed it on the ground and retrieved a twenty-round stick or "box" magazine from his pants pocket. He pressed the magazine straight up until it locked, pulled the cocking lever to the rear and got back into his stance. This time he drew a big letter "A" in the inky darkness, dropping a perfectly placed last shot for the period.

Lowering the Tommy Gun, Jelly turned and looked at Austin. "That's an A for Austin. That's for you, son," Jelly said as he smiled at his boy.

CHAPTER SEVENTEEN

Booming Business
April 1948

"JELLY SAW JIM KENNEDY from across the diner and waved. Kennedy stood up and walked around the long, white, curved counter. The men met halfway, shook hands and smiled warmly at each other. They were friends in the way that regardless of how long it's been since last seeing one another, it always seemed like picking up the conversation from where they'd left off a day before. And their conversations always started the same, perfunctory way.

"How's the family?" Jelly would ask.

"Good, good. How's yours?" Kennedy would quickly answer.

"Good, good, everyone's good." Jelly would reply in the same dismissive manner.

Then they would laugh and talk about work. It wasn't that they didn't love their families. They did. Loved them more than anything. But they'd always been obsessed with the work. They were addicted to the game. And like two stone-cold junkies with a bag of smack they would shoot up and get high on the hunt, forgetting everyone and everything else until they'd bagged their quarry. One way or another.

"So who's the bunny?" Jelly asked once they'd taken their seats in a red vinyl-covered booth.

Before answering, Kennedy dropped a nickel into the small jukebox mounted to the wall of their booth and pressed a few buttons. Frank Sinatra started crooning.

Talking low, Kennedy smiled and said, "Not a bunny–an owl. Willie 'The Owl' Green. Mob guy out of southern Illinois. Been on a one man killing spree from one end of the country to the other–at least that's what we're hearing. Started with contracts on the Shelton brothers, but it seems killing for business and money isn't enough for him anymore. Now he's taken to butchering prostitutes along the way. Almost like a hobby for him, I guess."

The Shelton brothers were bootleggers who'd graduated to full-scale racketeering in the late '30s. Early innovators, they'd adopted machine guns and armored cars well before most of gangland had thought of it. In 1926, they'd even gone so far as to hire a cropduster to drop dynamite bombs on a rival's fortified headquarters. The aerial bombing missed the intended target, one Charlie Birger.

Birger got creative himself in his response–instead of bullets or bombs, he'd had the Shelton brothers framed for mail robbery. That plan fell apart when one of Birger's men rolled over and confessed to the perjury.

The Shelton brothers returned to power after that and were doing just fine until they became an annoyance for the Chicago Syndicate. That's when The Owl was hired to put the Shelton brother's problem to bed in a more traditional, blood and bullets manner–which he did.

"Why 'owl?' " Jelly asked, more out of politeness than real curiosity. Everyone had a nickname, it seemed, and it was getting old.

"Don't know. Don't care." Kennedy apparently felt the same.

Jelly nodded. "So, what's his deal?"

"Oh, this guy's a beaut. His professional work he uses a pistol, silenced .22; puts a few in the hat, dumps the body or just leaves it in the trunk of a hot box until someone complains about the smell. But his personal work, that's something different." Kennedy shook his head and leaned further across the table toward Jelly. "Fancies himself a real Jack the Ripper, apparently. There's no mistaking his work. He takes pieces of the girls with him. We don't know if he's keeping trophies or eating the parts. We've seen both as you know. Either way he's a sick fuck."

Jelly nodded again. "Swell. So what's the play?"

Just then the waitress stopped by with two white coffee cups and a pot of coffee. Placing the cups down, she filled them without asking, then looked wearily at the lawmen. "Cream?" Both men shook their heads. In response she pulled a pencil and small green pad out of her apron pocket and stood there, waiting for their order. They both opted for the breakfast special, stack of pancakes and coffee. As Kennedy outlined his plan, Jelly watched the waitress walk to the short-order cook and pass him the order slip from her pad. The cook had prison written all over him, and by the way he was looking at them, he'd apparently sensed which tribe they belonged to as well.

As Kennedy laid out the plan to catch or kill their criminally insane bird of prey, Jelly kept an eye on the cook. He didn't like anyone messing with his food and this guy looked like the type who would. His hunch was proven right a few minutes later as he watched the cook flip one of the pancakes right off the spatula onto the dirty floor. When the cook cast a glance Jelly's way, Jelly appeared to be looking at Kennedy, deep in conversation. But Jelly was watching in his peripheral vision as the cook bent over and picked up the pancake, wiped it off on his dirty white apron and put it back on the griddle.

Looking into the coffee cup, Jelly saw something tiny with legs floating in it. He put his hand over Kennedy's cup and shook his head. "This place is fucked. Let's get out of here."

Their conversation completed anyway, Kennedy nodded and the men stood up and walked to the counter.

"Something wrong?" the waitress asked disinterestedly.

"Yeah, we gotta go," replied Kennedy diplomatically.

The cook turned from the griddle, holding two white plates with a stack of tan, yellow-ringed pancakes on each. "What about your order?" he asked, a surly edge to his voice.

"Next time," Kennedy said.

"Fine," said the cook, unceremoniously tossing the plates on the counter and then planting his hands, palms down, beside them, "but that's still seventy-five cents for the coffees and pancakes, Mack."

As Kennedy was about to reply, he saw the cook's eyes swivel toward Jelly; the man's aggressive attitude suddenly vanished and he stepped back from the counter. Kennedy looked to his right and saw Jelly standing there calmly, Registered Magnum in his hand lying flat on the counter top.

"How much?" asked Jelly.

Without missing a beat, the cook replied, "I said that will be ten cents for the coffee."

Jelly's mouth curled into a grin but the rest of his face didn't join in. Reaching into his jacket pocket with his left hand, Jelly fished around and pulled out a dime. Placing the dime on top of his thumbnail, he placed the tip of his thumb into the crook of his curled index finger and flicked the dime into the air. It spun over the counter in a perfect arc and came down on top of the griddle, instantly stuck in the film of sizzling grease.

The cook, waitress, and Kennedy watched the coin travel up, over and down. The image of their synchronized head movements amused Jelly, though his face stayed frozen in the same oddly disturbing expression.

The cook swallowed hard, looked back at Jelly. Jelly's

hands were empty. The gun had vanished. The lawmen walked out of the silent diner.

Once outside the men walked for a block before Kennedy started laughing so hard he had to stop for a minute.

"You crazy bastard."

Jelly smiled. "Aw, fuck him. If he hasn't done time, I'm a monkey's uncle. Besides, he dropped your pancake on the floor and put it back on the plate."

Kennedy stopped laughing and looked at Jelly. "Really?"

Jelly nodded.

"How do you know it was my pancake?" Kennedy asked.

Jelly smiled and said with conviction, "It certainly wasn't mine."

The men started walking again and Kennedy said, "I recently heard a story about you in another restaurant where your heater made a guest appearance. What I heard was you and the Boss were waiting to be waited on and it looked like you were being ignored, so you took out your pistol and put a round into the ceiling."

Jelly grinned. "Who told you that?"

"Doesn't matter. Is it true?"

Jelly kept smiling and picked up the pace. "Come on," he said, "we've got work to do."

* * *

Exactly one week later, Willie "The Owl" Green was lying on the table of the Illinois Medical Examiner's Office.

Jelly and Kennedy had tracked him down fairly easily; the Owl was used to being the hunter, not the hunted. When the two lawmen made their approach as the contract killer was leaving a saloon, Willie miscalculated just how fast and dangerous he was with his specially-modified .22 Colt Woodsman. Jelly shot him once in the throat, the booming Magnum round taking a chunk of spine with it as it blew out the back of his neck and drilled lead, blood and bone into the mortar of the brick wall behind the instantly deceased psychopath.

The little Colt fell from the Owl's hand, eleven rounds unfired and intact in the magazine and chamber.

It had all happened so fast, and the two agents' reactions were so calm, that the lone couple walking a block away who'd heard the loud sound of the shot and looked in the direction from which it had come saw nothing to make them think it had been more than a car backfiring.

Inside the saloon, the few patrons who were still somewhat sober barely noticed the noise, absorbed in the fight being broadcast on the radio at full volume.

As the gun smoke wafted away, Jelly and Kennedy bent over, grabbed Green under the arms, picked him up and dragged him into a seated position against the wall. Jelly slumped the dead man's head forward, arranging his hat so it looked as though he were passed out. A quick pat frisk of the body turned up a Maxim suppressor in a jacket pocket. Jelly was glad that was the only evidence of The Owl's criminal activities found. He'd been afraid of finding some poor girl's body part in a bag.

Taking out a cigarette and lighting it, Jelly sedately smoked while he waited for Kennedy to go back into the saloon and telephone an ambulance to take them all back to the morgue.

Neither agent saw any reason to bother the local police with the matter. The case was closed and the little trace of their work they'd leave behind was quickly congealing on the wall.

* * *

The next afternoon, at Hoover's insistence, Jelly met with the press. Hoover had set up a conference in a hotel in town, and all his media contacts had been encouraged to send people to attend. They did. The small room just off the lobby of the hotel was packed with reporters and photographers. After introducing himself, Jelly gave a brief statement, describing the background and criminal record of one Willie Green. He then explained that "Mister Green had been located in town, and in the process of effecting the arrest, he resisted violently, resulting in his death."

A few flash bulbs popped, and a couple of softball questions were tossed Jelly's way. He answered them all professionally, efficiently, and politely. Then a woman at the back of the pack raised her hand. Jelly smiled and acknowledged her with a friendly "Yes, Ma'am."

The attractive brunette reporter smiled back at him, then snapped off what she apparently imagined would be a knuckle ball.

"Agent Bryce, isn't it true this is far from the first suspect you've had 'violently resist you' as you put it, when making an arrest?"

Several of the other reporters turned to look at her in surprise. This wasn't the usual type of question asked at these things. Then everyone turned to look at Jelly, curious about his response.

Jelly stood calmly, smile still on his face. A moment passed. The woman felt emboldened. Just before she asked a follow up question, Jelly replied, "It *is* true, Miss…?"

"O'Neil. Bertie O'Neil, Illinois Chronicle."

Jelly remembered the woman's name. This was the reporter who'd blown up Charlie Winstead with the commie question back in '42. Apparently she'd relocated from the southwest.

"True, but not really surprising, is it?" Jelly asked kindly, giving nothing away. "These are, after all, violent criminals we're dealing with. You did hear my description of Mister Green's history, did you not?"

The reporter nodded and felt her face flush a bit. She was not going to be intimidated by this patronizing, cocky lawman. She recognized Agent Bryce and all these policemen for what they were: violent, oppressive thugs. "I did," she said, an edge coming into her voice, "I was just wondering if you'd ever considered bringing a suspect back *alive*?"

Jelly's gaze locked on her for just a heartbeat before he said, "Actually, Miss O'Neil, I'm more concerned with bringing me back alive."

The room erupted in laughter. O'Neil's face flushed hot again, and before she could follow up with another remark Jelly thanked everyone for coming and ended the press conference.

As the reporters filed out of the room, talking and comparing notes, Jelly watched the woman push through them, all business and anger in her stride. Several of the male reporters looked at her and chuckled as she passed.

'Fuck her,' Jelly thought. The woman was an aberration. Most reporters understood the police were the only thing standing between the public and the vicious thugs that would prey on them unchecked if the lawmen didn't do their jobs.

As for his response to her question, even though he'd delivered it with the intent of getting a laugh and making her look silly for asking it, his answer had been honest. He *was* more concerned with bringing himself back alive. He'd never considered the idea of sacrificing himself as viable. In his experience, the only people who ever thought it was a good or noble idea to put your own life at more risk than necessary while dealing with criminals were the people who weren't involved in the actual doing of it.

"Silly, naïve fucksticks," Jelly mused quietly as the hotel's maintenance crew entered the room and started breaking down the podium and chairs.

He was relieved most people could see the insanity of equating as much value to a violent criminal's life as an honest lawman's.

CHAPTER EIGHTEEN

Enjoy it All, Little Brother
19 January 1950

"DELF, HOUSTON IS ILL."

Jelly's heart sank after hearing Vivian Wilder say those four words over the telephone line. It wasn't just the heartbreaking way she said it, her voice catching; it was the words themselves. H.V. Wilder was never "ill." He was made of iron and let everyone know it. This conversation could only have a bad end. Vivian went on to explain H.V. had been feeling unusually "under the weather" for several months. She'd finally badgered him into seeing a doctor. When he'd come home later that afternoon he'd been "pale as a ghost," Vivian said. She'd started crying. Jelly had told her to hang up. He was on the way.

When he'd pulled up outside their house Vivian had come out to meet him. She apologized for breaking down on the phone then broke down again in his arms. "Oh, Delf," she said, "Whatever will I do without him?"

"What is it, Viv?"

"It's his liver. Cancer. They say he doesn't have long." Vivian took a few deep breaths and steadied herself. She was wearing a white apron. She lifted the bottom to her eyes and wiped them and her face. Then she straightened herself up, forced a smile at Jelly and said, "Okay, come in. He wants to see you."

To Jelly's surprise Wilder wasn't laid out in bed. He wasn't even sitting down. He was bent over fiddling with the radio trying to fine tune a station. Vivian called out,

"Houston, look. Someone's here to see you."

H.V. turned, saw Jelly, and smiled. "Well looky here! Mister F.B.I. himself in my very own parlor!"

The two men shook hands, H.V. sandwiching Jelly's right hand between his big mitts.

"Sorry it's been so long since I've been here, H.V.," Jelly said, shaking his head. "Things just got away from me last few years." Though the two men saw each other occasionally at the police station while working cases, they hadn't had much time to socialize, even since Jelly's transfer back to Oklahoma City.

H.V. waved him off. "Don't be silly. I know you're busy. We're all busy."

Vivian watched the two men, remembering all the scenes that had played out in the house over the years between them. H.V. had basically adopted Jelly when he was a rookie officer, and helped groom him through the years into a competent, distinguished detective. The legendary gunman stuff was something else. That was all Jelly. "How about something to eat? Coffee and pie?" she asked hopefully.

Jelly was about to answer when H.V. gave him a look and Jelly held off. The two men had been friends and partners so long they could communicate in subtle ways. Words weren't always necessary.

"That would be lovely, darling," H.V. said nodding at her. "Me and Delf are just gonna sit down and catch up for a bit, okay?"

Vivian picked up the bottom of her apron again and nervously wiped her hands on it, smiled, then walked out into the kitchen and started assembling the food.

H.V. waited until he heard her moving things around in the kitchen before he prodded Jelly toward the dining room table. "Sit," he said, indicating the chair at the head of the table. Jelly glanced at the seat back and saw the old rub marks from the grip of his holstered lucky gun were still there. He sat down on the chair, careful to position himself so the holstered Magnum revolver wouldn't do the same.

H.V. pulled out the chair directly to the side of Jelly's and sat down. The two men looked at each other for a minute. "She told ya, didn't she?"

Jelly nodded. "She did."

"Well, all right then. Seems I'm in a bit of a fix, don't it?"

Jelly nodded again. "I suppose. What about another doctor? You've gotta see someone else, H.V. You can't trust the opinion of just one man, not with somethin' like this."

H.V. looked down at the table. "I know what you're sayin', Delf. But trust me, little brother, there's no need. I can feel it. Been coming on a while. I should have had it checked sooner, but I was stubborn."

Jelly nodded. "Hard to believe, you bein' stubborn."

H.V. looked up and smiled. "I know, so unlike me, right?"

Both men smiled.

"'Bout a week before I went to the doctor, I had a weird coughing fit, you know? Coughed from so deep, then something came up. I spit it out." He nodded. "I was hoping that was it. Thought I'd gotten rid of whatever had been making me feel so bad, you know?"

Jelly nodded.

"But it weren't. And it didn't. So I went and the doctor ran a bunch of tests and he told me it was a cancer. In my liver and spreading fast. I asked how long and he just patted my shoulder and said, 'I'm sorry, Mister Wilder. You should have time to get your affairs in order, and I would do it as soon as you can.' And so, I guess that is that."

"But H.V.," Jelly started to say when his friend cut him off. "I know, second opinion, but I'm telling you Delf, that won't do no good." He looked at Jelly and smiled again. "I can't tell you how happy I am to have you here, little brother."

Jelly didn't know what to say, so he just nodded, whispered, "Of course."

Vivian came out of the kitchen carrying forks and two plates with big slices of blueberry pie. She set them down on the table, then just as quickly walked back to the kitchen, returning a moment later with two cups of black coffee. "Here you go," she said with a sad smile. "You two visit. I've got a few things to do."

H.V. and Jelly thanked her, then watched her leave the room.

H.V. leaned in and whispered, "Viv is the one I'm really worried about, Delf. My daughter's livin' her own life, you know? As it should be. And with our boy, Jason, gone in the war, well, I just can't stand to think of her bein' alone out here." The big man's eyes got a little watery. In all the years he'd known H.V., despite all the awful things they'd witnessed together, Jelly had never seen a tear from him. He'd even been a rock when his son was buried, giving a eulogy that had everyone both laughing and crying before he'd finished.

"Don't think about that right now, H.V. And you know–both of you know, that if either one of you needs anything, I'll be there. Always."

H.V. took a deep breath, blew it out and nodded. The steel came back into his eyes. "I know that. I've always known that." He smiled at his old partner, picked up his fork and sliced off a piece of pie. "Have some pie, Delf."

Jelly just looked at him.

"You know," H.V. said, holding the fork up to his nose and breathing in the sweet aroma, "my old man always used to say, 'You never know when you're putting on your last shirt.' " He put the pie in his mouth and closed his eyes, chewing slowly. After swallowing, he opened his eyes and looked at Jelly, then said calmly, "And, you never know when you're eating your last piece of pie. Enjoy it all, little brother."

*   *   *

As usual, Houston Vard Wilder did things his own way. His doctor had wanted him in the hospital for some experimental treatments using both radiation and chemicals that had been derived from mustard gas. As soon as H.V. heard the words "mustard gas" he'd adamantly refused to have anything further to do with it. "I spent too much of my time in the Great War dodging that shit to go and let you all use it on me now."

Despite the doctors' best efforts to explain how the compound, called nitrogen mustard, might help slow the spread of the cancer, H.V. was unmovable after they'd answered his question: "If I let you experiment on me, can you guarantee me even one additional day in this world?"

The doctors had silently shaken their heads in response.

"No thank you, then, gentlemen," he'd said with finality. "If the good Lord wants me home with Him, His son, and my son, then I won't be interfering with that none."

Over the course of the next few weeks H.V. deteriorated quickly. The whites of his eyes turned a sickly yellow shade followed by his skin. Weight started to fall off him at a shocking rate. His abdomen swelled noticeably. Though he tried to hide it, it was obvious he was in a lot of pain.

Jelly visited him regularly. When H.V. had first checked into the hospital, Jelly had smuggled in a hip flask filled with Jameson Whiskey. Vivian would later tell Jelly that H.V. would take a swig now and then, proudly telling whichever visitor was present that Jelly had given him the flask. When one visitor asked if the whiskey helped, H.V. had honestly answered, "Can't hurt."

* * *

One afternoon while Jelly was at work running a meeting about a case currently under investigation, his secretary interrupted. "Mister Bryce, Lieutenant Wilder's wife just called, said you need to get to the hospital right away."

The several agents and stenographer present all looked at Jelly, worried he may feel obligated to finish the meeting; for one of the few times in his career, Jelly walked away from the job to attend to a personal matter.

When he got to H.V.'s hospital room he was greeted by Vivian, her daughter, Olivia, and Olivia's husband and children. Both Viv and Olivia had tears in their eyes. Vivian took Jelly's hand and whispered, "The doctor's with him now. He says this is it, Delf." Jelly looked at the bed. The big white drape had been slid closed around it.

A few minutes later the doctor emerged, reached up and slid the screen open. H.V. was lying on the bed looking like a cadaver. "He doesn't have much time," the doctor said quietly, patting Vivian gently on the shoulder as he walked slowly out of the room.

"We've said goodbye, Delf," Vivian said. "You go ahead and talk to him. He was asking for you this morning before he took a bad turn."

Jelly nodded and went to H.V.'s side. "It's me, H.V., it's Delf." Jelly placed his hand on top of his friend's. H.V.'s hand was cold and waxy to the touch. His eyes were closed but he smiled.

"Delf," H.V. whispered weakly.
"It's me, brother."
H.V. smiled.

Jelly leaned in, kissed H.V. on the top of his head. "I love you, my friend," he said quietly.

H.V. whispered back, "Thank you." Then he grimaced in pain.

Jelly, trying to comfort him, said, "It's all right, Houston. You're just falling back. It's time to fall back and regroup."

H.V.'s eyebrows knitted together. "Regroup?" he asked quietly.

"Yes," Jelly said. "Time to regroup."

H.V. nodded. "Yes," he said, slightly louder, "Time to regroup. This is just a temporary situation."

As Jelly watched, a transformation took place before his eyes. H.V. started to breathe deeper. His hands started to flex. He opened his eyes.

Twenty minutes later, H.V. Wilder was sitting up in bed. "I could use some scrambled eggs," he said.

No one could believe it, including the doctors who came into the room and checked H.V.'s vitals. "This should not be happening," H.V.'s doctor said to Jelly. Then he asked, "What did you say to him?"

"I just said it was time to regroup. You know, I meant like fall back to Heaven and regroup with his son and the men he'd served with who'd gone on ahead."

The doctor shook his head. "Well apparently, it had a very different meaning to him."

Jelly stayed at the hospital for another two hours. H.V. had rallied completely it seemed. He ate a big plate of scrambled eggs, drank some coffee–even had Jelly pour a little whiskey from the flask into the cup.

Vivian was exhausted by the sudden turn of events, pleasing as they were. Her mind had just accepted the love of her life's death and now he was sitting there smiling, holding court, telling some of his corny jokes to the doctors examining him.

"I haven't spoken a word to my mother-in-law in two years," Vivian heard him saying, watching as one of the doctors politely asked why. H.V delivered the punchline, "Didn't want to interrupt her," then started laughing. The doctors joined in.

Standing next to the doorway, Vivian smiled up at Jelly as he kissed her cheek on the way out.

"Toughest son of a bitch I've ever known in my life," he said admiringly in her ear.

"I know he is," Vivian answered proudly.

*   *   *

The next morning Jelly received a call from Vivian.

"Houston's gone, Delf," she said calmly and quietly. "He went during the night. He'd rallied so strongly the doctor told us all to go home and get some sleep, come back tomorrow. We finally did though I really didn't want to."

"I'm so sorry, Viv." Jelly said.

"The doctor said he checked on Houston about three a.m. and he was laying back on the pillows with his eyes open. When he saw the doctor, he saluted him, smiled, then closed his eyes and was gone."

*   *   *

They buried H.V. with full military honors in his World War One, US Army uniform. Jelly and Clarence Hurt prepared the uniform, polishing the boots, making sure all the ribbons were displayed properly.

Officers from the Oklahoma City Police Department stood post at either end of the casket during the service for the 35-year police veteran.

Before the funeral staff closed and locked the casket, Jelly slipped the fully-filled flask into H.V.'s inside right-breast jacket pocket; in the left-breast pocket he slid a blued, Colt Police Positive revolver. The chambers were loaded with .38 S&W cartridges. "Not sending you into the afterlife unarmed," Jelly whispered in H.V.'s ear before he kissed him on the forehead.

Clarence Hurt waited until Jelly moved away from the casket before he placed a silver dollar in H.V.'s cold right hand. "For the toll," he said, patting his friend's shoulder for the last time.

*   *   *

Following the death of her beloved husband, Vivian mourned for two months. Then one morning she took out H.V.'s Smith and Wesson Model 10, cleaned and oiled it like he'd taught her, and made a decision.

She filled out an application for a deputy sheriff's position with the Oklahoma County Sheriff's Office. She'd get the job, serving proudly for 26 years until retiring in 1973.

On August 1, 2000, after a short illness, Vivian would pass away surrounded by family and friends, and be laid to rest next to H.V. at the Sunny Lane Cemetery in Del City, Oklahoma. She would live to be 97 years old. She never remarried.

CHAPTER NINETEEN

The Bryce Effect
October 1955

THERE WAS AN EVERGREEN tree in the front yard of Jelly's home, a windswept, Eastern red cedar. It was a handsome specimen, standing off by itself about twenty yards from the house next to the driveway. The thick trunk and limbs wore heavy bark, an appropriate skin for a tough old Oklahoma native. During the winter the old tree produced crops of blue cones among the almost delicate deep green needles, small cones that looked like berries and attracted a variety of birds. Francine and Jimmy loved the tree. So did the neighbors and all of the visitors to the Bryce homestead. Its dramatic shape and presence rarely went unnoticed or unappreciated by all who saw it. The only one who didn't like the tree was Jelly. He actually loathed it.

His hatred for the striking cedar tree began one night as he drove home after dealing with a hostage situation. He'd turned the corner up his drive, the tree greeting him as always, solid and solitary, but as the headlights of his Cadillac panned across the trunk Jelly had seen something in the shadows behind it. His heart had revved up as the adrenalin hit his bloodstream and everything else slowed way down for him. His mind worked at lightning speed, causing the perceptual slow motion effect, but Jelly–so used to operating in this state–didn't even realize this was happening. Everything seemed to be happening in regular time. And in regular time his foot crushed the brake pedal to the floor, he palm-slapped the gear selector on the steering wheel into park, threw open the door and rolled out of the car, coming up with his big blaster in his hand and cleared around the tree.

Nothing had been there.

'But there could have been,' the voice warned.

Each and every time after that, as Jelly approached his house on foot, in his car, or on horseback, he eyeballed that damned tree that would provide a perfect ambush point for someone wanting to use it to hide behind, gun in hand, waiting to pump rounds into his body.

He thought about cutting it down but didn't want to have to explain why to Francine or the boy. So he just lived with it. Each and every day.

*　　*　　*

One afternoon as he drove down his street heading home to take the family out for an early dinner, Jelly spotted his son, Jimmy, walking by the side of the road carrying his book bag home from school. Jimmy was walking determinedly, little body leaning forward against the weight of the bag on his back, head down, eyes locked on the ground beneath his feet.

Jelly smiled, proud of his kid, then pressed the button on the console and lowered the power window on the passenger side. "Hey, you," he said quietly.

In response to his words Jimmy tipped forward further and broke into a dead run. He never looked over to see who was in the car by the side of the road or who'd spoken to him. He just rocketed away on a beeline toward the house as if being chased by an angry bear.

Jelly smiled wider. He hadn't meant to scare Jimmy, but that had been a perfect response. No one would be grabbing his kid up off the road. *'This kid's got the survival instinct all right,'* he thought happily. He was relieved.

He'd done his best to ensure his son wouldn't become one of the victims in this world. His son was small and defenseless, and while Jelly would rain hellfire down on anyone who'd dare threaten his child or–God forbid–lay hands on him or injure him in any way, the reality was Jelly couldn't always be around to protect Jimmy. So he'd worked hard to imbue his boy with the knowledge of the realities of the world, and tried to help him get his mind right so he'd be able to protect himself. Naturally, the plan was, as his boy got older, Jelly would train him to the best of his abilities; his son would no doubt be better, faster, and more deadly than Jelly could ever be.

Jelly had already introduced his son to firearms, taking his time, carefully explaining about the dangers, teaching him how to properly hold, load, unload, and fire a gun, starting with a small .22 caliber bolt rifle. Jimmy's first ever shot from ten yards went right into the middle of a little white circle on the target, and Jelly could not have been more proud. Then he'd moved on to pistols, again a little .22 to start, this time a Colt single action. He hand-crafted Jimmy a red leather gunbelt and holster, carving fancy designs on both, then taught the boy how to draw and fire from the crouch, just like he did.

Jimmy seemed to take to it naturally, beaming up at his father each time Jelly told him he'd done it right. This became a nightly ritual for them. "Ten repetitions a night, Jimmy," Jelly would say. "Just ten a night and you will be blindingly fast in no time."

Another ritual they had was repeated each day when Jimmy went out the door to school or play. If Jelly was home as his boy was leaving, he'd call out, "Hey! Remember now, keep your eyes and ears–"

"Open," Jimmy would reply by rote, pausing in the

doorway.

"And keep your left and right–"

"Up."

"And be–"

"Ready."

Then Jelly would smile, say, "Have a good day, son," and out the door Jimmy would go.

One morning after watching the little ritual, Francine looked at Jelly and said, "Do you really have to do that every time?"

Surprised, Jelly asked, "What are you talking about?"

"I think it makes him nervous, Delf. You might not realize it, but he's afraid a lot of the time."

Jelly found himself getting a little angry, heard it creeping into his voice as he told Francine she had no idea about what was out there. About the monsters that lurked in the world. "I just want my son to be aware. Not everyone is good, Fran. There's lots of sum'bitches out there and they look for victims. *Not my kid*. My kid's not gonna be one of them."

Francine looked pained. "I know, Delf, but still, he's just little…"

"No, Francine," Jelly said shaking his head, conviction in his voice. "I'm sorry, but you *don't* know. You may think you do, but until you've seen this stuff up close and for real, you have no idea. Your eyes are closed to it, like most people, because you don't want to think about it–don't want to think it's real." Standing up, he walked to his wife and took her hands in his. "Darlin', I so wish it wasn't necessary. But believe me, he needs to know what the world is really like."

Francine looked into Jelly's eyes. "I just hope you know what you're doing, Delf."

"I do. Trust me."

* * *

Even though Jelly was sure he was right about the approach he'd taken with Jimmy, there were a few unfortunate incidents he'd regretted. One night as they were driving home from a visit with his parents in Mountain View, Jelly saw a state trooper scout car with its red bubble light activated up ahead on the highway. Slowing down as he approached, Jelly saw the trooper had an old Buick sedan pulled over, and the trooper was wrestling with a large man Jelly assumed to be the operator. Jelly swung his Cadillac in front of the Buick and parked, instructing Francine that if anything went wrong she was to drive her and Jimmy away from there as fast as she could. Francine didn't even reply, just nodded, all clear-eyed and business; she slid across the seat behind the wheel, her eyes locked on Jelly as he moved toward the struggling men.

"FBI," Jelly said loudly so the trooper wouldn't think he was being flanked, then he reached out and grabbed the driver's wrist, pulled the arm straight out and put the man into an armbar and a lot of pain. In seconds the man was face down on the ground, the trooper wrapping his steel bracelets around the driver's wrists and closing them up tight. "My wrists!" the driver bellowed, "You're breaking my wrists!"

"You'll be lucky if I don't break your fuckin' neck before this night is over," said the trooper as he stood up, leaving the driver prone and whining on the roadway. Then he turned to Jelly, shook his hand and thanked him for the help.

"No problem," Jelly said smiling as he started walking back to his Caddy. That's when he heard the screaming. As he got closer he saw Jimmy's horrified, wide-eyed stare over the car's rear deck. His son was crying hysterically, big tears streaming down red cheeks. Francine was turned around, leaning over the front seat trying to comfort him. Jimmy, terrified, was nearly hyperventilating by the time Jelly opened the rear door.

"Jesus Christ, what's wrong with him?" Jelly asked. "Did something happen?"

Francine just looked at him before saying, "He doesn't understand that's what you do for work, Delf. It scared him."

Jelly had the uncomfortable thought there may be something wrong with his son. It was obvious Jelly knew what he was doing. It had been a simple, textbook takedown. He couldn't understand this reaction. "Son," he said, stroking the boy's head. "It's all right. Daddy's fine. It's okay, kid, honest."

It took twenty minutes for Jimmy to calm down.

* * *

That evening after dinner Jelly had a shot of Jameson and went to bed. He had an early flight to catch to DC next morning and he wanted to get some sleep. Francine and Jimmy were still up, sitting on the couch in the parlor, talking.

As he listened to their voices in the other room the feeling came over him there was more than one wall between them. He was isolated even when with them. He'd felt this way for several years, ever since Jimmy had started talking. It was odd, he knew, this feeling. But he couldn't shake it. And he certainly couldn't discuss it with Francine. She'd never understand.

He lay in bed and felt himself starting to fade off to sleep when something triggered within him. He snapped up into a seated position on the bed, heart pounding; his chest got tight and he started to feel like he was suffocating, unable to take a full breath.

What is this? *What is this?* He placed his hand on the sawed-off, double-barreled shotgun he kept hung from a hook behind the night table next to his side of the bed, picked it up and held it across his lap; then he pulled it close to his chest, trying to catch his breath and slow his heartbeat. After a few minutes of this he lay the gun on the floor, stood up and walked around the dark room, still trying to breathe normally. Something was wrong but it made no sense to him. Was he having a heart attack? A stroke? His left arm started tingling and he became more lightheaded. It *was* a heart attack. His legs got weak; he sat back down on the edge of the bed. *'This is it,'* he thought.

He was about to unload the two double-ought buckshot rounds from the gun so it wouldn't pose a danger to anyone who found his unconscious body when the symptoms started to subside.

Gradually, his breath came easier and his heart slowed and the room stopped closing in on him. His head slowly cleared. He stood up again. He was okay. He looked at the bed and his wife was there sleeping soundly, slight rhythmic snore rising up from beneath the blanket. He'd never heard or felt her come to bed. He looked at the round, white alarm clock ticking away on the night table: 3:00 a.m. He'd been sleeping for hours apparently. Something had happened to elicit that little episode, he thought. There must have been a noise in the house.

Picking the shotgun up, muzzles down, Jelly silently walked into his son's bedroom. The boy lay on his side, breathing deeply, covers pulled up tightly around his head, two stuffed animals standing guard on either side of the pillow. Jelly stared down at his little son for a few moments. He loved his boy more than anything. Then he went and checked the rest of the house, room by room.

*   *   *

The next morning Jelly had pretty much forgotten about the strange symptoms of the previous night. *'Just an aberration,'* he figured–as he'd done quite a few times when having similar experiences in the past. The little episodes never seemed real except when he was in the moment, trying to calm himself while trapped within the overwhelming feeling of impending doom. These weren't the only odd experiences he'd been having.

A few months before, while taking a shower one night after work, his heart had started galloping in his chest. It was an odd sensation to not only be aware of your heartbeat, but to feel it pounding out a disturbing, irregular rhythm. In the first few minutes after it had started, he'd thought he was having a heart attack, even though he otherwise felt fine. When he hadn't lost consciousness after several more minutes of the crazy pounding beat, he figured it was just a more severe form of a similar experience he'd had in the past.

Sometimes, when he'd been running on little sleep and lots of coffee he'd feel his heart dance around a bit, but it had always resumed normal after a few flips and skips.

This time it didn't. It just kept pounding out the weird, asymmetrical drumbeat. Not only had it continued for the rest of the evening, but went on for three days before he finally mentioned it to Francine. "What?!" she'd said, alarmed. "Three days? What's wrong with you, Delf?"

"I don't know," he'd replied seriously. "It just started and it's still doing it."

She looked at him as if he were insane. "No," she said. "I mean what's wrong with *you*? Why haven't you gone to the doctor, for heaven's sake?"

"I figured it couldn't be that bad, Franny. I'm still

walkin' and talkin'. I don't feel like I'm dying."

Later that day, at Francine's insistence, Jelly listened to the doctor say the same thing. "Oh, yes, I absolutely hear it," Doctor Longine said, stethoscope pressed against Jelly's chest. "It's a pretty pronounced arrhythmia."

"Arrhythmia, Doc?"

The doctor sat back and looked at Jelly. "Yes, they're not that uncommon. Yours sounds like a premature ventricular contraction. It's like when your heart skips a beat. Funny thing about yours is it just keeps on going. Usually these don't last too long."

"Great," Jelly said. "So then I'm not going paws up–at least not right now, because of this?"

The doctor shook his head as he placed his index and middle fingers on Jelly's wrist to take his pulse. After ten seconds of staring at his watch the doctor said, "No, I don't think so."

"You don't think what, Doc?"

The doctor smiled at him. "My prognosis would be no paws going up, at least not because of this."

Jelly nodded. "So what caused it?"

"Could be too much coffee, too much smoking, too much stress. Any of these play a part in your life?"

Jelly smiled. "I'll cut down the coffee. When will it stop?"

"Could stop anytime. Could keep going just like it is. You'll either have to get used to it, or wait until it goes back to normal. I wish there was more I could tell you."

His heart resumed normal two weeks later, the night he killed his sixteenth man.

*   *   *

His name was Dirk English. He was having a bad run of

luck. Got into debt with some serious people. Started taking money from the joint savings account without telling his wife, Annabelle. Ran through all the cash, started selling stuff like his watch, then his car. Next came her jewelry and some money they'd been putting away for her daughter's wedding. Dirk was Annabelle's second husband. She'd known he had a criminal record when they'd married. Mostly petty crimes, he'd told her. Things he'd done as a kid when he'd fallen in with the wrong crowd. He'd left out the part about the armed robbery and the manslaughter charge when he was twenty-two.

The previous day they'd had one heck of an argument. Dirk had been drinking like he promised he wouldn't and the matter of the missing money was brought to the table by an angry Annabelle. That's when she met the man she'd married. At one point, Dirk had grabbed her by her long, thin neck and squeezed. "He started choking me," she'd later describe it. But it wasn't choking. It was strangling. Luckily for Annabelle, Dirk had stopped just after the tiny red pinpoint marks started appearing in the whites of her eyes, but before she'd lost consciousness and died of asphyxia.

Next thing they knew it was near midnight and the Oklahoma City Police were at the door. Annabelle's daughter Sophie had phoned them after hearing her mother's screams inside the locked apartment when she'd come home from a late shift at Rothschild's Department Store.

The police pounded on the door. Dirk answered by firing three .45 caliber slugs through the cheap plywood door back at them.

The two responding police officers pulled their own handguns and prepared to fire back the same way. Sophie screamed that her mother was inside and a hostage situation was born as Dirk yelled out, "Come in here and I'll kill her!"

After figuring out who the shooter was in the apartment, the police ran their checks and discovered there was an active federal warrant for Dirk. In addition to his other accomplishments, he'd been convicted of interstate transportation of stolen property, a motor vehicle. The local police called the feds. The agent on duty, following orders, immediately called the Special Agent in Charge.

"Yes," Jelly said picking up the telephone after the first ring. He kept it by his bed on the floor at night.

"Got a situation, Boss. Guy with a federal warrant in an apartment with a gun and a hostage."

Jelly swung his legs over the edge of the bed, snapped on the lamp and picked up his pocket notebook and pencil from the night table.

"Go with the address."

* * *

Half an hour later Jelly pulled up near the scene in his Bureau sedan. He never liked to get too close to a given address. He'd done that once years before in El Paso, pulling in behind a marked scout car to assist with a similar situation. The uniformed officer had met him on the street, and explained to Jelly that a man inside the house had shot at his scout car with a rifle a short time before.

"A man in *this* house," Jelly had said, pointing at the two-story clapboard structure they were standing in front of.

"Yes," the officer had nodded, pointing at a window on the second floor. "From that window right there." Then the officer had pointed at the door of his scout car, indicating two oblong shaped holes in the sheet metal. "He hit my car right there."

Jelly had taken a deep breath and exhaled slowly as he'd

started to back around his car in order to put it between his body and the suspect's muzzle. "Here's what I want you to do," he'd said calmly to the officer as he drew his .357 Magnum revolver and locked his eyes on the house. "I want you to get in your scout and pull it down the street to the corner. Then radio for more cars and tell them to set up a perimeter, but keep their distance from the house. Got it?"

The officer had looked at Jelly crouching behind his car, then at the house, then the holes in his cruiser. His face had gone a little pale as he'd crouched down and run around to the driver's side of his own car and climbed in. Staying low in the seat, he'd started the scout and pulled down the street.

'Some people,' Jelly had realized that day, *'just have no sense of danger.'*

The Dirk English incident had been managed differently from the get-go. To begin with, Jelly was home. He knew the Oklahoma City police and they knew him and–with only a few exceptions–they knew what to do. Jelly had trained them for these types of situations. He'd taught them to set up a good perimeter, stay alert, keep it contained–and to call him immediately.

Jelly knew that more than a handful of officers died needlessly each year when responding to these types of incidents because they had no experience dealing with them, they had no sense of danger, or both. Some of the things he'd seen policemen do over the years had shocked him.

On more than one occasion he'd been horrified as he'd watched officers walk toward an armed gunman, first stopping to take off their gunbelt and place it on the ground, showing the suspect they were unarmed and "just wanted to talk." Sometimes that insane gambit actually worked and the suspect would be talked into surrendering. Other times the suspect would drill a hole in the lawman's chest, and then either suck on the barrel of their own gun and kill themselves, or be dropped in a hail of gunfire fired by other officers at the scene. Either way you ended up with a dead cop, and there was no reason for it. "Cops aren't expendable!" he'd railed at officers on more than one occasion.

After arriving too late to one such incident after being reassigned to Oklahoma City, Jelly had instituted his contain and call protocol. Technically speaking, unless there was a federal violation somewhere in the mix, he'd have no jurisdiction. But practically speaking, everyone who knew him felt it was better to call him to the scene. It was his thing. He was Jelly fuckin' Bryce.

"Hi Jelly," one of the detectives assembled at the scene said as Jelly walked up to the command post. The command post in this situation consisted of two scout cars pulled in nose to nose just half a block away from the apartment.

"Hey, Bobby."

Detective Bobby Bruno calmly explained the situation to Jelly as Jelly scanned the area, focusing on the one-story apartment building. It was low and long, the suspect's location in an end unit.

"Did you evacuate the other apartments?"

"We did," said Bobby, "and we cleared the houses across the street just in case."

"Perimeter been secure since this started?"

"Yes, sir. The first two responding patrolmen knew what to do. One's been posted at a corner on the left rear, other one, right front." Posting men at opposite corners of a square or rectangular building allowed them to each watch two sides, meaning all the sides of the structure were covered except for the top. That's why they'd also been taught to look up occasionally.

"Good job," Jelly said nodding. "When was the last communication?"

"Talked to him twice on the phone, last time maybe twenty minutes ago. He didn't cotton to me much. Got pissed and hung up. Nothing since."

Jelly nodded again, drew his revolver and opened the cylinder. Fully loaded. He gave the cylinder a spin, then stopped it, and gently pressed the cylinder closed. It locked up tight.

"Think it will work?" Bobby asked.

"It always works," Jelly said with a smile, slipping his pistol back in the holster.

"Not that," Bobby replied. "You know. The thing. The *Bryce effect*."

Jelly smiled again. "Well, I certainly hope so."

*   *   *

The "Bryce effect" was a term officers had started using to describe a weird sort of phenomenon that had been occurring in situations like these. An armed criminal would be barricaded somewhere, either with hostages or simply alone in a good defensive position, and refuse all efforts at conversation. Then Jelly would show up, say a few words over the bullhorn or the telephone–words almost exactly the same as what had already been said by other officers–and the suspect would give up. Usually almost immediately. Once or twice when the suspect had refused to respond to the telephone or shouted commands, Jelly had taken a calculated risk and walked right up to the door, standing to the side as he pounded his fist on it and ordered the suspect to surrender "right the fuck now," Magnum blaster clenched in his other hand pointed toward the door. No one could figure out why, but in these instances the suspects had also immediately complied, dropping their weapons and exiting with their hands on their heads, "like in the war movies" as

Jelly always instructed.

During the very last barricade incident Jelly had been called to, no sooner had he arrived in his Bureau sedan and stepped out than the suspect–who'd threatened death before surrender–mysteriously had a change of heart and gave up. Officers at the scene had stared in bewilderment at Jelly, who'd simply smiled and said, "You're welcome," then climbed back in his car and left.

That had put the icing on the "Bryce Effect" cake for sure.

*   *   *

"Where's the daughter?" Jelly asked.

Bobby pointed to a scout car fifty yards away from the scene. Jelly walked over and spoke gently to her for a few minutes. She was very scared for her mother. Apparently, she'd been fending off Dirk's advances since before her mother had married him. He'd threatened to kill her and her mother both if she told. Jelly patted her reassuringly on the shoulder and returned to the command post.

"What do ya think?" Bobby asked.

"I think I'll go have a talk with him." Jelly took in a few deep breaths to calm himself, though it wasn't truly necessary. At this point in his life, he hardly got stressed at all from this type of work. He actually felt best at moments like these. His confidence and calmness were palpable things, spreading to those around him in an almost organic way.

'It's reassuring and kind of eerie at the same time,' Bobby thought as he watched Jelly stride silently across the wide street toward the center of the apartment building. Jelly's mere presence made the situation seem dreamlike, non-threatening, completely under control.

Once Jelly had crossed the street, he looked to his right

and nodded at the officer standing there behind the corner of the apartment building. The officer nodded back, his shotgun held with muzzle pointed at the door. As Jelly approached the door, the officer lowered the shotgun toward the ground. Jelly stood next to the door, back to the wall, and slipped his revolver from the holster with his right hand. With his left hand he knocked on the door as if he were a salesman.

"Get away!" came Dirk's muffled voice behind the door. "I'll kill her, I swear to fuckin' God I'll kill her if you come in."

"Mister English," Jelly said clearly, "you know we can't leave. That's just not gonna happen. But right now all we've got is a man and his wife having an argument. I can help you get through this. Please let me."

"Nobody can help me!" Jelly could hear the desperation in the voice. That wasn't good. Anger was one thing, that could be shaped. Desperation and despair–that often ended in death. Best case scenario, the man would ice himself and leave the woman alive. These types of men usually didn't play it that way though. They liked to make a mess on the way out.

"Listen, my son," Jelly said, getting a strange look from the officer at the corner, "my name is Father Ford. I'm the department chaplain. They've asked me to come here and try and talk to you, help you find a good way out of this situation and back to the Lord. Will you at least talk to me? Please, son?" Sophie had also mentioned to Jelly that her creepy stepfather went to confession every Saturday, then church every Sunday.

"You're a priest?" English asked through the door, his voice wavering.

"I am."

Jelly could hear talking inside the room. A woman crying. "What's your name again, Father?" English asked, all the energy gone from his voice.

Something about that voice put Jelly on edge. He nodded to the officer to get ready, stepped back from the wall and pointed his blaster toward the door. "Ford. Father Ford. Will you please let me help you?"

"Please forgive me, Father." Jelly could barely hear the words through the door. Then he heard the distinctive sound of a hammer being cocked back.

In one motion Jelly booted the door, extended his arm, and fired his gun. It looked too fast to be good. No sooner had the muzzle flash lit up the room than the door bounced back, broken lockset keeping it from latching closed. Jelly kicked the door open again and entered the room, the patrolman right behind him.

Dirk and Annabelle were seated on the floor facing the door, backs against the refrigerator. Her head was slumped forward onto her chest; Dirk's head lay back against the refrigerator door. He had one arm wrapped around her shoulders. In his other hand was a cocked .45 semi-auto, his finger still in the trigger guard. The safety was off. A hole had been punched through Dirk's face, right on the bridge of his nose. Blood and brains were sprayed on the white refrigerator door behind him. His eyes were open.

Jelly turned his attention to Annabelle, already thinking about what he was going to say to her daughter, to break the news as gently as possible, when the woman stirred. Her head swiveled on her neck; she raised it up, eyes locking on Jelly's face as she tried to focus. Even the skin on her face had little petechial hemorrhage spots. Dirk must have cut off the blood supply to her head again to knock her out so she wouldn't be conscious in the moments before he blew her brains out. Because that's what he'd been planning to do.

That's the image Jelly had seen in that fleeting moment

as the door swung open: Dirk had his pistol against the side of her head, finger on the trigger, a resigned, defeated expression on his face. He'd made his decision. She would go first.

Jelly interrupted his plan. Dirk would go first. Annabelle would follow, probably in about thirty or forty years.

"Nice work, Father," the patrolman said, looking at the profile of Jelly's face as other officers ran in to the scene, a medic kneeling down to attend to Annabelle.

Jelly turned his head toward the young patrolman, his eyes focused and intense even as the calmness oozed out of him and filled the room. "Thank you, my son," Jelly said. Then he held up his revolver, muzzle toward the ceiling and made the sign of the cross with it. "Go in peace."

*   *   *

When Jelly got home an hour later, he found the house still dark and secure, his wife and son sleeping soundly. Francine didn't even wake up anymore when he'd get called out. Jelly liked that. He liked that she was so confident of him and his abilities she could stay asleep while he was out taking care of dangerous matters.

"But don't you worry about him when he's dealing with all these criminals and murderers?" Francine's mother had asked once she'd realized exactly what Jelly actually did for work.

"Honestly, Mother," Francine had replied with a wry smile, "I'm more worried for them." It was a joke because she didn't worry about them at all, naturally. She knew her husband always did the right thing for the right reasons. She also knew that sometime in this world it was necessary to take a life in order to save a life. It's just how the world worked. Her husband, the man she'd married, was something special. He was the smartest and bravest man she'd ever known.

She just wished she could make him see what he was doing to his son.

*   *   *

The Bryce Effect took other forms. Jelly's presence, his intensity, his aura–whatever you chose to call it–was always turned on, always pulsing. So was his vigilance. Though he couldn't see it, Jelly was indeed "wound up tight" as Donnelly had described him years before. It had only increased since.

Once in the Oklahoma City office a new agent made the mistake of walking up behind Jelly and tapping him on the shoulder to get his attention and ask a question. The next moment the agent was looking into his boss's eyes from inches away, the blue lamps on fire, boring into him. It took a moment for the agent to realize Jelly also had his blaster in his hand pointed up under the agent's chin. "Speechless" summed it up.

It had taken a few seconds for Jelly to unwind, but once he did he reholstered his pistol, smiled at the agent self-consciously and said, "Please don't do that to me."

The shaken agent shook his head in agreement. "I won't, I'm sorry."

On the homefront things were similar–but different.

Jelly tried to keep a lid on himself, though he startled easily, springing into a fighting posture whenever Francine or Jimmy came around a corner unexpectedly, drawing his ever-present pistol if there was a loud, unexpected noise.

"I don't know," he'd say sheepishly when this happened, shaking his head and smiling.

As his son had grown older, Jelly had started to see

some changes in the boy, too. Like him, Jimmy seemed to startle easily. He'd also started to be fresh to his parents, something Jelly couldn't understand. Both he and Francine doted on the boy, tried to make sure he was happy and well fed, had plenty of toys to play with.

    Jelly tried to spend as much time as he could with Jimmy, but work called practically every day and night; there was always something that demanded his attention. To make up for it, once a year Jelly took Francine and Jimmy away, usually on a trip to the ocean to do some deep sea fishing. Hoover had recommended a place in Florida Jelly liked. They had a good time in the sun and salt water, catching more than a few sailfish on their adventures. While it was nice to get away, Jelly always felt a sense of relief once he got back to Oklahoma and his job.

    When Jimmy was around eleven, the profanity started. Jelly had been careful with his language around the house, but sometimes when talking on the telephone or if one of his friends stopped by, the many creative variations of "fuck" or another curse word they used on a regular basis would slip through. When it happened in Jimmy's presence, Jelly would look at the boy and say "Belay that." That was the code they'd worked out meaning Jimmy should mentally erase what he'd just heard.

    Apparently, that system didn't actually work too well.

    One afternoon while Jelly and Francine had guests over the house for a barbeque, Jimmy picked up a plate with a big piece of cake on it and was walking toward the living room when the cake rolled off the plate and bounced on the wooden floor, sending chocolate crumb and white frosting shrapnel in every direction.

    Jimmy, eyes wide as he watched the cake bounce across the floor, let loose with an explosive series of professionally strung together expletives that would have made a sailor blush.

"James Fel Bryce!" Francine said, embarrassed in front of their company. "What have I told you about using that kind of language!?"

When Jelly laughed, Jimmy took off on another profanity-laced tirade. Francine turned her angry eyes on her husband. "Don't encourage him, Delf." Then, looking at her guests, Francine said, "I'm so sorry, I just don't know what to do about it."

One of the guests, recently-retired Clarence Hurt, looked at Jimmy, then Jelly. He kind of grinned then said, "You should probably give him another piece of cake."

CHAPTER TWENTY

Shakin' Hands with the Governor
10 January 1958

IN FEBRUARY 1956 JELLY moved his wife and son to a ranch he'd bought in his hometown of Mountain View. He'd started to think seriously about retiring from the FBI and this was his first step. He'd get the ranch set up, get his family settled in, then commute to work in Oklahoma City until he was ready to pull the pin and put in his papers.

H.V. Wilder's untimely death coupled with the retirement of Clarence Hurt in 1955 had put the idea in his head there may be life after the Bureau. Hurt in particular seemed determined to show Jelly the upside of moving on. He'd put law enforcement behind him and started farming up in McAlester, Oklahoma.

"I'm tellin' you, Delf," he'd said to Jelly a number of times, "you won't believe how deep in you are until you get out."

Jelly hadn't understood what his first boss and police mentor was trying to tell him.

"I mean," Hurt went on, "it's like being under water. Bein' deep, deep down you get used to the pressure, you know? Then suddenly you don't have to be down there anymore, and as you start to rise the pressure comes off you in waves. Only then do you start to realize just how much pressure you were under. Gotta say, Delf, the longer I'm out the more I feel it. It's like being able to breathe normally again, you know?"

Jelly sort of did, or thought he did. But his trust in

Clarence Hurt was absolute. Clarence was one of his tried and tested friends. If he was telling Jelly this, there was a reason.

He was also worried about his son, Jimmy. The boy had gotten more wild with each passing year. Jelly couldn't understand it. It seemed no matter what Jelly said to him, Jimmy had a smart-alecky remark loaded up and ready to fire. It was more than just the normal rebellion of youth and it was starting to wear on Jelly and Francine. All they wanted was the best for their only child. They couldn't figure it out. Jelly had also run out of ways to deal with it. His usual tactics for achieving control didn't apply. Apparently, Jimmy had figured that out before Jelly. One afternoon as they were driving into town for supplies, Jimmy had started acting up, talking disrespectfully to Jelly. Jelly suddenly found himself angry at his son like he'd never been before. The voice in his head started ranting, *'Who the fuck does this kid think he is? Does he not know who I am? Does he not know I would give the back of my hand to anyone else who dared talk to me like this?'* Then the voice spilled out Jelly's mouth.

He pulled the car over to the side of the road, knuckles white on the steering wheel and glared at Jimmy. "You better think twice, Jimmy, before you open your mouth again. I'm not in the mood, and I'm sick to death of your nonsense. Do you understand me, mister?!"

To Jelly's surprise and horror, Jimmy had smirked at him in return, then challenged him: "What are you gonna do, hit me?! Go ahead! I don't care! Hit me all you want!" The longer the boy talked the more hysterical he became. His face glowed red and hot, his eyes watered but he wasn't crying. Jelly was bewildered. He immediately lost his own anger and began trying to calm his son, finding himself apologizing for having yelled at Jimmy.

By the time they got back home Jelly was a mess. His heart was pounding as his brain tried to figure out the path clear of this situation. "What do I do with *this?*" Jelly repeated quietly to himself as he walked away after parking the car and watching Jimmy storm into the house, slamming the door behind him.

*   *   *

Shortly after that incident Jelly started renting a room at the Roberts Hotel in Oklahoma City so he wouldn't have to make the long, two-hour commute back and forth to Mountain View every day. The ride had started to wear him down. That's what he'd told Francine, anyway.

The room was small but it was only a ten-minute walk from the hotel to his office. On the nights he stayed in the city Jelly would often find himself feeling restless after work. It wasn't unusual for him to head out to the streets, often accompanying an Oklahoma City Police patrolman on his rounds.

One evening, bored and wandering, Jelly stopped by his old police station. On his way to the staircase leading to the second floor detective unit, he paused and watched one of the new patrolman seated in a chair getting his shoes shined. The young man providing the shining service seemed to be struggling with the job. The patrolman having his shoes shined was watching with growing concern as his shift was starting in five minutes and his sergeant was a stickler for detail. If your metal and leather uniform parts weren't buffed and glowing you'd not only hear about it, you'd pull the worst patrol assignments for a month or better with no relief.

Jelly approached them and tapped the shoeshine boy on the shoulder. The boy, about thirteen years old, looked up first at Jelly, then the patrolman. The patrolman didn't know who Jelly was and was really getting anxious. He was about to say something to the shoeshine boy when Jelly took the rag from the boy's hand, knelt down and spit on the patrolman's shoes, and started snapping and popping the rag across the toe of the first shoe. In a matter of moments, the leather went from a dull black to a mirror-reflective shine you could comb your hair in. Jelly smiled at the boy, handed him the rag and pointed at the other shoe. The boy imitated what he'd just seen, and though it took a little longer and wasn't quite as shiny as its twin, the shoe looked good enough to pass inspection.

When he'd finished, the boy and the patrolman looked up from their reflections in the leather to see Jelly's reaction. But he was gone. The patrolman gave the boy a dime, smiled and tousled the boy's hair as he hurried in to make roll call.

*   *   *

Jelly walked into the empty detective unit offices on the second floor. Little had changed since he'd shared this space with H.V. Wilder and the other "old timers" back in the day. Moving slowly around the room, he let his hand run over the tops of the chair backs until he arrived at Wilder's old desk. Pulling the chair out, he sat down and looked across at his own old desk.

'This was the view H.V. had all those years,' Jelly thought. He could just imagine what his old partner had thought as he'd watched Jelly tirelessly pounding away at the typewriter, always resisting H.V.'s attempts to get him to be more open to things other than work.

"Thanks for never givin' up on me, partner," he said quietly. In his mind he saw Wilder smiling back at him.

* * *

That night at the hotel Jelly had a late dinner at the restaurant on the first floor then went up to his room. He turned on the radio and sat back on the bed, his little metal flask on the desk next to him. When he was alone like this his brain would start working on him. Sometimes the slideshow of bodies and violence would start, images flashing through his mind one after another. Then his heart rate would elevate, thoughts of heart attacks and strokes replacing the disturbing images. Those thoughts would trigger a stronger physical reaction and his heart would really start pounding away, followed by a tingling sensation in his arms and chest, then light-headedness and an urge to get up and flee the room.

He knew the drill by now. This had been happening practically every night for years. On one level he would be convinced he was sure to die before morning. On another level his mind would try to reason its way clear of the oppressive feelings. *'This happens all the time. You always feel like you're about to die–but you never do. You always wake up in the morning and you'll wake up again tomorrow. Just stop this nonsense now!'* And he'd try. After experimenting he'd found that a few things made the torture stop.

Work was number one. Whenever he was consumed by a job the feelings of weakness and dread were absent. The more complicated or dangerous the assignment, the better he felt.

Exercising worked sometimes. So did alcohol. Not necessarily enough booze to get plastered, just a belt or two would smooth him out. The only problem with alcohol was that its effects were short-lived. He had no intention of becoming an alcoholic. Moderation was the key, but also limited the duration of relief.

Sex worked too. And sometimes food. If he started feeling uneasy, either one would seem to short-circuit the slide into dread and uneasiness.

This particular night, his wife was miles away and he never cheated. Food wasn't the answer either–he'd already eaten.

Jelly took a couple of swigs from the flask. Jack Daniel's Old Number 7 had replaced the Jameson whiskey he'd long favored. "Good enough for Sinatra, good enough for me," Jelly said as the smooth whiskey left a mildly burning trail down his throat.

Half an hour later, after he'd gotten washed up and undressed for bed, Jelly sank into the hotel pillows and closed his eyes. In his mind's eye he visualized a kite; blown hard by a strong wind it strained against the thin string that kept it anchored to the earth so far below. He could see and feel the tension on the string, but the kite itself was strong and intact, like iron–*'An iron kite,'* he thought, amused. But the string was not metal, it was just string, and he felt the string could break at any moment and he was afraid because he didn't know what would happen to the iron kite once it broke its tether.

Then he was dreaming, and in his dream he saw Francine and she was crying. "You failed them, Jelly," she said between sobs. "You took care of everyone and everything else but your own family. We always came second. Always."

"That's not true," Jelly replied in the dream, listening to his own voice as if it came from someone else. The voice was calm but inside his mind rocked back and forth like a ship at sea in gale winds. *'Was it true?'* his mind asked, doubting now. "No," Jelly said aloud, "It is not true. I've always done my best for my family."

Then he was asleep for a few hours until he awoke to

use the bathroom; he quickly slid back into bed, hoping sleep would return before the torture began again.

* * *

During this time, as his career was winding down as far as he was concerned, Jelly did his best to give the Bureau its money's worth. He found, however, it was getting harder with each passing day. He was only barely aware of how his inner turmoil had started to affect his outward actions. He became more on edge, even in the office, and would sometime find himself feeling angry and aggressive toward those around him.

One afternoon as he was leaving the office building he ran into a few of the secretaries coming back from lunch. One of them, Miss Marfleet, smiled at him as they passed and politely asked, "How are you, Mister Bryce?"

Jelly tersely replied, "Worse."

Without pause or thought Miss Marfleet responded, "Oh, Mister Bryce, you couldn't possibly be worse."

No sooner had the words left her lips than all the secretaries' eyes opened wide in recognition of what she'd just unconsciously told the Oklahoma City SAC.

Jelly, hearing the words, stopped walking in the middle of his stride just for a heartbeat. Without turning around, he ruefully smiled then continued walking away at a fast clip.

* * *

In late November 1957, J. Edgar Hoover called Jelly and told him there was going to be another "routine periodic reorganization" after the first of the year. Jelly knew what that meant. Hoover sometimes referred to these as "career enhancement transfers." Jelly was going to be switching posts with the SAC in Albuquerque, New Mexico. Though the idea of going back to New Mexico appealed to him on many levels, resistance to the idea of moving again trumped them all.

That afternoon Jelly drove home to Mountain View and sawed a one-foot wide plank into a three-foot long section. He nailed a length of picket fence to it, pointed end down. Then he painted the plank white. After the paint dried, he took out a small can of black paint and hand-lettered the words, "DUN MOVIN" across the front of it.

As Francine and Jimmy watched, Jelly carried the sign into the yard in front of their house and set the picket into the cold ground with a hammer. Jelly got his camera out and had Francine and Jimmy stand on either side of the sign.

"Now smile and wave, please," Jelly said brightly, his breath visible in the air. As they waved Jelly snapped a photograph.

One week later an envelope arrived at the Seat of Government with Jelly's Mountain View return address. The address caught Miss Gandy's eye as she sorted the mail. She stood up and brought the envelope into Hoover's office. "I thought you might want to look at this," she said, placing it on his desk. Hoover looked first at it, then her. Miss Gandy didn't move to leave.

In all the years Jelly had worked for the FBI, he'd never sent anything to Hoover from his home address.

Hoover opened the envelope and took out a letter, unfolding it. A black and white snapshot contained within fell out. Hoover picked it up, holding it away from his eyes so he could make it out. He held the photo out to Miss Gandy, and after she took it he started reading the letter aloud.

"Dear Mister Hoover:

Please accept this as notification that I will be retiring from active duty as of February 1, 1958. I respectfully request leave without pay starting January 10, 1958 until my retirement officially begins. I would also like to inform you that, as we discussed last June, I have decided to run for the position of Governor of Oklahoma." Hoover's eyebrows raised up as he read that part.

"It has been my sincere honor to serve as a member of the Federal Bureau of Investigation these past 24 years, doubly so to have been able to serve under your exclusive command. You have accomplished what Machiavelli described as the thing most difficult to do: you took the lead in the introduction of a new order of things." Hoover looked up at Miss Gandy and smiled before finishing the letter.

"I am forever grateful for your guidance, wisdom, and friendship. Respectfully submitted, D.A. Bryce, Special Agent in Charge, Oklahoma City, Oklahoma."

Hoover placed the letter down on his desk and looked up at Miss Gandy.

"Governor of Oklahoma?" she said incredulously. "Is he serious?"

Hoover looked across the room, eyebrows knitted in thought. "Son of a gun," he said admiringly. "I guess he *is*."

*　　*　　*

A few months earlier, Jelly had walked out of the men's bathroom on the fifth floor of the Justice Department Building just in time to see Edgar Hoover shaking hands and saying goodbye to a well-dressed, distinguished-looking man. As the gentleman turned Jelly recognized him: it was Raymond Gary, Governor of Oklahoma.

If the governor had seen Jelly, he might have recognized him as well. Jelly had met the man once or twice during official business but had never developed any kind of relationship beyond that–and for good reason. Jelly had learned from Hoover that politicians could be one hundred times more dangerous than any street thug or crime family. Especially the smart ones. But that was only part of the story.

Jelly remembered being surprised years before, when first starting out in law enforcement, to discover that many successful politicians weren't necessarily all that bright. Later he'd come to understand they didn't need to be if they were connected. It was the people they were connected *to* that were the true danger. Usually these people were wealthy and powerful, having achieved both through their intelligence, cunning, and sometimes ruthlessness. *They were bright*. And they were actually running the show from behind the scenes, using their politicians as fronts to move the levers.

Jelly wasn't sure about Gary. Though the man had done a pretty decent job as governor, he was still considered to be a bit of an arrogant elitist. The former president of the Sooner Oil Company, Gary was also definitely connected. Before becoming governor he'd served as a state senator for fourteen years and acted as President Pro Tempore of the Senate until running for–and winning–the Governorship in 1955.

As Jelly observed, Hoover watched Gary walk away, then pulled a clean and creased white handkerchief from his pocket and began fastidiously wiping his hands with it. Glancing down the hallway, the Director spotted Jelly standing outside the men's room and smiled. Jelly nodded in return as Hoover strolled over to him and stopped. "Did you see who that was?" Hoover asked.

Jelly nodded, then pointed with his thumb toward the restroom behind him. "I just finished shakin' hands with the Governor myself," he said with a grin.

Hoover laughed. "Where are you staying tonight?"

Jelly was in DC for two days, then headed to Quantico to help oversee some modifications to the firearms training program for the rest of the week.

"Probably the Statler."

"Nonsense," Hoover said. "You'll stay with me tonight. Why spend the money if you don't need to." It wasn't a question. An invitation to spend the night as a houseguest of the Director was something you didn't turn down. Many agents considered that one of the highest forms of regard in the Bureau, something only a select few ever received.

Jelly smiled. "Thanks, Boss. I would appreciate that greatly."

*   *   *

A few hours later Jelly parked across the street from 4936 Thirtieth Place NW in DC. It was a large brick-faced, two-story building, well-kept with carefully pruned shrubs and handsome trees out front. Jelly walked up to the door carrying his small overnight bag and rang the doorbell. He could hear a series of gonging chimes coming from within.

A pleasant looking, conservatively-dressed black woman answered the door. She smiled at Jelly and said, "Mister Bryce?"

Jelly smiled back. "Yes, ma'am."

The middle-aged woman said, "My name is Annie. Mister Hoover told me you'd be arriving this afternoon. Please come in."

Jelly thanked her and entered the house, taking off his hat as he crossed the threshold. Then he stopped and just looked. He was a bit startled to see that practically every inch of the place was jammed with furniture, carpets, trinkets, books, and antiques of all kinds. The walls weren't spared either. Framed paintings, photographs, souvenirs–*covered*. Even though everything was also spotless and dust free, it made Jelly claustrophobic. It didn't help that the windows were all shut tight, shades drawn, curtains pulled over the shades.

"I'm to show you to the guest room," Annie said, "then Mister Hoover would like you to come down to the recreation room."

Jelly nodded and started to follow her up the heavily-carpeted staircase. The floors were completely covered with layers of oriental carpeting, thick padding beneath those. The effect was moving silently through the place as you walked, almost like walking across a bed.

"Dinner will be served this evening promptly at 5:15," the woman said, speaking quietly as if in church. "And in the morning, you'll be having breakfast at exactly 7:30 in the dining room with Mister Hoover." She looked back at Jelly as she arrived at the top of the staircase. "Mister Hoover always has the same thing for breakfast: two soft-boiled eggs, white toast with butter and black coffee. If you'd like something different you just let me know."

"That sounds fine for me, ma'am. Thank you."

"All right," she replied sweetly as she opened a door. "This will be your room here. You go ahead and put your bag on the bed. If you'd like, I'll lay your things out for you."

Jelly walked into the bedroom and looked around. Here too, it was neatly and tastefully packed to the gills. He put his bag down on the floor and smiled at her again. "Thank you, ma'am, but that won't be necessary."

"Very well," she said. "There is a bathroom two doors down on the right if you'd like to freshen up. You just come downstairs when you're ready and I'll bring you to the recreation room."

Jelly had the oddest feeling he should tip her, but of course that would be totally inappropriate. He smiled warmly instead, said, "Thanks so much," and placed his hat on the bed as she left, closing the door behind her.

Jelly sat on the comfortable, quilt-covered bed and scanned the room. This was not what he'd expected. He'd always envisioned the Boss's house as more austere, more organized. This place looked like an antique shop on steroids. Smelled like one, too. Not an unpleasant odor, just slightly musty, like old books.

"Interesting," he said quietly. The thought of the place being bugged suddenly skipped across his mind. He shook his head in response. *'Ridiculous,'* he thought. But he'd be careful of what he said nonetheless.

*   *   *

Hoover took Jelly on a tour of the house after Annie brought him to the basement recreation room. Later, when they'd finished dinner, they'd retired back there to have a drink.

As Jelly listened to Hoover talk he took in all there was to see in the recreation room. It too was cluttered, but had a decidedly different feel than the rest of the house. A large fireplace dominated the room, its bricks painted white. A stuffed deer head hung over the fireplace, the mantle below it packed with smaller examples of the taxidermist's art, along with cowboy statues, powder horns and other knick-knacks, in an effort to give the room a strong masculine motif. This was especially evident by the artwork hung on the walls. In addition to photographs of Hoover with movie stars and other Hollywood celebrities, "pin-up" art, pictures of scantily-clad starlets smiling into the camera, competed for prominence. An original copy of Marilyn Monroe's nude calendar shot signed by the photographer, Tom Kelly, held a place of honor above the rest.

Hoover pointed out the Monroe photograph and smiled at Jelly as he told him how he'd gotten an original print. "Kelly's a friend of mine. He took that picture in '49, paid her fifty dollars. Imagine? Who'd have guessed she'd be such a big star just a few years later?"

Hoover poured them each a drink and ushered Jelly into one of the big white overstuffed chairs facing the fireplace.

"I'm really happy to have you here, Jelly," Hoover said smiling. "There's not a lot of people I can trust enough to bring into my home."

"I'm sure, Boss," Jelly agreed.

"Things have changed significantly ever since the war ended, as you know. We're heading into unchartered waters now like never before in the history of mankind."

Jelly nodded, taking a sip of his drink. It was really strong. "This is good," he said holding up the glass. "What is it?"

Hoover smiled. "That's Johnnie Walker–*White Label*. They haven't made that since the first World War."

Then Hoover took a drink from his own glass and started talking. For the next hour and a half, he talked practically non-stop, only interrupting his stream of consciousness a few time to refill their glasses or ask Jelly for some minor feedback about some point or another. The Boss was on a roll.

He rambled from one subject to the next, covering everything from the gangster days to the last war to the current political situation. It was talking politics that got him most fired up. He started with the death of Roosevelt.

Six weeks after the President died the new President, Harry Truman, had fired the attorney general, Francis Biddle. In his place Truman appointed Tom Clark. Clark, whom Truman would later describe as "a dumb son of a bitch," and the "biggest mistake of my presidency" would later accept a huge bribe in return for fixing a war profiteering case.

"He was a piece of work, Clark was," Hoover told Jelly, "but I loved him." Clark had left Hoover alone and let him run his own shop in whatever way the Director had seen fit for the four years he'd headed Justice. In 1949 he was made an Associate Justice of the Supreme Court.

"Naturally," Hoover said shaking his head.

During the post-war years the fight against international Communism had really taken off. The FBI became embroiled in a number of high-profile matters ranging from the Rosenberg spy investigation to a series of "Cold War" scandals and questionable activities. Chief among these were the Alger Hiss case in which the Bureau was accused of rigging evidence and the Senator Joe McCarthy "Red Scare" hearings of the 1950s. Through it all, Hoover's steady hand was on the wheel.

"Joe was a bit of a screwball and an alcoholic," Hoover mused, "but I fired him up Truman's asshole like a heat-seeking missile."

Hoover had disdained Truman almost from the get-go. It had been mutual. Right after the war had ended, he'd gone to the new President and proposed a modified plan for the secret worldwide intelligence agency he still wanted to create and lead. As Roosevelt had done before him, Truman listened carefully and quietly as the Director of the FBI had laid it all out for him. Unlike Roosevelt, Truman didn't need time to think about it and get back to him. He told him there and then.

"That certainly is an interesting plan, Edgar," he said in his short, clipped and pointed manner. "But that's never gonna happen."

On January 22, 1946, Harry S. Truman signed an executive order creating two new entities: the National Intelligence Authority and the Central Intelligence Group (CIG). The CIG would be responsible for providing strategic information to the President and the management of clandestine activities abroad. He tapped Rear Admiral Sidney Souers, the Assistant Chief of Naval Intelligence, to be the first Director of Central Intelligence.

Hoover and his FBI would be limited to operating only within the confines of the United States. Nowhere else.

Hoover had gone ballistic at the news, going so far as to insist on a private meeting during which he vehemently argued his point with the Commander in Chief. "I should be in charge of both FBI and the Central Intelligence Group," he'd stated adamantly.

Truman had just stared at Hoover, watching as his subordinate's chest heaved under his three-piece suit. Then he'd said clearly and directly, "You're getting out of bounds, Edgar."

That had brought Hoover back to the reality of his current situation. "Fine, Mister President," he'd responded stiffly, then got up and left the room. He'd never forgotten nor forgiven Truman for putting the final nail in the coffin of his greatest ambition.

That's why Hoover had carefully cultivated "Tail-Gunner" Joe McCarthy and fed the man's own distorted dreams of power and notoriety. He'd loaded McCarthy's Communist infiltration gun with ammunition from his secret files, launching round after round against the State Department, the Voice of America, the US Army and most of all, Truman's administration. To Hoover's delight, McCarthy even publicly attacked the president, calling him "a drunkard" and "a son of a bitch who should be impeached."

McCarthy, however, quickly became addicted to the

public attention and power. His cravings for more couldn't be controlled by Hoover or anyone else. Eventually the Director had to cut him loose. Shortly afterward, the junior US senator from Wisconsin was censured by the United States Senate then spiraled out of control politically and personally. He'd died in the hospital just the month before Jelly's visit to Hoover's home.

"Drank himself to death," Hoover said, shaking his head. "Poor, dumb bastard."

After resting for a minute, Hoover looked at Jelly and asked, "Have I told you anything about COINTELPRO yet?" COINTELPRO was short for Counterintelligence Program. The brainchild of one of Hoover's top men, it was intended to help the Bureau deal a devastating blow to the Communist Party of the United States and other "subversives."

Jelly shook his head. He'd heard a few rumors about a new secret program, but Hoover hadn't mentioned it.

Hoover looked at Jelly, thinking. The Director had aged considerably during the war years and didn't have the stamina he'd once had. "You know what?" he said shrugging, "Another time. I don't feel like getting into that right now."

"Okay, Boss," Jelly said. He knew better than to try and pursue it. Hoover would tell him when he was ready–if that time ever came.

After refilling their glasses, Hoover sat up in his chair and said, "Jelly, let me ask you something. What would you think about the idea of me running for president? I mean, if Ike doesn't run again?"

Dwight D. "Ike" Eisenhower had succeeded Truman in 1953. Though Hoover adored Ike, there had been some speculation that the former Supreme Commander of the Allied Forces in Europe would not be running for reelection due to health concerns.

Jelly tried hard not to show his surprise at the question. "President?"

Hoover looked at him appraisingly. "Yes. President. What would you think?"

Jelly took a sip of whiskey and thought about it. "I think you'd be a great president, Boss. Who better than you?"

Hoover stared closely at him for a moment, then a smile broke over his face and he sank back into his chair. "Thank you, Jelly," he said sincerely. "I mean, it most likely won't ever happen, but I'm exploring all options just in case, you know?"

Jelly nodded. *'Would Hoover make a good president?'* he thought. The man had brought the Bureau along from a non-descript bureaucracy of about 650 employees, including 441 special agents in 1924, to being the premier organization of its kind in the world employing 6,147 special agents and 7,839 civilian support personnel with an annual operating budget of 105 million dollars. *'Why not president?'* he mused.

"Or," Hoover continued, "I suppose I could always go to Hollywood and start a film career." He smiled at Jelly. "Did you know they're making a movie out of *The FBI Story*? They asked me to be in it, as myself, you know? Me and Jimmy Stewart."

The FBI Story was a recently published book by Don Whitehead. An authorized history of the Bureau, Hoover had shaped it by the access given to Whitehead while doing his research. Once it was released, the Bureau's Crime Records Division ensured it received good reviews and plenty of exposure. Hoover loved the book.

"Good for you, Boss," Jelly said, raising his glass in toast. "I'll bet you give Stewart a run for his money."

Hoover smiled again, then asked, "Why haven't you

asked me why the governor of your home state was at the S.O.G. today?"

Jelly shrugged. "Figured you'd tell me if I needed to know."

Hoover nodded. "That's why we get along so well, my friend. Your governor was in because he was thinking about taking another run at the senate. Wanted to know if I'd support him."

Jelly raised his eyebrows in question.

"Oh, these politicians, Jelly. Things happen with them all the time. They go out with their mistresses, get drunk, run over some poor schmuck... we hear everything. Once *they* know *we* know, we never have an issue with them again. It's a dirty, dirty business. But it keeps *us* in business and running without interference for the most part."

Jelly stayed silent. He wasn't sure he wanted to hear any more. Hoover was the one who'd taught him long ago there were some things it was better to be ignorant of.

"You know what I think?" Hoover asked, suddenly animated. "I think what this country needs are some politicians with integrity. *Real* integrity."

Sensing they were heading back to the topic of Hoover running for president, Jelly started thinking up some way to delicately change the subject when Hoover pointed at him.

"*You!*" he said. "You oughta run for something, Jelly. You'll be retiring in a few years, maybe. You should get out and run for office. Do some good for the country that doesn't put you in harm's way at the same time."

Jelly smiled. "I could always run as your vice-president."

Hoover laughed. "No, Jelly. I'm serious now." He sat up straight in his chair. "You, Mister Bryce, *you* should run for governor. Governor of Oklahoma!"

Jelly laughed again. "No experience, Boss man. No money either. Never gonna happen."

"Hmmm," Hoover said, thinking. "You've got plenty of experience leading men and managing multiple government offices. We'll get you the money. A lot of people would like to see you at the helm there, I'm sure. And besides," he said conspiratorially, "I have enough information to blow any of your potential opponents out of the water." He winked at Jelly.

Hoover suddenly stood up and walked to the fireplace. He picked up three small framed paintings that had been stacked on the mantle face down. Bringing them over to Jelly, he handed them to him and stood back. "What do you think?"

Jelly looked at them. They appeared to be miniature paintings of Eleanor Roosevelt. He looked up at Hoover and raised his eyebrows. He knew Hoover detested the former First Lady.

"Now turn them upside down," Hoover directed, pointing at the painting and spinning his index finger in a circle. Jelly did. Upside down the images unquestionably appeared to be depicting a woman's sex organs.

"Do you see it?!" Hoover asked.

Jelly nodded. "I do." He didn't know what else to say.

Hoover laughed out loud. "I got those from W.C. Fields. He gave them to me as a gift. He can't stand that cunt any more than I can." Hoover took the paintings from Jelly and carefully placed them back on the mantle. Then he filled his glass once more, dropped a few ice cubes from a sterling silver bucket with matching tongs into it and sank back into his chair.

"Oh, she is a vile creature, Jelly. That bitch is nothing but trouble. She accused me of setting up an American gestapo. Me! Imagine? Meanwhile, she was having affairs with men, women, niggers, communists–practically anyone who was able to close their eyes and bear it." Hoover shook his head. "I'm telling you, my friend, she was one of the most dangerous enemies the Bureau ever had. Lucky for us, that poor bastard FDR knew it. He once said to me–and this is the Gospel truth, Jelly–he once said, 'Edgar, if you think you've got it bad, think about me. I have to live with her.' That's a true quote."

Jelly had stopped enjoying the conversation a while before, but now he was just worn out from listening. He was about to excuse himself and head up to bed when Hoover looked at him and started talking again. "Yes, a vile creature she is."

Hoover's eyes were glassy by this time. Jelly was convinced his boss was more than "half seas over" for sure. He'd landed on the opposite beach.

Hoover sank lower in his seat, dragged a footstool over to his chair with the toe of his slippered foot then plopped both feet up on it. "Vile," he repeated. Then he shrugged and said, "But we all are, I suppose. All vile creatures driven by base impulses. We're no better than a virus on this planet, really. *A scourge.* And now that we've got *the bomb–*" he sniggered– "we'll probably rectify *that* problem in short order." Hoover rolled his head toward Jelly, his eyelids heavy. "Honestly Jelly," he said gloomily, words slightly slurred, "I don't see us surviving much longer. Someone will push the damned button. One of these sniveling, conniving politicians. American, Soviet–doesn't matter. Someone will. Then that will be that, I suppose."

Jelly looked into the sad eyes of the man who would be president, finished his drink and stood up. He carefully placed his empty glass on a coaster on the table. "Good night, Hoover."

Hoover watched Jelly walk a little unsteadily across the thick carpet toward the door. "Goodnight, Jelly. Sleep well."

CHAPTER TWENTY-ONE

T-34s on the Bridge
March 1961

THE BABY BLUE CADILLAC Eldorado Seville gleamed in the early afternoon sun. The weather had been cool and comfortable and Jelly'd felt like taking a ride alone. He'd told Francine he was going to bring a couple boxes of old FBI reports to the Oklahoma City office for safekeeping. It was mostly true.

Though he'd been retired nearly three years, he'd held onto some pieces of his old life, the files among them. There was nothing of a sensitive nature in them, just information relating to cases that had still been active when he'd left. He'd worked with the agents who'd inherited the investigations, providing them copies and direction as needed. But now these cases were resolved, trials over or bodies planted in their graves and he was tired of looking at the big brown cardboard banker's boxes in his basement. He'd called the office the day before and arranged to meet the filing clerk later that afternoon.

It was nice to get away from the ranch for the day, even though he truly loved his new, post-Bureau life. He had cattle and horses to attend to, buildings to fix up and barbed-wire fences to mend. He could go fishing and hunting pretty much whenever he pleased–which was pretty often. He'd also been spending more time with Francine and Jimmy, trying to mend fences there too. That hadn't been going so well as far as his boy was concerned, but he and Francine had never been better.

The job pressure that Clarence Hurt had told him about, and his description of the "decompression process" had been spot on. Jelly and he'd had many conversations both in person and over the telephone. Clarence had been a great help as Jelly'd learned how to adjust to civilian life. Then Clarence had surprised him by throwing his hat in the ring for Sheriff of Pittsburgh County. The renowned FBI agent, one of the men who'd put lead into Dillinger outside the Biograph Theater so long ago had won easily and was already getting ready to run for a second term.

"I don't know, Delf," Clarence had told him, trying to explain why he'd been compelled to walk away from farming and go back into the mix. "I just found myself thinking about police work more and more. Then I started dreaming about it. I figured, hell, I must miss it. So I'm trying this for a spell."

Jelly'd heard through the FBI grapevine that Charlie Winstead had also gone back to law enforcement after the war, working as a Sheriff's Deputy down in New Mexico.

As for Jelly, he'd had enough. The longer he was out, the more it started to seem as if the whole thing had happened to someone else. It was strange. He'd loved the Bureau with everything he had, had given himself completely to it, and now that he was out he felt no nostalgia for it at all. In fact, after the first few months, the opposite effect started taking hold of him. If he saw a police scout car, heard a siren, or even thought too much about the job, his heart would start pounding for no reason, he'd get light-headed and feel like he was going to be sick. At first he'd been mystified by this; later on he'd come to expect it. When he'd worked up the courage to ask Clarence Hurt about it, he'd been immensely relieved to hear his friend laughing on the other end of the line, then say, "Well thank the good Lord it ain't just me who's fucked up to a fare thee well! That's just more of the decompressin' goin' on, Delf. It'll wear off over time."

Now approaching his three-year retirement anniversary, Jelly wanted to get rid of more reminders and the boxes were full of them.

He swung the big Caddy into the parking lot of Cattlemen's Café, picked out a good spot and backed the car in fins first. He loved driving the car backwards as much as forwards. Whichever direction you faced gave you a view filled with Breton Blue curves and shining chrome. The 1959 Eldorado had taken his breath away the first time he'd seen it. In addition to the soaring fins flanking the trunk with their high-riding, dual red, bullet tail lamps, the car had a huge curve-top windshield and jeweled grills front and back. The ride was fit for a king, packed with power everything–windows and doors, air conditioning and air suspension. It was an engineer's love letter to ostentatiousness and comfort–and class.

After putting the Caddy in park Jelly shut off the motor, pushed the trunk release button and got out. He walked around to the trunk and lifted the lid, taking a quick peek at the boxes to make sure he'd remembered to bring everything. He had. Then he reached deep in beyond the boxes and unzipped the long leather gun case lying on the shelf above the main trunk compartment. Standing up straight for a moment, he adjusted his fedora as he glanced around, then bent back in and slipped a wood-stocked, 12-gauge shotgun out of the case, keeping it hidden inside the confines of the cavernous trunk.

The shotgun wouldn't be getting turned in. It was one of his own personal guns and it always rode with him. He'd had the Number 0 Riot Grade Remington Model 10 pump-gun for a long time. It was set up special with a 20" barrel and six-shell magazine extension. He'd had it so long and used it so much for shooting demonstrations that all the bluing had rubbed off, making it look like stainless.

The story he'd been told by the old man who'd sold it to him was that only ten of these specially-outfitted guns were ever made. The man had been a guard back in the early twenties at the Oklahoma State Penitentiary and had bought the gun when he'd retired. That was his story anyway. Jelly'd overlooked any possible complications involving the gun when he'd bought it as a young Oklahoma City policeman partly because the old man had seemed decent, but mostly because the shotgun had a unique characteristic Jelly appreciated: if you held the trigger back while firing and cycling it to reload, the gun would slam fire each time the slide was driven forward. It made for an impressive cyclic rate of fire, and Jelly could drill with the gun even though it only had a small bead front sight and nothing on the receiver other than the serial number and the *REMINGTON ARMS COMPANY* marking.

Jelly pressed the action bar release and pulled the slide back just enough to confirm the chamber was empty. He didn't intend to have any ventilation holes added to the Caddy's quarter panels. After closing the action, he pulled an oily yellow cloth from the bag and wiped the gun down before returning both to the case and zipping it up.

Checking the shotgun was one of the ways Jelly had found to stay calm while off the ranch. Feeling the weight of his .44 Special lucky gun on his hip was another. Jelly had started carrying the gun again after retiring, even though Hoover had made a gift of the duty .357 Magnum Smith. Though he loved them both, the .44 felt right.

He remembered how he'd read up on the Samurai after meeting Donovan, and been fascinated to learn the ancient Japanese warriors believed their swords were imbued with a soul. He could understand that. Guns had always been like living things to him, in their own way. Guns and cars. They were machines with souls. The good ones anyway.

Satisfied all was in order, Jelly closed the trunk, checked his wristwatch and headed into Cattlemen's for lunch. He had more than an hour to relax and eat before his meeting. He unzipped his short leather Eisenhower jacket as he approached the door, feeling the nickel-plated blaster in its holster beneath the jacket with his right elbow.

Pushing the door open, he walked in and turned to the right. The fancy dining area was to the left but Jelly preferred the opposite side with the old tables and sit-down counter. He nodded to the girl behind the cash register and started down the far aisle heading for his favorite table when he saw someone already seated there. The salt-and-pepper-haired man with a distinctive scar running up the side of his face was facing the door, both hands wrapped around a glass filled with whisky and ice. His eyes were lasered on Jelly.

It took but a few milliseconds for Jelly's brain to adjust for the aged appearance of the man but then it clicked and the identity was certain: it was Donnelly. He was waiting.

When Jelly recognized him he felt himself unintentionally freeze up just for a moment, so briefly that no one watching him would have even noticed. No one other than Donnelly. Donnelly saw it and smiled knowingly at Jelly, then shook his head slightly side to side. Jelly read the movement as indicating no danger. His senses, already on high alert at the sight of the man he hadn't seen since the war, ratcheted up another notch at the unspoken reassurance of safety.

"Hey," Donnelly said amicably as Jelly walked slowly to the table.

Jelly's eyes narrowed. He wanted to scan the room but didn't want to take his eyes off Donnelly. Something was up. Though they'd shared a past in the shadows the man seated before him was no friend. Jelly had never truly been sure just what Donnelly was–other than dangerous. Even with all the FBI assets at his disposal, Jelly had never been able to find out who Donnelly really was.

"You're in my seat," Jelly said with a nod.

Donnelly's eyes went kind of dead for a moment as he considered that. "Don't trust me having your back?" he asked. It was almost a challenge.

"I don't trust anyone with my back anymore. Why are you here?"

Donnelly extended his leg and slid the chair opposite him out with his foot. "Just saying hello. I was on a job nearby. Heard from a friend you'd be in town today. Figured you'd show up here. You've become a real creature of habit." He smiled. "Buy you a drink?"

Just as he said that the waitress came by the table with Jelly's regular glass of Jack Daniels and ice in her hand and a wide smile. "Your friend Albert here told me you'd be wanting this as soon as you came in," the middle-aged woman said, glancing at Donnelly. Donnelly looked back at her and winked. She blushed and her smile widened. Donnelly had been working her. "Are you boys ready to order now?"

"Thanks, Myrna," Jelly said as he took the glass from her with his left hand, "but Albert won't be staying long."

Myrna's face fell and she looked at Donnelly again. He shrugged in response and said, "Actually, sweetheart, I may have just enough time for something quick. Can you suggest anything?"

As Myrna's smile returned she opened her mouth to reply but Jelly cut her off. "Fine then, just something quick. Bring us two orders of lamb fries, would you please?"

"You've got it!" Myrna nodded and hustled off toward

the kitchen.

"Lamb fries?"

"Yeah. The house specialty. I eat 'em every day. You don't like 'em, I'll have yours too."

Donnelly started to ask what they were when Jelly interrupted and said, "Chair."

Donnelly sighed, said, "Fine," got up slowly with his glass in his hand; the two men circled around so Jelly was facing the door, his back to the wall.

Donnelly stared at Jelly for a moment before shaking his head and sitting down in the chair. "Nothing's ever easy with you, is it," he said flatly as he placed his drink on the table, keeping both hands circled loosely around it.

Jelly carefully sat down onto the seat, placing his left hand around his drink, the other below the table. "So why the visit? Or are you just gonna drag this out?"

Donnelly's eyes tracked downward into his glass on the table. He seemed to relax. "Honest Injun, Bryce, I just wanted to stop by and see you. Nothing's going on, no mystery, no intrigue. Just saying hello to a kindred spirit and fellow traveler. That's all."

Now Jelly sighed as his eyes scanned the room behind Donnelly. Nothing unusual or out of place caught his attention. All the reflections in the glass windows showed only the regulars at their normal tables eating and drinking like he wanted to be doing right then. On the other side of the windows the street looked right. But that didn't necessarily mean it was.

When Donnelly looked up his eyes told Jelly he was telling the truth. He looked tired, Jelly thought. Tired and a lot older than the last time they'd met.

"All right," Jelly said. "A social call. So go ahead. Start being social."

Donnelly laughed. "You really are bad at this, aren't you?"

Jelly stared back.

Donnelly shook his head, still smiling. "You try, Bryce, and you're pretty good at making people think you're like them when you want to; you can be funny and charming, make people trust and like you. But I know you're not like them at all. You're more like me. You're a wolf among sheep." He smiled knowingly and, spotting Myrna approaching, added, "You'd just as soon eat them as you would your lamb fries."

Jelly thought about that as Myrna brought two plates to the table and set them down. Both were filled with breaded and fried pieces of tender meat, cut almost to look like shrimp. Small bowls brimming with red cocktail sauce and big slices of lemon nestled against the fries added to the seafood-like appearance of the food.

"Here you go, boys, enjoy!" Myrna said as she flashed Donnelly another big smile. "Can I get you anything else?"

Jelly smiled at her and gently shook his head. Myrna started walking away then looked back and threw Donnelly another smile.

Donnelly didn't catch it. He was watching Jelly pick up one of the fries and dip it in the sauce. Then he put it in his mouth and chewed slowly. Donnelly followed suit. It was delicious. A little tangy, but sweet and tender. "These are really good," he said, picking another off the plate.

Jelly nodded.

"That's where you're wrong, Donnelly," Jelly said, picking up the earlier conversation. "I'm not a wolf. I'm more like a sheepdog. My thing is protecting the sheep from the wolves. Always has been. You sitting there telling me you're a wolf isn't a smart move. I was never really sure before. But I'll believe you if that's what you tell me."

Donnelly's eyes narrowed as he chewed. He swallowed and said, "Wolf, sheepdog, what's the difference? Dog will eat a sheep if he's got a good enough reason. Or even if he just has the opportunity."

Jelly shook his head. "Only a wolf would think that way. So why the visit, Mister Wolf?" Jelly smiled and added, "Now there's a good name for you to use. You must be getting tired of Donnelly by now?"

"Haven't gone by that name in quite a few years. Albert Toulane's the name."

"If you don't mind I'll just call you Donnelly. Not a fan of the name game."

"Is that so, *Mister Peterson*?" Donnelly smiled, using the assumed name Jelly had travelled to New York City under many years before on an assassination mission. Jelly just stared back and put another lamb fry in his mouth.

Donnelly did the same then looked around as he chewed. On a shelf across from where they sat was a stack of board games. Donnelly nodded toward the games, swallowed and asked, "How about *those* games? Ever play any of them?"

Jelly glanced at the stack and shrugged.

"What about Monopoly?" Donnelly asked as he picked up his glass and took a sip of whisky. "Ever play that?"

"Yeah, sure," Jelly replied. "Sometimes with the family we play it. Why?" He'd decided to just roll with the bizarre visit and conversation. Sooner or later the point of it all would come out. Either that or there really was no point, and Donnelly was just losing it or lonely. Jelly could understand that. Loneliness ate some men to the bone, especially in the secret killing professions. No one to talk honestly with, be yourself around. After a while you became no one, nothing–even to yourself.

"Do you like it?" Donnelly asked.

"Monopoly? Yeah, it's all right. It's a game."

Donnelly sat back against his chair. "Just indulge me for

a minute. Okay?"

Jelly raised his eyebrows. Nodded. Squeezed some lemon on his lamb fries and popped another one into his mouth.

"So you play the game, go round and round the board. You buy shit, you pay fines, go to jail. Right?"

"Right," Jelly replied after swallowing. He took a sip from his glass.

Donnelly continued. "Get out of jail, buy more shit, charge the other players when they land on your property. Yes?"

Jelly nodded. "That's how you play."

"Okay then, so who wins?"

"Whoever ends up with the most money and property."

Donnelly shook his head. "Nope. I mean, who *really* wins?"

Jelly scratched his eyebrow. Chewed the inside of his cheek. Waiting.

Donnelly sat forward and started talking again. "You're looking at it too close. Back up a little bit. You're just playing the fucking game. The people who *sold* you the game are the real winners."

"Can you just talk straight for a change?" Jelly said, tiring of whatever game Donnelly was actually playing at. "What are you trying to say?"

Donnelly smiled. "Sorry," he said quietly, looking down at the table again. "Metaphors just amuse me I guess. What I'm saying, Mister Sheepdog," looking back up at Jelly, "is that the people who *sold* you the game–the people who have sold all of us the game–*they're* the ones who really win, who profit. It doesn't mean a damned thing at all to them who wins or loses the stupid fucking game. They get paid either way."

Jelly watched Donnelly closely and waited.

"When I was in Palestine after the war," Donnelly continued, lowering his voice, "I got to know a guy who'd been a prisoner in one of the concentration camps. We spent a lot of time together. He was a good man. A mensch. One night we're drinking and he starts telling me about how he was used as slave labor at one of the plants. The plant was making trucks for the Nazis. Do you know the name of the plant?"

Jelly shook his head.

"*Ford*. It was a Ford plant. Nice, huh? While these trucks were bringing supplies to the Krauts so they could kill Americans, old Henry Ford, back here safe and sound in the United States of America, was getting paid. He's one of them."

"A Nazi?"

"No. Well maybe, kinda sorta. But mostly no. He's one of them that owns the game. See it?"

Jelly was disturbed.

"Ford–and men like Ford–own the game itself, Bryce. The Allies win, the Axis wins, it doesn't really matter to these people. Because they own the game, they win no matter what. Us, the dopes *playing* their game, thinking it's all real, well we're just going round and round the board trying to figure out how to make enough money and stay out of jail long enough so we can finish the game without going bust."

"Fuck you, Donnelly," Jelly said shaking his head. "Millions of people died in that war. It was no fuckin' game. What's wrong with you?"

Donnelly stared at Jelly steadily for a few moments before grinning. "Naw," he said dismissively, "You're right, Bryce. I must just be getting too cynical in my old age." He picked up his glass and downed the whiskey that remained, ice cubes stopping at his lips then sliding back to the bottom of the glass as he set it down. "I always liked you, Bryce. I liked that I always knew where I stood with you. In some weird sort of way, I feel almost like we're connected somehow. You know? On a deeper level. Does that sound strange?"

Jelly's eyes narrowed again. "What the fuck. Do you want. From me?"

Donnelly sat back again. His shoulders sagged. His hands on the table trembled a bit. He slowly shook his head then looked Jelly in the eyes. "Nothing."

Jelly held Donnelly's gaze. The man's eyes were bloodshot and watery. Donnelly was drowning. Jelly could see it. "You need to find a life for yourself, Donnelly. Before it's too late. The war is over. You made it home. Let yourself up now. Get the fuck out of the business while you still have some time. Enjoy things a little. Loosen up."

The weakness left Donnelly's eyes and his shoulders slowly straightened. "Thanks, Mister Pot," he said with a tired smile. "Mister Kettle appreciates the words of wisdom and advice."

With that Donnelly slowly stood and extended his hand. Jelly stood up and shook it. "Is the social visit over?" he asked.

"Yes, sir. It's over. You won't be seeing me again."

"Should I read something into that?"

Donnelly shook his head. "Nope. I hope you have a good life, Bryce. You deserve it."

"You too," Jelly replied, still unsure of what this visit was about.

Donnelly picked up the last lamb fry from his plate and put it in his mouth. "These were great," he said after swallowing. "What are they again?"

"Lamb fries."

"I'll have to remember that. What part of the lamb are they made from?"

"The testicles."

Donnelly stared at him for a moment, then smiled and said, "Fuck you," disbelievingly with a chuckle. Placing his snap brim hat on his head, the man Jelly knew by several names gave him a salute, turned and walked out of the restaurant.

Jelly watched him through the window as he walked across the street, climbed into a turquoise-colored sedan and left. Jelly chewed the inside of his cheek as he considered the timing of Donnelly's surprise visit.

He wondered if the former OSS man had known that if he'd pulled this stunt any time before 1957, Jelly most likely would have broken his jaw.

* * *

The meeting that saved Donnelly a lot of pain had taken place in June 1957 at Walter Reed Army Medical Center in Washington, DC. This was around the time Jelly had started considering retirement.

One morning while reading the paper at his office he'd seen an item about General Bill Donovan that caught his attention. According to the article, Donovan had suffered some kind of stroke. While Jelly knew without doubt this news had elated Hoover, it had made him incredibly sad. Jelly believed Donovan was not only a good man, but a great one.

For years people who knew Jelly had been referring to him as a "legend" of the FBI. This generally amused him. He'd usually respond, "Yeah, I'm a legend in my own mind."

Hoover was a different story. Lots of people described Hoover as being a living legend in a much broader way, both in print and in person. The Director of the FBI not only agreed with this assessment but encouraged it.

While it was nice to be thought of in that way, Jelly never really took it to heart. Even when it came to Edgar, Jelly only half-believed it was warranted.

But Wild Bill Donovan *was* that. He was truly legendary in word and deed. He'd led a life of honor, courage and fearlessness like no one else Jelly knew of. The stories of the remarkable, bravely-insane things he'd done just went on and on, yet Donovan had also come across as humble and dedicated to causes greater than himself when Jelly'd met him.

Unfortunately, he'd also proven the adage that "No good deed goes unpunished."

A month after Japan surrendered President Truman fired then-Major General Donovan and abolished OSS with barely a by-your-leave. In a one-page letter of thanks and goodbye, Truman laid out how he'd carved up the organization Donovan built and given its parts away. Both the Research and Analysis Branch and the Presentation Branch were transferred to the State Department. The rest of OSS was fed to the War Department.

Donovan, however, having been on the ground all across the globe as events had unfolded and exploded around him, understood the coming dangers of the post-war world better than most. He knew intelligence would be a critical key, and lobbied hard for the creation of a permanent intelligence agency that could both compile and analyze foreign intelligence as well as conduct covert intelligence operations throughout the world.

Just as Hoover had done, Donovan went to Truman and presented a proposal of his own for the creation of such an agency, and suggested he should lead it.

Truman's blunt approach to delivering bad news remained consistent. "Yeah, well, General, that's just not gonna happen."

Donovan had made one more run at it. Realizing that the FBI, State Department, War Department, and many other pieces on the US Government chessboard had been set in motion against him, he'd tried to win popular support by having his contacts in the press write stories about OSS adventures during the war. It was a case of too little, too late.

Hoover's long-entrenched propaganda machine had already been humming along, pushing the narrative of how the FBI had won the spy war on the home front. He also made sure that mistakes and bungles committed by Donovan and OSS operatives during the war were publicized to a much greater degree than the successes.

It was soon over. Neither Donovan nor Hoover would ever lead America's future intelligence agency.

Truman's executive order of 22 January 1946 creating the National Intelligence Authority (NIA) and Central Intelligence Group (CIG) was soon followed by the passage of the National Security Act of 1947. As a result of this act, CIG was transformed into the Central Intelligence Agency–an organization strongly resembling that proposed to Harry Truman by Wild Bill Donovan.

Instead of walking away from the government that had treated him so poorly after the war ended, Donovan answered the call to duty once again, agreeing to serve as special assistant to the chief prosecutor at the Nuremberg War Crimes Tribunal.

Ever the soldier, and ever bound to the code of honor he lived by, Donovan quickly found himself at odds with the approach taken by the Tribunal. While he looked forward to the Nazi criminals being prosecuted and executed, he didn't believe the German general staff and officer corps should be prosecuted alongside them. Not all Germans were Nazis, he'd reasoned, any more than all Americans are Democrats.

Once again he found himself standing alone as Truman and his advisors disagreed. Holding fast to his code, Donovan stayed true to himself and resigned from the prosecution team. He owed Truman nothing. He'd paid all his debts and honored all his responsibilities.

He went home.

Five years later a new president would call him back to duty. Eisenhower, knowing Donovan's sterling character and appreciating it, appointed him ambassador to Thailand in 1953. Donovan, then seventy, was disappointed at not being put in charge of CIA but grateful for the opportunity to serve again. Two years later he resigned. His health was waning, his enthusiasm, spent.

A series of strokes in 1957 would land Donovan in the hospital where he was diagnosed with arteriosclerotic atrophy of the brain, a severe form of dementia. He deteriorated quickly. On 23 September 1957 President Eisenhower arranged for his old wartime comrade to be admitted to Washington's Walter Reed Army Medical Center.

Unlike many of the Washington bureaucrats who fled whatever ship they were on once it started taking on water, the men and women who'd served with Donovan in OSS were loyal. Not only did he have whatever he needed to be comfortable in the hospital, but his security was looked after as if he were still the commander of the wartime secret intelligence agency.

Jelly would discover this the day he went to visit Donovan at Walter Reed.

* * *

Jelly tracked down Donovan's location to a large, rose-brick Georgian Revival style building at the north end of the post. He walked past the Seahorse Fountain into the building, approaching one of several people seated behind a long information counter. When he told the young man he was there to see General Donovan, the orderly opened a log book and looked up the name. "Down this hall until you get to the elevators," the orderly said pointing to his right. "Third floor, left off the elevator, then down the end of that hall you'll see the nurses' station. They can help you."

Jelly followed the directions, moving through the crowded hallways. When he got off at the third floor, he turned left and found the nurse's station. Expecting a nurse to be there, he was surprised to find instead a large, serious-looking, bald man dressed in a suit seated behind the small counter. The man's neck filled the shirt collar straining the button. The suitcoat barely wrapped around his barrel chest. As Jelly approached, the man's eyes locked on him and tracked him all the way to the station.

"Can I help you, sir?" the man asked. His voice was gravelly but pleasant.

"Yes," Jelly said, taking out his FBI identification and holding it out. "I'd like to see General Donovan."

The man stared at the identification, then looked at Jelly's face. "I'm afraid the General isn't taking visitors, sir. Is there anything else I can do to help you?"

Having already scanned the man both as he'd approached and while talking with him, Jelly realized there was no outward display of identification showing on his clothing or on the counter. He'd also made out the unmistakable bulge in the material of his tight-fitting suitcoat indicating a pistol on his right hip. Jelly looked left and right. A doorway to his left led into a hallway marked with a sign reading, "Walter Reed Army Convalescent Center: Radiology." To the right was another door, closed and apparently locked. There was no sign by or above this door.

"This is a matter of some importance, sir," Jelly said calmly. "Is there anyone else I can speak to?"

Jelly detected a hardening of the man's features as he took in a slow, deep breath, straining the small white button at his neck even more. Jelly half-expected it to break free and be launched across the counter.

"Sorry," the man said evenly, "No one allowed to see the General without family approval. You're not on the list."

Jelly closed his identification wallet and held it up. "This no good?"

The wall of a man shook his head, eyes on Jelly's.

Jelly looked back for a minute, thinking. The man just stared. Not in a threatening way. But Jelly could see there was no fear. Jelly slipped his identification back inside his suitcoat. Then he slowly reached into his overcoat pocket and withdrew the sheathed spike he'd taken off Donnelly years before. He'd kept it along with other unusual and interesting things he'd acquired over the course of his professional life. He'd thought to bring it this day so he could return it to Donovan as a token of respect. Placing it gently on the counter, he said nothing. Just watched the giant's eyes looking at the spike for a moment.

The sentry–for that's what he was–looked back up at Jelly and said, "You've got ten minutes. Don't stay too long. He gets tired fast." Then he reached under the counter and pressed a button. The door to Jelly's right buzzed and unlocked. Jelly picked up the spike, placed it back in his pocket and walked through.

Inside the door he was greeted by another well-dressed sentry. This one, closer to human size, asked for Jelly's identification, then held his arms up, indicating Jelly should do the same in order to be pat-frisked. Jelly submitted to the frisk, something he would normally never allow. But he'd come too far, and wanted to see Donovan one last time. The man quickly and expertly patted Jelly down without putting his hands in Jelly's pockets. When he'd finished he stepped to the side and pointed to an open metal box on the table next to him.

"Guns and gear in there. You take the key with you. Pick up your stuff on the way out."

When Jelly hesitated the man added, "I'll keep an eye on it. Can't let you pass otherwise."

Jelly nodded. He took out the spike first and placed it in the box, then his small, bone-handled sheath knife. Pulling his set of gun-blue handcuffs from his coat pocket he held them up with a questioning look. The sentry nodded and Jelly placed them in the box. His six-inch, brown leather flat sap went next. Then he took the Registered Magnum from its holster and gently set it inside, leaving it loaded. Six loose .357 Magnum rounds taken from another pocket followed. Looking up at the sentry's eyes, he could see the man was still waiting.

"You're very good," was all Jelly said as he reached into a small inner pocket he'd had sewn into his suitcoat and retrieved the little .44 derringer Winstead had gifted him. He placed that in the box.

The sentry nodded, closed the lid, turned the brass key to lock it, then handed Jelly the key. He picked up a telephone from the table and pushed a button on the handset. "One coming down."

"Through those doors," he said, pointing to the end of the long hallway. "Don't overstay. The Old Man's having a fairly good day today so far, but that can change. Okay?"

Jelly nodded. "Thanks."

When he passed through the final set of doors he was greeted by the sight of William J. Donovan across the room lying in a big hospital bed next to a tall, double-hung window. The upper half of the bed was elevated so the General was sitting up. An orderly in a white uniform stood beside him. Donovan was wearing blue hospital pajamas covered by a thin white robe with the Walter Reed Medical Center unit insignia embroidered on the right chest with red thread. On his otherwise bare feet he wore a pair of handmade, soft leather slippers.

Jelly looked at Donovan, then the orderly, a young black man with clear, intelligent brown eyes. The name tag on the orderly's shirt read "Brooks."

"He seems to be doing okay today," Brooks said by way of greeting. "The company will do him good."

Jelly nodded and walked across the bright, sterile room to the bed. Donovan was staring out the window, gazing at a green wooded area with a creek running through it, water reflecting the morning sun wherever it peeked out through the trees.

"Hello, General," Jelly said quietly.

Donovan slowly swiveled his head, his penetrating blue eyes now softened and jaundiced. He smiled sweetly. "Hello."

Jelly looked at the man he'd only met once, but who'd left a lasting impression like few others had. Donovan's skin was nearly translucent, his white hair thinned so much it barely concealed his scalp. Blue veins showed across the backs of his hands, one of which had an intravenous tube set in it, held in place with white tape, feeding a clear liquid from a bottle suspended from a rack attached to the bed.

"How are you, sir?" Jelly asked without betraying the shock he felt at the old man's appearance.

"I'm fine, David. I'm glad you're here, son."

Jelly looked back at the orderly who was standing nearby. He'd apparently heard Donovan's comment. "David is his son," Brooks said, speaking normally.

The General was nodding. "Have you seen your mother lately?"

"General…sir," Jelly said gently, "it's Delf Bryce. *Jelly. Jelly Bryce from FBI.*"

Donovan nodded. "Yes, the FBI. Hoover's a son of a bitch, I'll give him that." Donovan smiled. "Knows how to leverage people all right. Him and all his files. Has a file on me, did you know that?"

Jelly shook his head, thinking it had been a mistake to come.

Donovan's expression turned serious as he leaned slightly toward Jelly. "I've got my own damned files on him, too. Enough material–*including photographs*–to put that bastard out of business most riki-tick." He relaxed and settled back against the pillows, smiled again. "But I'll never use them. That's his game, not mine. He's a clever, miserable fuck but he's weak of character. Hides behind his files like battlements."

Brooks walked over and checked the IV. "Nice that you have a visitor today, General," he said cheerily. "FBI agent no less, right?" looking at Jelly.

"Yes," Jelly said, looking back at Donovan. "Jelly Bryce. We met a few years ago, General Donovan. In El Paso."

Donovan looked at Brooks then back at Jelly. "Yes, of course. Good to see you."

Brooks glanced at Jelly before moving back across the room and smiled encouragingly. "He's in and out. Stay with it, he may surprise you."

"Do you know what FDR said once?" Donovan asked. Without waiting for a response he continued, "Before the war, he said he was thinking he should put me on a nice, quiet, isolated island where I could scrap with some Japs every morning before breakfast. He said that would keep me out of trouble and entirely happy." Donovan laughed.

"Son of a bitch was right! It would have!"

Jelly laughed with him. He'd decided to stay just a few more minutes and then leave. The man he'd come to see was already gone. "So are they treating you all right, sir?"

"Oh yes. Fine as kine." Donovan looked back out the window. "You know, I was thinking about all the things I'd seen and done. I was blessed, son. Truly. Even the worst of it was worth experiencing, just because it was real–unvarnished." He nodded. "I'll never forget those camps, I'll tell you that. The Nazis were pure evil incarnate. I walked into one right after our boys had liberated it. *You couldn't imagine*. I just stood there and cried like a baby." Donovan's red-rimmed eyes suddenly welled up with tears.

Jelly looked to Brooks, worried he was upsetting the old man. The orderly was standing by the door reading a newspaper opened on the table. Jelly pulled his silk pocket square from the breast pocket of his suitcoat and handed it to Donovan. The General looked at it, took it and wiped his eyes. "Thank you," he said when finished, keeping it clenched in his hand.

"But even with that, David," Donovan said, clear-eyed again, "I still believe, as bad as we can be, as awful the things we're capable of doing, so are we just as capable of doing the greatest of good. *Our potential is limitless*. We'll find our way through this dangerous time. Like Lincoln said, 'the better angels of our nature,' you know?"

Jelly smiled at the words spoken by the old man on the bed. Wild Bill Donovan was still in there; trapped in an old body and deteriorating mind, but still there. Jelly could just imagine him walking around with a burning torch held high, trying to find his way back to the world.

"It was wonderful to see you again, General. Thank you for seeing me." Jelly reached out and patted Donovan gently on the shoulder. "You're one of the best men I've ever known, sir." Now Jelly's eyes got a little teary. He took a breath and settled it down.

Donovan was staring at him.

Jelly nodded and turned to leave but Donovan said, "Wait!"

Jelly looked back and waved, "Take care, sir."

"No!" Donovan said, "Wait. I need to tell you something."

Brooks glanced up and looked over as Jelly walked back to the bed. Donovan reached out his hand. Jelly took it and Donovan pulled him in close. "I'm glad you're here, son. I wanted to make sure you knew–it wasn't a mistake. Did he tell you?"

Jelly nodded. "I know, sir, it's okay."

"No," Donovan insisted. "Listen to me. *Jelly*." His eyes were clear and focused. "It *wasn't* a mistake. It was the woman. The woman was the target. No one else knew."

"General?" Jelly asked, seeing recognition in Donovan's eyes.

Donovan nodded strongly. "Yes, Jelly. The man in the mirror, remember? You need to know. The woman was the target. You did the right thing."

*   *   *

As Jelly walked through the parking lot outside Walter Reed he felt a tremendous weight had been lifted off him. Similar to the way Clarence Hurt had described the pressures of the job, Jelly hadn't really been aware of just how much guilt he'd been carrying until it was removed.

"The woman was the target," he said, repeating Donovan's words. The General had fought his way to the surface just long enough to put Jelly's mind to rest. It didn't matter that a few minutes afterward Donovan had disappeared again, looking out the window where his mind fed him an image of Soviet tanks coming across the Queensborough Bridge. "They can't be allowed to cross, goddammit!" he'd railed as Brooks rushed to the bed and prepared a syringe. "The tanks, the fuckin' Soviet tanks! Can't you see them? There's T-34s on the bridge. They can't be allowed to cross. They'll take Manhattan!"

Brooks had injected the needle into a Y-shaped port on the IV tube close to Donovan's hand. Almost immediately the General had visibly relaxed, settling back into the pillows, eyes half-closing.

"Tell Dulles to handle this," Donovan had said drowsily. "He's a good man. He'll know what to do." He'd then closed his eyes and drifted off to sleep as Brooks checked his pulse.

Jelly had stood in silent witness as the orderly attended to his only patient. But in his mind he'd been far from the hospital room, transported back to 1944 and his one and only OSS mission.

* * *

June 1944

After Jelly's surprise meeting at the Roswell bookstore with Donnelly, he'd taken the small canvas bag and secured it in the trunk of his car. He'd initially been a little wary of the bag for a few reasons: if it *was* a bomb inside–which he believed it was–it might go off unintentionally and kill him. If Donnelly or someone else wanted him dead for some reason, it might also go off *on purpose* with the same result. Either way it would be a bad day for Jelly Bryce. His logic quickly overruled both possibilities. The device had to be a world class construct so it wouldn't go bang until it was supposed to. And if these people wanted him dead, there were plenty of easier and less attention-attracting methods to get that done.

Into the trunk it went.

Jelly left Roswell that afternoon and drove for an hour or so until he found himself on a long stretch of empty desert highway. He pulled off the side of the road next to a barbed wire fence that seemed to run forever in both directions. There was no traffic visible for miles. Jelly walked around to the back of the car, opened the trunk, unzipped the bag and looked in. What he found was a metal container. He unsnapped the latch, carefully opened the top and saw a neatly packaged device comprised of three parts with an unmarked envelope on top. He opened the envelope and read the hand-written note within. It was short and sweet, reading: "Good luck, Samurai. –D." Just enough to convince Jelly that Donovan had written it. Below that was written the name of the airfield, time and date of take-off and the aircraft's tail number.

He turned the paper over. On the back was a set of assembly instructions written in plain language along with a series of crudely-drawn illustrations. "Are you shittin' me, Donnelly?" he asked incredulously. "I gotta put this thing together?"

Though he hadn't had a lot of experience with bombs beyond a Bureau-sponsored familiarization class, he had to admit this looked to be a good one. Some years before during a car chase, a couple of gangsters he and Wilder were after had thrown sticks of dynamite at them. Luckily only one had actually detonated, but the blast generated by one measly stick had been pretty impressive. That's sort of what he'd been expecting with this: a bunch of sticks of TNT taped together with wires and a big ticking clock attached.

Instead, according to the drawings, the device looked

almost like some kind of sap-like impact weapon when assembled. There was a six-inch long metal pipe, about an inch-and-a-half in diameter; a smaller tube that fit in one end of the pipe; and a flexible cloth tube about a foot long filled with a putty-like material. According to the directions, the small tube was a "booster." It fit inside the metal pipe which housed the triggering mechanism. The long cloth tube would be attached to the end of the pipe over the booster. The putty material was actually a pound's worth of plastic explosive.

Jelly read the directions.

"The triggering mechanism is activated by the drop in external atmospheric pressure when the plane rises to an altitude of approximately 1500 ft. above take-off level. A diaphragm forms one wall of a pressure chamber which is sealed at take-off level by removing the metal strip and tightening a counter-sunk screw. The safety pin is then removed which will arm the unit."

Jelly rotated the pipe in its little cut out slot in the case until he saw the flat metal strip that served as screwdriver and the safety pin taped to the side.

"Changes in temperature have been compensated for, and the device will work satisfactorily in low, high, or rapidly changing temperatures."

'Okay,' Jelly thought. *'Good to know.'*

"The assembled unit should be concealed in a location on the aircraft that is not usually checked in pre-flight inspections. Best examples of these are the weight-lightening holes in the wall of the wheel wells, accessible when the wheels are down. These holes open directly under the wing fuel tanks insuring total destruction. The weapon can also be placed in the tail assembly where the lifting bar is inserted."

One of the line drawings showed a man inserting the device, metal tube first into an opening on the underside of a plane's wing. The cloth tube was shown bending as he did this. Jelly got it. "Doesn't look too complicated," he said.

He knew he could do this job. He was actually intrigued by the whole operation. The hardest part would be getting out on the airfield and placing the device without being seen.

"Hell," Jelly said aloud as he placed the instructions back in the box and shut the lid. "I'm a fuckin' Indian. They won't even know I'd been there."

* * *

The news about the mysterious plane crash in Mexico broke a few days after Jelly had returned home. Though there was nothing in the local newspapers about it, the Bureau intelligence feed had picked it up. Jelly read the report with interest.

The aircraft, a Canadian-made Noorduyn Norseman C-64A was a single-engine bush plane made for taking off from, and landing in rough environments. Some had pontoons affixed. This one didn't. Just two fixed wheels protruding from the lower fuselage like Donnelly had described and a small tail wheel in back.

This particular plane had been modified by the addition of two fuselage belly tanks which dramatically increased its range. They'd also dramatically increased the size of the fireball when the device exploded at 1,534 feet killing all five aboard.

The description of those killed was vague enough. Two military Peruvian pilots, a Peruvian Army Colonel named Amaru, an American expat named Johnson–and his fiancée.

Jelly's breath caught as he read the last part. *A woman had been on board.* Some poor girl who'd done nothing to deserve death other than being on the wrong plane at the wrong time.

Though he understood that millions of innocents had already died during this war which was still not over, *he* was responsible for this. He didn't even attempt to rationalize it as "following orders" or casualties of war.

He'd set the device, no one else. He owned the deaths of the people aboard that plane as surely as if he'd shot each of them one at a time.

Like all the others he'd sent across the river, he would have to live with them.

The difference was, with the exception of the people on that plane, all the others he'd killed had brought it on themselves. Their actions at the moment he'd pulled the trigger *caused* him to pull the trigger.

This was a different animal altogether. And though he knew he could live with it because his mind and will were strong as iron, he also knew the fact he'd caused the death of an innocent woman would torture him for the rest of his life.

Or so he'd thought until Donovan had fought his way back through the barbed wired trenches of his mind to save him from that life sentence. For even though Jelly would never know the backstory, Donovan had told him the woman had been the target.

Donovan's word alone was good enough.

* * *

On February 8, 1959, Wild Bill Donovan died at Walter Reed Army Medical Center. He was 76 years old.

Allen Dulles, Director of CIA, had a cable sent to all station chiefs around the world: "The man more responsible than any other for the existence of the Central Intelligence Agency has passed away."

Donovan, the man President Eisenhower called "the last hero" after his death, is still the only American to receive the nation's four highest awards: The Medal of Honor, the Distinguished Service Cross, the Distinguished Service Medal, and the National Security Medal.

TOP SECRET

OFFICE OF STRATEGIC SERVICES
WASHINGTON, D.C.

Her name had been Marta Muratova. Born in Saint Petersburg, Russia to wealthy parents, she'd been spirited away to Paris by her family when they'd fled the Revolution of 1917.

Though they'd lost most of their wealth and possessions, her father managed to preserve enough to provide them a comfortable life in France.

She received a classical education in Paris, becoming fluent in English, French and German. Hired as a journalist by a French newspaper, she travelled extensively throughout Europe during the mid-1930s.

Being young, beautiful, and educated, Marta was invited to countless social functions and introduced to the powerful and famous. At one of these functions she met several members of the Nazi Party who were quite charmed by her. In addition to attempts to seduce her into bed were several attempts to seduce her into intelligence work. She'd initially refused them all.

Then when France fell in June 1940 she had a change of heart and agreed to work for the Abwehr. In exchange, her family would be protected. Her German handler trained Marta in spycraft for several months. Marta was bright and learned quickly. She had a knack for intelligence work and was soon given an assignment in Spain. Once in Madrid, she used her new skills to locate and contact the British MI5 representative, revealed who she was and offered to work for them as a double agent. They checked her out and took her on.

Though she performed exceptionally well for the Brits, sending her German handlers false information for months, she also started to become temperamental. Her demands grew. She enjoyed a lavish lifestyle which she felt entitled to. She was, after all, risking her life for the British Government.

Soon her demands turned to threats. She'd been seeing an American expat businessman while on an operation for the Germans in Bolivia, and had not only told him she was a spy, but that she was doubled. When her MI5 handler found out, Marta threatened to send a secret signal to her German handler that would alert them she was under British control. If that happened, all the work she'd been doing for the Brits would be undone. Quite a bit of erroneous information had been given to the Nazis during her time working for MI5.

If it came undone, numerous operations and agents would be compromised, and worse- the fact the Brits had broken the German Enigma encryption machines would come to light. Many of Marta's specially-prepared messages to her Nazi handlers had been re-encrypted in the Enigma machines, the British using them to verify the accuracy of their de-encryptions by comparing Marta's known text against those intercepted and translated back in Bletchley Park.

It couldn't be allowed. The opportunity

to set things straight presented itself when Marta accompanied her now-fiancé, Felix Johnson, on a trip to Mexico. Johnson had been working with the Nazis for years in Bolivia before and during the war. It had been profitable for them all. Johnson would never jeopardize his position or relationship with his Nazi business partners by revealing Marta's duplicity. It would mean both their deaths. He'd decided to just ride it out, especially since a new venture was underway.

The Germans were interested in expanding into Peru and had been for some time. In early 1943, Johnson had made contact with a high-ranking member of Peru's fragmented government, a cold, calculating man named Alvaro Amaru. Amaru had no qualms about working with the Nazis, any more than he'd had about working with the French. It was all just business to him. Being placed in charge of Peru's government by his Nazi handlers after the existing government was overthrown in a coup carried out by his loyal troops was a perfect outcome as far as Amaru was concerned.

Not surprisingly, all of this intrigue had gone largely unreported by the FBI's assets in Latin America. Back in New York someone had decided the rumors of Nazi influence in Bolivia and Peru were simply red herrings fomented by the Communists.

What the Brits needed was a simple solution that would tie up all these loose ends without giving away Marta's double-agent role. Stephenson had reached out to Donovan whose first thought hadn't been of Jelly.

It had been Donnelly who'd put the pieces

together. He'd suggested they utilize the competent FBI agent for the job since the timing was perfect. Donovan had agreed. Donnelly had made the preparations.

Jelly had carried it out.

CHAPTER TWENTY-TWO

Alone
1973

THE DAY SHE DIED he was by her bed in the hospital. The car wreck had taken the drunken driver instantly but Francine had suffered for a week. Jelly tried to tell himself it was a blessing she was finally at rest. He kissed her gently on the lips, held her hand for a long time. The nurses left him alone like that for more than an hour. He didn't cry.

When he finally was able to get up and leave her, he walked slowly to the car, feeling numb. Climbing behind the wheel of the Cadillac he started it up and began the long drive home.

That's when the crying started but it was unlike any crying he'd ever experienced. His left hand gripping the steering wheel, Jelly piloted the car slowly and steadily down the roadway. In his right hand he held a small towel he kept on the front seat to wipe dust from the dashboard and gauges. He held the towel over his mouth and nose, and as he drove in traffic, his chest heaved as he sucked in lungs full of air and exhaled that air in the form of low moans that grew in intensity. His breathing was steady, his driving perfect. Tears streamed down his cheeks into the towel as mile after mile passed. Part of his mind was in complete control of the vehicle and his thoughts were calm and reasoned. That part of his mind accepted the other part and left it alone–the grieving animal part that was inconsolably sad, that shifted from grief to momentary anger and back again. He steered onto the ramp to the highway and drove on like that for a long time. Then it would stop and he would catch his breath, the calm mind in complete control for several seconds or minutes. Then the next wave would come from deep, deep in his chest, his heart breaking all to pieces, tears and sobs pouring from his body like blood from a wound mile after mile until he arrived home.

He pulled into the driveway, rolled the window down and shut the car off and sat there staring up into the late afternoon sky. A cool breeze touched the red, hot skin of his face. The crying stopped.

He got out of the car and walked into the house, leaving the Caddy's window down. *'Might rain,'* the controlling part of his mind said, though only halfheartedly. It was running on autopilot it seemed, reminding him of things he would normally be unable to leave undone. Jelly didn't even pause or respond to the thought, just walked into the house, went up to their bedroom and fell to his knees not in prayer, just doubled over by the tremendous weight of the grief that started rolling through his body wave after wave again. Without the distraction of driving the car, the grieving animal inside him took over completely, and Jelly listened with a sort of awe as his body shuddered and shook, moans becoming louder and more intense with each breath, tears streaming down his face in such magnitude that he worried about becoming dehydrated.

This went on for five days–though not continuously. When after an hour or so the sobbing would stop he'd drink some water, eat some food, talk on the telephone. He had arrangements that had to be made, friends and family would call, people stopped by the house. Jelly greeted them all and said what had to be said and listened as they talked but inside he was wailing and moaning, the animal pushed down deep but tearing him up, demanding to be let out.

He went to the funeral home and picked out the box she'd be laid in and the headstone that would mark her resting spot and brought the dress, jewelry and makeup she'd wear for the wake and the banality and perfunctory nature crushed him because the raging animal wanted to destroy something, destroy the thing that caused this, but the son of a bitch was dead and Jelly couldn't dig him up and shoot him or tear him to pieces or maybe he could but it would change nothing.

"It's just what happened," he would say again and again when the tears stopped, his face and teeth aching from crying. "No reason for it, no sense to it, no greater purpose or meaning. It's just what happened." Then the words, "I can't believe she's gone. What do I do now?" would spill out of his mouth and the next wave of grief and tears would hit.

The night of the wake he stood by the wall with his family and greeted the people who'd come to pay their respects and thanked them for their condolences and never left his spot despite the fact the line went out the door and down the sidewalk in front of the funeral home.

Five hours later the last person left and Jelly used the bathroom then went out back and smoked a cigarette. When he finished it he just tossed it aside without the usual field stripping ritual and slipped his stainless-steel flask from his jacket's breast pocket, unscrewed the cover and took a long pull. The whiskey went down easy into his empty stomach and almost immediately started to do its job. He screwed the cover back on, put the flask away and took out the last cigarette from the pack and lit it up. Holding the empty cigarette pack in his hand he studied the image of the camel standing in front of the pyramids for a moment, then crushed the pack in his hand.

Jelly let the pack fall to the ground and the memory of dropping the old cigar box he used to keep his pistol in that first day at the range when he'd met Clarence Hurt came rushing back to him and just for a moment he wondered what ever happened to it as he took a few more drags on the smoke. He'd liked that old box. It had been his grandfather's.

Then the thought passed and Jelly tossed the second butt to the ground and went back inside to sit next to his wife for a while longer.

The night after they'd buried Francine, Jelly was lying in bed staring at the ceiling thinking he was doing okay when his head started to swim and his chest began pounding out a strange beat. His legs and arms went suddenly cold and he began shivering uncontrollably. He knew he was dying and should get to the telephone to call for help but instead he wrapped the blankets around him and waited for his heart to stop or the blood vessels in his brain to burst and he felt no fear. His youngest son was grown and on his own path for better or worse. His oldest son was a stranger to him and would be better off without him. The rest of his family would grieve him and so would his friends but everyone left sooner or later and if now was his time that would be fine with him. Losing Francine had torn the joy from his life. The world was a darker, grayer, colder place–more so than it had ever been to him before. If it would all just end here and now, he thought, it would be a blessing. He shivered like that in their bed, waiting for it all to disappear. Hours later he opened his eyes, back from a deep sleep, surprised he was still alive but not overjoyed. "Another day above ground," he croaked, rolling onto his back.

Eyes on the ceiling he reached out to the night table by the bed, his hand instantly landing on the pack of cigarettes. He shook one out, put it in the corner of his mouth, then slipped the book of matches from the cellophane that covered the cigarette pack and lit the first smoke of the new day. Before he was finally able to get himself out of the bed he'd smoke three more, one after another.

Six weeks after they'd buried Francine in her spot in Mountain View Cemetery, Jelly stood by the grave looking down at the new grass that had grown in the dirt that covered his beloved wife.

He spoke to her softly, first sadly, then laughing as they remembered some funny thing they'd shared when she was still in the flesh, not simply alive in his mind.

Afterward, he drove thirty miles to Sentinel and located the cemetery where they'd buried the drunken bastard who'd taken his Francine from him. Jelly walked a grid pattern until he located the spot. He read the name on the new stone and checked the date of death. Satisfied he'd found the right grave, he didn't even look around to see if anyone was nearby as he drew his .44 Special and pumped six rounds directly down into the ground above the casket six feet below. He knew the rounds wouldn't penetrate more than a few inches into the soil but it just seemed like the thing to do in that moment. Then the moment passed and he realized he felt no differently and his Francine was still gone.

Standing there like that, big blaster warm in his hand, Jelly felt a thousand years old and empty as his pistol. "I'm all alone," he said and the world seemed like a lost and empty place to him.

His head hung forward toward the grave below him and he cried for the last time.

Soon after that the image of the rope returned to him. Only at night. Only as he lay alone in his bed. He knew he'd never do it. There wasn't even a question. He'd never do that to himself, or his family. Especially the boys. Suicide was an evil thing. It could almost be contagious. If someone in your family does it, it sort of becomes an acceptable alternative for someone else when they're going through their own dark times.

Jelly's favorite author, Ernest Hemmingway had gone out that way, same as Hemingway's father Clarence had years before. Both of them used guns–the father, an old Civil War Smith and Wesson .32 revolver; Ernest ended it with a W. & C. Scott & Son shotgun. Another Hemingway, Ernest's sister Ursula, was believed to have been a suicide as well. She used pills.

"An evil thing, suicide." Jelly said aloud each night.

But now he better understood those who chose that exit. He thought of Tom Wilson.

Sometimes it just seemed the better path. Sometimes his mind told him it wasn't just better, but correct. It was time to go. His life had been spent. There was nothing left here for him. *But no*. He would never do that. Not that. Wouldn't do that to his sister. His dad. His family and friends. And most of all, he wouldn't do that to his boys. Not his boys. He wouldn't leave them that for a legacy.

But it was a struggle.

On top of all that was the night torture. That's what he'd taken to calling them, those episodes that felt like physical death was imminent and unstoppable, only to have it and all the symptoms pass again and again with no aftereffects or physical damage–that he could see.

Jelly Bryce was feeling worn out.

CHAPTER TWENTY-THREE

Shangri-La Resort
Grand Lake O' the Cherokees, Oklahoma
12 May 1974

"JELLY? JELLY! WHERE ARE you, man?" Jim Rutherford was speaking to him. Jelly looked up from his glass. He'd been deep in thought for quite a while apparently.

"Sorry, Jim," he said seriously.

Rutherford smiled. "It's okay, my friend. I've just been blathering on and on here, thought you'd maybe like to tell these young agents a different story."

Jelly looked at Frank Brandt and Jerry Hennigan seated there, drinks nearly empty, smiling kindly back at him.

"You know, gentlemen, if you don't mind, I think I'll take the dog outside to do its business."

The older agent, Brandt, looked disappointed. Jelly was surprised to see the younger agent who needed a shave and a haircut did as well. He'd been sure they were just listening to be polite.

Hennigan spoke up. "Mister Bryce, before you go, could I just ask you something?"

Brandt grew nervous, worried Hennigan was going to ask something about killing men. Some young guys who didn't know better felt it was an appropriate question.

Jelly looked back at Hennigan. "Sure."

"Would you mind giving me a little advice? I'm looking forward to a long career with the Bureau. Anything you can tell me that might help me not screw it up?"

Brandt was relieved. The question was actually a good

one. He was curious to hear Jelly's reply.

Jelly looked down at the table for a moment. Quietly he said, "Let me ask you a question first."

"Okay," Hennigan said, leaning forward.

"What do you think happens to us when we die?"

Hennigan's eyes narrowed. Then he smiled. "I'm kinda hoping I'll do enough things right so I get my ticket punched into Heaven."

Jelly smiled back at him. Then he looked at Brandt. "What about you?"

Brandt shook his head. "I have no idea, sir."

Jelly glanced at Rutherford. The big man looked at his drink. He was staying out of it.

Jelly turned his gaze back on Hennigan. "See, I believe when I die, the world will come to an end." He waited to see the response. Hennigan's eyebrows went up and he looked at Brandt. Brandt remained steady, eyes on Jelly.

"Do either of you remember what it was like before you were born?" Jelly asked seriously.

Both men shook their heads.

"Yeah, me neither. That's what I believe death will be like. Nothing. Just nothing at all. And if that's true, gentlemen, that means all we have is the here and now. This life. Now some people look forward to the afterlife. Hell, some people invest more into their life after death than the one they're in the middle of here and now."

Brandt nodded.

"But see," Jelly said leaning forward, hand around the dog's little torso, "If this is all there is, then we have an opportunity to do great things with our time on Earth. To make it all count. Because if this is it, then this will be our only chance to do that."

Hennigan settled down. Now he was nodding.

"For me, fellas," Jelly said sincerely, "all I want, at the

end of my life–which I'm closer to than either of you–is to be able to look at myself in the mirror and know I did the best I could while I was here. That I stayed true to myself and did the right thing, even when it would have been easier not to. If you can do that, Mister Hennigan, then no matter what else happens, you will have lived a successful, honorable life."

Jelly sat there looking at the two younger men. Then he smiled. They smiled back, both of them nodding. Jelly stood up, holding the dog with his left hand under its front legs, its little body supported by his forearm. "If you'll excuse me now, gentlemen."

Both agents stood; Hennigan walked around the table and extended his hand. Jelly took it and they shook. "Thank you, Mister Bryce. Thank you very much, sir."

"Jelly," Rutherford said, still seated, "Are you coming back for the interview?"

"I think I'm gonna have to pass, Jimmy. Feeling more tired than I ever have right now. Think I just need a good night's sleep."

*   *   *

"Another drink, Mister Rutherford?" Hennigan asked after Jelly had left. "Bureau's buying."

"Way I figure it," Rutherford replied with a grin, "the Bureau owes me at least one drink."

Brandt smiled, held up his hand and waved to the waitress, indicating another round for the table. She squinted her eyes, pointing her index finger at them counting, then smiled and waved back.

"He gonna be okay?" Hennigan asked, nodding toward Jelly who was talking to their waitress as he slowly made his way to the exit.

Rutherford turned his large frame around in the chair and looked, just catching a glimpse of Jelly as he disappeared out the doorway. "That guy's always okay. Don't let the little old man appearance deceive you. He's one tough hombre, gentlemen. The stories I can tell you about Jelly Bryce would curl your hair."

Brandt nodded, then asked, "Didn't I hear something about him running for governor, too?"

Rutherford nodded. "He did. Back in '58 when he retired from the Bureau. I actually spent some time with him, working on his campaign."

"How'd it go?" Hennigan asked.

"Well, let me put it this way: Jelly threw his hat in the ring and was immediately approached by a lot of people with their hands out. The Democrats were interested in him, but the going price tag for the nomination then was three-hundred thousand. Jelly refused to play, even though he had enough wealthy supporters that he could have easily raised the money."

Brandt shook his head. "Nice to know nothing's changed."

"Just the price," Rutherford said smiling. "Now I hear the cost for admission is a half-million. Anyway, Jelly ends up filing as an Independent candidate and goes to war with the establishment on both sides–Dems and Republicans. He also swore he wouldn't attack any of the other candidates individually, and he didn't. He attacked them as a whole, saying the entire system had been corrupted, and that if the people of Oklahoma wanted an honest, straight-shooting man to lead them then he was their guy. He pledged to clean up the mess and run the political parasites and unscrupulous characters out of the state house, and by God, I truly believe he would have done it."

The waitress brought the drinks to the table, including

another round of shots. "Your friend paid for these on the way out. You know, the gentleman with the little dog."

The men smiled at her. Brandt reached into his pocket for a tip but the waitress held up her hand. "Oh no, he took care of that too." Then she walked back toward the bar through the now-thinning crowd. It was getting late.

Rutherford lifted the shot glass and held it up. "To your health, gentlemen." They all downed the whiskey, then turned to the cold beers that accompanied them.

"So how badly did he lose, if I'm reading your story right?" Brandt asked.

Rutherford looked down at his beer. "Well, I'll tell you." He looked up and glanced around, then turned back to the agents. "And this stays at this table, yes?"

Both agents nodded and leaned forward in their seats.

"Well," Rutherford began, lowering his voice, "around the middle of the election cycle, Jelly is getting trounced. The other candidates are outspending him, out-advertising him, out-talking him. So back in DC, Hoover–who always had a special affection for Jelly–Hoover's been monitoring this whole thing. One afternoon he calls me up, tells me he's sending a package by courier for Jelly, wants me to pick it up. Now this is Hoover calling himself, mind you. That was a big deal. Around that time, too, he'd started to get a little…eccentric. Made people uneasy if you had to deal with him directly."

"Like what?" Hennigan asked. Brandt shot him a look. Rutherford didn't notice.

"Well," Rutherford said, "he was getting older then, you know. Had become a bit of a hypochondriac, washing his hands like a thousand times a day, stuff like that. Then the word started coming down that if you were ever near him, you couldn't step on his shadow or he'd go ballistic."

Hennigan's eyebrows stretched to their apex. "What?"

Rutherford nodded. "For real. Got a little fucky toward the end, old J. Edgar did." Rutherford sat back and narrowed his eyes. "Actually, I guess that wasn't really too close to the end at all. He lasted another fourteen years now that I think about it."

"So the packet?" Brandt said.

"Yes, the packet." Rutherford leaned in closer. "So I get this packet and give it to Jelly. It's got no markings on the outside–sterile, you know? An' Jelly looks at it and says, 'What's this?' So I tell him it's from the boss. He goes to his desk and sits down, opens it up, and I can tell from across the room what it is. They're files from the "Do Not File" file."

Before Hennigan could ask, Brandt looked at him and said, "Don't ask."

Rutherford nodded. "Right. Anyways, if I had to guess, I'd guess there was enough information in those files to blow up all the other candidates in the race. I'm talkin' Hiroshima and Nagasaki quality devastation. Once those puppies dropped, Jelly would be the only man left standing in Oklahoma state politics."

Hennigan looked confused. "But you said he lost?"

Rutherford smiled again. "That he did. And here's why. After looking over those files Jelly just sat there for a few minutes. I could see he was thinking. Then he stood up, picked up a metal wastebasket and set it by the window. Opened the window, took out a cigarette and his lighter and lit the smoke. Then he picked up the files, looked at me, and touched the flame from his lighter to the edge of the paper till it caught. Once it was burnin' good, he dropped it into the basket and we just stood there watching those yellow flames consume his election."

Hennigan's eyes narrowed in thought.

Brandt smiled. "Good for him."

Rutherford looked at him and smiled back. "That's what *I* said."

*   *   *

Jelly pulled the wrapped-up leash from his pocket and snapped it to the poodle's collar. The leash was light like the dog. Light and strong. Bending over he set Tequila on his four little paws on the sidewalk in front of the convention center building. The dog looked up at him expectantly, checking to see if everything was all right. For ten years Jelly had been the big dog in their pack.

Looking down into the animal's trusting eyes, Jelly could read every thought and impulse sparking through his little buddy's dog brain. He smiled at his loyal companion, nodded and quietly said, "Go ahead."

Reassured, the poodle stretched, butt in the air for a moment, then straightened up and began carefully checking for messages along the walkway. It was important to find just the right spot for leaving a turd. Life was good in Tequila land.

Francine had loved the little dog from the moment Jelly'd brought it home as a pup. It had been a cold fall day so Jelly'd placed the poodle inside his leather jacket to keep it warm. He'd never forgotten the look on his wife's face when he'd unzipped the jacket and the tiny head popped out, all black nose, big brown eyes and downy gray fur. Francine had immediately fallen in love with the puppy and vice versa.

Jelly had hoped the poodle would help add a dimension to the family that had been missing ever since Jimmy left shortly after his eighteenth birthday. It had. The longer the dog was with them, the more Jelly and Francine treated it like a child rather than a pet.

The dog didn't see it that way, though. Decades of careful breeding couldn't eliminate its core DNA programming. It was a pack animal, and quickly identified Francine as the human mate of the leader.

As a result, while Tequila was extremely loyal to, and affectionate with Francine, the little high-strung dog had become neurotically obsessed with the man. Jelly was the alpha in their pack. In Tequila's world that was everything. The sun rose and set on the flawless leader whose every glance had meaning. Even when Jelly was sleeping in his big chair in the living room the poodle would sit and just watch him, waiting for the slightest movement of the inspirational, charismatic being who only had to open one sleepy eye to trigger a tail-wagging, excited greeting.

It was amusing for people to witness the relationship. Jelly accepted the situation with humor and respect, paying a great deal of attention to the pup, always aware of Tequila's nervous temperament and doing his best to keep him calm.

For nearly a decade the little family dynamic had been working for the Bryces in their home in Mountain View. In many ways it had improved Jelly's and Francine's relationship because the dog was so in tune with them that their slightest actions would set it off like some kind of stress detector.

If Jelly and Francine ever argued or even raised their voices in agreement while making a point on some rant, the little fella would take a position between them, his whole body shaking, the worried look in his eyes stopping them in their tracks. Whatever issue they were discussing became irrelevant as they focused their attention on restoring his faith in them, for without doubt they'd failed the simplest expectation of the junior member of their pack–the expectation of unity. Jelly, who hadn't had a dog since he was a kid, felt he understood Tequila better than he'd ever understood most humans.

"Right, little fella?" Jelly said, looking down at the dog as he led it slowly into the lobby of his hotel and pressed the elevator call button. The poodle looked up at him and whined. Jelly bent down, rubbed Tequila behind his ears then picked him up and held him as he waited for the elevator, standing conspicuously off to the side of the doors.

When the doors finally opened he waited there for a moment, then slowly changed his position until he could see the elevator was completely empty. Stepping inside, he stood in the rear left corner so he wouldn't be immediately visible to someone in the hall when the doors opened again.

On the short ride to the third floor several memories of similar elevator rides flashed through Jelly's mind. Slow motion rides that had too often ended in violence. Though the slideshow of death and mayhem in his head had faded in both frequency and intensity over the past 16 years, he could still bring images up easily when he wanted. Occasionally, something as innocuous as an elevator ride would still trigger a vivid memory with no prompting on his part.

When the quiet chime announcing they'd passed the second floor sounded, Jelly glanced into the copper-colored reflective panel mounted to the wall in the elevator and saw Agent Tom Spenser's shredded face staring back. Part of Jelly's mind combed through the internal filing cabinet and instantaneously recovered the facts of the case: *'New York, January 1935. Tom Spenser, permanently disfigured and blinded by a mid-level killer-for-hire-piece of shit gangster, Luke Ferrengamo.'*

The events of the case flooded back to him. Thanks to some excellent police work by the NYPD, Ferrengamo had been caught within hours. The FBI agents who'd originally gone in to capture the man had fucked up the operation to a fare-thee-well. Ferrengamo had fired a sawed-off shotgun through the door of the room he was in, nearly murdering Spenser and seriously wounding several other agents. Then he'd gone out the window and escaped by sliding down some sheets from the seventh floor. That mission had been a turning point for Jelly. He'd been there when it happened. After that day he never worked with anyone he didn't know or trust unless forced to by orders or circumstances, in which case he would assume absolute control of the operation–and God help the man who opposed him doing so.

The elevator stopped and the doors opened with a distracting metallic rolling sound, drawing Jelly's eyes from the disturbing image on the panel to the dimly-lit hallway outside the elevator. He stepped out and turned to the left, counting the numbers on the doors until he arrived at his. The "Do Not Disturb" sign still hung from the doorknob. His eyes followed the seam of the door on the hinged side. He'd placed a paper match between the door and frame a cigarette's height above the floor before he'd left, pushing it too far in to be seen from the hallway.

Jelly set Tequila down on the carpeted floor, then removed the match book from his pocket. He watched the dog for a moment, sensing no anxiety or stress about any strange human odors coming from inside. Opening the matchbook, he gently slid the flap down inside the seam until he felt it hit the match. It was there, at the right height.

Straightening up, Jelly slid the key into the lock and turned it. It rotated effortlessly. *'Six well-worn pins,'* he thought. *'Take less than a minute to pick.'* Touching his elbow to his holstered pistol, Jelly pushed open the door, stepped inside and scanned the room before allowing the door to close behind him. He'd shut the drapes and left some lights on when he'd gone out earlier so everything in the room was visible but no one could get a bead on him from outside. Tequila walked in beside him, looked around, then stared up at Jelly.

Jelly leaned over, unsnapped the leash and made a double clicking sound with his tongue against his front teeth and nodded. The dog walked into the room ahead of him, then jumped up onto the bed. Jelly rotated the deadbolt, slid the chain lock into its track, then reached into his pocket and took out a wedge-shaped rubber door stop. Bending over he slid the stop in place, then gave it a few encouraging taps with the toe of his shoe to set it under the door.

On a table near the bathroom door stood an ice bucket and some glasses. Jelly opened the bucket he'd filled earlier from the machine down the hall, dropped a few cubes in a glass, then took out his new 8-ounce hipflask and poured himself a double. He looked at the stainless flask. "PLAN B" was engraved on the front. He smiled. "Always gotta have a plan B, Tequila."

The dog, eyes locked on Jelly, raised its eyebrow-like ridge and whined. Jelly smiled back. "It's okay, baby," he said. "Daddy's fine."

He slipped his jacket on a hanger and put it in the closet, then kicked off his shoes. Taking his lucky gun from the holster, he walked over to the bed, pulled the spread down with his left hand then slid the .44 Special under one of the pillows. He pulled his wallet from his back pocket and set it on the night table, then walked back to the closet, took off his trousers and hung those up as well, leaving his belt through the loops, holster still in place. Last to come off was his pearl tie pin, necktie and shirt. Once they were neatly hung he picked up his glass and swallowed the whiskey down.

He sat heavily on the edge of the bed. Tequila yawned,

stretched, and huffed as he low crawled into a better position next to Jelly, then placed one of his little paws on Jelly's leg. Jelly placed his hand on the dog's neck and rubbed the loose skin; scratched gently behind the animal's soft ears again.

Then Jelly grimaced and shook his head. He'd lied to the dog. Daddy wasn't fine.

* * *

Earlier that evening, when the attractive brunette who'd reminded him of Francine had walked off with Walter Walsh, she'd told Jelly and Rutherford to "collect your thoughts and think about what you'd like to tell us about your lives, okay?"

It was a completely natural thing to say considering they were going to be interviewed. But an unsettling thing had happened as Jelly had sat there at the table thinking, reviewing his life in his mind. After going over his story from his early days in the Bureau through to the end, he suddenly realized he'd never even thought about his wife or children. *Not a moment's thought.* He'd compartmentalized his life so completely in his mind that it wasn't until he'd finished internally narrating his story that it even occurred to him. *'What the hell?'*

It was an uncomfortable moment of self-realization. What had he done? What had he become?

The work had apparently consumed him. *'No,'* Jelly thought, *'the work had been my fortress.' He* had placed himself inside of it; *he* had built the walls stone by stone.

God, he was tired. And in his exhausted state, with just enough alcohol in his system to relax him, his mind finally rolled on itself, and he could see himself from some distance.

It was in that moment he realized with shocking clarity

the primary lever that had moved him all those years was fear. He'd been afraid. Nearly his whole life, it seemed, he'd been afraid of loss. His mother's death when he was a boy had taught him about the excruciating pain of loss.

* * *

The morning she'd died he'd thought he would surely die as well. He'd suffered like that, trapped in his adolescent mind with those thoughts until she was buried.

His cousin, Little Jimmy had taught him about distraction the day of the funeral. That was the day Jelly discovered he could get lost in the work, in doing the thing he loved, in the pure art of the gun. How even when the world was crumbling around him he could shut off the fear and the pain and the noise in his head by focusing on something else.

That day it had been shooting his old .22 rifle at bottles hanging by strings from a tree.

Jelly had aimed not at the bottles that day, but at the strings, and though it had looked ridiculously fast and easy to his cousin watching him, for Jelly the time had slowed way down, his focus and concentration a singular thing; as he'd lined up each shot and pressed the trigger smoothly back he'd watched the bullet race from the muzzle and track down range toward the string. Then the next bullet, same process. Then the last.

And in those few fleeting moments the overwhelming sadness of the world coupled with the raging voice in his head–raging against the loss of his dear, beautiful mother; raging about his father's absence while she'd grown sicker; about the unfairness of the world and *his failure to get the doctor in time*–all of it had blessedly evaporated. And in that moment, in the absence of the noise and anger, he'd been given a gift, a precious break–just enough time to throw the switch in his head and stop the relentless, pounding pain and guilt.

That focus, that moment, lost in doing what he did best, lost in the process, in the work, *had saved him*, gotten him through that awful experience.

Lesson learned.

Jelly had found an effective approach to dealing with the pain of the world. He would focus on work, focus on skill, and everything else would fade into the background.

Work became a blessed refuge.

Then slowly, surely, it had become home.

"Or a prison?" Jelly asked aloud as these thoughts slowly circled one another in his mind.

Reaching over to the night table next to the bed he picked up his wallet and opened it, gold FBI retirement badge flashing in the lamp light. Shoving his fingers into the compartment behind the badge he slid out some well-worn photos, then dropped the wallet on the bed next to Tequila. The dog sniffed it disinterestedly then placed its head back on the blanket.

Jelly had been carrying the black and white photographs for years. One was a group shot of him with his mother, Maggie, dad Fel, and sister Lila a few years before Maggie had passed. Fel and Jelly had serious expressions. Maggie and Lila were smiling sweetly. Jelly remembered keying off his father. "Photographs are historical documents," Fel used to say. "A man doesn't want to be remembered as a flibbertigibbet."

The other two photographs were of his sons.

Jelly held up the photograph of Austin, moving it closer to the lamp light. He smiled, remembering. It was from the day he'd taken him to the range. His boy was wearing Jelly's fedora and cradling a Thompson Submachine gun. The gun was nearly as long as Austin.

Jelly clearly remembered Austin's face right after Jelly had drawn the letter "A" in the night sky with the tracer rounds fired through the Thompson. His son had looked up at him and smiled back happily, proudly, gazing at him as if he were Superman or something.

Then as Jelly'd watched, a shadow had clouded over Austin's face from the inside and the happy look faded, replaced with the normal look of contempt and scorn, as if he'd remembered something terrible about his father.

Against his best instincts Jelly had grown resentful at Austin's inability to accept him as he was. He knew he wasn't perfect but he'd been trying. He knew Austin was just a boy but Jelly hadn't created the situation. Austin's mother had.

After that day Jelly had stopped trying. He'd figured he'd give the boy some time to think things through. If Austin wanted to see him again, he could just ask and Jelly would be there.

Austin never asked.

Jelly wouldn't see him again until 1946 when he would refuse to help him with money for college and tell his first-born son to join the Marines.

Jelly sighed, remembering that day. He'd been going through some tough times at work, had recently completed a couple of brutal cases. His emotional armor plating was as thick as it had ever been. When his secretary had told him over the intercom his son was there to see him, Jelly had immediately thought his wife Francine had brought their new baby to the office to surprise him. He'd reacted badly to Austin and he knew it. Knew it as he was speaking with the young man in his office. Regretted the things that were coming out of his mouth even as they were spilling out and fatally poisoning the relationship.

Jelly sighed louder, shaking his head. *'What was I*

thinking?' he thought grimly.

He placed the photograph down on the table next to the first. The last one in his hand was of Jimmy. Jelly looked at it and smiled. Jimmy was about eight, wearing a cowboy hat and the gunbelt Jelly had made him. The boy was standing in a crouch as he'd been taught, holding the little .22 single-action revolver as Jelly had shown him to.

'Those were better days,' Jelly thought as he closed his eyes tightly, trying to ward off the images of the days that had followed.

* * *

Jimmy had started drinking as a teenager. Started getting into trouble. More and more often he showed contempt for Jelly, then Francine. The day Jelly witnessed the boy being disrespectful to Francine was the last straw. He'd gone after his seventeen-year-old son that day, fury in his heart and violence on his mind. For the first time in his life Jimmy had seen that look–the Jelly Bryce death gaze that froze hardened criminals in their tracks. Jelly hadn't realized he was wearing the look, showing it to the person he loved most in the world, his little boy, his son, until he saw terror in the young man's eyes. Jimmy had fallen backward; stumbling over his own feet he'd landed hard on his ass. Then he'd jumped immediately up, face red and tears in his eyes.

Jelly made himself slow down, consciously reset his face into its normal appearance. "Now you listen to me, Jimmy…" he began.

Jimmy, no longer facing the terrifying visage but seeing only his father's familiar face again, screamed, "No! You listen!" The teenager was practically frothing at the mouth. "You never hear me. You never listen! Do you know my whole life I've been afraid? Do you know that?"

Jelly took a step toward him. "*What?* Jimmy, son…"

Jimmy stepped back. His eyes were wild. Jelly was suddenly afraid for his boy.

"No!" Jimmy screamed, his chest heaving, fists balled up tight. "We hardly ever saw you–even when you were home you weren't with us. But that was better. Because when you were here all you did was make me afraid!" Jimmy's hands unclenched. He started panting, bent forward with his hands on his knees. He looked like he was about to collapse.

Jelly didn't know what to do. He wanted to help his boy, wanted to protect him. But here his son was telling him that Jelly was the thing he needed protection *from*.

Jimmy took a few deep breaths; he started to calm down a bit. He looked up at his father's face. "My whole life I've been afraid because of you." The words hung in the air between them as they stood looking into each other's eyes.

Jelly couldn't respond. He'd never seen it before that moment but suddenly the memories came flooding into his mind–all the things he'd said and done over the years, thinking he was doing the right thing to help protect his boy–suddenly and clearly he saw them from his son's perspective.

'Of course he was terrified,' his mind told him. *'He had all the awareness of danger, but no way to protect himself from it.'* Jelly felt his stomach drop. Before he could say anything Jimmy had turned and run off around the house. Jelly could hear him crashing through the brush into the field beyond.

He'd let him go.

Jimmy had moved away soon after that. Last Jelly'd heard his youngest son had gotten married and divorced. Had been bouncing from job to job.

"He'll come back, Delf," Francine had told him. "We're his family. Of course he'll come back. He just needs time to figure things out. He knows you'd never hurt him on purpose."

*   *   *

Jelly sat there on the edge of the bed, head in his hands. "What the hell. What the hell did I do? What the hell have I been doing all these years?"

After what felt like half an hour but was really only ten minutes or so, Jelly lifted his head and nodded. He'd made a decision. He would not let this stand.

He breathed in deeply, filling his lungs. Then he blew the air out slowly. "I will make this right, boys."

Jelly stood up. His legs felt weak. He attributed it to the whiskey. He walked into the bathroom, little dog jumping off the bed and staying close.

Filling the sink with warm water, Jelly stood there, hands braced on the sides of the sink and breathed deeply and slowly. He didn't feel right. He rubbed the thin bar of hotel soap between his palms, then scrubbed his face, rinsing off with the warm water in the bowl. Picking up one of the soft white towels on the counter Jelly dried the skin of his face, then dropped the towel to the floor and looked in the mirror.

He looked odd. Different. It was his eyes; the eyes were absolutely different. Jelly stared at the reflection for a full two minutes before it dawned on him: the "killer eyes" were gone.

His heart beat lightly and his breath seemed to come easier than it had in years. He knew what had happened. Jelly was finished. Jelly was complete. Jelly had no more things to set right, no more missions, no more battles.

Looking back at him were the eyes of Delf Bryce.

Delf walked to the night table and picked up the photograph of Austin. The likeness was undeniable. "My son," he said with conviction. His mind was settled. He knew what he would do. Delf's mission was clear.

He sat back down on the bed and picked up the telephone next to the table lamp, dialing a number from memory. After more than a dozen rings a woman's sleepy voice answered.

"Lila, it's me, Delf."

As his little sister listened Delf told her he was sorry for calling so late but he needed to tell her: needed to tell her she was right–had been right for years. He needed to make it right with his son, Austin.

"Hell," he said, "I need to make it right with them both. Will you help me?"

Lila was happy, so happy for her brother. He was the best man she'd ever known–even though she loved her husband dearly–but Delf had always been the strong one, the one who always knew what needed to be done and who always did it. Delf was and always had been larger than life in so many ways.

The only thing her big brother had been blind to all these years was what he'd done to himself and those closest to him. He'd shut his family out of large segments of his life, locking himself away in secrecy.

Jelly felt lightheaded he was so relieved and happy. "The boys need to meet, Lila. They've never even met." Perhaps the three of them, Delf thought, the three of them together could make a whole. Help each other become the best versions of themselves. They were family. They were all they had in this world.

Lila cried over the telephone, happy for her brother and nephews. "Yes, Delf. Of course I'll help. I'll do whatever you need me to."

Delf's heart started beating quickly again, and he suddenly felt a little dizzy. "I'm going to get some sleep, now, Lila," he said calmly. "I love you, little sister."

Lila gripped the telephone tightly. "I love you too, Delf," she said, waiting for him to hang up before she went back to bed to tell her husband the wonderful news.

After hanging up the receiver Delf sat there for a moment just smiling. Only a few hours before he'd felt his life was over, that he'd had no further purpose or use. Now the mission that had always been in front of him–the most important mission of his life–was seen clearly. He knew what he had to do and he knew he would find the right way to do it.

He was Delf Bryce, but he still had Jelly's years of experience, Jelly's nimble mind, and most important, Jelly's iron will.

He would make things right by his sons.

Tequila yipped once at his feet, then jumped up on the bed, turning around twice on the mattress next to Delf before settling in close, just as Delf remembered something Walter Walsh used to say.

"We grow too soon old and too late smart," Delf whispered, nodding. "You're a smart prick, Walter. A lot smarter than me, I guess."

Delf went to put his hand on the little dog when he felt something pull in his shoulder followed by the brief familiar galloping of his heart in his chest. Just for a moment the impulse to flee, to escape came over him. Then a slight twinge of pain in his chest.

"Fuck you," he said out loud to the internal demons that had tormented him for so many years. He made himself stay put. "This will pass, I am fine; when I wake up in the morning I have things to do so fuck off and leave me be."

He found it odd he felt so tired so quickly, as if he'd just run a great distance and for a long time. He actually had to struggle to lift his legs, one at a time, onto the bed.

Then he felt a pressure in his chest. This was different than the usual pain but hardly unbearable. His left arm began to tingle and went numb. He smiled.

"Fuck you very much," he said again to the pain. He knew what this was. It would pass like it always did, either in a little while, or it would be gone when he woke in the morning.

Delf sank back against the pillows. The little dog adjusted his position on the bed, crawling across the mattress until he was along Delf's left side, all the while staring pensively at the leader of their pack of two with his brown, soulful eyes.

Delf turned his head, looked at Tequila and smiled, too tired now to even pat the dog reassuringly. "It's ok, buddy," he said soothingly. "I know what we need to do now. We have a mission."

Delf closed his eyes. After just a few moments he was sound asleep. That's when the vivid dreams began.

He saw Clarence Hurt, Charlie Winstead, and H.V. Wilder. They were standing together, smiling at him. H.V. nodded, grinning crazily as if he'd just told one of his awful jokes, then reached out to pat Delf's shoulder.

The images changed and Delf saw his dad as he was when Delf was a child, young and strong, full of life. Aunt Susan was there, talking to his cousin, Little Jimmy. Delf could see her lips moving but couldn't make out her words.

Then Lila was there, standing before him, eyes clear and honest as always. Two young boys stood next to her, one on either side, each holding one of her hands. Delf looked at their faces and recognized them: Austin and Jimmy. *'They're so little,'* he thought. *'Just children, really.'* He felt a deep sense of pride as he looked at them. *'My boys.'*

"I'm sorry, boys," he said aloud in the room, eyes

still closed.

Tequila's ears folded back at the sound of his voice; the little dog raised his head to look at Delf's face.

"I'll make it right. I will," Delf said, his voice fading.

Breathing slowly as he fell into a deeper sleep, Delf saw a shadow walking toward him, growing clearer as it approached. The image brightened as if the sun were quickly rising, allowing him to see the contours of the specter's face.

She was walking silently in a field of green grasses and wildflowers, no shoes on her pretty feet, blue sky and billowing white clouds behind her to the horizon. She smiled at him and held out her hands. A warm breeze swept across the field, making the flowers and grasses dance and bow beneath her.

Delf smiled back sweetly. "There you are," he whispered contentedly.

The little dog shifted on the bed again, moving closer against him.

And sometime during the night, the world came to an end.

Delf "Jelly" Bryce

1906-1974

Top: Special Agent D.A. Bryce cracking up the troops.
Bottom: Jelly "skywriting" with a Thompson SMG.
(Images courtesy the Bryce Family)

ACKNOWLEDGEMENTS

The production of the Jelly Bryce trilogy was not undertaken lightly. Delf Bryce was a real man who led an interesting and consequential life. He lived during an era when the country he loved was undergoing dramatic and substantial changes in many areas, from the development of modern law enforcement to the defense of our form of government from subversive elements both within and without.

In addition, he served as a member of the Federal Bureau of Investigation during both the tumultuous gangster era and while the United States was involved in the greatest global war the world had ever seen. His unique career path inevitably brought him into direct and personal contact with criminals, psychopaths, spies and saboteurs as well as those involved at the highest levels of government and society.

To accurately portray any man's life without having been present to observe it is difficult, but made easier when there is an evidential trail to follow. In the case of Jelly Bryce, the trail was difficult to follow at best. Bryce was an extremely private man and for most of his adult life was involved in confidential, secret, and top secret activities. While I have done my best to uncover the bits and pieces available in old articles, police records and declassified FBI records, again, the amount and quality of solid, verifiable evidence found is spotty.

Bryce's life is camouflaged in many ways, despite the hard evidence that is known about him. There are a number of photographs, newspaper articles, factual stories, tall tales and legends that surround him, all serving to wrap the actual man in a Ghillie suit of mystery. This mystery is further compounded by the cloak of secrecy draped over Bryce's FBI career by the Bureau itself. (Ron Owens,

Bryce's biographer, was the first to discover that 469 pages had been purged from Jelly's official FBI personnel file soon after his death in 1974.)

That is why I am deeply indebted to a number of people who have been interested in Bryce's life and examined it themselves, or who actually knew him personally and were willing to share their knowledge with me during this project. I am also proud to be able to say that over the five years spent writing these three novels, not only was a collaboration established, but so were a number of friendships I have come to cherish.

In chronological order:

I would like to thank author and friend, Ron Owens, whose ongoing assistance was invaluable. Ron's biography, *Jelly Bryce: Legendary Lawman*, served as the basic reference work during the production of the trilogy. Through a stroke of extremely good fortune, Ron's book on Jelly and my first effort in this series, *The Legend Begins*, caught the attention of the production crew for the American Heroes Channel program, *American Lawmen* in 2014. We were both asked to participate in the show dedicated to telling Jelly's story–for the first time ever on film. This project gave me the opportunity to not only visit Oklahoma and meet Ron in person, but also to take a road trip across the state to visit many of the actual sites Jelly frequented and scenes where incidents portrayed in the trilogy happened. In a word it was awesome. Ron and I hit it off like two old cops who'd been patrolling the streets together for years. I had a blast and thank him sincerely for his hospitality, humor and friendship. He is also a wealth of information on all things related to the history of Oklahoma lawmen. I highly recommend any of his books to those with an interest in subjects ranging from southwestern law enforcement to a compendium of Medal of Honor awardees.

Faded Glory: Dusty Roads of an FBI Era is a website owned and operated by retired FBI Special Agent Larry Wack. Larry spent over 30 years in the FBI, and is a proud former member as well as an excellent representative of the best the Bureau has to offer. Larry's website is packed full of information about the early years of Hoover's Bureau. I spent many, many hours poring over it and want to thank Larry for preserving this material and working so hard to ensure the historical accuracy of the information he provides. Please note that I cannot make that same claim in my novels! The Jelly Bryce trilogy is historical fiction. While based on real people and events, much of it has been either modified, changed, or completely created for obvious reasons. My intent was to tell a story, staying as close to actual events as possible, but not to document confirmed facts. If you're looking for facts, check out Ron Owens' biography on Jelly or go to Larry's website.

Delf Anne Bryce, Jelly's niece, was the first member of the Bryce family I contacted when I began the project. She was understandably wary of the unexpected call from a man she didn't know who spoke with a bizarre Boston accent. She gave up very little. I understood. The first installment of the trilogy hadn't been written yet so she had no idea of what I was actually doing. Unfortunately, after *The Legend Begins* was released I found out Delf Anne had passed. This was told to me by her devoted partner who was still dealing with the recent loss. Thank you both for your graciousness.

Delona Sue Bryce, Jelly's treasured granddaughter, is another member of the family who provided me with tidbits of memories, photographs and information about her Grandpa. One of the things I found both telling and consistent about Jelly's character was that while growing up, she'd never known her grandfather had been a policeman or an FBI agent. For many years she'd thought he'd been a rancher his whole adult life. Thank you Delona, for taking a chance on me and for the feedback you provided about the first two books. I hope you like this one as well.

Jelly's elder son, Bill Bryce, is a wonderful man. I wanted to start off my acknowledgement to him and his family that way because it's the first thing that comes to mind when I think of him. I promised Bill that I would preserve his privacy to the best of my abilities and I will keep that promise. I also want to thank him sincerely for speaking with me and giving me a glimpse into a well-lived life–his own. Bill and his lovely wife, Sarah, raised their children in an exemplary manner. While I know my wife, Kathy, did an outstanding job, I only hope I did half as well as Bill with my own two kids.

To Bill's son, David Bryce: thank you my friend for all you shared and for opening the door. I believe things are better for the opening and I truly hope you agree.

To all the other kind folks who shared memories of Jelly with me through emails, letters and telephone conversations–thank you. I hope the books serve to jog a fond memory or two, provide a laugh or inspiration. I know they did all that and more for me during the writing process. Socrates is believed to have said, "The unexamined life is not worth living." One of my hopes in writing this trilogy was that by examining Jelly's life, others–including myself–might possibly gain some insight into their own.

That brings me to my final acknowledgements. First, thank you to my wife, Kathy, not only for your assistance proofreading and editing, but putting up with all the time lost over the years while I worked, wrote, and pursued whatever demons I was chasing, both internal and external. Thank you for understanding.

To my parents, Margie and Jim, thank you for my life and for preparing me for the world.

To my children, Kate and Nick, I couldn't be prouder of you both. You are the brightest lights in my life and always have been. You inspire me to do and be better and I thank you for that.

Thanks also to my good friends who read each of the Jelly Bryce books prior to publication to provide feedback and guidance: Paul "Yoda" Damery, Richard Lane, and Tony Abreu. As always, your assistance is deeply appreciated and won't be forgotten.

I am also grateful for another new friend made as a direct result of this project: Chip Pearsall. Chip offered to cast his professional editing eye on *FBI Odyssey* and did such a crackerjack job that I couldn't imagine publishing this final installment without his assistance. Thank you, sir. Your kindness and efforts are eternally appreciated.

Finally, to my best friend for forty years, Pat McAdam, who not only read a lot of my stuff during those four decades including the first two Jelly Bryce novels, but always inspired me to be a better man, thank you for everything, Duke. Your loss is immeasurable, my Brother.

ABOUT THE AUTHOR

A second-generation police officer, Mike Conti retired as a lieutenant from the Massachusetts State Police after more than twenty-four years of service.

The President and founder of Saber Group, Inc., a private training and consulting company, he also serves as Rangemaster and Physical Education Firearms Instructor for the Massachusetts Institute of Technology in Cambridge, MA.